AFTER THE SILENCE

ALSO BY LOUISE O'NEILL

Only Ever Yours
Asking For It
Almost Love

AFTER THE SILENCE

Louise O'Neill

riverrun

First published in Great Britain in 2020 by

riverrun

An imprint of

Quercus Editions Limited
Carmelite House
50 Victoria Embankment
London EC4Y 0DZ

An Hachette UK company

A CIP catalogue record for this book is available
from the British Library.

Hardback 978 1 78429 889 0
Trade Paperback 978 1 78429 890 6
Ebook 978 1 78429 891 3

10 9 8 7 6

Typeset by CC Book Production
Printed and bound in Great Britain by Clays Ltd, Elcograf S.p.A.

Papers used by Quercus are from well-managed forests and other responsible sources.

In memory of Granny Murphy.
You were so, so loved.

'I dream of moor, and misty hill,
Where evening closes dark and chill;
For, lone, among the mountains cold,
Lie those that I have loved of old.'

Emily Brontë

There were three of them, in the beginning, and we called them the Crowley Girls.

They were born of this island, as we were; sister-children, brethren, kin. Soil and bone. A common blood running through our veins, for our ancestors had been family, once, if you went back far enough. We tell you this for you must understand the ways of Inisrún before we begin our story – we were all connected here.

But those girls were not like us.

Since they were children, we had whispered to one another of their other-worldly beauty. Their golden waves of hair, their eyes so green, their long legs in short skirts or tight jeans. We watched them but they watched each other. They had no need of anyone else.

Three is a magic number, of course. Three wishes granted.

1

The Wayward Sisters. The Moirai. The Holy Trinity – the Father, the Son and the Holy Spirit. Those girls were protected when they were still three. They were blessed, they were charmed. Born under a blood moon, made of stardust, shimmering bright.

But then the island was swallowed whole by the night and one of the Crowley Girls was taken from us, breaking the spell. Death came to this land and we were never the same after that.

Which one of the girls, you might ask? Which one of the sisters lost her life on that terrible day?

Oh, but the best one.

The best one of all.

CHAPTER ONE

Keelin Kinsella

'Everyone on the island knew the Kinsellas. Even before Misty Hill was set up—'

'Can you briefly explain to us what Misty Hill is, Keelin?' the young man interrupted, looking up from the camera monitor in front of him. She wondered what she must look like, her body trapped in that small square of glass. An echo of herself, a reflection on water. A shadow. 'Sorry,' he said, screwing his face up in apology. 'It's just that some of the viewers in the UK might not be familiar with the place.'

Henry wouldn't like that, she thought. *The only name that gets mentioned more than Misty Hill in award speeches is God,* was his oft-repeated line at parties, the fifth glass of champagne slurring his voice. The women would gaze at him

3

in a way that made Keelin take a step closer to her husband, call him 'darling', remind them that Henry Kinsella was not for the taking, not without a fight anyway. *He's mine,* Keelin would think fiercely, taking Henry's hand in hers. *This man belongs to me.*

'Misty Hill was the artists' retreat centre that the Kinsella family built on the island of Inisrún,' she said, reaching for the bottle of water that was by her feet. If Evie was here, she would scold her mother for continuing to use single-use plastic. Why aren't you using that BPA-free container I bought you for Christmas? she would ask, with all the affront a sixteen-year-old girl could muster. Climate change! Marine pollution! The end of the world as we know it, Mum, not that *you* seem to care. Evie always waited until Henry was in the room before she began the lecture on how her mother was destroying planet earth, and though her eyes never left Keelin's, it was clear for whom the performance was really intended. Her daughter would pause ever so slightly, giving Henry the opportunity to interject, lavishing praise upon the girl for her sense of civic responsibility. Evie would smile at her mother then, slowly, as if to say, *See? I win. Daddy loves me the most.*

But Evie rarely came home to the island now. Too difficult, she said. After everything that had happened with the Crowley Girl.

'Keelin?' the man behind the camera said. *Noah, that's his name. Noah Wilson.* These two men had arrived to Inisrún

4

yesterday, and they'd asked if they could interview Keelin first, before anyone else. Your voice is going to be integral to the whole documentary, Noah Wilson had said, and she tried to pretend that was a good thing. 'Are you all right, mate?'

'Yes,' she said, taking a sip of water. 'Sorry. The Kinsellas built the artist retreat in the nineties.' *Build it and they will come – that's the Kinsella way.* 'And the main centre, the place where the residents had dinner and shared their day's work – that was part of the deal, you see; they had to eat together every night. The Kinsellas wanted to foster a sense of community here, a creative hub where artists could take inspiration from one another – that site was what we would have called *Cnoc an Cheo* in Irish. There's mist on the hill, you know.'

Emily Brontë was his favourite writer in school, Henry's father always said. 'I dream of moor, and misty hill,' he recited aloud every time he took the ferry from Baltimore and the island began to emerge on the horizon, rising from the sea like Atlantis. Jonathan Kinsella claimed he had wanted to create something special here, something that would benefit everyone on Inisrún, islanders and artists alike, but he was a businessman too. He had a bottom line to think about. There were always going to be people who would be upset, those who would find fault with his efforts, he said later, but he had done his best. That was some comfort to him, he said.

Jonathan Kinsella refused to return to the island after Misty Hill was razed to the ground and the islanders stood and watched it burn. For days, he would think he smelled smoke; he would wake in the dead of night choking on ashes. And then he'd remember what had happened on the island of Inisrún.

'Where was I?' Keelin asked. She often had moments like this, as if her brain had short-circuited, and she lost her train of thought midway through her sentence. It's just the medication, Henry reassured her when she turned to him, waiting for him to fill in the blanks and guide her home. I'll take care of you, darling.

'You were telling us how everyone on the island knew the Kinsellas,' Noah said, and the man beside him nodded in agreement. Jake, that was the other young man's name. Jake, with his closed mouth and his doubting eyes. Keelin had a feeling she would need to be careful around Jake.

'They did,' Keelin said, crossing her legs and instantly regretting it. Did her skirt ride up, showing too much thigh? Henry had suggested she wear the cream bouclé Chanel suit today; he said it would look respectable. It was important they made the right impression, he reminded her. They wouldn't get a second chance at this. 'Obviously.'

'Why "obviously"? Because it's such a small island?'

'Well, yes. But also . . . Look, you have to understand what life was like on Inisrún in the eighties,' she said. 'There was no money here. I mean, you could argue that no one on the mainland had money then either, but things were even worse on the islands. We were a problem, most of the time, as much

6

as the politicians liked to rhapsodise about how "precious" the islands were, how we were the "last bastions of Irish culture".' She snorted. 'Being a bastion of culture wasn't going to feed us, was it? We had to depend on ourselves. The people here tried to lean into the tourism angle and the Irish colleges had only just started up—'

'Sorry, Keelin,' Noah said, his hand in the air to slow her down. 'And the Irish colleges were . . . ?'

'Schools set up in the Gaeltachts, areas where Irish was still the native tongue,' she said, trying not to sound impatient. She needed these men to like her, Henry had warned her. 'Parents would send their children here during the summer holidays so they could immerse themselves in the language. The college on Inisrún had only started in '86, my mother was a Bean an Tí, one of the first, and—' Noah winced, *sorry, sorry*, and Keelin backtracked quickly. 'Bean an Tí means woman of the house,' she said. 'We would have students stay and Mam would cook for them and make sure they spoke in Irish all the time.'

Her mother had been strict with the lodgers, she remembered. There were tears from the teenagers who had been caught speaking in English, threats to send them home to their parents or, worse, have their ketchup privileges revoked at dinner time, nothing to temper the plates of lamb chops and floury potatoes thrown in front of them. That'll soften their cough, Mam would say. Keelin didn't like it when her mother yelled, particularly not when it was at the girls from

7

Dublin. Those girls were wild: singing Madonna songs as they danced around the spare bedroom, fixing their tight miniskirts before they left for the céilí, chattering loudly about which one of the local boys they would shift behind the old dance hall that night. Keelin felt self-conscious for the entire summer the Irish-college students were in the house, especially when her mother chatted to her in Irish about the errands she needed Keelin to do, the shifts Keelin had to cover in An Siopa Beag that week, the freshly baked soda bread she wanted Keelin to drop over to Mrs Ní Ghríofa, who was still recovering from the flu; there was talk of bringing the doctor in from the mainland the old lady was so bad. The Dublin girls would stare at them open-mouthed when they spoke, as if they were time travellers from a different era, half stifling giggles whenever Keelin called her mother 'Mammy'. *Mum*, she practised in the bathroom mirror afterwards, enunciating the word carefully. *Mum*.

'When did the Kinsellas arrive on Inisrún?' Jake asked, and when their eyes met, Keelin had the strangest sensation of recognition. He knew, she felt. Somehow, this young man knew what had happened to her. What she had done.

'Henry would be the best person to ask about that,' she tried.

'We want to hear it from you, Keelin.'

'It was a year or so before I was born,' she said, beads of sweat forming beneath her breasts, dripping slowly onto her stomach. '1970, 1971 maybe. They didn't actually stay here, mind, it was just day trips at first. Henry's mother was born on Rún, you see. She still had second cousins on the island, and both she and Jonathan, that's Henry's father, became very involved in life here. It used to be the priest who would lobby on our behalf, writing letters to the newspaper about how poor the living conditions were, complaining we were being ignored by the government. But before we knew it, Jonathan had somehow become that person for Inisrún, our ambassador, I suppose you could call it. He and Olivia were even here the day electricity was brought to the island.' An early beacon of hope, they had thought. *Let there be light.* 'They bought the old house soon afterwards. Spent a small fortune doing it up was the story around the place.'

'And what did the islanders think of them?' Noah asked, still staring at the camera monitor.

'Oh,' Keelin said, hoping she sounded suitably vague. Henry could be sensitive about his status as a blow-in; he liked to see himself as half-native at this point, fond of pointing out his mother's birthright to anyone who asked how he ended up here. She didn't want to say anything stupid and hurt his feelings. 'They were different to us, I suppose. Impossibly glamorous, particularly the Kinsella brothers. All of the girls were in love with Henry, and his brother, Charlie, too.'

The islanders would know well in advance when the Kinsellas were on their way. In the early days, Mrs Breathnach, the caretaker's wife, would have received a letter, which then became a phone call, asking her to have the house ready for their arrival. All the bedrooms have their own toilets! she would tell Keelin's mother as she picked up milk and butter from the siopa. You've never seen the like, Cáit, you'd swear you were in America. The delivery boys picked up the extra messages from the ferry, things that couldn't be bought in Keelin's mother's shop, cardboard boxes with names like Fortnum & Mason and Marks & Spencer stamped across the top. Then, finally, that day in mid-July would be upon them, everyone watching out of the corners of their eyes as the four Kinsellas disembarked from their specially chartered ferry. Jonathan holding Olivia's hand as she stepped onto the pier, a silk Pucci headscarf covering her ash-blonde hair. The boys followed, Charlie and Henry in Ray-Ban sunglasses, looking like film stars with their thick, auburn hair and blindingly white teeth. Every girl on Inisrún took a collective inhale at the sight of them, but the brothers didn't seem to notice, barely looking up from their Walkmans as they made their way through the village.

'Were *you* in love with the Kinsella brothers?' Jake asked her, tilting his head to the side.

'No,' Keelin said, and she was glad it was true. Somehow, she felt that Jake would be able to tell if she was lying. 'I thought they were both gorgeous, like, everyone did, but I had a boyfriend, sure. Seán and I—' She stopped.

'Seán?'

'Yes.'

'Seán Crowley?'

'Yes,' she said again.

'Nessa Crowley's uncle?'

Keelin shifted in her chair. She didn't want to talk about Nessa, she didn't want to even *think* about her ever again. But all anyone wanted to talk about was the Crowley Girl and what had happened to her that night in the dark.

'Keelin?' one of them asked, and she didn't bother checking to see whether it was Noah or Jake, their Australian accents blending into one. She looked straight down the lens of the camera, allowing herself a rare moment of defiance.

'Are we done here?' she asked.

CHAPTER TWO

Keelin wasn't sure how she was supposed to react when Henry told her that he had agreed to participate in the documentary. 'It'll be on Channel Three in the UK,' he said, cracking his knuckles one by one. He always did that when he was excited, the snap-snap noise making Keelin grit her teeth. 'It's a huge opportunity for us, darling.'

'An opportunity for us to do what, exactly?' she asked.

Could Henry truly believe that by agreeing to this – this documentary meant questions, it meant people in their home, riffling through their belongings in search of clues – that Misty Hill could somehow be resurrected to its former glory? The mere thought of more interviews gave Keelin an unpleasant swoop in her chest. What on earth was her husband doing?

'It's the ten-year anniversary next March,' Henry said as if she might have forgotten about it, the date simply slipping

her mind. 'And with the success of all these true-crime podcasts and what not – people are rather keen on them, aren't
they? – there's an appetite for this kind of story, it seems.'

It was two Australian men who would be here filming, he
explained. One of the men had family in west Cork; he'd
heard the story about Misty Hill from his Irish cousins. Henry
showed Keelin the email they'd sent, waiting for her to find
her reading glasses so she could see the phone screen clearly.

We don't have an agenda, Mr Kinsella, and we don't
have any theories about what happened that night either.
We just want to give you and your wife a chance to tell
your side of the story.

It was blatantly untrue; everyone had theories about the
Crowley Girl and who, exactly, was responsible for her death.
Keelin very much doubted that these men would be any
different. She handed Henry back his phone in silence. 'Marvellous,' he said. 'I'm glad we're in agreement, darling.'

Later that evening, she picked up her husband's iPad and
crept into her dressing room. It was at least three times the size
of her childhood bedroom: a cream carpet in deep pile, delicate wallpaper in swirls of vanilla and pearl. Two of the walls
had silver racks lined with heavy wooden hangers, another
had glass shelves for shoes and accessories, everything perfectly lined up in its correct place. Sitting at the marble-top
vanity table, she googled the two documentary makers. She

left the door slightly ajar so she would have time to hide the device if she heard Henry approaching, but all she could make out was the sound of his feet slapping against the belt of the treadmill in the gym downstairs. *Noah Wilson, film-maker, Australia*, she typed, finding an article in the *Sydney Morning Herald* the man had written about the role of St Patrick's Day in Coogee, the suburb he'd grown up in. His pale, freckled skin and blue eyes betrayed his Irish heritage; even without the article she would have guessed he was the one whose mother hailed from west Cork. The *Herald* piece linked to his Twitter account, which was mostly retweets of praise their previous documentary, *Closed Doors*, had received, but his Instagram account was a more enlightening illustration of his life in Sydney. She scrolled through photos of Noah surfing, his hair tied in a high man-bun, poached eggs and avocado for brunch at beachside cafes, hikes taken up the Blue Mountains, but rather than the blonde girl Keelin had pictured by his side, Noah was holding hands with an attractive black man, smiling shyly at the camera.

Jake, that's what Henry had said the other film-maker was called. He's Chinese or something, he added, waving away the unfamiliar surname. I can't remember exactly.

Jake Nguyen wasn't Chinese, as it turned out, but of Vietnamese descent, as he explained to a chat-show host when he and Noah were on morning television to promote *Closed Doors*. Keelin had found the clip on YouTube, and she was struck by how handsome Jake was, his dark eyes deep set in perfect, smooth skin, a small cleft in his stubbled chin. He and Noah were the same age, she'd read, both in their late twenties, but Jake seemed the older of the pair. Noah nodded at every question eagerly, tapping his fingers off his knees; he was one second away from turning to the camera and waving to his friends watching at home. Jake, however, gave increasingly short answers; his mother was born in Hanoi, he said, but she'd moved to Sydney in her twenties to work as a nanny for a family there. 'Your reasons for wanting to make this *particular* documentary are understandable, Jake.' The host smoothed back an errant strand of hair as she looked at him with sympathy. 'Jake's mother was married to the infamous Lucas Taylor,' she said, her voice hushed, 'the man who *slaughtered* his wife and his daughters while they were sleeping before taking his own life in a tragic murder–suicide. It's a story that shocked all of Australia, and one I'm sure many of our viewers will remember.' A photo of a petite Asian woman flashed on screen, flanked by two grinning pre-teen girls, miniature versions of Jake in Day-Glo T-shirts and shorts. 'Lucas Taylor,' the presenter continued, 'was said to be suffering from undiagnosed depression at the time of the incident. Coupled with the loss of his job at a local factory, he snapped under the *tremendous* pressure. Such a terrible story – that poor, poor woman.' The camera on Jake's face then, his jaw tight. 'That woman was my mother,' he said. 'And her name was My Nguyen.'

'What do you think?'

Keelin froze, jabbing at the off button. 'I didn't hear you come in, Henry.'

He reached down to take the iPad from her. 'They're good, aren't they?' he said, squinting at the screen, holding it out at arm's length so he could see.

'They're on the bed stand,' she said, but her husband ignored her. He hated his reading glasses and refused to wear them in public, as if no one would notice he was almost fifty as long as he pretended his eyesight was still perfect. You're getting older, Henry, she wanted to say. We both are.

'You really should watch *Closed Doors*, darling,' he said. 'It's beautifully shot, and a rather damning indictment of the manner in which society deals with domestic violence. It's had a huge impact in Australia, or so I'm told.' He shook his head. 'The things these women have to endure, Keelin. It would break your heart.'

'Hmm.' Keelin resisted the urge to remind her husband that she had seen plenty of things that had broken her heart all the years she'd worked in the women's shelter in Cork city. She reached for the bottle of cleanser on her desk, pumping some into her palms and massaging it into her skin. 'I thought you were in the gym,' she said, wiping the mascara off with a cotton pad. She usually preferred to remove her make-up in private, staring at the mirror while Keelin Kinsella disappeared and her old face returned to her. She was still Keelin Ní Mhordha then, she would think, underneath all the artifice. Still the island girl, born and bred. 'I heard the treadmill.'

'Couldn't have been me,' he said, gesturing at his shirt and pressed chinos. 'Not exactly dressed for working out, am I?'

'But I heard th—' She stopped. There was no point in having this conversation, she knew. 'Have you talked to Alex about the documentary?' she asked, changing the subject.

'I thought you should probably do it. He'll take it better coming from you.'

'Henry,' she said, struggling to keep her voice level, 'he's not going to be happy about this, especially if they're staying in his cottage. You know how particular Alex gets about his things. I don't know if—'

'He'll understand how important this doc is, for all of us. Alex is smart.'

'Alex is fragile.'

'And that's my fault, I suppose,' he said. 'Really, why must the parents be blamed for everything these days? It hardly seems fair.'

He's not your son, she thought, dropping her head in case he would see the flash of anger spiking through her. *He was never your son.*

'Keelin.' Henry crouched down, resting his hands on her knees for balance. 'I know you're not happy about this. I'm not exactly thrilled either.' She could feel a smile twisting on her mouth, and she pressed her lips together to suppress it. She loved her husband, but she wasn't blind to his faults,

17

not least of which was his insatiable need to be the centre of attention. Henry had been born searching for a stage, a spotlight in which to shine. He was withering away on this island without it. 'But these men are coming to Inisrún whether we like it or not,' he continued. 'This film is going to happen, even if we don't take part. But I think we should, all three of us.' He took her hands in his. 'It will look bad if we refuse to cooperate with them. It'll look *suspicious*. We can't afford for anything to look suspicious, can we?'

'No,' she replied, for what else could she say? 'You're right, Henry. Email the Australians back and say we'll do it.'

CHAPTER THREE

'This is, like, batshit insane. You know that, right?' Evie said, staring at her mother from the screen of her iPhone. Keelin had thought someone had died when she'd answered her daughter's FaceTime, such was the extent of Evie's weeping. 'What is it, darling?' Keelin asked in alarm, unable to get a coherent answer for the first five minutes of their conversation. 'You, you . . . Dad . . . I can't . . .' the girl sobbed. Her eyes were swollen, mascara smearing down her cheeks. 'This, this *documentary*,' she finally managed to spit out, and Keelin was almost relieved that it wasn't anything worse.

'Why are you doing this to me, Mum?' Evie said. 'Isn't it bad enough that I was forced to go to school in, like, *Scotland* of all places, to get away from this shit? Can't I just *live*?'

'I know, pet,' Keelin said soothingly, although, as she recalled, no one had forced Evie to go to boarding school.

She wasn't entirely sure it was possible to force Evie to do anything she didn't want to do; Keelin certainly hadn't been able to do so in the last sixteen years. She had initially objected to the idea of boarding school, reminding Henry of how much Alex had hated it, and then, in desperation, she'd cited the girl's age – her daughter was only eleven at the time, practically a baby. But Evie persisted. She'd been miserable at the island school since Nessa Crowley's death, treated like a pariah by her classmates for something she had played no part in. Boarding school would be a fresh start, she told her mother, a chance to be *Evie* again, rather than just the daughter of the infamous Henry Kinsella. She showed her father the glossy brochures over breakfast, talking about the 'opportunities' such a place would afford her, promising that she'd spend the weekends with her Grandma and Grandpa Kinsella, whose Scottish estate was only forty miles north of the school grounds. Finally, Evie reminded him that her first cousin had gone to the same school, and Henry, never able to bear the thought that his brother might have something that he himself did not, transferred the considerable deposit the same night.

'And, and . . . it's so cold here,' her daughter said.

'But it's May. I thought it would be getting warmer at this time of year,' Keelin said, prompting another bout of sobbing for some inexplicable reason. 'Shh, love, it's okay,' she murmured, waiting for her daughter to calm down.

'I just don't get it,' Evie said eventually, sniffling loudly.

'It's bad enough that everyone at home is, like, obsessed with the case, but if you do this thing on Channel Three, and Daddy said it might even get picked up by, oh my God, *Netflix* –' she paused, her voice trembling – 'then my friends here will find about it too. Are you *trying* to ruin my life?'

'Don't your friends have Google?' Keelin asked. 'I presumed they all knew about it anyway.'

'I go by Evie Moore at school – I told you that when I first enrolled. *God.* You never listen to me, do you, Mum?'

It was odd – Keelin could recall with perfect clarity everything that had happened before the night Nessa Crowley was murdered: her childhood, running wild across the island with her best friends, Seán and Johanna; those painful years with her first husband, whom she'd married because she was pregnant and it had still seemed vaguely shameful in Ireland to have a baby out of wedlock in 1991. Alex's birth was seared into her memory, how she had counted his fingers and toes, each tiny nail a miracle; the death of her father, then her mother soon after; the day she married Henry, and his face when he held a newborn Evie in his arms and he looked as if he had found home, for the first time. But since the night Nessa died, Keelin's ability to retain the minutiae of day-to-day life had weakened, her fingers prised off her memories, one by one. She felt like she was trying to piece together fragments of half-fading dreams, people wearing the wrong faces and answering to the wrong names, static

21

buzzing around the edges of their words, none of it quite making any sense.

'I do remember,' Keelin lied. 'I think it's lovely you're using my maiden name. I—'

'Get a grip, Mum. It's not for any, like, *sentimental* reasons.' Her daughter said the word with disdain, as if gravely offended Keelin would dare to assume any such thing about their relationship. 'And I'm not even using Ní Mhordha – no one would be able to pronounce that anyway. It's just so I don't have to deal with this crap.' She tilted her jaw at the screen. 'Well, you can forget about me coming home for the summer holidays. I'll stay with Grandma and Grandpa instead. I can't believe you're doing this; it's so selfish of you.'

'Me? Why are you blaming me?'

'Don't yell at me, Mum.'

'I'm not yelling at you. I think you'll find that I'm speaking in a very calm voice, actually. And I was under the impression your father spoke to you about this matter already.' (Did you tell Evie? she'd asked Henry that morning. Of course, her husband replied, buttering a slice of toast. She took the news rather well, I thought.)

'He did,' Evie said, her chin quivering. 'He phoned yesterday.'

'So why are you—'

'This isn't my fault,' she wailed, the way she always did when she felt backed into a corner. I've told you a million times, take your shoes off at the door before coming into the

22

house, Keelin would say in exasperation when her daughter was a child and dragging sand through the kitchen after a day on the beach. Evie would glance around shiftily, looking for someone else to blame it on, shrugging off any responsibility as easily as a snake shedding its skin. Henry found it funny, their daughter's inability to admit she was wrong. The girl has the makings of a great politician, he would say. But it bothered Keelin. There was something sneaky about Evie's behaviour that left a bad taste in her mouth.

'I was *also* under the impression that you told your father it was fine to go ahead with this documentary,' she said.

'I didn't want to upset Daddy – he seemed so excited about it.'

'Right,' Keelin said, quashing the temptation to ask Evie why she was never worried about upsetting her. 'Well, I'm afraid this is your dad's decision, so any concerns you have about it "ruining your life" will have to be taken up with him. OK?' The girl didn't reply. 'OK, Evie?' Keelin said again, waiting until her daughter met her eyes.

'Fine. I'll talk to Daddy.'

'Great,' Keelin said, even though they both knew Evie wouldn't say anything. She could never bear to disappoint Henry or risk jeopardising her role as his little princess. 'I'm glad that's settled then.'

The girl blew her nose into a clean tissue. She was so like Henry, with those hazel eyes that turned green when she'd been crying, the same auburn hair, though she wore hers in a messy topknot. Evie was attractive in a way that wasn't particularly fashionable at her age. She had been almost six feet tall by the time she was thirteen, her pale skin burned in the sun rather than tanned, and Henry had banned her from getting blonde highlights. Not a hope, Evie Diva, he'd told his daughter when she phoned home, crying because a boy from a nearby school had called her 'ginger pubes' at a local disco, her friends snickering in agreement rather than defending her. Keelin was secretly relieved that it had been from her father Evie had inherited her red hair – this humiliation would have been all Keelin's fault, otherwise, and she'd never hear the end of it – but she felt sorry for the girl too. *It gets better*, she wanted to say, but she couldn't lie to her daughter. Keelin had told enough lies.

'Are you all right, my love?' she asked gently, straining to see the screen as the sun emerged from behind a patch of cloud, filling her bedroom with brilliant light. She turned her back on the window to shield her phone from the glare, and waited for her daughter to respond.

'It's just hard, you know?' Evie said. She looked heart-breakingly young then, the veneer of adulthood she was so determined to wear dissolving, revealing the child hidden underneath. No one will play with me, Mummy, she'd told Keelin in the months after Nessa Crowley's death. The invitations to birthday parties dwindled, there were no more play dates with her best friend, Alannah. Evie had always been the queen bee in the small island school, playing one classmate

24

off against the other to ensure they were all vying for her affection, and the girl was left floundering by her sudden demotion in status. She started to complain of stomach aches, refusing to go to school because she was 'sick'. Keelin ought to have been firmer with her, she should have insisted Evie go to school anyway, should have arranged a meeting with the teacher to discuss the situation, but she didn't have the energy in those early days. Fine, she had said, and her daughter would crawl into the bed beside her. They would lie there all day, waiting for Henry to come home.

'I'm sorry, Evie.'

'S'OK,' she said, attempting to smile. 'It's not your fault.'

But it is, Keelin thought. *This is all my fault.*

'Anyway –' Evie brushed her fringe out of her eyes – 'you look nice. Give me a proper look at the outfit.' Keelin stood in front of the full-length mirror, flipping the camera around so Evie could see her reflection. 'Oooh,' her daughter said. 'The new Gucci collection! It's flames.'

'Is it?' Keelin adjusted the navy cardigan with red and green trim. 'I thought it seemed a bit . . .' She paused, checking to make sure she could hear Henry pottering about downstairs before continuing. She didn't want him to hear her call the outfit boring, not after he'd been so helpful last night. He'd found Keelin in her dressing room alone, sitting cross-legged on the floor, watching particles of dust dance in the sunlight streaming through the window. What's wrong? he'd asked, concerned. She pointed at the racks of clothes, silently

25

praying for her husband to make it better, she couldn't do this without him. He had picked out the clothes then, talking Keelin through all the possible options, explaining the image she should project. He was so much better at this kind of thing than she was. 'I don't know, pet,' she said. 'It just seems like an old geansaí your mamó would have worn.'

'You're hopeless, Mum.' Evie rolled her eyes. 'This shit is wasted on you.'

'Language,' Keelin said half-heartedly. 'And you know I'm not into this stuff. I never have been.'

Her daughter frowned. 'This can't be easy for you either,' she said, as if the idea had only just occurred to her. 'How are you doing, Mum?'

'I'm fine,' Keelin answered automatically. That's what she always said when anyone asked how she was – I'm fine! Great! Busy! – not that many people were interested in hearing about how Keelin Kinsella was these days. 'But I'd better go, Evie. The documentary makers will be here soon – we're just waiting on the text from Baltimore to say they're on the ferry.'

'Showtime!' her daughter called out in a booming voice, like a ringmaster at a circus. 'It's showtime, children.' Keelin's hand jerked involuntarily, almost dropping the phone in fright. 'Don't say that, Evie. I can't—' she began.

'What's wrong, Mum? You've gone totally white.'

'Nothing,' she said. 'It was nothing. I love you.'

'Love ya right back,' Evie replied, blowing a kiss.

The screen turned blank and Keelin saw a woman in its

reflection, an outline pencilled in the black glass. *Who was that person? That stranger?* she thought, before remembering what she looked like these days, the creation she had remade herself into.

That's you. That's you now, Keelin.

CHAPTER FOUR

Later that afternoon, they both started when Henry's phone beeped. It was a message from the man at Baltimore pier, the man her husband paid handsomely to keep them informed of imminent arrivals to the island. Forewarned is forearmed, he always said. 'Two young men with Australian accents have just boarded the ferry to Inisrún,' Henry read aloud. 'They're nearly here,' he said to Keelin. 'Are you ready, darling?' And she nodded, ignoring the dizzying sensation that felt like she was falling, as if in a bad dream, waiting for the bottom of her nightmare to rise to meet her. She would have to be ready, she said. There was no going back now.

'You found the place all right then?' she heard her husband ask as he opened the front door to their guests.

'It would have been hard to miss,' a male voice answered. Keelin stood at the top of the stairs, a hand clutching at the banister, as she watched them walk into her house, these men who had the potential to set her life on fire, and probably wanted to do so, all in the hope of making their reputations. Laughing, throwing well-worn suitcases and backpacks and camera equipment at their feet. They looked younger in real life, their clothes like those of students, low-slung jeans and scruffy trainers, beanie hats pulled low over their foreheads.

'Hello there,' she said, joining them. 'Welcome to Inisrún.' She shook their hands, hoping her palms weren't sweating. 'May I take your coats?'

'I'll keep mine, thanks,' Jake said, stuffing his hands into the pockets of his navy-blue rain jacket. He was taller than she had imagined, his untidy curls tucked behind his ears, and he was in need of a shave.

'You're not cold, surely?' Henry slapped him on the back. 'It's nineteen degrees outside. That's tropical for Ireland, my friend.'

'That's what I told him,' Noah said, laughing. 'But he didn't believe me. He's been moaning since we set foot on the tarmac at Cork airport.'

'It's lucky you came now then,' Keelin said. 'May is a good month for your first trip to the island. There's a grand stretch in the evening these days.' She sounded inane, like a cliché of an Irish woman unable to talk about anything other than the weather, but she couldn't help herself. 'It can get very bleak here, in the winter.'

'I guess,' Jake said. 'Although it's a pity we weren't green-lit before March. It would have been useful to be here for Nessa's anniversary.'

An uneasy silence spilled between the four of them at the mention of her name, lapping at their toes. Keelin could feel Jake's eyes on her, interested to see her reaction, and she kept her face very still. She couldn't become complacent, she told herself; she had to remember why these men were here, why they had come to this house and this island. It was all because of *her*.

'It's always a difficult time for the island, the anniversary,' Henry said quietly. 'We hope your programme will bring some peace to the Crowleys at last. That poor family.' He let out a deep sigh. 'But please, come in and make yourselves comfortable.' He motioned at the young men to follow him into the kitchen. The heart of the home, the architect had pronounced, outlining his desire to create a space that would make the most of the natural light and stunning sea views. The interior designer had selected the island carved from Italian marble in gleaming white, the bespoke fitted cabinets in stainless steel and glass, the overhead lighting fixture that resembled an art installation in misshapen orbs of silver. One of the Australians let out a low whistle as they walked in, muttering, 'Very nice,' under his breath.

'What'll you have?' Henry asked as he opened the fridge door, peering inside to see what had been delivered from the mainland that morning. 'We have still and sparkling water, and there's tea in those canisters by the Aga, isn't there, darling? It's rather a scandal in this part of the world if you don't prefer the traditional breakfast tea, and it has to be Barry's, naturally. I'm sure you're well aware of the interminable tea war, being a Cork man,' he said to Noah, who chuckled politely. He was already charmed by Henry, Keelin could tell, a ready smile on his lips whenever her husband made a quip. 'But there's a selection of herbal teas as well,' Henry continued. 'And we have a Nespresso machine if you'd prefer coffee. Or you might be in the mood for something stronger?' he raised an eyebrow mischievously.

Looking at him now, Keelin thought that it could have easily been ten years ago, before their lives had fallen apart. Henry had always enjoyed having people to the house, filling its many rooms with music and laughter, relishing his role as the magnanimous host. He would sit at the top of the dining table, presiding over whatever heated debate was currently raging on among their guests, refugees or taxes or social welfare housing, everyone repeating arguments they'd read in the *Guardian* or *Spectator*, depending on their political allegiances, and passing them off as their own. Henry had been dazzling, his opinions incisive, his quick wit defusing any disagreements that threatened to turn nasty. What do you think, Henry? people would ask, giving him the last word on the subject. Keelin had felt lucky then, watching her husband, the candlelight soft on his handsome face. All these people would have to leave once the party was over, go back to their mundane, ordinary lives, but she would

31

get to wake up next to Henry Kinsella and call him her own.

'Ooh, white wine would be lovely, if you have it,' Noah said, sitting on a tall stool and slapping his hands on the marble island, leaving fingerprints behind. Keelin gazed at the smears, wondering how to wipe the countertop clean without appearing rude. 'I could do with a proper drink after that journey. Two planes, a bus and a boat, all within thirty-five hours. I'm cooked.'

'I couldn't believe how long it took to get to Inisrún from Cork airport,' Jake said, taking a seat next to Noah. 'It must feel quite isolated, living here. You're so far away from everything.'

'It's not for everyone, island life.' Henry grabbed a bottle of Chardonnay from the Neff wine cooler and poured Noah a glass. He offered some to Jake too, but the young man politely said no. 'You have to be comfortable with yourself, is the best way of putting it. You're surrounded by water on every side, and left alone with your own thoughts for a great deal of the time. It can drive some people mad, particularly in the winter months. But we've always loved it here, haven't we, darling?' he said to Keelin, and she nodded in agreement.

'You have a beautiful home, Mrs Kinsella,' Noah said, gesturing towards the sunroom adjoining the open-plan kitchen, cut from glass, ceiling to floor, so all you could see was a forever expanse of grey sky, the sea breaking its spine against the rocks below.

'Keelin, please,' she said. 'And thank you, that's very kind.'
A beautiful home – that was what everyone said the first time
they came to Hawthorn House. An Tigh Mór, or the Big
House, as it was known on the island. Henry used to find
the nickname amusing. It's like we're in an Elizabeth Bowen
novel, he would say to his friends from school, laughing.
They burned those houses down, Keelin had wanted to
remind him. They smoked the unwanted strangers out.

'How long have you lived here?' Noah asked, holding on
to the edge of the counter and leaning back on his stool in
a precarious fashion, as if defying gravity to do its worst.
Her son used to do the same thing when he was a small
boy, she remembered. In the old house at the other side of
the island, the stove lighting and Keelin's mother beside it,
her shoes thrown off, her feet webbed by thick tan tights.
The older woman was peeling a mandarin, throwing its
skin onto the fire, the sharp scent of citrus rising through
the air. Look at me! Alex cried, standing on the uphol-
stered armchair like it was a surfboard and dipping low
until it almost touched the ground. Look at me, Mamó!
Look what I can do! His grandmother had gasped and
stood up in panic, her hands outreached as if to catch him,
and the little boy stopped immediately. He steadied himself
and climbed down from the chair, rushing to his grandmother's side. Don't be scared, Mamó, he said, wrapping
his arms around her waist. I'm a big boy now, I can take
care of you.

'Darling?' Henry touched her arm. 'Noah asked you a question.'

'God, sorry, I was away with the fairies there. The house, wasn't it? We've been here for fifteen years, give or take,' Keelin said. 'Almost a year after our daughter was born.' She coughed, trying to think of something else to say. 'And you've family in Cork, don't you, Noah?' she tried.

'Yeah, my mam's from Beara originally. She moved to Sydney in the early eighties but me and my two brothers were shipped off to my grandparents during the school holidays. It was like another world, the freedom of it! Out the door every morning and we didn't get home until after sunset and no one was worried about us.' He looked around the kitchen again. 'My nan's house is pretty different to this one though.'

'I bet,' Jake half laughed, unzipping his jacket and pushing it down around his waist. There was a tattoo circling his forearm, winding underneath his elbow, swirls and dots in black ink. A message, Keelin thought, a code. And then, flash-quick, a picture in her mind's eye. Another tattoo, on another body. That had been a message too, but one she hadn't deciphered in time. She swallowed, a familiar clamp-ring of nausea around her neck, squeezing tight. She couldn't think about that now, not in front of these men. It wasn't safe.

'Those are great,' he said suddenly, pointing at the wall behind her. 'We might use them for cutaway shots, if that's OK with you guys.' It was hung with various photographs: one of her and a teenage Alex on a water slide in Cyprus, their

34

mouths gaping in giddy laughter; a two-year-old Evie sitting on her brother's shoulders in the stands at Páirc Uí Chaoimh, wearing a football jersey in the county colours of red and white; a faded photo of Keelin's mother and father, taken before a céilí in the fifties, her mother's waist tiny in her swing skirt.

'He looks like you.' Jake stood up and walked over to the wall, tapping the edge of a silver frame. It was a recent photo, Alex with his face half turned from the camera, Keelin beside him, her arm around his shoulders.

'Like me?' she asked, surprised, for no one ever said Alex looked like his mother.

'No,' Jake replied. 'Like you,' he said to Henry.

'We get that quite a bit,' her husband said. Alex was tall, around the same height as Henry, with a similar aquiline nose and well-defined jawline. 'He may not be my biological son –' he reached across to rub the back of Keelin's neck – 'but I love him as if he was my own. Don't I, darling?'

'You do,' Keelin replied, for it was the truth. He had been amazing with Alex from the very beginning, despite her son's dogged resistance. Henry was the first boyfriend Keelin had ever brought home and Alex refused to acknowledge him, he wouldn't even look at the man, but Henry had been patient, giving her son enough space and time to adjust, reassuring the child that he wasn't trying to replace his father, or steal his mother away. He just wanted to be a part of their lives, in whatever way possible.

'And where is Alex? He still lives on the island, doesn't he?' Noah asked.

'He does indeed,' Henry said. 'It's a difficult time for young people, isn't it? Almost impossible to get a mortgage, or so we hear from friends on the mainland. Alex is luckier than most. Ordinarily, he lives in Marigold Cottage where you will be staying—' He waved away Noah's apology. 'Don't be silly,' Henry said. 'He'll be fine. We converted the attic into a self-contained apartment for Evie a few years ago because my wife says it's important for young adults to have their independence. She's the therapist, so I tend to bow to her superior knowledge.' *I'm not a therapist any more.* Keelin pretended to smile at her husband. *I'm nothing now.* 'Alex will stay in Evie's studio while you're filming,' Henry finished.

'But won't your daughter be coming home for the summer holidays?' Jake asked. 'We'd like to include her in the doc, if we could.'

'She's spending the break with my parents in Scotland,' Henry said, a tiny muscle pulsing in his neck, so faintly that only Keelin would have noticed. 'And she's still a minor. We wouldn't sign any release forms for her participation, whether she wanted to take part or not. And I can assure you, she does not. She's awfully stubborn.' He started laughing. 'I can't think *where* she gets it.'

'And what about Alex?' Jake asked. 'Is he happy to be interviewed?'

'I'm not sure,' Keelin said. 'He's not very good with new

36

people, I'm afraid. It's been difficult. These last ten years, you know. Since . . .'

No one said anything, and Noah cleared his throat awkwardly. 'Hold up – is that one of your wedding?' he said, eyeing a small photograph almost hidden out of sight. Henry and Keelin on the steps of the registry office, their fingers intertwined. He was staring down at her, his mouth soft, but she was turning to say hello to a friend, her curly hair caught in a loose bun, her breasts spilling out of the dress's sweetheart neckline. 'I wouldn't have recognised you, Keelin,' Noah said.

She glanced at the photo. She was twenty-nine on her wedding day, and happier than she had ever thought it was possible for her to be. Nothing bad could happen to her now, she'd thought, not with Henry Kinsella by her side.

'That was a long time ago,' she said.

CHAPTER FIVE

Declan Ó Gríofa, former resident of Inisrún island

DECLAN: The papers said the Crowley Girls were almost identical but there were differences between them – you just had to be looking close enough to notice. And we were. (pause) Sinéad was the youngest, and she was shorter than her sisters; her hair was curlier too. She was the shy one, we decided, always hiding behind the others, happy enough to go along with whatever they wanted to do. She was easy, I guess you could say. Róisín was the middle sister, and the one who looked most like Nessa. The same height, the same build, but she had a gap between her front two teeth and she was conscious of it, we suspected; she didn't smile as much as Nessa did, anyway. Róisín was serious – she always had her nose stuck in a schoolbook. Not that it mattered. Even with all that studying, she still didn't do as well in her exams as Nessa did. None of us did.

JAKE: Tell us more about Nessa Crowley. What was she like?

DECLAN: She was something special. And I'm not just saying that now because she's dead, like. Even back then, we knew she was different. She was the most beautiful girl on the island, and when you put them together, the Crowley Girls . . . It was like staring straight at an eclipse. They were all any of us could talk about – where we seen them, who they were with, what they were wearing. We seen them in the siopa with their mam, begging her to buy a Viennetta for dessert. There they were at Mass, genuflecting before the altar like butter wouldn't melt. This one time, Róisín Crowley bent down to pick up her pencil case in class and Mikey Ó Súilleabháin swore he seen her bra, white lace he said it was, with a little pink ribbon in the middle. It's hard to believe there was a time when that was the biggest news on the island, the colour of Róisín Crowley's bra, but they had us driven demented, the three of them. (pause) Everything changed after the murder.

JAKE: In what way?

DECLAN: In every way. All the doors were locked for months after, which was unheard of on the island; sure, most of us didn't even know where our house keys were, half the time. Our parents wouldn't let us out alone at night any more, especially the girls; we weren't safe, they said. It was mad. Things like this didn't happen here, not to people like us.

JAKE: Declan, what do you think happened the night of the murder?

NOAH: We've heard some, eh, let's just say, *interesting* alternative theories.

DECLAN: Let me guess. Nessa had an overdose and the Kinsellas tried to cover it up. Nessa was kicked in the head by a mad cow on a rampage. The party guests were all members of the illuminati and Nessa's death was a sacrifice to appease their pagan gods. Have I missed anything, lads?

NOAH: (laughs) That's about it, I reckon. Do you think any of them are true?

DECLAN: Who knows? In my opinion, there are only two people who have any answers to your questions and their names are Henry and Keelin Kinsella. And I don't think either of them is going to be telling the truth any time soon.

CHAPTER SIX

Keelin was wearing her noise-cancelling headphones, so she didn't hear him come into the study and yet, somehow, she could sense him there, standing behind her. The knowing was in the stiffening of her spine, that uneasy prickle at the nape of her neck. She could taste him on her tongue.

Her eyes flicked to the corners of the computer screen, checking to see if she could find his shadow, but there was nothing. Her hand rested on the mouse, and she stopped scrolling through the article she'd been reading, waiting for him to speak first.

'She's young,' he said. There was a photo of a woman on the screen; it was taken on her wedding day, a slip of ivory silk clinging to her body. 'She can't be more than mid-twenties, can she?'

Nessa never even made it to that age. Nessa would never

turn forty-six and feel bone-deep tired all the time, like Keelin did. She wouldn't crawl into bed at ten p.m., barely able to keep her eyes open any longer, nor would she wake at four in the morning, her bladder fit to burst. Nessa wouldn't have to stare at her reflection in the mirror, pinching the new folds of skin around her jawline she was certain hadn't been there yesterday, wondering when, exactly, she had become old. The Crowley Girl would be young forever.

Her husband leaned over her and pressed the page-down key on the keyboard. An intake of breath as he skimmed the article. 'My God,' Henry said. 'The poor girl. Did you read this part, Keelin? Where her daughter had a tummy bug and was sick all over her bedspread? And when the husband found out, he made –' he checked the screen again – 'Sarah Watson *eat* the vomit.' He shivered. 'That's barbaric.'

Sarah Watson had married young, the journalist wrote, and the first time her husband hit her was on their honeymoon. By the time their youngest daughter was three, he'd hospitalised Sarah on two occasions, breaking her jaw and dislocating her shoulder by throwing her down a flight of stairs. But Sarah gave as good as she got, her mother-in-law was quoted as saying. That girl could start a fight in an empty room; they were as bad as each other, she said. After a particularly heated argument he choked Sarah until she lost consciousness, and she fled to a shelter, fearing for her life. The husband threatened to go to the police and file kidnapping charges if she didn't bring the children home and so, despite the staff's best efforts to persuade her to stay, she went back to him. I can't lose my kids, Sarah Watson said to the shelter's coordinator. He has rights in the eyes of the law, I'll still have to negotiate child-visitation rights with him. I've seen what the system does to women like me. It won't protect me. She was dead within two weeks, the story splashed across the front pages of the newspapers, friends and colleagues expressing shock that the husband could commit such a horrifying act of violence. He hadn't seemed the type, but you never know what goes on behind closed doors, do you? they said to each other for a few days before promptly forgetting all about it.

'I don't know why you continue to read stuff like this,' Henry said. 'It only upsets you. Why do it to yourself?'

Keelin continued to read 'stuff like this' for the same reason she continued to read her psychology books and journals. It was why she was still a member of the Psychological Society of Ireland and subscribed to their magazine, why she scrolled through the events sections on their website on a daily basis, imagining which conferences she would go to, the questions she would ask the speakers, if she was capable of leaving this island. Keelin had trained to become a counsellor special-ising in domestic violence because she'd wanted to support women, to show them that a life free of abuse was within their grasp. The work had been difficult, but it had been fulfilling too, in a way that seemed impossible to imagine now. So she read 'stuff like this' because she needed to pretend she still had a career, a *purpose*.

Henry turned the computer off. 'Honestly,' he said, 'it horrifies me how these men behave, if you can even call them "men". When I think about how Mark Delaney treated you, darling . . .' He gripped the back of her chair tightly. 'It's revolting.'

(Where were you? Her ex-husband screaming at her when he arrived home from work. I phoned the house a hundred times today and there was no answer. Where were you, Keelin? Are you fucking someone else, you cunt? Fists punching into her stomach, and she was doubled over in agony, begging him to stop, she would never do that, she would never betray him like that. I didn't mean it, Mark would always say afterwards, drawing a bath and gently lowering her into the water, tears coming to his eyes when she gasped in pain. I just can't bear the thought of you cheating on me, not after everything that happened with *her*. I'm terrified of losing you, that's all. I'll get help, he promised, and Keelin had believed him or she'd wanted to believe him. Maybe they were the same thing, in the end.)

Henry pulled her to standing, taking her place on the chair. He sat Keelin on his lap and she buried her face in his shoulder, breathing in the spicy scent of his cologne as she thought of that other house, that other husband. Henry would never raise a hand to her. She was safe with him.

'Look at that,' he said, checking his Patek Philippe watch, the delicate strokes of silver ticking in a platinum face. When Henry's brother turned fifty, Jonathan had given his first-born son his vintage Audemars Piguet as a birthday present; it was the sort of thing that should become a family heirloom, he'd said. He gave it to *Charlie*, of all people! Charlie would be as happy wearing a fucking Swatch! Her husband had seethed when he watched the videos of Jonathan's speech on Facebook, accompanied by photos of a lavish birthday party they hadn't been invited to. He spent weeks afterwards searching for the most expensive piece he could source and sent his father the bill. It's beautiful, Keelin told him when it was delivered to the island, hoping this would settle his prickly mood for a few weeks at least. But that same night she woke up and the bed was empty beside her. Henry? she called out, stealing downstairs and finding her husband in the sunroom. The new watch in his hands, staring at it. When will I be enough for them? he asked her, so quietly. Keelin sat at the foot of the chair, leaning her head against his thigh. You're enough for me, she said, wishing she could make this better for him. I love you so much. When she jolted awake the next morning, her neck aching, her husband was gone.

'I can't believe it's June 21st already,' he said now. He'd never become accustomed to this new, amorphous life of theirs, the undefined edges of each day where one hour bled into the next until finally it was over and they could go to sleep again. 'Remember when we used to—'

'Yes.'

Henry had always loved the summer solstice, waiting until the day fell fast into night before setting the bonfire alight, taking a breathless step back as it soared to kiss the sky. The flames crackling orange, bodies moving in and around its heart, dancing shadows cast against bare skin. The solstice celebrations were supposed to be cleansing, meant to purify the body and soul. The Misty Hill guests would run into the sea at midnight, gasping at the icy sting of the water, calling to the heavens to wash their sins away and make them worthy.

'Will you go down to Marigold Cottage and check on the Australians? They've been on the island for over a month now, I'm curious to know what kind of progress they're making,' he said. 'Why don't you ask if they'd like to join us for dinner? It's the longest day of the year – we should mark it in some way.'

Henry missed their old life, she knew, the dinner parties and the heavy thud of wedding invites through the letter box every spring, throwing confetti into the air outside charming little churches in the Cotswolds, the holidays to the south of France to stay in friends' plush villas. Was that why he had agreed to have the Australians stay in Marigold Cottage – because he was starved for company? Was her husband so desperate to fill the empty seats around the dinner table that he would put them all in danger?

'I have to check on Alex first. He's sick.'

'What's wrong with him?' Henry's tone was sharp. 'Has he done anything to—'

'He's fine, don't worry. It's just a twenty-four-hour thing.'

'Ah, OK. Poor Alex.' He kissed the back of her neck.

'But you can go down afterwards, can't you? To talk to the Australians.'

'I . . .' Keelin pictured herself walking down the garden path, knocking on the yellow door of Marigold Cottage, and she was so weary at the thought of it she could feel herself physically wilt. 'Please, Henry,' she said. 'I'm tired.'

'We're all tired, darling. And we all have to do things we don't want to do, now, don't we?'

She looked to the ground. 'You're right,' she said. 'You're always right.'

Upstairs, she knocked on her son's door. 'Alex?' she said, tiptoeing into the room without waiting for his response. She shouldn't have done that. She should have 'respected his personal boundaries', as her old supervisor would have said, but then again, her supervisor didn't have to deal with an adult child still living at home at the age of twenty-seven, a half-finished degree in French and Philosophy the only thing to his name. I can't do it any more, he'd told Keelin when he arrived home that day, midway through his second year at Trinity. I can't pretend I'm OK when I'm not, he said. He hadn't left Inisrún since.

'Alex,' she said again. It took her eyes a few seconds to adjust to the gloom, but then she saw him, lying on the bed, staring at the ceiling. This was Evie's apartment and the interior designer had taken the 'Teenage Girl' brief very seriously, using shades of millennial pink and rose gold, a four-poster bed with a sheer gauze canopy as the centrepiece. The last time she'd come home, Evie had plastered the walls with photos of her school friends: beautiful girls in short skirts and Adidas trainers. Friends Keelin had never met because her daughter had never brought them home to the island, and she never would.

She sat down on the bed, switching on the bedside lamp. Alex blinking, turning away from her. 'What is it?' he asked.

'I just wanted to check you were OK.'

'I'm grand, Mam. Just tired, you know.'

His face was pale, sharp cheekbones protruding and casting shadows on his jawline. He ate so little, scraps of sandwiches and half a biscuit washed down with a milky cup of tea, and only when Keelin forced him to do so. She could still see him as a new-born, wet and red and screaming. It's a boy, they'd said. What? she'd cried out, It's a what? (No. No. It couldn't be. A fortune-teller had once told Mark he would only have daughters, and so he had said throughout Keelin's pregnancy that the baby *must* be a girl. If the baby wasn't a girl, he would know Keelin had cheated on him, just like his ex had done.) You have a beautiful baby boy, the nurse said again, and Keelin wept as he was placed against her breast, wondering what Mark would do when he heard the news of a son, how he would punish her. But she had known too, in some primal part of herself that she couldn't quite understand, that this baby was more important than Mark now, and she would do whatever it took to protect him, including from his own father. Alex had grown from a demanding, colicky infant into a quiet child, one who had never played easily with other children, reluctant to share his toys. They'll only break them, Mammy, he explained, clutching his Tellytubby to his chest. He didn't need their company anyway, he said, not when he had Keelin's hand to hold. She'd hoped he would find it easier when he started at the island school; she had been shy too, yet she had found Seán and Johanna, she'd found her tribe. But her son became increasingly quiet, coming to her in the middle of the night in soaked pyjamas, whispering that he had wet the bed. It was months later when she awoke to the sound of him crying, choking back ragged sobs. (That was what hurt her most of all, she would think afterwards. That he had tried to hide it, that he hadn't felt he could confide in her.) What's wrong, mo stoirín? she said, one hand on his forehead to check his temperature. Are you sick? And then he told her. One of the big boys had informed everyone at playtime that Alex was *weird*, he was so weird he'd scared his dad away and that's why he lived in a house full of women; he was a sissy, a wuss, a mammy's boy. Why doesn't my daddy live with us? Did I do something wrong? the boy asked. The hurt in his voice, and Keelin's heart twisting in her chest to hear it. You did *nothing* wrong, she said, almost winded. I love you and your mamó loves you and your father loves you too, in his own way, of course he does. Our marriage didn't work out for other reasons – *nothing* to do with you. You're the best thing that ever happened to us, Alex, she told him. We will love you forever.

'I have to go see the Australians,' she said now, and her son stiffened.

'Why?'

'It's summer solstice. We thought it might be a good idea to have a dinner party.'

'Henry thought it was a good idea, you mean.'

'They seem like nice enough lads.' Keelin brushed his hair away from his forehead, feeling how lank it was beneath her fingertips. When was the last time he'd showered? Was he taking his medication? She wanted to ask him, but she knew Alex would snap at her, tell her to mind her own business, he wasn't a child any more.

'Don't.' He pushed her hand off him. 'I can't believe you're doing this, Mam.'

'Henry—'

'Henry would do anything for attention.'

'That's not fair. Who's been the one taking care of us for the last ten years? I wouldn't have survived without him in the beginning and I think you know that. This documentary was going to happen, whether we liked it or not, and now they're here, we have to stick together and get on with it.' She waited for his reply. 'Alex,' she said in a softer voice when he remained silent, 'please. I need you to promise me that you'll just try, OK? That's all I'm asking, mo stoirín.' She stood up, and when she was at the door her son spoke again.

50

'These true-crime programmes are disgusting. They're voyeuristic and exploitative. Someone died, Mam. She's *dead*,' he said. 'Nessa is . . .' He curled into the fetal position, his arms around his knees, holding himself together. He could barely say her name, Keelin realised. Her son still loved that girl, even after all this time.

CHAPTER SEVEN

The Crowley Girl

'I don't know what to do, lads,' Keelin said. She'd texted her two best friends that afternoon and asked them to meet her in Cupán Tae, the island's oldest cafe. The owner had been one of the few who refused to sell to the Kinsellas when Misty Hill was set up, much to their frustration, so there was never any danger of running into Henry here. She hadn't yet met another human being who could nurse a grudge quite like her husband. 'What do ye think I should do?' she asked them. Seán Crowley, with his weather-beaten face and unkempt blond beard, was as much of the island as Keelin was, his family had been here for generations, but Johanna Stein was the daughter of blow-ins, a pair of German artists who moved to west Cork in the early seventies, looking for the end of the world, and they had found it on Inisrún. As children, the three of them spent their days exploring the island; racing down narrow, winding roads with tufts of grass sprouting in the middle, shouting *Seachain!* when the odd car would pass, a shell of metal belching black clouds and half held together with twine, squeezing the children up against stone walls stuffed with moss and weeds. They would go down to An Siopa Beag and beg Keelin's mother for salt-and-vinegar Taytos, sitting side by side on the stone ledge outside, licking crumbs from the foil crisp packets, their voices echoing in the cocoon of a beach surrounded by the high sea cliffs on the right and the pier to the left, watching as the boats arrived from the mainland to see if anyone new was coming to the island. Apart from Seán and Keelin's brief attempt at romance as teenagers – This is a terrible idea, Keelin had said after a few months of dating. Can we go back to normal, please? and Seán had laughed, and said he thought she'd never ask – they had always been a gang of three, and utterly inseparable.

'Henry will go mad if he sees these marks.' She gave Seán the report that her son had brought home from school the day before. He took it from her, making a face as his eyes skimmed down the page.

'Yeah,' he said, passing it to Johanna. 'Not great and that's coming from me, like.'

'Alex is more creative,' Keelin said defensively, taking the letter from the other woman, folding it in two and putting it back in her handbag. 'And you know how much I hated maths in school – I was pure useless. Alex takes after my side, unfortunately for him.'

'He did brilliantly in french,' Johanna tried to comfort her. 'He's obviously more inclined towards languages. There's no harm in that.' The café's proprietor, wearing the same worn-out GAA jersey and acid-wash denim jeans he did every day, placed a slice of homemade coffee cake on the table for her, apple tart for Johanna. 'Go raibh maith agat, Cormac,' Keelin said, smiling at him. She waited until the older man had gone behind the counter again before continuing. 'Henry won't be happy about this,' she admitted, frowning at Seán when he rolled his eyes. 'Excuse me, Crowley. Don't be like that about my husband. If Alex wants to go to university, he'll need to get better marks than this, and that's the reality of it. We agreed that he could sit his final exams on Inisrún, but only if he kept his grades up. If Henry hears he's failing maths . . .' She sighed, taking a bite of the cake. Her son had been miserable at the boarding school outside Dublin that a friend of Henry's had recommended; he felt isolated, never quite fitting in with his rugby-obsessed classmates. I miss the island, he said every time he phoned; please let me come home, Mam. She had gone to Henry then, wheedling and cajoling, promising that Alex would be an exemplary student if he came back to Inisrún, he wouldn't get lower than a B in any of his subjects and if he did, there'd be hell to pay. She didn't want to admit that her efforts were as much for her own benefit as Alex's; she'd missed her son terribly when he was away at school. 'I don't know what to do,' she said again, slicing her fork into Johanna's apple tart, ignoring her friend's complaint.

'Maybe it's time . . .' Jo paused, glancing at Keelin uncertainly.

'Maybe it's time to what?'

'Alex is almost an adult,' her friend said. 'He'll be off to college soon. You won't always be there to rescue him, Keels.'

'I'm not trying to "rescue" him; he's my son. I just want him to be happy. I don't think that's a crime, is it? Especially after everything he's been through.'

'Of course.' Johanna put her arm around Keelin's waist and squeezed tightly. 'I'm sorry, I shouldn't have said anything. You're the most loyal, supportive person on Inisrún. That's why we love you, isn't it, Seán?' Their friend snorted, and told them to leave him out of this. 'And I don't even have kids,' Jo said. 'What do I know?'

'Wait,' Seán interrupted, tapping the side of his head as if he couldn't believe he hadn't thought of this earlier. 'I have the perfect solution.' He paused for dramatic effect, pretending to do a drum roll on the wooden table. 'Nessa!'

'Nessa, your niece?'

'Do you know another Nessa on Rún, d'ya?' he asked, and Keelin stuck out her tongue in response; she always regressed to acting like a ten-year-old when she was around him. 'I'll have you know my goddaughter got an A1 in honours maths in the Leaving, and she's in second year of Mathematical Science at UCC now, no less.'

'Yeah, we're well aware of that. You wouldn't stop going on about it last year.' Jo smirked. 'You'd swear it was you who was doing your exams.'

'Nessa is giving grinds to earn money.' Seán ignored their friend. 'She's got the grant, but Cork is still an expensive city to live in.'

Nessa Crowley's results seemed to be the only topic of conversation on the island for days after they were announced. *Did you hear the eldest Crowley Girl got six hundred points in her Leaving, and all higher-level subjects?* Keelin was asked at Mass and when she was picking up Evie from school and down by the pier waiting for the ferry, until she wanted to reply in exasperation, *You do realise other people sat their exams too, don't you?*

'But . . .' Keelin hesitated. Wouldn't Brendan Crowley mind if his daughter came to work in Hawthorn House? she wanted to ask. Her husband thought Brendan adored him, assuming the school principal was eternally grateful to the Kinsellas for the money they'd sunk into the island's education system, but Keelin was from Inisrún and she knew how these things worked. The more money Henry spent trying to fit in, the less people here liked him. She could see them suppressing an eye-roll when her husband attempted to speak Irish, or when he mentioned, yet again, how his mother had been born here, his accent suddenly sounding more foreign, more *English*, than it ever had before.

'Won't Nessa be busy with her college work?' Johanna said, a side-glance at Keelin telling her that her friend understood her reservations. 'She's hardly going to want to traipse home every weekend to give grinds to a teenage boy, is she?'

'Ah, you know what those girls are like,' Seán said. 'They can't survive without each other. Róisín and Sinéad were wailing the day Nessa left – you'd swear she was after getting on a coffin ship rather than the ferry to the mainland. She'll be home every weekend anyway, mark my words. I'm telling you, she'd jump at the chance to work for you.'

'Nessa Crowley,' Keelin said, relenting. She stirred sugar into her coffee. 'Well, well. You might be the solution to all my problems.'

CHAPTER EIGHT

Keelin Kinsella

KEELIN: I met my ex-husband in my first year of college. He was ahead of me in the checkout queue and he turned and said, Have you ever heard of a vegetable, girl? because my basket was full of baked beans and pasta, you know, typical student stuff. When I'd paid, he asked if I needed help with my bag and he walked me home. And that was that, I guess. Within weeks, we were boyfriend and girlfriend and he was telling me I was beautiful, I was special, that he'd never felt like this about anyone else in his whole life. It was very full on.

JAKE: Did that set off any alarm bells?

KEELIN: It didn't, to be honest. I'll admit, I'd been lonely up until that point, I missed Seán and Johanna so much, and my ex-husband was the only person to show any real interest in me since I'd arrived at UCC. At the start of second year I fell pregnant, and by Christmas I'd dropped out of my course. I'd go back after the baby was born, I said. We were married by the time I was four months gone – a registry job, my parents weren't even there; he said it would be more romantic if it was just the two of us. He made it sound . . . anyway, it was done before I knew it, really – and then he wanted to move back to Carlow, where he was from. He said his mother could help out with the baby. It made more sense, he said.

NOAH: What was it like in Carlow?

KEELIN: Oh God, it was *awful*. It was in the middle of nowhere, the nearest neighbour was miles away. I wanted to get a job; I was so young and I thought it would be a good way of meeting people, but my ex said I should concentrate on the baby. All I had to do was ask him for money if I needed it, I wouldn't go without. But the house was so isolated, I said, I was afraid I'd be lonely. And he told me it wasn't isolated, it was *private*, there was a difference. (pause) I soon found out what could happen with that man in private.

NOAH: I'm sorry, Keelin. Did you ever call the police about the abuse?

KEELIN: Ah, look. The worst of it happened at night-time and the local garda station wasn't open twenty-four hours a day. I'd have had to wait until morning to talk to someone and by then . . . well, things always seemed better by then.

59

(pause) And a friend of his from the rugby club was a guard – we used to have dinner with him and his wife sometimes. It was too embarrassing, I guess, the thought of having to make a complaint to him, knowing he'd go home and tell his wife too. I wasn't sure if he would even believe me, everyone always said what a great guy my ex was. Salt of the earth, you know.

JAKE: You were still in Carlow when you heard the news about your father, weren't you?

KEELIN: Yeah. When the phone rang – I wasn't supposed to answer it during the day, my ex didn't like the idea of me chatting to my parents or Jo and Seán; he said they'd only be filling my head with stupid ideas about moving back to the island. But the phone kept ringing and ringing, and Alex was screaming, and I couldn't take it any longer so I picked it up. It was just weeping at the start; it took me a few minutes before I even realised it was my mother at the other end of the line. Mam, I said. Mam, what's wrong? But I didn't need her to tell me. I already knew.

JAKE: What did you do then?

KEELIN: I had to wait until my ex-husband came home. He checked the petrol and the mileage every night to make sure I hadn't gone anywhere; I wasn't allowed to use the Toyota by myself. He said I was a bad driver and he didn't want his son in the car with me, it was too dangerous, he said. So I sat there and I waited.

★

Mark had found her sitting on the floor that evening, the phone still cradled in her lap. I don't think you should go, he said when she told him. *My father is dead.* She said the words carefully, one by one, trying to make them real. Keelin stared at him, shocked. But it's Daddy's funeral, she said. He never liked me, did he? Mark replied, and Keelin wondered if this was another test. Was she supposed to ring Mam back and tell her no, she wouldn't be coming? But she couldn't do that, she realised. She packed hurriedly, grabbing nappies and a change of clothes for Alex, shoving a black dress and shoes into an overnight suitcase for herself. As Keelin drove to Cork, she thought of her father, how gentle he had been, how loving, how much he'd adored his only daughter. But she didn't cry. She was too afraid to cry.

'I got home in time for the funeral,' she said, swallowing hard. Jake passed her a box of Kleenex from the kitchen counter and she smiled gratefully at him, dabbing her eyes with a tissue. 'And that was all that mattered really.'

'I've heard there are some cool funeral traditions here,' Noah said from his corner, headphones on as he checked the audio levels again. 'My grandparents have told me a little bit, but I'd love to hear you describe it, Keelin.'

She could have told them about meeting her mother in the hospital that night, the older woman collapsing into her arms. How thin Cáit had felt, how much weight she'd lost since Keelin had last seen her. What will we do now? she asked and Keelin didn't know how to reply. The boat trip back to the island, the ferryman quiet. The lights at the pier, the islanders holding candles to welcome Tomás Ó Mordha home for the last time. Walking up the steep hill to their cottage, the coffin balanced on the shoulders of six strong men. The wake – the songs and the stories, the tea and the scones – and then the coffin going into the ground, a bed of flowers awaiting him, and Keelin thinking, My father is in that grave. *My father is dead.*

'No,' she said. 'I'm too tired to go into all that now, Noah. I'm sorry.'

'What about your mother's death? I understand Alex was—'

'No,' she said again. 'That's it for tonight.'

'Too right,' Jake said, shooting Noah an annoyed look. 'You've been great, Keelin. We really appreciate it.'

The Australians had called to Hawthorn House earlier, asking if they could 'borrow' Keelin for the evening. She'd been in the kitchen but she could hear them on the porch, Henry joking, saying he'd *have to check with the missus.* When the front door closed, Keelin walked into the hall, waiting for her husband to speak.

Do you want to go, darling? he asked.

Do you think I should, Henry?

It couldn't hurt, he said so she went upstairs to fix her make-up. Be careful, he said as she left. I always am, she replied.

In Marigold Cottage, she copied Jake and took her boots off, leaving them on the shoe rack inside. She had sat at the kitchen table with a cup of tea as the two men set up for their interview, chatting easily about their plans for the documentary. It was July now; they'd been on the island for two months and they weren't scheduled to return to Sydney until January. That's a long time, Keelin said. We've been lucky with you guys giving us free accommodation, Noah admitted. That makes a huge difference to our budget.

But there are only so many people here to interview – sure, there's barely two hundred people living on the island these days, she said, and they explained that they wouldn't be on Inisrún all the time, they'd be travelling to the mainland and to the UK as well, they had plenty of interviews set up over there. Listen, Jake said, his eyes on her, we want this documentary to be different from anything else that has been made about the Misty Hill case. That's why we've moved here; we want to fully immerse ourselves in island life. We want this to be an in-depth exploration of a community torn apart by violence and we can't do that over a couple of weeks. This has to be done properly.

'Keelin,' Jake said now, motioning at his friend to help him tidy up their equipment, 'do you want to stay for dinner?'

'Nah, yeah,' Noah said, putting the camera lid back on. 'Jake is a brilliant cook – the first thing he did when we visited Cork city was find an Asian supermarket to stock up on spices. He likes that expensive shit.'

'I don't know if I'd call it "shit",' Jake said drily. 'You're really selling my skills here, mate.' He smiled at Keelin. 'We'd be glad to have you though, if you'd like.'

She checked her phone. It was eight p.m., and she had told Henry she'd be home by nine thirty at the latest. 'OK.' She made her mind up, thinking of that dark, silent house, and all the questions Henry would have for her when she arrived home. Asking how the interview had gone, what the men had asked her, what she'd said in response, circling around and around until she would want to fall down in exhaustion. 'That would be lovely, thank you.'

She and Noah sat at the rickety old table while Jake cooked, the kitchen full of sizzling heat and the smell of frying onions, garlic and ginger. He had his back to them but it was clear he was listening carefully to their conversation, stifling a snort when Noah made one of his ridiculous jokes, becoming very still whenever Keelin said anything, as if he wanted to make sure he didn't miss a word. 'It's just beef pho,' Jake said when he was finished, placing steaming bowls of noodle soup on the table. 'And not even a proper version – my ma would be disgusted that I didn't boil bones for the broth.' He faltered, ever so slightly, when he mentioned his mother, and Noah rushed to fill the silence, chattering about his boyfriend, Jamie, who was a doctor ('Creative people need to date someone who has a proper job, Keelin – at least one steady pay cheque should be coming in, don't you agree?') and his parents' reaction when he came out as gay ('Mam just said, yeah, we thought as much, and Dad said he was proud of me and promptly left the room and never mentioned it again.') He teased Jake incessantly – about his terrible surfing skills, his love life, how obsessed Jake was with work. Jake took it with good humour, rolling his eyes and calling Noah an obnoxious gronk. Keelin asked what a gronk was, and the two men competed to find the most outlandish Aussie slang they could teach her, shouting over one another until Keelin was giggling helplessly and wiping tears from her eyes. She couldn't remember the last time she had enjoyed herself so much, staring at her empty plate in astonishment when Jake asked if she wanted a second helping. She had eaten the entire portion. She never did that any more.

'Top of the morning to you, Mammy,' Noah said as he answered his phone. Keelin could hear an indignant tone on the other side. 'Oh, I'm sorry,' he said. 'Is that not how the fine people speak on this here Emerald Isle? Begorrah, be God.' He started to laugh at whatever his mother's reply was. 'OK, OK.' He put the phone on speaker. 'Say g'day to Jakey and Keelin,' he said, holding the phone out, and an Irish voice said, 'Hi, Jake. Hi, Keelin.' Noah tilted his head towards his bedroom, mouthing 'ten minutes' at them.

'Was that actually *Keelin Kinsella*?' his mother asked, the phone still on speaker, as Noah closed the door behind him. 'Tell me everything! What's she really—' and then it went silent, and all they could hear was the muffled sound of Noah's voice through the walls, the creak of mattress springs as he sat on the bed.

'I should go,' she said.

'Don't,' Jake said. 'I'm sorry about that. Noah's mother doesn't mean any harm. She—'

'It's all right.' She looked around the cottage, the only one that had been salvageable after Misty Hill burned down. The thick wooden beams across the ceiling and the cracked slate floor, the súgán chairs with their woven seats, the half-door in a bright yellow. It was a cliché: stone walls painted white and a thatched roof – what a foreigner would think an Irish cottage should look like. But that was the image the Kinsellas had wanted to create for Misty Hill. Traditional sells, Jonathan Kinsella said, and he had always prided himself on being a good salesman.

'Please stay,' Jake said. 'Have some more wine?'

She looked at her iPhone again. There was a text from Henry, wondering where she was. *Do you need me to rescue you, darling?* She turned it face down. 'Maybe half a glass,' she said.

They talked for another two hours after that. Jake asked about growing up on the island, the changes she had seen in her lifetime, if she'd ever considered leaving Inisrún. It didn't feel like an interview this time; he appeared genuinely interested in learning more about her. She wasn't sure if it was the heat of the fire or the red wine – she wasn't used to alcohol any more, she'd barely drunk since the night of the party – but Keelin felt like her tongue was stirring loose, all the words she had swallowed during the last ten years re-forming on her lips, eager to be spoken.

66

'You dropped out of uni when you were pregnant but you went back as a mature student when Alex was a little kid, right? That's pretty impressive.' Jake said, going to top up Keelin's drink.

'Not really,' she said, putting her hand over the glass to stop him.

'How would you describe it then?'

'Selfish, probably. I should have stayed at home with Alex; it wasn't right leaving him here with my mother. Not the way she was.' Keelin gestured at Jake to pass her the water jug instead. She couldn't go home tipsy; it wouldn't be fair to Henry. 'He was the best kid though,' she said, smiling as she remembered her son waving her off at the pier every Sunday, blowing kisses and squealing with joy as she pretended to catch them. 'He never complained about me being away for most of the week. He made it easy for me.'

'You trained to be a psychiatrist, I read,' Jake said. Of course he had read up about her – he probably had dossiers full of information about Keelin, about her childhood and her education, every relationship she'd ever had, all in the name of research. It was uncomfortable, and a stark reminder of the imbalance of power between the two of them, the advantage this man had over her.

'No, that was yet another thing the papers got wrong,' she said deliberately. 'It was a course in Counselling and Psychotherapy.'

'Did you ever use your degree?' He held his hand out for

Keelin's plate, stacking it on top of his own. She gathered the cutlery and followed him to the sink.

'I worked in a shelter for battered women on the mainland, but you already know that, don't you?' she said, leaning against the counter as Jake loaded the dishwasher. 'It was the hardest work I've ever done in my life but I loved it too. Well, "love" is probably the wrong word. But it felt . . . necessary. Like I was doing something important, something that would actually make a difference in other people's lives. That sounds a bit grandiose, doesn't it?' She cleared her throat, embarrassed. 'Not that it matters any more. I was told my services were no longer needed after . . .'

'Nessa died?'

'Yeah.'

'That must have been difficult for you,' he said, but Keelin didn't reply. 'Did you always want to work in that sector?' he tried instead.

'Domestic violence?' Keelin asked. Jake sat back down on the súgán, nodding his yes. 'Not when I was in school or anything. I never gave it much thought, to be honest. My dad was a quiet soul – the only time I heard him raise his voice was when Cork were playing Kerry in the Munster final and he didn't like a decision the ref had made. He would never have hit my mother; he'd have been shocked at the very thought. Domestic violence was something I thought happened to *other* women. This is going to sound awful, but I thought it happened to women who weren't as smart as I was or as well

68

educated, women who were used to being slapped around because they came from "bad families",' she said, using her fingers to make air quotes. 'I didn't have a clue.'

'You know what's funny?' Jake asked, leaning forward in his chair. 'As a kid, you think that everyone else's house must be the same as yours, that everyone's family behaves exactly like yours does. It's only as you get older that you learn life doesn't work like that.'

'How do you mean?'

'Well, when I was little I just assumed all fathers were like mine, wanting things done in the exact right way, which meant *his* way. He demanded dinner on the table at seven p.m. sharp, and the cutlery had to be laid out how he liked it. If they were even half an inch out of line, he would flip the table, just tip it right over. Then he would make my ma get down on her knees and eat the food off the ground, like she was a fucking dog. And I actually thought that was *normal*. My sisters did too. I'd look at them when my father was on one of his rampages and they'd barely respond, their eyes glazed over like it was nothing new. And it wasn't new, not to us anyway.'

Keelin kept very still, maintaining eye contact with Jake so he would know he was being heard, that she was holding a space for him, bearing witness to his story. Old therapy tricks die hard, she supposed. 'Tell me about your mother,' she asked gently. 'I'd love to know more about her.'

'Ma came to Australia when she was seventeen,' Jake said,

69

fingering the frayed edges of the cloth place mat. 'She met Lucas Taylor a year later and she was pregnant with me almost immediately. My sisters—' He broke off, his throat pulsing with something unsaid, words that were unspeakable. 'Ashleigh and Brooke – they were twins – they came ten months after me.' He tried to laugh. 'What's that called here again? Noah told me but I've forgotten.'

'Irish twins,' she said. 'Although I guess it's Irish triplets, in your case.'

'Yeah,' he said. 'Irish triplets.' He blinked rapidly, as if to stop himself from crying. 'Jesus. I don't know why I'm telling you all this – I never talk about it. This isn't very professional of me, is it? But I guess I just wanted you to know that I understand what it's like to be famous for something you didn't do.'

'Jake . . .' she started but she couldn't find the right words. 'I'd better go home,' she said instead, gathering her phone and her bag. 'It's late.'

It was cool when they walked outside. 'Hard to believe it's July,' Jake said as Keelin shivered, rubbing her bare arms vigorously. It was a clear night, the stars sharp in the sky like scar tissue on velvet, seeming so close you could almost touch them.

'I'll walk you home,' he offered.

'No.'

'Right,' he said. 'I understand.'

And as he waved her goodbye, Keelin thought he just

70

might. She turned to walk up the hill to Hawthorn House. The lights were off, the outline of the building looming black against the night sky, and it was then she looked at her phone. Five missed calls, six unread messages. *Darling,* Henry texted. *I'm worried about you. Please let me know you're safe.*

'Jake,' she said, looking back over her shoulder, 'this might sound like a weird question, but . . . were you ever angry with your mother? For everything that happened?'

He leaned against the half-door, his arms dangling over the edge. 'If I'm being totally honest, I wish she had at least *tried* to leave,' he said. 'I wish she had protected us more. That she'd been stronger, I guess? She should have made the choice to leave him years ago; he was never going to change. She knew he was dangerous and still she stayed. Maybe my sisters would still be . . . I know that's not fair of me to say, but it's how I feel.'

'Sometimes,' Keelin said slowly, 'leaving isn't a choice that's yours to make.'

CHAPTER NINE

The Kinsellas could never determine who had sold what to which outlet, but in the months that followed the murder, photos from the party were splashed across the newspapers. Henry with his shirt unbuttoned too low, a smidge of cocaine burrowed in his left nostril, bottles of champagne littering the ground behind him. An actress from a beloved BBC period drama, a joint in hand, her nipples visible through her sheer dress. Two of Henry's school friends doing a pretend jig while wearing green leprechaun hats, the sort of cheap thing you'd find in shops selling Paddywhackery to tourists at an indecent mark-up. Ireland had been at the beginning of a recession when Nessa Crowley was murdered. People were losing their jobs, they were worried about how they would pay their mortgages and feed their children, and the photos from the party touched a nerve, like an exposed wire. Didn't the Brits realise that Ireland was a free country now? They couldn't just come over here and treat the locals like indentured servants. And was it true Misty Hill received funding from the Arts Board? they wanted to know, becoming increasingly indignant. Despite denials, there were persistent rumours a high-ranking government official had been in attendance that night. Was this what their taxes were being used for? And now a young woman was dead, an innocent caught up in something she didn't understand. Seduced, no doubt, by the glamour and the privilege. And the money. The Kinsellas had always had plenty of money. Maybe too much, the islanders whispered. The money had been the start of it all. The money paid for the parties, and the parties had brought the outsiders. It was only then the trouble came.

What is she doing here? Keelin had asked Henry when she saw Nessa arriving at the party, a bottle of wine in hand. I don't know, her husband shrugged, bored already. Alex must have invited her. Her son, his face lighting up at the sight of the Crowley Girl, hugging her hello. Their heads close, talking in low voices, sharing their secrets. Keelin couldn't help but think of his diary, what she had seen in its pages, and she felt queasy at the sight of them together.

There was only one photo of Nessa taken that night. She was in a filmy black dress, cut tight to her body, and Keelin was beside her. Nessa's arm around her waist, both of them smiling at the camera. The girl had smelled of apple shampoo, crisp, fresh. Keelin would remember that smell for the rest of her life.

That same photo accompanied the articles about the Misty Hill case in the years that followed, printed and reprinted in every outlet in the country. The story was irresistible, it had it all: beauty, celebrity, wealth, sex. Then there was Nessa, with her big eyes and long legs, that perfect face – she would haunt the Irish people for the decade to follow. Who had killed the Crowley Girl? they asked. Who could have done such a thing to someone so young, so beautiful? When would there be justice?

CHAPTER TEN

Johanna Stein, Keelin Kinsella's childhood friend

JOHANNA: I've never talked about Keelin in this way before.
I'm only doing this interview because . . .

JAKE: Because?

JOHANNA: I'm sick of hearing other people talk about her,
I guess. People who barely know her, who have no idea
what the real Keelin is like.

JAKE: What is the real Keelin like?

JOHANNA: Where do I start? (pause) I'm almost forty-seven
years of age, and in all my life I've never met anyone who
loves like Keelin does. She was never Miss Popular or
anything, never the person who had dozens of friends,
not like Henry was. When she would come and visit me
at Mary I – that's the teaching college in Limerick, where

I studied – my housemates would tell me afterwards they thought she was a bit standoffish. She didn't make much of an effort, they complained. But Keelin was just shy. She didn't let everybody in, but if she did, if you were lucky enough to be her friend, my God – that woman would go to war for you.

NOAH: Can you give us an example?

JOHANNA: Oh Christ, let me think, I could be here all day. OK. OK, I remember this time, the first year of college it must have been, I'd come down to visit Keelin in Cork for the weekend. We were dressed in our finest, only delighted with ourselves, and we were standing outside a club when a group of guys started jeering at me, calling me a 'fucking dyke', and I just froze. I hadn't even admitted I was gay to myself at that stage, let alone to other people, and it was terrifying to think that it might be so *obvious*, that strangers on the street could see it in me. And Keelin marched up to them, and it was almost comical – she was half their size and she had her finger in their faces, telling them they were bullies and they were pathetic and how dare they speak to me like that? I had to drag her away before she lost the plot entirely, started something she couldn't finish. (pause) Just as we were falling asleep that night, she said, 'You know that I love you, no matter what? I hope you know you can tell me anything, Jo.'

NOAH: That's all you need to hear in that moment, isn't it?

JOHANNA: Yeah. And look, I knew my parents would be fine with it, no matter what my sexuality was, but I didn't realise until that moment that I'd been worried about what Keelin and Seán would think; there wasn't exactly a thriving gay community on Rún in the nineties. (laughs) I should have known it would be fine.

JAKE: What did you think of the Kinsella family?

JOHANNA: Well, I was the only island girl who wasn't in love with Henry or Charlie. That should've been my first clue. (laughs) Look, my parents weren't from Inisrún; we were always seen as blow-ins, even though I was born there. That gave me the ability to observe, I guess. And it was obvious to me the Kinsellas were never going to fit in on the island, no matter how hard they tried.

JAKE: Why not?

JOHANNA: Where do I start? Olivia wasn't too bad; I think she had some sense of how she should behave around the locals, and Jonathan was grand too, really, although he liked the sound of his own voice after a few whiskeys but as for the two lads ... The posh accents, and the *clothes* – I once saw a friend of theirs rocking up in a tweed cape and Hunter wellies, just play-acting at being 'Oirish', they were – and the money didn't help either. It was like Monopoly notes, the way they threw it around. (pause) There was always this tension between the islanders and the Kinsellas, in my opinion. They needed that family, and no Irish person likes to feel beholden to an English man for their survival. The resistance is embedded in their very DNA. It was never going to end well.

JAKE: And what about Henry himself? Did you like him?

JOHANNA: I did. (pause) In the beginning, anyway.

CHAPTER ELEVEN

The Crowley Girl

'We don't know anything about this girl,' Henry said, taking a carton of milk from the fridge. 'Have you seen her exam certificate? She could be a complete charlatan.'

'Oh my God, you're right. Nessa Crowley is probably an international scam artist. Hide the silver, quick.'

'Very amusing.' Henry poured cornflakes into a misshapen clay bowl Evie had made for him in art class, shaking a teaspoon of sugar on top. 'I can't even picture her; all those girls look the same to me. How on earth is one of them old enough to be in the second year of uni?'

'Well, she is. I told you about the piece in the *Examiner*; her Leaving Cert results were among the best in the county. Were you listening to me at all?' Keelin glared at him, her hands on her hips. 'Seán and Johanna think it's a great idea, anyway.'

'Oh, *excuse me*. If Seán and Johanna think it's a good idea, then that's that. I don't know why we're even bothering to discuss the matter.' He took a spoonful of cereal. 'And really, darling, I'm not comfortable with you seeing Seán Crowley so much. How would you feel if I was going on "tea dates" with my ex-girlfriend all the time?'

'They're not dates.' And I wouldn't mind, she wanted to tell her husband, if your ex-girlfriend was alive for you to have tea dates with. But they weren't allowed to talk about Greta Ainsworth, she and Henry. Not ever. He'd made that clear from the beginning. 'You're being ridiculous, babe. Seán is one of my oldest friends and we sort of dated for two minutes when we were teenagers. I'm not going to stop seeing him now because you've decided to throw a temper tantrum. You're worse than Evie at times – do you know that?'

He froze, his spoon halfway to his mouth. He looked so outraged that Keelin couldn't help but smile, patting her husband on the head as if he were a small child. 'There, there, baba,' she said in a mollifying tone, but he didn't laugh like she expected him to do.

'Babe, I—' she began, when the doorbell rang. 'That'll be her now,' she said, relieved. 'Come here to me, ya dope. You've bits of cornflake stuck to your chin.' She wiped his face clean, waving her hand at him to get rid of the bowl.

'Be nice,' she warned as she dragged her husband into the hallway after her. There was a young woman standing on the front porch, a neon-pink satchel swinging from her shoulder. Five foot ten inches of her in skinny black jeans and a ribbed vest top, freckles dusted across her nose, a blonde fringe sweeping over one eye. 'Hi,' she said shyly. 'I'm Nessa.'

'You don't have to introduce yourself to me, don't be daft. Thank you so much for doing this, pet,' Keelin said, reaching out to hug the girl. 'I can't get over the height of you, and the *figure*! You're only gorgeous. We're all so proud of you; I can't go anywhere on the island without someone falling over themselves to tell me how well you're doing at UCC. Congratulations.'

'Aww, thanks a million, Keelin.' Her eyes widened as she walked into the hall, taking in the split staircase lined in pale grey velvet carpet, the delicate chandelier hung from a twisting silver spire, the oversized paintings on the eggshell walls. 'Oh my God,' she said. 'Your house is stunning.'

'Would you stop, it's grand. Now, you must make yourself comfortable here. Treat the place like it's your own. Right, babe?' She nudged her husband in the ribs.

'Absolutely, Nessa. We want you to feel at home here,' Henry said, turning around at the sound of footsteps on the stairs. 'Here's the man of the hour,' he said. Alex came to a skidding halt when he saw who was standing beside his mother, the tips of his ears burning bright. He stammered a hello, scratching the back of his neck furiously. 'Hi, Alex,'

Nessa said, half waving at him. 'Do you want to get started?'

Why didn't you tell me? he asked Keelin later. Why didn't you say that it was one of the Crowley Girls who was coming to give me grinds? You could have at least prepared me, Mam.

She's just a person, Keelin said, taken aback. Her son didn't behave like this, not about girls anyway. He was usually too absorbed with his music and his video games to notice anyone else around him. Nessa Crowley is not some sort of mythical creature, Alex, she said.

But it was clear her son wasn't listening to her.

CHAPTER TWELVE

When Keelin woke the morning after dinner with Noah and Jake in Marigold Cottage, she had a headache, a tightness forming around her temples and across her eyes. It was still dark outside, no sign of sunlight straining beneath the heavy drapes, but Henry wasn't in the bed next to her. She slipped her hands under the duvet to pat the sheets on his side, but they were cool to touch. She stretched her arms out, yawning, the stiff bones of her neck clicking into place, and she reached to grab her phone, unplugging it from the wall, and tapped in her passcode.

And tapped it again.

And again.

'Henry?' she called as she got out of bed, wrapping a dressing gown around her. She padded downstairs, pausing on the bottom step and listening so she could hear where he was. 'Henry,' she said when she walked into his study. He was sitting in the antique chair he'd bought at auction a couple of years previously, a dark mahogany with forest-green leather upholstery, an exact replica of the chair his father had in the Kinsella Group headquarters in London. His eyes were closed as an eerie piece of classical music blasted from the sound system.

'Henry.' She prodded him gently on the forearm. He opened one eye, saw it was her, and pointed the remote into the air, silencing the music instantly. 'Camille Saint-Saëns,' he said. 'It's beautiful, isn't it?'

'Very nice,' she said. 'I'm sorry, I didn't mean to disturb you.'

'That's fine, darling.' He looked down at her bare feet. 'Keelin, you need to wear your slippers around the house. You'll catch a frightful cold. We've talked about this.'

'Yes, sorry, you're right,' she said. 'I'll remember next time.' She held her iPhone out to him. 'There's something wrong with my mobile.'

'What seems to be the matter?' he asked, taking it from her. The wall behind him was mirrored and Keelin could see her reflection: her blotchy skin, patches of red breaking out around her nose and chin, her breasts hanging low under the silk gown. Nessa had had perfect breasts, she thought, swallowing the shame. But Nessa had been young, and she hadn't given birth to two children, now, had she? Of course her breasts had been perfect.

'It won't let me . . . The passcode doesn't seem to be working.'

'How odd,' Henry said, turning it over and peering at the screen. 'Did you change the code?'

'No, of course not.'

'Are you sure? You were home late last night, and you *were* rather tight. God knows I've done some stupid things in my time after a few drinks.'

'I only had two glasses of wine. Surely I would remember if—'

'I don't know, darling. I'm not an expert.' He dropped the phone back on the table. 'But you can use mine for the time being, if you'd like. Just ask when you need it.'

'Thank you.' She paused. 'And I'm sorry for being late last night. We were chatting, and I lost track of the time.'

'These things happen, don't they?' He switched the music back on, a roar of a violin solo swooping through the room.

'And I—' she tried to say over the music. 'Henry, I can't hear you with that racket.'

'I'd hardly call Saint-Saëns a "racket",' he said, but he turned the volume down. 'What is it now?'

'I just . . .' She watched him carefully. 'Maybe it's not a good idea for me to speak to them by myself any more – the Australians. What do you think?'

'Goodness,' he said. 'That's not really for me to say, is it? You should do whatever you think is best for you, darling.' He closed his eyes again, tapping his fingers against the desk in time to the orchestra. Keelin stood there, watching him, wondering if she should leave the phone or take it with her.

In the end, she left it there.

'Dinner time,' Henry said later that day, as the grandfather clock in the hall chimed seven times. They had been sitting in the sunroom, he and Keelin, neither of them speaking. Keelin was kneeling by the glass wall, resting her palm against its weight, staring at the restless sea before her. She counted the waves crashing against the cliffs, one by one. It was best to keep her mind busy; she had learned that trick years ago. She could never be sure of what she might start thinking about otherwise, what she might remember.

'Excellent,' she said, getting to her feet and following him into the dining room. The table was beautifully set, thin ivory candles in Waterford Crystal holders, freshly laundered linen napkins, a vase of lilies in the centre. She sat in her usual place, at Henry's right side, smiling at the housekeeper as she presented their dishes with a flourish, telling Keelin that she'd left a plate for Alex in the oven, as always, despite her son's refusal to ever eat it. 'Thank you, Gosia,' she said, unfolding a napkin onto her lap. Keelin had always enjoyed cooking, and baking especially; it reminded her of her mother, how Cáit had allowed Keelin to weigh and sift the flour, teaching her how to make soda bread and apple sponge, a pavlova that was as light as air. But Henry was such a fussy eater – the potatoes wouldn't be creamy enough for his liking one day, the beef too tough the next – and Keelin began to dread putting the food in front of him, waiting for the inevitable criticism. She would sulk then, like a petulant child, and her husband became defensive. Would you rather I lie to you, Keelin? he'd say, and she wasn't sure how to tell him that maybe she would. It had been a relief when Henry suggested they hire a full-time housekeeper. I hate it when we fight, he said, especially over something as silly as this. Won't it be easier this way? My mother always had a chef, as well as a cleaner. Why shouldn't my wife have the same?

'It looks delicious, Gosia,' Henry said, checking his watch. 'But you'd better hurry or you'll miss the last ferry. See you tomorrow.'

'This is quite a small portion,' Keelin said when the house-keeper left the room, poking at the tiny piece of salmon and rocket leaves with her fork.

'I thought you might still be full after your blowout last night,' Henry said, cutting a slab of butter and letting it melt on top of his baked potato. 'I met Jake walking the cliffs this afternoon and he told me all about the Vietnamese broth he made for you. You were even looking for second helpings, he said.'

'I already said I wouldn't go down to the cottage again.'

'There's no need to snap at me. I was just worried about you; you know your IBS plays up if you eat spicy foods. I'm surprised you didn't tell Jake that.'

'I didn't want to be rude. I thought you wanted me to make a good impression.'

'And you're doing a wonderful job, clearly; they seem rather charmed by you, don't they? Oh, I meant to tell you . . .' He picked up his phone and scanned through the photo roll, turning it around so that Keelin could see. It was a picture of a model, raven-haired and fragile, her clavicle jutting out of pale flesh. 'I bought this dress online for you, it's the latest Simone Rocha. The website only had one size left, I'm afraid, so it's going to be a snug fit, but we can always send it back if it doesn't suit.'

Keelin eyed the plate before her, the knife and fork in her hands. Her skin was nearly translucent, spider blue veins and delicate bones, her blood pulsing through her, so close to the surface she could almost smell it. 'It's a stunning dress,' she said, cutting the fish into smaller and smaller pieces. 'Thank you.'

'Alex! Well, this *is* a treat,' Henry said as the young man walked into the room. Keelin turned around to stare at him in disbelief, stuttering her hello. Her son never ate dinner with them; he could barely get out of bed most days but here he was, plate in hand, and his portion was the same size as Henry's, she noticed, two baked potatoes, green beans, a large fillet of salmon drowning in a creamy white sauce. She couldn't recall the last time he had eaten that much food. 'Sit with me, a stór,' she said, patting the chair next to her. Henry raised an eyebrow at her behind

Alex's back, clearly as surprised as she was to see her son at dinner time.

'You look good,' she said. 'Doesn't he look good, Henry?'

'He does, rather,' her husband replied. 'There's colour in your cheeks – you caught some sun, Alex.'

Keelin's eyes drifted across her son's face, noticing the fresh freckles on his nose. 'Have you been outside?' she asked. 'Did you meet the Australians? You haven't talked to them, have you, Alex? We agreed you were to come straight to us if they asked for an interview.' She looked at Henry for support.

'Please do tell us if those men contact you,' her husband said. 'It's important we—'

'I know,' Alex cut across him, shaking out his napkin. 'I was just WhatsApping Evie there. She said you promised you'd ring her this morning, Mam, and you didn't. She's raging, you know how girls can get.' He speared a green bean with his fork. 'Did you forget?'

'There was an issue with your mother's phone,' Henry explained.

'What issue?' Alex asked, but Keelin said she didn't know. 'Well, you can use mine, if you want,' he said.

'I've already offered your mother the use of my mobile, if required,' Henry said. 'We have it under control.'

'My two boys, taking care of me,' she said. 'How lucky am I?'

The room fell silent, save for the scrape of a fork against a

89

china plate, the chewing of food, a slurp of water. The salmon tasted strange, as if it wasn't quite fresh enough, and Keelin could feel her throat close in revulsion. For distraction, she pictured herself in that new dress, Henry's eyes on her, dark, dark. Undressing her slowly and calling her beautiful. He would want her then. That was all Keelin had ever needed, she thought, Henry's desire for her. That would keep her satisfied.

'Is that what you're having for dinner?' Alex asked as she pushed the food away from her. 'There isn't a pick on you, Mam. You should be eating more.'

'You're one to talk,' she tried to joke, but her son's face was tight with concern. 'I'm fine, honestly. Just not very hungry today.' He nodded, but he kept sneaking glances at her plate while he finished his meal. When he was done, Alex stood up, the legs of the chair scuffing against the wooden floor. 'Do you want to go out for a walk, Mam?' he asked. A *walk*? She didn't dare look at Henry, to see her own shock reflected on her husband's face. 'It looks like a gorgeous day out there,' Alex said. 'Summer has finally arrived.'

'I . . .' A gorgeous day in July meant people. It meant stares and heads tilted in her direction, and Keelin pretending she didn't see them, talking louder and louder in an effort to distract Alex, until her voice would fall hoarse and she would be exhausted, yearning to be back in Hawthorn House, where she was safe. 'Not today, pet,' she said. 'Do you mind?'

A ripple of something across her son's face. Hurt, maybe, or disappointment, but it was gone before she could catch it. There had been a time when she had known all of Alex's faces, when she could read his expression instinctively, like a blind woman moving her fingers across a Braille plaque. But things were different now. 'Sure,' he said. 'But I think I'll head out anyway. I might call into the pub for one on my way home.'

'I'm sorry, Alex. You're going to the *pub* now? What are you going to do there?' Keelin asked, giving up any pretence of nonchalance. She was certain Alex had never gone to the island pub in his entire life. He hadn't been like Keelin, in and out of O'Shea's with Seán and Johanna since they were fifteen, the adults pretending not to notice because they had done the same in their time, and what else did young people have to do on the island? But that had not been Alex's way. They had never even caught him siphoning vodka from Henry's liquor cabinet, smuggling it over to the annual Good Friday bonfire in the dunes to be shared among his classmates. What was her son doing, going to the pub now, after all this time?

'Yeah,' Alex said, shrugging. 'I thought I should start making more of an effort.'

'That's wonderful,' Henry said, his hand on Keelin's knee under the table. 'We've been terribly worried about you these last few years. It's good to see you getting out and about.'

'Thanks.' Alex shifted from one foot to the other. 'I'm

91

sorry to ask, but would you mind, eh . . . would you mind giving me some money, Mam?'

'I don't have any,' Keelin said automatically. What did she need money for? She remembered that day, the last one she had spent on the mainland. It had been a year after Nessa's death and she was standing in line at the department store, two winter coats and a dress in her hands, but when she got to the till, she couldn't remember what to do next. Lady, the shop assistant said. Lady, I'm going to need you to give me some cash for this. Or your card? Which will it be? And Keelin had just stood there, staring blankly at the girl. She had come home to the island that evening, and begged Henry to help her. It was easier to let him take care of the money, she had decided. It all belonged to him anyway. 'But you can help him out, can't you?' she said, turning to her husband.

'No problem,' he replied, reaching for his wallet and pulling out a fifty-euro note. 'Here you go, Alex. Have fun.'

'Thanks,' Alex said, taking the money. He kissed his mother on the cheek, his breath warm against her skin. 'Go raibh maith agat, Mam.'

When he was gone, Keelin turned to Henry in a panic and said, 'The pub? A month ago, I had to check to make sure he had brushed his teeth in the morning, and now all of a sudden he's going to the *pub*?'

'It's surprising, I'll grant you that, but this is what we wanted, isn't it? For Alex to heal, to move on. I thought you'd be happy to see him leaving the house of his own volition.'

'But we don't want him *talking* to people. Jesus Christ, I don't want him—'

'Stop. We have to trust him.'

But what if he did something stupid? What if he had a beer too many and his tongue became loose, regaling the other patrons with the secrets of Hawthorn House? She didn't want her son to do something he would later regret. Of all people, she knew how hard it could be to recover from some mistakes, how deep the wounds could run.

The day she'd decided to leave her first husband had been a cold one, a January morning dawning grey and still. Her father wasn't dead a week then, and Keelin was weary from the shaking hands and saying *yes, it was so sudden, yes, a terrible loss,* cups of scalding tea pressed into her hands, mouthing the words of the rosary when the priest came to the house for the wake, the smell of incense clinging to her hair for days afterwards. Her mother had asked her to stay on the island for a bit longer, had begged, in fact. Please, a stór, Cáit said. I don't want to be alone in this house, not now. Not with your father gone. But Keelin couldn't stay. The fear was beginning to rise within her, like a fever. A sickness. Creeping up each bone of her spine, one by one. I have to get home to Mark, she said, hugging her mother goodbye.

He was waiting for her when she got back to Carlow, grabbing her by the wrist and pulling her into the house. She tripped over the door frame, falling to the ground, crying out as she hit the hard tiles, skinning flakes of flesh from her knees like she was a child in the playground.

Where were you? He leaned down and spoke softly into her ear but she didn't dare to get up. She didn't want to provoke him further.

The weather was bad, Mark, there were no ferries. I couldn't get home.

You said you'd be back straight after the funeral. That was two days ago.

There were no ferries! No one could get off the island, I swear to you, Mark. Please—

Why are you smiling?

I'm not, I'm not, I—

I'll teach you to laugh at me, you fucking cunt.

He kicked her in the ribs then, and it wasn't like before, when Keelin could convince herself that Mark hadn't meant to hurt her, he'd just been drinking too much or his foot had slipped, it had been an accident. He didn't know any better, it was the way he was raised; his behaviour was simply poor learning, copying his own father. It was Keelin's job to help him to heal. For better or for worse; she had taken sacred vows and she wasn't one to give up on those she loved. *Cunt*, he said again and then he spat at her. He kicked her again and again and something broke inside her, bones splintering, snapping. Get up, Mark said, you're grand. Stop faking it, for fuck's sake.

Alex was strapped into his buggy outside the front door;

Keelin could hear him bawling and she wanted to bring her son in from the cold, but she couldn't move. She lay on those tiles until Mark was finished with her. He left eventually, the sound of a car ignition, and tyres screeching against tarmac as he drove away. She clawed her way up to standing, gasping, her foot slipping in a small pool of blood, and she limped outside to a hysterical Alex. Shush, baby, she said, holding him close until he settled. Mammy's here. Mark returned home that night, his breath scorched with whiskey, telling her it wasn't his fault, what he had done, he hadn't meant it. He fell to his knees, nestling his head in her lap. I'm just like my da, he cried. I'm just like him. This time Keelin didn't deny it. She didn't tell Mark that he wasn't the same as his father, like she had so many times before; she didn't swear he was a good man, that she believed in him and they would get through this together. Instead, she limped upstairs to bed, Mark following, as he promised it would never happen again. It'll be different this time, he said. They should go back to therapy, to the woman whose office smelled of air freshener; lemon verbena, Keelin thought it was. The woman who had listened carefully and said, 'Please continue, this is a safe space,' whenever either of them hesitated. And so Keelin had talked. She had talked and talked and talked in those sessions while Mark stayed silent. But he listened to every word she said, she would soon discover. He had taken notes.

Six weeks later, the doctor confirmed her ribs were healing nicely – How did this happen, Keelin? he asked, raising an eyebrow for she had been into his surgery before, and always she had laughed, claiming to be clumsy, strangely accident prone. Now, for the first time, she told the truth, humiliation coursing through her at how easily the doctor believed her, how obvious it must have been to him all along. That night, she waited until Mark fell asleep and she crept out of bed. She didn't dare put on her shoes in case the noise would wake her husband. She had given Alex an extra dose of Calpol before bedtime, and he didn't stir as she picked him up from his cot and stole out of the bungalow, wincing at the bite of the gravel beneath her bare feet. Keelin let the handbrake release so it rolled quietly down the hill, only turning the key in the ignition when the tyres hit the country road outside the front gates. She kept looking in the rear-view mirror, expecting to see Mark running after her, screaming, but there was nothing. She drove to Baltimore, and she waited in the dark for the morning ferry to Inisrún.

What made you leave in the end? people would ask in the years to come. And there was only one answer she could give them. It was for Alex, she said. Keelin had to break the cycle. She loved her son too much to stand by and watch him become his father in turn.

CHAPTER THIRTEEN

Henry Kinsella

HENRY: She wasn't what people expected of me, Keelin. She wasn't quite what I was expecting for myself either – I'd always gone for the same kind of girl, girls who were part of our set in London, sisters of school friends, that sort of thing. Keelin was . . . well, she was not that.

JAKE: Did you know each other as children? As teenagers?

HENRY: Her mother ran the small shop on the island, so I'd see her occasionally but we weren't what you'd call friends. She barely looked at me, nor my brother, Charlie. She didn't shriek with laughter like the other island girls did when they saw 'the Kinsella brothers'. She looked *bored* by us. It was rather amusing, I must say.

JAKE: Tell us about when you started dating.

HENRY: OK, er, well, I suppose by the year 2000 I was living between Inisrún and the house in London. It was time I took an interest in the family business, my father said, but Charlie was rather territorial – it was clear there would be no room for me at KHG headquarters with him there. We all agreed it was best for me to take over Misty Hill. It wasn't as lucrative as the hotels but it was prestigious, even then; it was a huge boon to the Kinsella brand, and I was hungry to prove myself, to show I wasn't just some spoilt playboy. Especially after everything that . . . anyway. I needed this venture to succeed. And it was a delicate balancing act, Misty Hill, it wasn't the cushy number some people seemed to think it was. The artists were my main priority, naturally, but you had to keep the islanders onside too. There was a lot of champagne sent to local weddings and turning up to funerals to shake hands and offer condolences. That's where I met Keelin again, at her mother's funeral.

JAKE: Not the most romantic of occasions, mate.

HENRY: I suppose not. (laughs) But I couldn't stop thinking about her afterwards – how brave she had looked standing by the coffin, all alone. I remember hoping I would be as strong if I were to find myself in similar circumstances. And suddenly, I don't know how to explain it but it just made sense, me and Keelin. *Of course*, I needed to be with someone from the island. I couldn't believe I hadn't realised it earlier.

NOAH: What did your family think?

HENRY: My mother was delighted. An island girl, she said, just like herself. She found it rather thrilling, I think. And while my father was just happy to see me settling down, he was shrewd enough to know it couldn't hurt Misty Hill if I married a native. And everyone adored Keelin once they got to know her. How could you not? She was quieter than other women I'd dated, but I've never met anyone who *cared* as much as Keelin did. She was never too busy for her friends, always there whenever they needed her, and she was utterly devoted to Alex. I remember this time, it must have been after one of our first dates, when we arrived back to the cottage and the boy was waiting up for her; he wouldn't go to sleep until we came home, Johanna said. He had a joke he wanted to tell his mother. Keelin said, Hit me with it, kid. Alex couldn't stop giggling, he could barely get the words out, and then Keelin started to laugh too, as if this was the funniest joke she'd ever heard in her life. And looking at the two of them together, I wanted . . . I wanted to be part of it, I guess, a part of their little family. I wanted Keelin to be the mother of my children too. (pause) Not that we didn't face our own challenges.

JAKE: What kind of challenges?

HENRY: It took us longer than we had hoped to get pregnant and sadly, my wife struggled when our daughter was born – I'm sure she wouldn't mind me telling you that. She refused to breastfeed, saying she was afraid she would hurt the baby. She would wake me in the middle of the night in a panic, listing all the things that could happen to Evie – she might drop her, she might hit Evie's head against a door frame, she might roll over and smother the baby in her sleep. It didn't matter how often I tried to comfort her, Keelin wouldn't listen. I'd hear Evie screaming, and when I'd go to check on her, I would find my wife standing there, staring down at the Moses basket, just watching the baby cry. That was when I insisted we get a doctor. I was beginning to feel frightened.

JAKE: Why were you frightened?

HENRY: (silence)

NOAH: Henry, were you worried Keelin would do something to hurt the baby?

HENRY: It was better once the doctor came and prescribed the antidepressants. It wasn't my wife's fault, of course – post-natal depression is terribly common, and she's been a marvellous mother to our daughter ever since. But the fear never leaves you, that's what I'm trying to say. You never stop watching them, looking for signs, afraid it might happen again.

CHAPTER FOURTEEN

The journalists writing about the Misty Hill case would report that due to Storm Ida it had been two days before anyone could get on or get off the island. Everyone was stuck there – the locals, the party guests, the artists in residence. A dead body, and it was one of the Crowley Girls, the whispers began. *Nessa*. It was a head wound, they said. Had she fallen? Had she been pushed? Someone must know the truth, but no one was talking.

Keelin didn't remember anything, she told the guards when they finally managed to get out to Inisrún. The state helicopter landing unsteadily, a furious wind caught in its blades, stern men in uniform climbing out. The first thing they did was take everyone's names and phone numbers, explaining there would be more queries later, that all guests would have to make themselves available in the coming weeks and months. They wouldn't allow Henry to be present for Keelin's first interview – that's not how this works, Mr Kinsella, they said to him – but her husband insisted that he accompany Alex into the television room, where the guards had set up shop for their initial enquiries. He's a minor, Henry said, he's only seventeen. Alex staring into space, his hands shaking. It can't be true, the boy kept saying. *Not Nessa.*

The next afternoon, the guards asked Keelin and Henry to come to the station on the mainland for further questions. I've nothing else to tell you, Keelin said. She had been in a state of shock when she'd heard the news, she was distraught, and a guest at the party had produced a Xanax to help calm her down. She'd fallen asleep almost immediately.

– You slept for two days, Mrs Kinsella?

– No, of course not. I can't . . . I wasn't used to the tablets, I'd never taken them before. I didn't know the sort of effect they'd have on me.

– And what about your children? Who minded them while you had taken to your bed?

– My husband. He is their father, you know.

This would be the first question people asked of Keelin, she soon discovered. *And what about your children? Where were your children when all of this was happening?* Funny, she thought. They never asked Henry that.

As the two of them left Hawthorn House with the guards, she hugged Alex, promising him that everything would be OK. You're to go up to the Steins' cottage, she said, and take care of your little sister, do you hear me? Her son looked as if he was submerged underwater and couldn't quite hear what she was saying, blinking slowly in response. It's OK, Alex, Henry whispered as he embraced her son. Just wait for us to come home and say nothing. Do you understand me? *Nothing.*

Getting off the ferry at Baltimore, Keelin's flimsy ballet pumps slipping against the slime-covered concrete steps. She almost fell, but the female guard accompanying her steadied her. Be careful, Mrs Kinsella, the woman said, her hand in the small of Keelin's back as she guided her towards the garda car. It was a Volvo, unmarked, and it smelled new, like the plastic wrapping had just been peeled off the seats. Henry wasn't with her, and she opened her mouth to ask the woman where her husband was but she couldn't seem to talk, the words turning to dust in her mouth. She stared out the window as they drove to the station, at the men in mud-spattered overalls, carving fallen trees in half so they could be moved out of harm's way, the road littered with broken branches, bedsheets and knickers torn from some- one's washing line, brown water gurgling up from drains. It's a mess, the guard said. She was young, her face round, the boxy uniform turning her body shapeless. So many homes still without power too, she said and Keelin had murmured, Yes, it's terrible. The garda station was an ordinary two- storey house, pale green with yellow windowsills, and Keelin was brought into a room with a Formica dining table, four high-back plastic chairs around it, an unused fireplace stuffed up with yellowing newspapers in the corner. A young guard told Keelin that he was a distant relation of her father's. I'm one of the Ballyvourney Ó Mordhas, he said, smiling at her, but he fell instantly quiet when Joseph O'Shaughnessy came into the room. The older man put his bottle of 7UP on the table, his eyes sharp as he introduced himself, explaining he was a detective sergeant from the city. OK, Mrs Kinsella, he said, nodding at the younger man to start recording. Are we ready?

How long had you known Nessa Crowley? he asked. *How would you characterise your relationship with Nessa? You must have been friendly, if she was at your birthday party. Can you remember what time the power went out? Where were you when it happened? Who were you with? What did you do then, Mrs Kinsella? When was the last time you saw Nessa Crowley alive? Did you speak to her? For how long? What about? How did she seem at that stage? Was she upset? Was she drunk? Had you much to drink yourself?*

Keelin was there for hours, exhaustion creeping into her bones, turning her eyes bleary. The week leading up to the party smeared together, like running a finger down an oil painting before it had dried, smudging one colour into the next. She found her memories began to skip over one another, an hour from one day attaching itself to a completely different day, insisting that Keelin see them in chronological order even though she knew, logically, they could not possibly have

104

occurred that way. What did you say to the guards, Keelin? Henry muttered on the boat home, one eye on the ferryman to ensure he wasn't eavesdropping on their conversation. What did you say?

But she couldn't remember.

When they got back to the island, they found Hawthorn House had been cordoned off for further investigation. We can't let you in, the stony-faced guard said, ignoring Henry's attempts to cajole him, before threatening legal action if he was not allowed into his *own bloody house*. Henry went to his parents' holiday home to make some phone calls – I'm calling the solicitor, he said. This is ludicrous. They can't expect us to put up with this nonsense – and Keelin walked up to Johanna's parents' cottage to pick up the children. Oskar and Lena Stein, ashen, reaching out to hold her close. We are worried for Alex, Oskar said. We heard him crying last night. They were in love, *ja*? He and the Crowley Girl? Lena shushed him, wiping tears away from her eyes. Alex is heartbroken, the older woman said. We all are. Keelin thanked them for taking care of the kids, shaking her head when they asked her in for coffee. She waited until they had said their goodbyes before talking to her children.

Are you OK? she asked her son. He looked shattered, his eyes red and swollen, his skin mottled from lack of sleep. He turned away, as if he couldn't bear to look at her, and he walked down the hill to the pier. Keelin stood there, watching him leave, and she wondered where on earth she would go now. What would the autopsy show? Would Nessa's death be ruled accidental or . . . Keelin's breath drew short at the thought of a murder investigation, and what the guards might find if they looked too closely. She imagined them taking handfuls of her secrets, scattering them to the wind like ashes. She would never be able to find them all again and put them back where they belonged.

Evie was tugging at her sleeve. Mummy, she said, what's happening? Why's Alex so sad? and Keelin felt a rush of fury, pushing her away and shouting at the little girl to stop whining. Evie burst into tears and Keelin knew she should apologise, reassure her daughter everything would be all right, but how could she do that when her ribs were tightening into her chest, pressing her lungs together, and she couldn't seem to catch her breath? The guards had taken over Hawthorn House and they would find the porn she and Henry kept in their bedroom, women in full restraints, screaming for mercy as men did whatever they wanted to their helpless bodies. Unwilling flesh forced to do terrible acts of depravity. *You like this*, Henry said when they first watched the videos together, reaching down to touch her, inhaling sharply at how wet she was. She had been equally surprised. Up until that point, Keelin's sex life had been unremarkable. She'd lost her virginity to Mark Delaney when she was nineteen, and while she didn't come, it hadn't hurt either, which seemed about as much as she could ask for. After their marriage broke down and Keelin limped home to the island, she had dated a few other men before Henry. They were safe, decent men, men she knew she would never fall in love with and therefore presented no threat to her new life. But from the first time she slept with Henry, Keelin understood this man was different to the others. There was a knife edge of violence to the way he took her, threw her on the bed, wrapped a hand around her throat and held her down until he was finished with her. She and Henry still fucked at least once a day, if not more. He would arrive home in the evening and she would be waiting for him, begging him to do whatever he wanted with her. They couldn't get enough of one other, testing each other's boundaries, seeing how far the other would go before they admitted defeat and gave in. As Keelin thought of what the detectives would find in their room, vomit forced its way up her throat. Soon, she thought, everyone would know what kind of person she really was.

Keelin needn't have been worried. The detectives found the porn, yes, they found the restraints and the harnesses, holding them up with half-smirks and lewd remarks, *Look at this lads, wha'?*

But they discovered the photo too. And that became the only thing anyone ever talked about.

CHAPTER FIFTEEN

The Crowley Girl

'Oh, hello,' Keelin said when she arrived home to find Nessa Crowley in her kitchen yet again. The girl was leaning against the Aga, those endless legs in frayed cut-off jeans despite the autumn chill. Keelin lifted her shopping bags onto the marble island and began to unpack the groceries. 'We weren't expecting to see you so soon, Nessa,' she said, gesturing at her son to move out of the way so she could put the sliced pan in the bread bin. 'I thought Alex's grind wasn't until eight.'

'I got my times mixed up.' Nessa stood up straighter, pulling the shorts down her thighs. 'I thought we said four. Alex was free so we just did it earlier.' Her cheeks turned pink. 'The grind, I mean.'

Keelin checked the Salvador Dalí melting clock on the

opposite wall. It was six thirty p.m. now. 'I'm sure you've better things to do than hang around here all evening though,' Keelin tried, but Nessa shrugged and said she didn't mind, with a side-glance at Alex that made Keelin's jaw clench.

'Where's Henry?' she asked, looking between the two of them. She wanted her husband here as a witness. I'm not being paranoid, am I? she would say to him. There's *something* going on, right?

'He went down to Bluebell and Foxglove.' Her son folded his arms across his chest. 'The Final Screams checked out yesterday and he wanted to get an estimation of the damage.' He tilted his head at Nessa. 'Punk group,' he said casually, as if he were a band member himself. 'Lots of drugs, crazy shit.'

'I thought you were in charge of inspecting the cottages, Alex. That's why we give you so much pocket money every month, remember?' Keelin said, ignoring Nessa's giggles.

'Henry said he'd do it for me today. Because of the grind, like.'

'And your sister?' Keelin asked. 'Where has she disappeared off to, may I ask?'

'She's in the playroom watching a DVD,' Nessa said. 'I bought her the new Narnia one. Henry mentioned he was reading the books to her so I thought she might like it.'

'That was very kind of you,' Keelin said, looking at the clock again, pointedly. There was a moment of silence, before Nessa grabbed her satchel and said she should be on her way. 'Let's do some trigonometry next time,' she told Alex. 'Have a go at last year's exam paper and we'll look at it together when I see you.'

'Cool,' he replied. 'Thanks, Ness. I'll walk you out.'

Keelin hovered at the back of the hall, hiding behind a bouquet of white roses, watching as the two said goodbye on the front porch. She couldn't hear, but her son must have made a joke because Nessa threw her head back in laughter, hitting Alex playfully on the upper arm. They leaned in to hug and – Keelin's heart beat slowing to a dull thud – she thought they might have kissed but she couldn't be sure from this angle. Alex closed the door, leaning against it, his eyes half closed.

'What?' he said, when he saw his mother standing there, staring at him.

'Is something going on with you two?' she asked.

'No,' he said. This was Alex's reply to everything Keelin asked him these days. Did anything strange or startling happen in school today, mo stoirín? *No.* Do you want to go for a walk with me? *No.* Do you want to invite some friends over to the house? I could cook a pizza. *No.*

Separation was a natural part of adolescence, she reminded herself. It was an important step in her son's psychological development. But they had always been so close, she and Alex. She hadn't realised how much she'd liked it that way until Nessa Crowley had arrived into their lives and it became abundantly clear whom Alex preferred.

'I'm not sure I feel comfortable with Nessa giving you grinds if there's some kind of . . . *romance* happening between the two of you. That's not what I'm paying her fifty euro an hour for, Alex.'

'Mam,' he snorted, 'you sound about a hundred. Next you'll be asking if we're doing a line, or if I'm taking her out courting.'

'Please don't talk to me like that. I think I'm allowed to have some reservations about you dating a twenty-year-old woman, especially one I'm employing to help you study.'

'Oh my God, *Mam*! She's my friend. You were the one who was so anxious for me to make friends here, and now that I've found one, you don't like it?'

'Of course I want you to have friends.' *But not like this,* she thought. Keelin wanted her son to hang out with boys his own age, a gang of lads sheepishly waving hello as they snuck cans of beer into the house. Friends who could see past Alex's intense, awkward manner and appreciate how sweet he was, how funny he could be. She didn't want him spending all his time with a college student, and a disconcertingly beautiful one at that. 'I just . . .' She paused. 'I don't want you to get hurt, Alex.'

'Why do you have to assume that I'd be the one to get hurt?' he asked as he pushed past her, taking the stairs two at a time, slamming his bedroom door so loudly that it shook in its frame.

Because, she thought, stopping at the foot of the stairs and looking up towards his room. *Because I know girls like that. Girls like Nessa Crowley don't fall in love with boys like you.*

111

CHAPTER SIXTEEN

'You need to get your hair done, darling,' Henry said at the start of August. Keelin was in the sunroom, sitting cross-legged on an old cushion Johanna had bought her in Mexico years ago, green silk embroidered with Frieda Kahlo's face in fine stitching. She had been very still, watching the evening light ripple lavender across the waves, when Henry stood above her, touching her scalp with the tips of his fingertips. 'These roots are frightful,' he said, and she tensed, opening her mouth to say that she would dye it herself, she could easily order a home colour kit on Amazon, but he cut her off before she could speak. 'I'll email the salon for you today,' he said. 'Tell them to send one of their girls.'

Nicola was the name of the hairdresser they dispatched to the island this time, a nineteen-year-old with a peach-coloured bowl cut and an aggressive amount of black kohl smudged underneath her eyes. Keelin told her where she could set up her tools and stood at the kitchen table awkwardly until they were ready to begin. She felt the way she always did when an outsider came into Hawthorn House: torn between fear at what they might bring with them, like settlers carrying disease to the New World, and her strange desire to *consume* them, to eat them – and their freedom – whole. She sat on a wooden stool, the hairdresser wrapping a silk cloak around her shoulders. 'Yeah, yeah, yeah,' she said as Keelin explained what style she wanted done today, breathing out each *yeah* like it was costing her something. It was clear the girl had never heard of the murder or Misty Hill, or if she had, she didn't care. Instead, she kept up a running commentary on the latest celebrity gossip as she combed Keelin's wet hair, talking about an Instagram influencer who had shared a herpes diagnosis on her Stories ('I don't know why everyone is making such a fuss, apparently we all have the virus and we just don't know it, like.'), a former *Love Island* contestant who was releasing a fitness video ('I gave up on that shite last year, would it kill them to have anyone over a size ten on the show? It's so *boring.*') and then, finally, she told Keelin about a girl she'd been at school with who had since broken into the porn industry. Well, her ex-boyfriend filmed them having sex and uploaded it to RedTube when she dumped him. 'It's desperate, what he done to her,' Nicola said. 'Not to mention illegal. But I can't tell you how many fights I've had with friends of mine about it. And with girls, like. Saying, what did she think was going to happen? She should have known better, and all this crap. It's mad.'

Keelin stayed quiet, hoping the other woman would take her silence for agreement. But she had often wondered why these young girls *did* agree to have their most intimate moments recorded, send naked photos of themselves to men they barely knew. Surely they had to realise such messages could be used against them? Screenshots taken, and shared in group WhatsApp chats. It's just banter, anything to impress the *lads, lad, lads*. It didn't matter that the men's texts were equally crude, for they were men and men had always been allowed to express their sexuality however they wanted. That was how the world worked and Keelin was too old to think it would change; she had seen too much to believe in fairy tales. As the hairdresser painted the dye onto her hair, Keelin had a burning desire to phone Evie, to make her daughter swear she'd never be so stupid as to send those kinds of photos to a boy, who would pass them around his school dormitory, snickering with his friends and rating her body out of ten. Evie's naked flesh, her vulnerability; it would declare him a man, damn her a whore.

But she hadn't spoken with Evie in weeks, not since her passcode stopped working. Don't worry about it, Henry told her when she asked to borrow his iPhone to ring their daughter. Evie is having a great summer in Scotland, hanging out with her friends. She's not going to want to talk to her parents every five seconds, now, is she? Just relax, darling.

But the girl was always happy to talk to Henry, naturally. Her father controlled the purse strings, it was his money that paid for the expensive make-up and the new sneakers she just *had* to have on the weekend shopping trips to London. Evie couldn't afford to ignore him.

After the hairdresser had blow-dried Keelin's long bob and declared it 'stunning', she packed her styling tools in her leopard print suitcase, and left, the house falling silent in her wake. Keelin touched the shining blonde hair and repeated the word in a low voice. 'Stunning.' She watched herself in the mirror, mouthing it over and over. *Stunning. Stunning.* She went into the study, to the bookshelves lining the far wall, and she ran her fingers along the spines, the academic texts about psychology she knew Henry would never bother looking at. She stopped when she came to a textbook called *Domestic Violence and Psychology*. She pulled it out, and the book beside it – a memoir written by a man who had been raised in an abusive home – and in the space left behind, she saw the old binder. Her name scrawled in black ink on the inside, and it was bulging with newspaper clippings and torn-out magazine articles, the edges raw and curling. She sat on the floor, opening the folder before her.

Keelin wasn't sure why she kept these newspaper clippings. All she knew was that on the days when she could not quite believe that Nessa was dead, she needed to feel this folder in her hands. She couldn't reconcile that limp body face down in the grass with the Nessa she had known, the baby in a lace christening gown in Seán's arms, mewling in displeasure as she was doused in holy water. Are you ready to help the parents of this child in their duty as Christian parents? the priest asked the godparents, and Seán, solemn in his new suit and cheap shoes, said that he was. Nessa the toddler sitting on Seán's shoulders, calling Kee-Kee, Kee-Kee, chubby palms on Keelin's cheeks, leaning in for a smacking kiss. The little girl in a swimsuit with a frill across the bottom, dipping low so her long hair trailed into the water, digging clumps of wet sand to build a wall around her sandcastle, handing out orders to her obedient sisters. The young woman who turned up on their doorstep, smiling, I'm Nessa. Where was the real girl in all of the mythologising of the last ten years? Keelin couldn't find her, but she was determined to keep looking. On the nights she was unable to sleep, she would sneak downstairs, cautiously treading on the stairs to avoid the sections where the squeaking floorboards would betray her, and come into the study to find this folder. *There*, Keelin would think, as she stared at a photo of Nessa, *there you are*. She wondered if she was obsessed with Nessa Crowley; if she loved the girl or she hated her. Maybe it was both.

'Mam? Cad atá . . .'

Keelin bent over to hide the folder; she didn't want Alex to see this. But her son crouched beside her before she could stop him, picking up one of the newspapers. Alex sat on his haunches, his eyes scanning back and forth as he read the report, and Keelin watched him. She could see a tiny nick on his jawline from where he'd cut himself shaving, flakes of dry skin around his nostrils, the shadows beneath his eyes.

'Alex,' she tried. 'Don't, a stór. Please.' But he didn't listen, staring at the photo on the front page, Nessa flanked by Róisín and Sinéad. The Crowley Girls were so similar, with those slanting green eyes and that tousled blonde hair, but it was always the oldest sister to whom your gaze was drawn. The other two were squinting into the sun, but not Nessa. The light bathed her, surrounding her like a halo, setting her on fire. 'She was something special, wasn't she?' Alex said, picking up an old photo of Seán holding a doll-like Nessa in his arms at her third birthday party. 'It's hard to believe that . . .'

'A stór,' she said, but he dropped the photo to the ground. 'I'm sorry, Mam,' he said, his voice wavering. 'I can't do this.'

'Alex,' she called after him, but he was gone, leaving her alone again. Sighing, she gathered the photos and the newspaper clippings together, filing them neatly back into the folder. She stuffed it behind the textbooks, making sure it was safely hidden away where Henry wouldn't see it. She stood there, leaning against the bookshelves, nostrils twitching as the swirling dust crept into her nose. And she allowed herself to remember.

It was a few months before Nessa's death, and Keelin was in her son's bedroom. She wasn't snooping; she'd just wanted to give it a cursory tidy before the housekeeper arrived. That's her job, Henry would tsk when he saw Keelin running frantically about the place, but Keelin wasn't having that woman telling tales around the island that Keelin Ní Mhordha was slovenly, saying she had notions after marrying a Kinsella, and her children were even worse. Alex's room had been particularly revolting that day; three mugs of cold tea under his bed, each growing a film of mould across the top, a jam-smeared knife on a plate sticky with breadcrumbs, and the room smelled of dirty socks and Lynx deodorant. She had been stripping the sheets, trying not to gag, when she noticed something peeking out beneath the mattress. It was a photo of her son and Nessa, she found, the girl holding the digital camera at arm's length to take the shot. A quarter of her face was out of frame, but Alex wasn't looking at the camera, he was staring at Nessa, an expression on his face that Keelin had never seen before. It made her son seem like a stranger, and something twisted in Keelin's gut at the thought of that. She went to shove the photo back under the mattress when she saw what else was hiding there. A notebook, A5 size, an image of Van Gogh's *Starry Night* on the cover. Pages and pages of Alex's handwriting inside, the scrawling script that had tested his teachers' patience since he was a child. *Don't, Keelin.* But she couldn't resist. This notebook might explain Alex to her, maybe the pages within contained all the secrets he had started to keep from her.

She opened the cover, and she read one page, then another, barely able to make sense of what she was seeing.

– Tight little pussy

– You want me to destroy you

– Fuck you in every hole

– My cum slut

Keelin closed the diary, her hands trembling, and she placed it back where she had found it. They were just words, she told herself as she hurried out of the room. It didn't mean anything. There was no point in talking to Alex about it, was there? That's what boys his age did, they had disgusting, stupid fantasies. It was because of porn and peer pressure and everything else that came with being a teenager, nothing more. They were all the same. He would grow out of it, of course he would. And she couldn't ask him about this. Their relationship was strained enough as it was right now – she didn't want her son to be angry at her for violating his trust. Evie was Henry's pet – Keelin could barely get a look in with her daughter these days. All she had was Alex; she couldn't risk losing him too.

Everything OK? Henry asked when she went downstairs and Keelin hesitated, wondering if she should tell her husband what she had seen in the diary. She couldn't help but think about the things she and Henry did to each other in bed, the words they called one another. Had Alex overheard them? Had he stumbled across something in their room – a video, a book, a toy – that he was too young to understand? All this time, Keelin had been afraid that Alex would inherit the badness from his father, but what if it was *she* who was broken? Keelin, Henry said, are you quite all right, darling? And she just smiled at her husband, and she said yes, everything is fine. Nothing to worry about. She didn't know what to do so she did nothing. She stood back and watched as it all unfolded before her, and she remained silent throughout.

She would regret that, when it was over.

CHAPTER SEVENTEEN

Henry Kinsella was never charged with the murder of Nessa Crowley but neither was anyone else. That was the problem, you see. We were left devastated, keening the loss of our most beloved daughter, and we wanted blood vengeance. We wanted answers and still, ten years later, we had none.

The guards were excited about a potential witness at one point, an Ellen Tiernan who had sworn blind that she'd seen a tall man with reddish-brown hair that night, a rock in hand, madness in his eyes. But as much as we wished we could believe this account – and we did very much want to believe it; it would have been much more convenient if Henry Kinsella was behind this, the Outsider, the Sasanach – we couldn't allow ourselves to hope, for we knew the Tiernan woman well. She was a blow-in, living on Inisrún these last fifteen years, and notorious for her tall tales and exaggeration. Sure enough, it emerged that Ellen Tiernan had been in Tipperary the weekend of the party and she had 'seen' all of this in a vision; she had the second sight, she was a Bean Feasa, she claimed. Thus her story was worthless.

Many of us came forward with our own theories about what happened that night. It had been Keelin Ní Mhordha, we said, and didn't she have good cause to do it? Besides, everyone knew how much she hated the Crowley Girl spending all that time with her son. No, it was one of Henry's posh friends, we said, Miles Darcy was a dubious character. We heard he made a pass at Nessa Crowley at the party and she rejected him, something a man like that wouldn't take lying down. There were even some who thought it might have been Alex Delaney, so wildly in love with Nessa was he, but he was a gentle type, we argued, incapable of such a deed, and more importantly, he had been seen that night, before Nessa was taken from us. Unconscious in bed, a puddle of vomit on the floor beside him. Dead to the world.

As time went on, we became eager to turn on one another. There were furtive visits to the guards, whispering rumours in their ears, using the murder to settle old scores with neighbours who'd bought land we wanted for ourselves, school bullies, and the ex-lovers who spurned our proposals. But none of our gossip would hold up in a court of law either.

And so, there was nothing else we could do. Henry Kinsella came back to the island, to reclaim his home among us.

An innocent man, he said, but we knew it wasn't true. We knew what he had done.

CHAPTER EIGHTEEN

Keelin wasn't surprised when the Kinsellas' lawyer phoned to say the case against Henry had been dropped because the Director of Public Prosecutions decided there wasn't enough evidence to prosecute. The lawyer had predicted this would be the outcome – the bar for such things was high in Ireland and there had been no physical evidence to link her husband with Nessa Crowley's death, nothing that could prove his guilt beyond a reasonable doubt. Henry seemed to expect everything would return to normal then, that the islanders would forget, in time. But it was he who had forgotten, he who had been foolish enough to overlook what the Irish did to outsiders who stole what was rightfully theirs. On the second anniversary of Nessa Crowley's death, the Kinsellas went to sleep and they awoke with the smell of smoke on their breath. Fire, Henry shouted. *Fire.* He ran outside, shouting for help that refused to come, and he watched Misty Hill burn to the ground. All I ever wanted was to belong, he cried as Keelin pulled him away from the blaze, the flames so close she could smell her hair singeing. I know, she said, and it was at that moment she understood she would never be able to leave him.

There was a noticeable shift in public sentiment in the years that followed the fire, pious op-eds denouncing this kind of 'parochial vigilantism'. More letters began to arrive, but these letters were different to the ones that had come before; they were far less frightening to read, for one thing, containing fewer death threats, fewer promises to rape Keelin. Women who'd seen photos of Henry and had been struck by his good looks and expensive suit, writing to tell him they'd love to meet him in person if he was 'ever in the area'. Men's Rights Activists, furious Henry had been implicated at all, given the lack of evidence. This 'Believe Women' movement has gone too far, they wrote in their rambling missives. It's a dangerous time to be a man, wouldn't you agree? Activists wanting to expose garda corruption, who thought the Misty Hill case would be a perfect place to start. Invitations for Henry to be the keynote speaker at Free Thought events, requests from literary agents wondering if he was interested in writing a memoir about life after Misty Hill. Her husband read these letters out loud to her, an edge of excitement in his voice. The world wants to hear your side of the story, they said.

No one wanted to hear Keelin's side of the story. Oh, they

claimed they did, but she knew it wasn't true. On occasion she had been contacted by journalists, usually women, who promised a 'sympathetic' audience for the wife of Henry Kinsella. They could help her, they wrote, she could trust them, but Keelin knew what they really meant. They wanted her to cry on camera and admit that she knew what Henry had done, but she'd been too terrified to tell her story until now. They wanted her to shout about female empowerment, to pledge her allegiance to the cause and say she was determined to find justice for the Crowley Girl, as if Nessa was Keelin's first priority while she sat outside her devastated son's bedroom to make sure he hadn't harmed himself during the night. If she could hear Alex's breath, she would know he was still alive.

The interview requests had intensified in recent years. Powerful men had been exposed, the decades-long whispers that they'd touched what was not theirs to touch turning to a primal scream. Keelin thought this 'movement', whatever it was, would not last. Men always made excuses for one another no matter what their crimes; they would band together and close ranks, as they had always done. She watched as women took to the internet to rip open barely healed wounds, as if a hashtag could save them from bleeding out. 'We're reclaiming our stories from the lens of the patriarchy,' she was told in emails from feminist blogs written by millennials high on their sense of self-importance. Monica, Lorena, Hillary, Sinéad, Courtney; they would crown all the difficult women as queens in this new world order, and wanted to do the same for Keelin, if she'd let them. 'Share your story for the good of the culture,' they wrote but she knew her story wouldn't fit the narrative they wanted to create. It wasn't a simple tale of a bad man and a good victim.

Keelin's story was far more complicated than that.

CHAPTER NINETEEN

It was the last days of August now and Henry still hadn't returned from his trip to the mainland. It should have been peaceful, having the house to herself while her husband was away on yet another 'business trip'. It meant Keelin didn't need to worry about wearing make-up, she barely changed out of her dressing gown and slippers, and she could happily watch what Henry termed 'trash' television, shuddering at the sight of a Kardashian or a Real Housewife. But she couldn't fully relax because she never knew when Henry would be back; he was always vague about his travel dates, which meant Keelin was on edge all the time, awaiting his return. He would email at irregular times, and if she didn't respond within the hour, he would worry. Why did it take you so long to reply? he would ask. Are you OK? Do you need me to come home? It was easier when Henry was here, and he knew she was safe.

Keelin was outside, dead-heading roses, wearing the Cath Kidston gardening gloves Evie had given her as a birthday present, a sign, if one was needed, that she truly was middle-aged now. There was real heat coming from that sun, as her mother would have said, despite it being almost September. Keelin could feel it burn across the back of her neck, sweat forming beneath her breasts and at the edges of her hairline. She had been uncomfortably warm this week but it had to be the weather, she was too young for hot flushes, surely? Cáit had been forty-three when she gave birth to Keelin, a great age in those days, but Keelin had no idea when her mother started perimenopause or what the experience had been like for her – had Cáit suffered with mood swings, an intense irritability climbing out of the days where she'd felt weepy, maudlin? Had Cáit missed her period for three months, and then bled continuously for weeks, the stains seeping through her underwear and her trousers, leaving both ruined? Keelin wondered why she hadn't asked her mother these questions when she'd had the chance; she was twenty-eight when Cáit died, she hadn't been a child. Cáit would have been prepared to have that kind of conversation with her then. But Keelin had been preoccupied, dealing with her ex-husband, who was still making weekly pilgrimages to the island, begging Keelin for a reconciliation. You're the love of my life, he swore. I'll kill myself if you don't take me back. In the midst of all that drama, she didn't have time to be sitting around with her mother, having casual chats about their menstrual cycles. Later, when she was starting the college course in Cork, she hadn't given her mother much thought at all, outside of the convenience of having a live-in childminder. Keelin had presumed that Cáit would always just be there and she would answer all the questions Keelin had when she was ready to ask them.

'Why aren't you wearing your visor?' Henry asked, the squeaking of the garden gate behind him. Keelin put a hand over her eyes to shield them from the sun, peering up at her husband. He was dressed in a light shirt and linen trousers, and as he pointed at her bare head, she noticed his armpits were perfectly dry despite the weather. His body probably wouldn't countenance the indignity of perspiration.

'Welcome home,' she said. 'How was your trip?'

'I'm not sure if there's much point in paying a dermatologist to come to the island if you're just going to sit outside and scorch yourself,' he said, standing closer to her so his shadow blocked out the sun.

'I used factor fifty . . .' she trailed off. 'Sorry,' she said. 'You're right. I wasn't thinking.'

'Come on,' he said, reaching down to pick up the Louis Vuitton overnight bag that was at his feet. 'Let's go inside.'

That night, he watched as she did her bed-time yoga routine, stretching her body to the soothing voice of the YouTube instructor. *Upper arm bones still rotating out, we're breathing here, yes, we're starting to find that vital prana, yes, that's it . . .*

'You look fantastic,' he said as she pushed back into a downward dog. He placed his novel on the bedside locker, taking off his reading glasses and putting them on top of the hardback. 'You're in such good shape, darling.'

'Thanks,' she said, moving through a chaturanga extra slowly, showing off her body for him. She'd already gone to the gym that morning, pushing herself to run 15K on the treadmill as she ignored her stomach grumbling. *You're not hungry*, she told herself, running faster. *You're stronger than that.* She kept thinking of that photo, and how thin the girl had been. The image haunted her. The exposed clavicle and delicate ribs, the bones so lovely in their aching fragility. Keelin wanted to be like that. She wanted to be clean; and not just for Henry, for herself too.

He waited until she had completed her final vinyasa and was resting in child's pose before saying, 'Will you try on the Simone Rocha I bought? I'd love to see it on you.'

In the dressing room, Keelin held her breath as her husband pulled the dress over her head, praying silently that it would fit, that the sacrifices she'd made during the two weeks he was away would pay off. The zip stuck for a second, Henry meeting her eyes in the mirror, but he tugged on it again and it glided the rest of the way up easily. She smiled in relief, proud of how she looked in the red silk slip with a sheer sleeveless tulle layered over it, embroidered with a delicate floral lace, daisies dancing across the fabric. Henry pulled her hair out of its ponytail and shook it loose around her face.

'You're beautiful,' he said, but she wasn't; Keelin knew that. She had never been beautiful. But she was thin now, thinner than she had ever been in her life, and maybe that was just as good. She looked at her reflection, her gaze moving from her manicured toes to her toned arms, her taut, slightly waxy face. It had been Henry's idea to hire the dermatologist to give her Botox twice a year, as well as injecting her lips and her cheeks with subtle fillers. Keelin had been complaining of feeling tired, and worse, looking so, and Henry only ever wanted to make her happy. I've found someone who can come to the island, if you'd like, Henry told her when she turned forty. He handed her a glossy leaflet, before and after photos of an ordinary woman on the front, grinning, a body and a life transformed. Entirely your decision, darling, her husband said. You know I think you look perfect just as you are.

But when Keelin looked in the mirror, she could see her mam's face, Cáit's distinctive features emerging on her skin. She didn't want to look like her mother, not now. She didn't want to be reminded of all she had lost. So she asked Henry to help her forget, and he had whittled her into this new wife, like Frankenstein with his creature, remaking her into a woman who was small and neat and tidy, someone who took up as little space as possible.

'Beautiful,' Henry said again, unzipping the dress to the

waist. He knelt down, lifting the tulle skirt. He grabbed her hands, placing them at the back of his head, and then he buried his face between her legs. Her knees trembled as he picked her up, carried her out of the dressing room and lay her on the bed, nodding as she murmured, 'The KY is in my locker.' Henry warmed the lubricant between his hands, and Keelin closed her eyes as he entered her, hard. 'Oh God,' he said. 'Oh fuck, that's good.' As she closed her eyes, she imagined that Nessa was watching them. The girl was standing by their bed, her hair clumped with blood and mud, still in her party dress, and she watched as Henry fucked Keelin, as she cried out, telling her husband to do it harder, faster. It was Nessa's face that she saw as she came, falling apart.

Henry allowed himself to come too, collapsing on Keelin's body with a gasp. He rolled off her quickly, pulling the locker open and grabbing a packet of wet wipes to clean himself with. Inside the drawer, in among the earplugs, lip balm, the random selection of batteries and antacids, there was a small brown bottle. Henry took it out, shook a pill into his palm and handed it to her.

'You don't need to check up on me all the time, you know.'

'I'm not checking up on you,' he said. He went to the chest of drawers against the far wall, riffling through them. 'You were the one who asked me to remind you to take your Lexapro, weren't you? Why ask for my help if you don't want it? Sometimes I feel like I can't win with you, Keelin.' He pulled on an old T-shirt and boxer shorts and sat down on the bed beside her.

'I just . . . I was thinking maybe I could come off them. Even just to see what it's like. It's been such a long time since—'

'You need the medication.' He cut across her. 'I don't want things getting bad again.'

'Neither do I,' she replied. 'But I'm fine, I promise. I don't see why I can't *try* at least, it might—'

'You took your tablets every night when I was away?' he asked, and she nodded. 'What about Alex? Has he been taking his as well?'

'I think so,' she said. 'I don't want to keep at him – you know how he gets if he feels like I'm monitoring him. He's been in better form anyway. He's still eating – he's gained some more weight back.'

'That's good,' Henry said, scratching at a patch of dry skin on his neck. 'Has he done an interview with the Australians yet? I don't think they're going to give up on him easily, you know.'

'He's not ready for something like that, Henry. I'm . . .' She paused. She hated to admit this, even to her husband. 'I'm scared for him.'

'Please, darling, don't worry. Didn't I promise you that I would take care of this?' He lowered his body until it was flat on the bed, pulling Keelin down with him. She nestled into his armpit, and, with her ear pressed against his skin, she could hear the sound of her own heart ticking. She was like the alligator from *Peter Pan,* a clock stuck inside its throat, *tick tock, tick tock.* Listening to her life pass her by with every beat.

'I missed you while I was away.' He pulled his knees up, the bones cracking in protest. He could do with some yoga himself, but she knew better to suggest such a thing. Henry didn't like any intimation that he was getting older. At nearly fifty, his hair remained suspiciously free of grey, his anti-aging skin products fighting for space with hers on their bathroom shelves. He'd always been interested in his looks – 'fond of himself', her mother would have said, which Keelin used to tease him about when they were first married. But it was different now; there was something disquieting about the way her husband took care of his appearance. He chose his clothes for the documentary with such meticulousness, selecting the most flattering of cuts, wondering aloud which colours would 'pop' on camera. Everyone was watching him, he said, so he may as well dress to impress.

'Was your trip a successful one?' she asked.

'Depends on what you define as success,' he said. Keelin waited for him to speak again, curling her fingers into her palms when she noticed a small chip in her scarlet nail polish.

'It was obvious people recognised me at the airport,' he said after a few minutes. 'They'd see my face and do a double take, and they looked frightened of me, Keelin. It was like I was some sort of ogre. I just . . .' He broke off. The pain was

135

etched into his skin, in the new creases cut deep across his forehead and around his mouth. 'I know I made mistakes. I know Nessa is dead and Alex is heartbroken, and I bear a degree of responsibility for that but I feel like I'm a bloody pariah,' he continued. 'I tried to contact Miles in London but he said he was in Norfolk, and Charlie bowed out of our lunch at the last minute, my own *brother*. Everyone's always too busy to meet me now. I used to be . . .' Henry sighed and Keelin could hear the heaviness in it, the burden her husband had carried with him for the last ten years. It wasn't made up of guilt, like hers was, but something stickier, more complicated; it was the frustration of a man who had lived a blessed life, who saw such an existence as their birthright, and could not understand why that was no longer the case. 'I was someone people wanted to spend time with,' he said under his breath.

Keelin intertwined her fingers with his, kissing his shoulder. 'I'm sorry, Henry.'

'I'm afraid this documentary is turning out to be a bad idea. Giving them so much access, allowing them to stay in the cottage,' he confessed. 'It's too risky. We don't need these men here for another five months. What if they discover something we don't want them to find?'

'That's why I said we shouldn't –' Keelin stopped.

'What was that?'

'Nothing.'

'Oh no, darling. Do tell me your thoughts on the matter.'.

'Henry, please. I don't want to fight about this.'

'You never wanted to do the documentary, is that what you were going to say? So it's all my fault again. Everything is always my fault, isn't it, Keelin?' He pushed her off. 'I've spent the last decade protecting you, trying to make sure you don't fall apart, *again*, and all you can do now is say, "I told you so." The Australians were going to make this film whether we liked it or not; I was the only one who was willing to face facts, as per usual. And now you're trying to throw it back in my face. Is it too much to ask that you support me, Keelin, just once?'

'I do support you!'

'Do you? Because I feel like I do an awful lot for you, and you don't appreciate any of it.' He gestured at the four-poster bed, the Egyptian cotton bedsheets, the House of Hackney wallpaper that had cost €250 per roll. Not a problem, Henry had said grandly to the interior designer when they'd received the bill, only the best for my family. He walked into the dressing room now, coming back with his arms full of her clothes, the designer labels he'd so carefully selected for her, and threw them in a heap on the floor. 'And what about your wardrobe? That doesn't come for free, you know. Everything in this house was paid for by *me* with *my* family's money and it would be nice if you could express even a fraction of gratitude for any of it, and for what I do for you and your bloody children. You sit there, rolling your eyes at the idea of a documentary, even

137

though it could change *everything* for us, it could fix Misty Hill, people might come back and we—'

'Henry, please. Please.' She knelt up on the bed. 'You need to calm down.'

His shoulders slumped and he dropped down beside her, visibly deflating. 'This isn't easy for me,' he said. 'I love you so much, Keelin, and it's like you don't feel the same way.'

'Of course I feel the same way.'

'Do you?' He looked at her. 'Because sometimes I get the impression our relationship is rather one-sided. It's not very nice, given what I've done for you.'

'Please don't think that,' she said. 'I'm so sorry I made you feel this way.' She wrapped her legs around his waist, shuffling closer so that her groin was pressed against his lower back. 'I'm sorry,' she whispered into his neck. His body was tense at first, and she waited for him to relax, to accept her apology. 'I'm sorry. I'm sorry.'

'When you act like this,' he said in a small voice, 'it reminds me of how my mother treated me when I was a child, how obvious it was that she loved Charlie more than she did me. It brings up all these old emotions when you do that, Keelin, and you make me feel *irrelevant*. I can't—'

'I know,' she said. 'Please, Henry. I'll do anything you want to make this better. Just tell me what you need me to do.'

He ran his hands down her legs. 'Will you do a joint interview with me tomorrow?' he asked quickly. 'The Australians have been wanting us to speak on camera together, and I don't think it's a bad idea, actually. It might force them to back off Alex for a while, give him some space. And most importantly, it'll give the impression we're united in this. Us-against-the-world-type thing, you know.' He half laughed. 'How could people believe I had anything to do with Nessa Crowley's death if my wife still loves me?'

Keelin hesitated. 'But I thought you said—'

'Oh, Jesus Christ. *Fine.* Forget I even asked.' Henry bent down to pick the clothes off the ground, telling Keelin to 'leave it' when she tried to help. 'You'll only do it incorrectly,' he said. 'Like you do everything else.'

'Henry, please. I'll do the interview, if that's what you want.' She picked up her dressing gown and wrapped it around her body. 'I just thought we'd agreed it would be better if I didn't talk to them any more.'

'When did we agree to that?'

'In your study? Remember? The morning after I had dinner in Marigold Cottage and I was late home. You thought it best that I stay away from the Australians for a while.'

'No, darling,' he said. 'That was *your* suggestion. It's not my place to tell you whom you can and cannot see.'

'Oh,' she said, trying to think back to that moment. He was right, she realised. It *had* been her idea. 'I'm sorry. I . . . I must have gotten confused.'

Henry's face softened. 'That's OK, silly,' he said, pulling her into his arms. 'Have you been feeling confused a lot recently? We might want to look at adjusting your meds

139

if that's the case – it's best to keep an eye on these things, isn't it? Now,' he said, without giving her time to reply, 'you should wear your Armani dress tomorrow, the burnt-orange one. With the Aquazzura pumps.' He tightened his grip. 'I bet Jake will like you in those.'

'Don't be daft,' Keelin said, laughing. 'There's no way Jake sees me in that way.'

'I didn't mean like *that* – goodness, you're old enough to be his mother. But he's intrigued by you, I can tell, and we can use that. You should befriend him.' Henry moved his hand under her dressing gown, tracing his fingertips up her rib cage. 'Try and find out about the other interviews he's conducted so far, what people have said about us. The direction they're taking with the doc.'

Keelin wasn't sure she wanted to know what the islanders were saying about her. It was odd, she supposed, given how eager she had been to leave this place after the murder, how hungry she'd been for a new world to call her own. She thought she could turn her back on her home and she wouldn't give it a second thought. But leaving would have been her choice; it was an entirely different thing to be rejected by the people whose blood ran in her veins. *I'm one of you*, she wanted to say. *I'm Tomás and Cáit Ó Mordha's daughter. You can't deny me my name, no matter how hard you try.*

'Noah is fine,' Henry continued. 'We don't need to worry about Noah – he's not exactly the brains of the operation here. He's technically skilled, I'll give him that, and I'm sure the footage will look beautiful, but I don't think he has any great investigative abilities. Jake is the tricky one. I can't figure him out and that, my darling, makes him dangerous. We need to be sure he's on our side.' He inched his fingers across her breasts, smiling as she gasped out loud. 'You should spend more time with him, Keelin. Make sure our guest is settling into island life.'

'But—'

'But what?' he said, removing his hand.

'You seemed so annoyed the evening I had dinner there.'

'Dinner where?' Henry asked, confused. 'What are you talking about?'

'In Marigold Cottage, when Jake cooked for me. I was late home and you were really pissed off with me. You said—'

'Keelin, you're being ridiculous,' he cut across her. 'How exactly was I "pissed off"? Did I raise my voice? Did I scream at you?'

'Of course not. You didn't say anything, really, but it was the way you . . . the way you looked at me, I guess? And the tone of your voice? I can't explain it. I could just *tell* you were angry with me.'

'Keelin –' he shook his head – 'are you psychic now? You'll give Ellen Tiernan and her second sight a run for her money yet.'

'But what –' Her mind went blank, as if she was an actress who had forgotten her lines on stage, looking desperately to the wings for a prompt. *Think, Keelin. Think.* 'But what about my phone?'

'What *about* your phone?'

'Yes!' she said in a rush of excitement. 'My phone. You wouldn't let me use it because I had stayed too long in Marigold Cottage that night.'

'I wouldn't "let" you use your phone?' He frowned at her. 'Keelin, I don't know what you're trying to imply here but it's making me very uncomfortable. The passcode wouldn't work – what on earth did I have to do with that?' Henry reached down to the leather briefcase neatly tucked in behind the locker, fishing out her iPhone. 'I brought it into the Vodafone store in Cork,' he said, handing it to her. 'The chap there said this kind of thing happens a lot – it's a glitch in the system, apparently.'

Keelin turned on her phone, typed her in her usual passcode with care, one number at a time. It worked perfectly.

'A glitch.'

'Yes,' he said. 'A glitch.'

CHAPTER TWENTY

Henry and Keelin Kinsella

HENRY: My apologies that we couldn't do this before now.
I was away on business for a few days.

NOAH: You go to the mainland regularly, I hear. That's what
the ferryman told us.

HENRY: Did he indeed? You can't do anything on this island
without the ferryman knowing. Keelin did warn me when
we decided to build Hawthorn House. Wave goodbye to
any semblance of privacy, she said. Pity I didn't listen.

NOAH: What takes you to the mainland so often?

HENRY: It depends. This time I visited my solicitor, and
then I flew to London to meet up with some old friends I
hadn't seen in yonks, have lunch with my brother, that kind
of thing. Someone even approached me at Cork airport,

can you believe that? A complete stranger. He wanted to shake my hand and say he thought it was a travesty what happened to me. A miscarriage of justice, he said.

NOAH: That's interesting.

HENRY: It's the era we're living in, you see. Trial by social media. Whatever happened to innocent until proven guilty? There wasn't a shred of evidence to connect me to this case – not that you'd know by the *appalling* manner in which the islanders have treated us. I was an easy target, you see. The Englishman up in the Big House. They'd much rather it was me who did this than have to grapple with the possibility it could be one of their own.

JAKE: It's not *quite* true to say there wasn't a shred of evidence to connect you to Nessa Crowley's murder, is it, Henry?

HENRY: I beg your pardon?

JAKE: There was some evidence, wasn't there? There were scratches on your face and your arms, compatible with the sort you would have gotten in a physical struggle. You had bruising under your eye as well, didn't you? You could see why it might make people suspicious.

HENRY: That was Keelin's doing, I'm afraid. She told the guards as much afterwards. Didn't you, darling?

KEELIN: Yes. We had been fighting, but I shouldn't have done it. Of all people, I ought to have known there's no excuse for violence. But I lost my temper, and I –

HENRY: My wife's engagement ring caught my eye – that was what caused the bruising. (silence) Look, they checked for

144

DNA under Nessa Crowley's fingernails and they didn't find anyth—

JAKE: The body had been left outside in one of the worst storms to hit Ireland in forty years; a lot of the evidence would've been contaminated by the time the guards even got to the scene. (pause) There were reports you lit a bonfire, is that correct? Seems odd, if you ask me.

HENRY: It was tradition. We lit a bonfire at every party we threw on the island.

JAKE: Even during a thunderstorm? And you positioned it underneath the balcony, on the other side of the house from where Nessa Crowley's body was found. That's convenient.

HENRY: Is it?

JAKE: A witness said they saw you throwing items into the fire. A shirt, a book of some sort.

HENRY: You wouldn't want to take that as gospel. Memories are not infallible things, you know, particularly when a great deal of alcohol has been taken. And I'm sure you're aware the guards combed through the ashes and they didn't find anything of note.

JAKE: You said you and Keelin had a fight the night of the party. Do you want to tell us more about that?

HENRY: The reasons are fairly well documented. I don't see the point in bringing it all up again, do you?

JAKE: Given the circumstances, it was probably the most significant fight you and Keelin have ever had. I don't think it's unreasonable for people to ask about it.

HENRY: Married people argue, Jake. You'll learn that yourself someday. And we've moved past that stage in our lives, haven't we, darling? We're stronger than ever now.

JAKE: Right. (pause) When the power cut, what happened?

HENRY: I went outside to switch on the generator and—

JAKE: But the guests said the power didn't come back on until early the next morning.

HENRY: Yes, that's right. I couldn't seem to work the blasted thing. My father had been warning me for years to get it upgraded, he said we needed one like the hotels had. I never got around to it, I'm afraid.

NOAH: So, you went outside to find the generator. What did you do next?

HENRY: Keelin followed me and it was then we ran into Nessa. A friend of mine had made a drunken pass at her, and the girl was distressed.

NOAH: According to the police reports, that was when you told Nessa to go home, Keelin?

KEELIN: Yes . . . I shouldn't have lashed out the way I did, but Nessa was always just *there*, in the house every time I turned around. Hanging off of Alex – and he was too young for her. He was so young then. I was tired and drunk and I told her to go home. She wasn't welcome in our house any more. (silence) It was a mistake. I see that now.

NOAH: What happened then?

HENRY: The girl was upset, naturally. She ran off and I tried to follow her. I wanted to make sure she was all right, but

146

she was too quick for me. I couldn't see properly, the rain was ghastly that night so I . . .

JAKE: You just let her go?

HENRY: Yes.

JAKE: You let a young woman run off in the middle of a storm by herself?

HENRY: She was from the island; she knew this place better than I did. I thought she would be . . . You think I haven't regretted that every day since?

JAKE: You were the last person to see Nessa Crowley alive.

HENRY: Apart from her killer, obviously.

JAKE: And what about your old girlfriend? Greta Ainsworth? You dated for four years before her death in 1999, is that correct? Young women seem to die in mysterious circumstances around you more frequently than is usual, don't they, Henry? Seems unfortunate.

HENRY: Excuse me? How *dare* you. Do not mention her name ever again. You don't have a bloody clue what you're talking about. That's quite enough.

NOAH: Wait, please don't go, Henry. He didn't mean to—

HENRY: I said, that's *enough*.

CHAPTER TWENTY-ONE

The Crowley Girl

'Do you know something,' Johanna said as she turned to face the sunroom, beams of light slashing through the thick glass walls. 'I never get sick of that view, no matter how many times I sit in this kitchen.'

Keelin snorted, handing her a cup of tea. 'Don't be such a plámásar. You'd swear you weren't from Rún yourself.'

'To be fair, I don't live here any more,' her friend said. Keelin was the only one of the three of them who still lived on the island. Jo rented a place in Schull, near the school where she'd recently been made principal, and Seán was away fishing for months at a time, renting out his two-bed bungalow in Castletownbere to cover the mortgage while he was gone. 'And there's a difference to being from here and having a house like this,' Jo said, gesturing at Keelin to pass the packet of biscuits. 'Oh lovely,' she muttered as she read the packaging. 'Gluten- *and* dairy-free. I would have called to Mama and Papi for tea if I'd wanted this shite.'

'Henry's orders,' Keelin said. She didn't want to talk about this house, not with Johanna anyway. Jo had been her best friend since they were babies, growing from a skinny child into a skinny adult – you'd miss her if she turned sideways, Keelin's mother used to say – with the same cropped black hair and buck teeth that were slightly too large for her mouth. They had been the only two girls born that year, and as they were both that rarefied thing on the island – the single child – they had become like sisters to one another. Keelin could not remember a time when Jo wasn't part of her life.

'A dairy-free diet doesn't seem like Henry's idea of a good time,' Johanna said, taking one of the offending biscuits. 'What's brought this on?'

'It's a long story,' she said. She didn't want to tell her the truth; she knew her friend wouldn't approve. Keelin had never dieted before now; her mother could remember rationing during The Emergency and had raised Keelin to believe that faddish eating was akin to a mortal sin: You'll finish that plate of food right now, young lady. Think of all the starving children in Africa. None of Henry's friends in London talked about diets either, it was considered terribly passé in their set. They ate butter and carbs, but the women still managed to be slender to the point of frailty, with spindly legs that looked as

149

if they might break if they stood up straight. Keelin was the only woman who wore anything other than a size eight and although she wished it didn't, it bothered her. She'd gone to Henry after the last party at the Darcys' house in Norfolk, and asked for his help. I'm useless, she said to him, and I've no willpower whatsoever. Will you keep an eye on me? Call me a heifer when I'm reaching for a second slice of cake? He'd laughed, told her she was no such thing. But of course, her husband said. If you want me to help you, I will.

'There are some benefits to living alone then,' Johanna said, pulling a face. 'At least I can buy whatever junk food I want.' She pointed at the magazine rack on the floor. 'I spy *Heat* mag. Gimme, please.' She flicked through the pages, turning it around to show Keelin a photo of a boy band from a reality television show, fanning herself.

'Not you too, Jo,' Henry said, walking into the kitchen. He'd been out running and he was red-cheeked, his damp hair clinging to his skull. 'They're practically children.'

'They're very hot children,' the other woman said, half standing to give Henry a hug before pretending to recoil at his sweat-stained T-shirt. 'You know I'm mad about you, Kinsella,' she said, backing away from him, 'but not that much, I'm afraid.'

'You win some, you lose some,' he said, filling a glass with water from the Brita jug. 'How are things with you, anyway?' Henry sat opposite Johanna, reaching across her to grab a biscuit. 'How's the lovely Susan? Still devoted to me, I hope?'

150

'But of course. She would leave me in a heartbeat if she knew you were available,' she replied.

Henry turned his hands up to the sky, as if in prayer. 'And I really think me and Susan could be happy together,' he said. 'But unfortunately, I love this lady too much to ever look at another woman.' He grabbed Keelin by the waist, and she squealed in protest. 'I'm beginning to feel rather rejected,' he said, pulling a pout as Keelin squirmed out of his embrace, complaining about how sweaty he was. 'Come, Ms Stein. Tell us news of the outside world, you know we're cut off from civilisation here.'

'Hmm, let me think,' Jo said. 'Well, I was just telling Keelin that I'm looking for a substitute teacher because Ríona is going on maternity leave next year. I'm up to my eyes in application forms. Zero craic.'

'That's a pity. Didn't she only start last September?' Henry said.

'She did,' Johanna replied. 'Good memory, my friend. But she's been married two years and she's in her mid-thirties so . . .'

'It must be frustrating,' Keelin said, pouring herself a cup of tea from the pot. 'I know it's not very politically correct of me to say this, but wouldn't it just be easier to hire a male teacher? At least you won't have to worry about a man going off on maternity leave.'

Henry and Johanna stared at her, open-mouthed. 'Keelin!' Henry said. 'Did I marry a Tory, unbeknownst to myself?'

151

He exchanged an outraged glance with Johanna. 'We have a daughter, remember? Surely you wouldn't want Evie to lose out on a job because she might need to take maternity leave some day? And you know how hard I've been trying to improve things here at Misty Hill. Jo, you'll like this.' He turned to her friend again. 'I've made it our mission to achieve a completely gender-balanced ratio of artists at the retreat centre by at least—'

'But you said the other day, you said, but, but, you *said*, Henry . . .' Keelin stuttered. 'You never stop complaining about how difficult that is.' She could feel tears pricking her eyes; she always wanted to cry when she felt embarrassed. 'You said loads of the female artists you invite here refuse to come because they have family commitments they can't get out of, even if you offer them a bursary. You said that—'

'Darling,' Henry said, taking her hand in his. His voice became gentler. 'We have to take into account how certain social structures make it more difficult for women to progress in their careers in the first place. No one seems to wonder why the *fathers* never have any issue with coming to Misty Hill for three months to finish their latest album or book or whatever.'

'Exactly,' Johanna said, pounding her fist on the table. 'No one ever asks men who's taking care of the children or how do they juggle it all. God, it's all such *bullshit* and I fucking love that you can see that, Kinsella.' She put her palm out to high-five him, Henry happily complying. 'You've a good one here, Keels,' her friend said. 'He's a keeper.'

'Yes,' she smiled tightly, putting her hand on the small of

her husband's back. 'Do you want to have a shower, babe? You'll catch your death.'

He wavered, clearly hoping Johanna would object, demand he stay for longer. Henry had always felt like a fraud, he'd confided in Keelin one night after too much Scotch, ever since he was a child. The boy who was sent to the best schools but who knew he was different; his family's wealth was too new, his surname too Irish. He knew he couldn't be one of them so he had, instead, made himself the *most* – the most fun, the most interesting, the most attractive. The life and soul of every party, the one who could be depended upon to say yes to one more drink or line or dance, always the last to leave. Keelin could see something in her husband, and she recognised what it was because it was within her too. A desperation to belong, maybe, or a yearning to be loved. Since her parents had died, she'd had no family except Alex, so when Henry proposed to her all those years ago, she had said, You and I can belong to each another now, Henry. I'd like that very much, he'd replied, his voice thick.

'I suppose I should probably . . .' he began, pausing when he heard a knock on the door. Keelin could hear a female voice calling out, 'Hello?', footsteps on the wooden floor in the hall, and there she was, *again*.

'I hope you don't mind but the door was open,' Nessa said. Her skin was glowing, even without make-up. Not for the Crowley Girls the blotchy complexion Keelin remembered from her own youth, the spots that would erupt around her chin and jawline when she was premenstrual. 'I was just passing by so I thought I'd pop in,' the girl said, plonking her cheap tan handbag onto the countertop. She had been 'just passing by' every day this summer, waving a quick hello before disappearing with Alex to his bedroom. They could be up there, alone, for hours. Keelin would walk past the closed door, listening for bedsprings, low moaning, but all she heard was music, low voices, the occasional peal of laughter. Keelin couldn't stop thinking about what she had read in her son's diary, but she couldn't tell Henry about that, she couldn't tell *anyone* what she had seen that day. She just said that she was unhappy about the situation, it wasn't appropriate, and her husband advised her to stay calm. Things will go back to normal when autumn comes and Nessa returns to UCC, he said. She'll be distracted by her friends in Cork and she'll forget all about Alex. But it was September now and here Nessa Crowley was, just 'passing by' Hawthorn House for the umpteenth time.

'Alex doesn't have a session with you today, does he?' Keelin asked her. 'Because he's not here, if he does.'

'That's fine – I'll wait for him.'

'Well,' Jo said to break the awkward silence. 'As I live and breathe, one of the Crowley Girls in the flesh. How are you, lovely?' She poured the young woman a cup of tea, Nessa shaking her head when Jo held up the sugar canister. 'Are the biscuits gluten-free?' she asked. 'I'm coeliac.'

'Are you now?' Jo asked, her eyes darting to Keelin. 'Well, then you're in luck! Here you go.'

'Thanks, Hanna,' Nessa said as she took the biscuit, slipping into her baby nickname for Johanna. She never did that with Keelin; she barely acknowledged that they'd known each other before she started giving Alex grinds. If Nessa could have called her Mrs Kinsella, Keelin suspected she would have. Had she been as nervous of Seán's mother when they'd briefly dated as teenagers? But that was different, she and Seán had been the same age, and they'd been friends for years. There was no chance she would have broken Seán's heart, just to prove she could.

'What were you all fighting about before I came in?' the girl asked. 'I could hear raised voices from the hall.'

'Nothing much,' Henry said, winking at Keelin. 'Just my wife setting back the feminist movement by twenty years.'

'That's not fair.'

'But surely you consider yourself a feminist, Keelin?' Nessa asked, her eyes widening. 'I know a lot of women of your generation think it's about man-hating and refusing to shave your legs or whatever, but actually, it's just about equality. Equal rights for men and women, like. That's all it is. It's nothing to be scared of.'

'Women of "my generation" have access to the dictionary too,' Keelin snapped. 'I don't need a twenty-year-old with zero life experience to explain the meaning of the word "feminism" to me.' She stood up, reaching across the table to grab the younger woman's cup, dumping the ware in the sink with a clatter. She stood there, not daring to turn around; she didn't

155

want to see the exaggerated grimaces, Johanna's mouthed *What the fuck?* to Henry. She gripped the edges of the counter as she tried to formulate a polite apology in her head, something to make her seem less ridiculous after that outburst.

'Erm, right, OK,' Nessa said. 'I'll head up to Alex's room, I think. I can wait for him there.' Keelin could hear the young woman getting up behind her, exchanging polite goodbyes with Jo and Henry as she gathered her belongings, her slow footsteps on the stairs. She wanted to scream after Nessa, to tell her to come back – *How dare you! The cheek of you going to my son's room without permission!* – and insist the girl leave Hawthorn House immediately. But Keelin couldn't do that, she had made enough of a fool of herself as it was.

'Are you all right?' Henry said under his breath, but Keelin was silent. *Not now.* 'Got it,' he said, hugging her from behind. 'We can talk later. I love you.'

'Jaaaaysus. What was *that* about?' Johanna asked when they were alone.

'Nothing,' Keelin said. 'I'm in bad form, that's all.' She took the biscuits and put them back in the tin before rinsing off the plates and tea cups and stacking them in the dishwasher. 'Just ignore me.'

'You know, Keels . . .' Her friend hesitated. 'There's been some talk around the island. Saying that one of the Crowley Girls is forever up in the Big House.'

'There's always talk around the island,' Keelin said, edging her way around Johanna, her hip grazing against the other woman's body. She walked into the sunroom, Jo behind her, and they looked out the window. It was a grim day, the water chopping angrily at the cliffs, spitting spray into the air, the clouds heavy with the threat of rain. The two women stood side by side, their fingers not quite touching, staring at the sea that had surrounded them for their entire lives.

'Do you remember when we were kids?' Jo asked her. 'God, I was never out of trouble, was I? I was non-stop talking,' she laughed. 'If I had a student like that in my classroom now . . . I don't know how Mr Ó Gríofa didn't murder me. But you –' she looked at Keelin – 'you were so well behaved.' She had been a quiet child, so quiet that the teachers rarely paid her much attention. Keelin Ní Mhordha was known as bright but not brilliant; she did her homework diligently but never raised her hand to answer questions, her face burning when the múinteoir called upon her in class. 'But whenever I was caught being bold,' Jo went on, 'you would insist you'd been messing too, that you deserved to be punished as well, even though you never did. And the two of us would be made to stand at the top of the classroom together, like a right pair of dunces. Remember?'

'What's your point, Jo?'

'My point is that I'm still standing here beside you and I'm not going anywhere either.' She touched her fingertips against Keelin's. 'You would tell me if you weren't fine, wouldn't you?'

Keelin didn't reply. She just squeezed Johanna's hand as tightly as she could.

157

CHAPTER TWENTY-TWO

Henry was furious for weeks after their disastrous joint interview for the documentary, although he claimed he didn't blame Keelin 'in the slightest', and she was being 'absurd' to suggest otherwise. It must have been a figment of her imagination then, how he slammed doors and stomped around the house like he was trying to dislodge the floorboards. In mid-September, he decided they needed to clean the house from top to bottom in preparation for autumn, inspecting Keelin's dressing area, querying why lids weren't on night creams and why cashmere jerseys didn't have lavender sachets tucked beside them. Did Keelin *want* her clothes to be destroyed by moths, was that it? Those sweaters were expensive but it was *his* money, so it didn't matter, was that it? And when she tried to apologise, he would tell her that she had nothing to say sorry for, he wasn't angry with her, for God's sake. Why did Keelin insist on behaving like he was some kind of tyrant? He just wanted things to be done correctly, he wanted things in their proper order, and no one else seemed to care.

But when night-time came, Henry was a different man. He would tell Keelin he loved her then, pulling his wife close and staring into her eyes. 'Isn't this nice?' he said. 'It's important we feel connected to one another, don't you think, darling?' She smiled her agreement, waiting until he fell asleep before attempting to wriggle out of his grip, but he refused to let go, his head tucked into her shoulder, the sounds of his snores grating against her ears. They would lie like that until the sun rose. 'I haven't slept this well in years,' Henry said when he woke, stretching his arms in satisfaction, and Keelin would smile and say *yes, me too*, but when she stood up she was dizzy, a rush of blood to the head, clouds swirling in her eyes. She became clumsy again, banging hip bones and knees against sharp edges, examining her skin for new bruises, and she was forgetful too. I'm so sorry, she said when she missed her daughter's first day back at school. Don't worry, Evie replied. Daddy sent a beautiful bouquet of flowers to wish me luck. At least *one* of you remembers that I exist.

'Jesus,' Henry spluttered. It was the afternoon and Keelin was sitting at the kitchen island, her head nodding forward and then jerking back as she tried to stay awake. He rushed to the kitchen sink and spat out a mouthful of tea. 'You've put salt in there instead of sugar,' he said, picking up the canister, dabbing his finger on the grains and holding it to his tongue. Had she? She couldn't remember re-filling that container in ages. 'Sweetheart, are you quite all right? I'm worried about you. Maybe we should get the doctor to pay a visit to the island, look at your prescription.'

'I don't think that's—' she began, but Henry was hugging her, murmuring, 'Poor Keels,' into her hair. She started to apologise, I'm sorry, I'm sorry, but he put his fingers to her lips. 'You need to rest, darling,' he said. 'Let's have some quiet time, just the two of us.'

He barely spoke to her for weeks after that. He would leave the room when Keelin walked in, and he checked her mobile every evening, looking at the phone calls made and received, scrutinising her search history. 'You need a digital detox,' he said, tutting when she asked for her iPhone back. 'We spend too much time on our screens these days. I read an article that links it with depression. We don't want to risk it, not with your history.'

Alex asked if she was OK. You've been very quiet recently, Mam, he said. And she lied and said she was fine, just a touch of laryngitis, that's all. She thought her son might question her further, he was usually so attuned to her moods, but Alex was distracted these days. He'd taken to going out at night in a waft of hair gel and aftershave, wearing a denim jacket with sheepskin lining that Keelin had never seen before. She badly wanted to ask where this new jacket was from and why he was making such an effort to go down for a pint in the local pub, and who was he meeting there? Who was he talking to? Was he being careful? Her son walked out the door every evening with such hope shining in his eyes. When was the last time any of them had a reason to feel hopeful? She wished she could discuss the matter with Henry, she was desperate to talk about anything really, the clamouring thoughts rapping their knuckles against her skull, whispering, *Hello, Keelin? We're here. Let us out, please.* She was going mad with the need of it.

It was a Saturday evening in late October and Alex was out, again, and Henry didn't like the TV show she had chosen. Do you mind, darling? he said, taking the remote control from her. The presenter's voice gives me a headache. His hand on her knee as they watched a documentary about the Holocaust, pictures of emaciated children, brittle bodies piled up in a cavernous pit, and Keelin could feel her gag reflex contract and she was afraid she might be sick all over the carpet. (A pity, she imagined Henry saying. That rug was Persian, and rather expensive.) Her mind was skipping over memories like a child jumping rope, over and over and over and – I am going crazy, she realised. I will lose my mind on this island, like my mother did before me.

'I can't do this any more,' she said, her voice hoarse.

'Can't do what?'

'This . . . *silence*. I can't—'

'I'm trying to help you, Keelin,' he cut across her. 'I do these things because I love you and I want to take care of you. I don't want you to become ill again. You don't know how frightening that time was for me, for all of us.'

'I do know,' she said. 'And I'm sorry I put you through that. But let me take care of you for a change.'

'How do you mean?'

'I'm going to go to Marigold Cottage,' she said. 'You were right about Jake. We will be friends, he and I. We have plenty in common, don't we? Maybe it's time I reminded him of that.'

Her husband hesitated, uncertain, but then something broke in him. 'Thank you,' he said, and for a moment she thought he might cry. 'I love you, Keelin. You know that, don't you?'

'Of course,' she replied. 'I love you too.'

It was obvious Noah hadn't expected Keelin to be knocking on their door. He was in a vest and pyjama bottoms, his long hair held back with a tartan bandana, and there was an open box of sweets in his hands. He froze when he saw it was her. 'Shit. I thought it was more trick-or-treaters looking for lollies,' he said. It was Halloween tonight, she realised; she'd forgotten. Keelin thought of October nights celebrating Samhain as a child, watching her mother bake the barm-brack, stirring a coin, a pea, a rag, a ring and a stick into the mixture. Tomás would cut Keelin a slice, slathering it with butter, whispering to his daughter that he bet she would find the ring, its golden sheen foretelling of a white dress, a walk up the aisle and a handsome man waiting for her at the end. Keelin took a bite, testing the brack for any hard edges, and for a moment she hoped she would find nothing there. She didn't want to grow up, she didn't want anything to change. She wanted this house and this island, her parents, Seán and Johanna. What need did she have of anything or anyone else? But she started to choke, spitting out half-masticated brack into the palm of her hand, spying a tiny wooden twig within its gooey mess. She whimpered, looking up at her parents in distress, but her father told her it was just a load of rubbish, and she wasn't to be worrying. He cut her another slice, handing it to her. Here you go, mo stoirín, he said. Everyone deserves a second chance, don't they?

'Keelin,' Noah said now. 'Keelin, I'm so sorry about what happened during the interview. Jake pushed it too far, he knows that. We didn't mean to upset Henry, or you for that matter. Jake gets really passionate about this stuff and he—'

'I'm here to see him,' she said. 'Jake.' It looked cosy inside the cottage, the fire lit, a half-eaten lasagne in a baking tray on the table. Noah nodded, disappearing into Jake's room, and she could hear them talking in hushed tones. 'All right,' she heard Jake say. 'I get it, mate.' Then he appeared, standing on the slab of stone outside Marigold Cottage, zipping up a North Face fleece, his persistent cowlick standing on end. His mother would have fussed over that, Keelin bet, wetting her fingers and trying to smooth it down as best she could, but to no avail.

163

'I've been trying to get in touch with you,' he said. 'I've been phoning and texting non-stop, Keelin. I was so worried about you.'

'Why?' she asked, genuinely curious. Why did all of the men in her life worry about her? What was it about her that prompted such concern?

'Because of Henry, he was fuming after the interview. Are you sure you're OK?' he asked, peering closely at her. 'You look exhausted.'

'Thanks,' she said. She didn't need Jake to tell her this; she was well aware of what she looked like. 'Let's go for a walk.'

It was very still as they picked their way down to the headland. The lighthouse on the mainland blinked slowly, and all across Inisrún the houses were lit up like jewels, smoke unfurling from chimneys in peels of grey. The bracken was turning at this time of year, dropping into a deep russet, but they couldn't see that now, not in the dark. They could only hear the roar of the waves, their feet against the ground as they walked to the cliffs, and their uneven breaths, a fraction out of sync with one another.

'Watch it,' Jake said, grabbing Keelin's arm to pull her back. 'You're too close to the edge.'

'There's a joke to be made there,' she said, 'but I can't quite seem to find it.'

She crept further, the stones loosening beneath her boots, crumbling into the sea below. Keelin had always needed to go to the cliffs and stand as close to the end of the earth as she could possibly go, staring at the flat expanse of sea and sky, tasting salt on her tongue. Next stop, America, the islanders said, and for the first time she yearned for that place. For dirt and car fumes and buildings so tall it would give you vertigo to look up at them. A place where no one recognised her name, and they'd never heard of the Crowley Girl. She could die in a city like that and no one would know, no one would even care. The prospect was oddly thrilling.

'Keelin,' Jake said again, a note of fear creeping into his voice. 'Be careful, please.'

Still she did not step back. She found that she could not, that the swirling vortex of water below was holding her in its trance. Would it hurt? she wondered. If she fell. Would anyone care as much about her death as they had done about Nessa's?

'Are you angry with me about what happened during the interview?' he asked. 'I only wanted to push Henry a little, see if I could get something new out of him. It's worked with other subjects, you know? And Noah and I need this doc to be a success if we're going to break out of the Australian market, we have to prove we're not just one-hit wonders. I misjudged the situation, clearly.' His hand on her elbow, making sure she wasn't going to jump off the cliff in front of him. 'But Henry says he won't give us any more interviews now. We can stay in Marigold Cottage if we want, he's not going to be petty about it, he said, but he won't be involved from here on.' Jake led Keelin back to a large rock, and pulled her to sit on it beside him. 'Noah is fuming,' he admitted. 'We're not totally fucked yet – we have plenty of other people to talk to; we've lots lined up on the mainland and in the UK for the next few weeks – but Noah says we'll be wasting our time with that, our whole USP was unrestricted access to Henry Kinsella.'

'What age are you again, Jake?'

'I'm twenty-nine.'

'Interesting.' She bent down to pick up a small pebble, worrying it smooth between her fingers. 'When I was your age, I was married for the second time with a nine-year-old son to take care of.'

'Is this your way of telling me that the documentary is meaningless in the greater scheme of things?' he asked. 'Because I don't think Noah is going to see it like that, or the production company for that matter.'

'No, that's not what I meant at all. I suppose it's funny, given how similar you and I are in some ways and then . . .' She trailed off, still rubbing the stone in her hand. 'When I was in my twenties, I couldn't have imagined travelling halfway across the world, like you've done – I'm not sure I was ever that brave. For a long time, I felt like I was just *surviving*. I loved Alex but I never thought I'd be a single parent, that this would be my life, you know? Mark – that's my ex-husband – he sent me a letter in '96, saying he wanted to start the divorce process. He wanted to marry his new partner. She was a nurse, he wrote, and he included a photo of the two of them, like I was a relative living out foreign who needed to be kept updated with all the Delaney family news.' Keelin had recognised Mark's handwriting on the front of the envelope immediately, her heart pulsing in her throat as she opened it, the small snapshot falling to the ground. She looked at that photo for hours, scanning the nurse's limbs for bruises, wondering if she could see a shadow of something in the other woman's eye. If she looked scared the way Keelin had done.

'That poor woman.'

'You know something,' she said. 'I never thought "poor woman", although I'm sure Mark did exactly the same thing to her as he did to me.' A tiny, terrible part of Keelin hoped that he had. For what if it had only been her whom Mark had decided to hurt? What if his new fiancée was simply easier to love? 'I was relieved,' she continued. 'I thought Mark would leave us alone then, he would forget about us. He used to come to the island, in the early years, begging me to take him back. And even when he finally accepted there was no hope left for us as a couple, he would still sit on the stone wall at the end of the garden and watch us. He wanted me to feel scared and to know he could do whatever he wanted, no matter how many times I complained to the guards. We can't arrest a man for standing outside a house, they told me. Call us when he actually *does* something. When I got the letter saying he'd met someone else, all I thought was: he'll leave us alone now . . . That was selfish of me, I suppose.'

'Alex was better off.' Jake looked away from her. 'No father is better than a bad one, I can safely say.'

'I'm sorry,' Keelin said. 'For what happened to you and your family.'

They sat in silence, listening to the waves crash against the pebble beach a hundred feet below them. The crests forming and re-forming and then breaking again. It had been the same for as long as Keelin could remember, and would be the same long after she was gone and everyone had forgotten about the Kinsellas and Misty Hill and the dead Crowley Girl. They were all inconsequential, at the end of it all.

'What happened after that? After Mark's letter?'

'I thought I was grand but a few weeks later, I don't know how to explain it, it was like I was coming down with the flu. I was tired all the time; I couldn't stop crying. You're grieving for what could have been, if that makes sense. The future I thought I'd have, the man Mark might have been if his childhood had been different, if he'd seen any kindness whatsoever from his own father. I had wanted to help Mark so badly and I felt like I'd failed him. Failed Alex too. My dad had been so important to me and the idea of Alex not having that broke my heart.'

'That wasn't your fault, Keelin.'

'Maybe not. I don't know.' She pulled her hand back, threw the stone as hard as she could into the sea below. 'But it was soon after I got the letter from Mark when I read an article in the paper about a course providing training in counselling for mature students, and I thought to myself that's what I'd do. I had a mind even then that I could help other women who'd been beaten, like I'd been. The services are bad enough as it is now – funding seems to get cut year on year; who cares when women and children are the primary victims of abuse, I suppose – but Ireland in the nineties? No one talked about this stuff. You were expected to get on with things. I went to a solicitor in Carlow once, I just wanted to see what my options were if I did decide to leave Mark. And the man asked me when was the last time I'd had my hair done and did I wear make-up around the house? It was important not to let myself go, he said. And even when I'd gone home to Rún, Mam didn't want to be hearing about all of that. When I told her Mark was getting re-married, I was expecting some sympathy, I suppose, but she told me I needed to get up off my backside and do something with my life. Alex deserved better than a mother sitting around moping all day, she said. I mentioned then I'd seen an ad for the counselling course, and it was she who made me apply.'

'And you got in,' Jake said.

'I did. I felt guilty at the start, leaving Alex with my mother, but I told myself I'd be back every Friday evening, he'd hardly miss me. The island is a good place to raise children, they have so much freedom here. They're –' her voice caught – 'safe. And I'd been having fun. I hadn't had fun since I was a teenager. I hated college the first time around, I'd been so shy – this felt like a do-over But I shouldn't have left Alex

169

here,' she said. 'Mam was getting bad at that stage. She was so forgetful – I was afraid it was early Alzheimer's for a while. It wasn't fair on Alex, but he seemed to be the only one who could do anything with her, and I just wanted some time for *me*, for once. I was only in my late twenties. I wanted . . .' She shook her head. There was no point in making excuses. 'I can still remember that day,' she said. 'I was coming home from the library, the cherry-blossom trees were blooming and I remember thinking, *I'm happy*. Then I heard someone yelling my name, and it was the woman from the digs, waving at me frantically. There'd been a phone call, she said, an accident. Is it Alex? I managed to get out, and the *fear*, I can't explain it. It was crippling, the idea of anything happening to him. But the landlady said no. It was my mother, she said. I was to go home immediately.'

'I'm sorry,' Jake said, gingerly placing an arm around her shoulders.

'She'd been on pills after Daddy had died, to help her sleep.' Keelin's voice was so calm, it was as if she was talking about someone she barely knew. 'She hadn't taken any of them in months, it turned out; she'd been stashing them away. And she'd phone me in the digs in Cork and she'd tell me she couldn't sleep. Go back to the doctor, I'd say, those tablets should be knocking you out cold. But she didn't want to go to the mainland alone, she said, and it was obvious she was hoping I'd bring her. And I should have. *I should have.* But I just pretended like I didn't know what she was hinting at. I didn't want to have to think about her, or Daddy, or even Alex, when I was at college. I wanted to be free.' She was afraid to look at Jake to see what his reaction was. 'You must think I'm a horrible person.'

'I don't, Keelin.'

You should, she thought. *You would, if you knew the truth about me.* 'It was Alex who found Mam,' she said. 'He'd been out exploring – he was always the sort of child who preferred his own company. He would roam the island all day, coming home spinning tales of pirates and smugglers, hidden coves in the sea cliffs. Mam had given him a packed lunch, told him to stay out as long as he liked. When he came home, he . . . he found her there, in her bed. He said it was like she was waiting for him.'

A doctor came from the mainland to pronounce her mother dead, a wake quickly arranged. It was a muted affair, the islanders huddled into the cramped parlour around the open coffin, everyone cutting glances at Alex. The poor lad, Keelin overheard a neighbour say through a mouthful of buttered scone, and that mother of his off gallivanting on the mainland when all this was going on. Sure the dogs on the street could see Cáit Ó Mordha was in a bad way. Terrible stuff all together, they agreed. Keelin took Alex's hand in her own and he stared up at her with those new eyes of his, eyes that had seen too much for one so young. I will never leave you again, she promised him silently, and she barely left his side in the weeks to follow. Not that her son seemed

171

to notice. He was practically catatonic, fighting sleep every night because he was terrified the spirit of his mamó would haunt him in his dreams, arriving at the breakfast table in the morning pale and drawn. It was Henry Kinsella who suggested a child psychologist, Henry, who was fast becoming a – a friend, maybe? Keelin wasn't sure. It had been years since she had last seen the younger Kinsella brother, and she'd tried to hide her surprise when he arrived at the funeral to offer his condolences, so tall in his long navy overcoat, smelling of expensive cologne. Her mother would have liked that, delighted her funeral had been graced by one of the Kinsellas, but Keelin hadn't given him another thought until ten days later when the phone rang, that deep voice and its plummy accent on the other end. Henry Kinsella here, he said. Just wanted to check in. He rang again, once a week in the beginning, then twice a week, and soon they were talking every day, or Keelin was talking at least, telling Henry things she had never told anyone else – about her first marriage and what Mark had done to her, the guilt she felt over leaving Alex alone with his grandmother, her fears for her son, this voluntary vow of silence the boy had taken. Henry didn't say much in return, but during their next conversation he told her a consultation had been scheduled with a child psychologist in Cork, a woman whose reputation was so renowned that even Keelin's supervisor hadn't been able to help her get an appointment. Henry shrugged when Keelin asked how he'd managed to skip the consultant's notoriously long waiting list. I had a friend make a call, was all he said. When the day of the appointment came, Keelin felt sick to her stomach but she smiled at her son as they stepped onto the ferry, leading him to a bench inside the poky cabin. He sat there, staring at the posters on the walls – safety procedures to be followed in case of emergency, B & Bs that had rooms for rent on the island, restaurants in Baltimore offering a ten-per-cent discount to anyone who presented their ferry ticket – while Keelin smiled at Murphy's, who were off to visit their daughter in Dublin. We're going to the mainland to get a new pair of school shoes for this one, she fibbed, and she pretended not to see Alex looking up at her sadly as she told the lie. Come, mo stoirín, she said, when the ferry docked. Let's go. And there, at the top of the steps at the pier, she saw Henry Kinsella, reaching out his hand to help her. I thought you might need some extra support today, he said.

'Keelin,' Jake said now, and she started. He was fumbling in his pocket, pulling out a small packet of Kleenex, and it was only then she realised she was crying.

'Thanks,' she said as he handed her a tissue. 'You came prepared.'

'Irish weather,' he said. 'I'm constantly sniffling. It's driving Noah mad.' He took a tissue himself, as if to prove the point. 'Thank you for sharing that with me, Keelin,' he said gently. 'I know it's not easy but I'm honoured you would open up to me like this.'

'I don't know why,' she replied, 'but for some reason, I feel like I can trust you.'

She said goodnight to Jake at the gate to Marigold Cottage, telling him she would call in the morning for her next interview, as planned. When she was at the bottom of her own garden, she looked up to see Henry standing at the bedroom window, waiting for her.

'Darling,' he said, when she slipped under the covers beside him, wincing at how cold the sheets were. 'Did it go well?'

'Yes.'

'Excellent,' he said. 'Thank you from the bottom of my heart.'

'Will you do something for me now?' she said, pausing until he nodded. 'Will you keep an eye on Alex? Find out where he's going in the evenings? I'm worried about him.'

'I'll take care of it,' her husband said, and he reached down between her legs, smiling at her intake of breath. He touched her until she came, silently shuddering. 'Goodnight,' he whispered, and he moved away from her, to his own side of the bed. For the first time in weeks, Keelin had enough space to breathe.

She fell asleep instantly.

CHAPTER TWENTY-THREE

Jonathan and Olivia Kinsella, Henry's parents

Archival footage taken from a 1998 programme, The Island of Secrets.

OLIVIA: We met in 1965.

JONATHAN: I thought we met in '64?

OLIVIA: No, darling. It was 1965. I was only twenty-two – can you imagine? I was a *baby*.

INTERVIEWER: Legend has it you first met in a Kinsella hotel.

JONATHAN: Yes, that's correct.

INTERVIEWER: Most of the people watching this programme will have heard of Kinsella Hotels; many will have stayed in one at some time or another. It's one of the most successful hotel chains in the UK.

OLIVIA: And Ireland, please. We've been a free state since 1922, lest you forget.

INTERVIEWER: Sorry, yes, my mistake. The UK and Ireland. And you built it from scratch, Jonathan, you're entirely self-made. It really is a remarkable story.

JONATHAN: I got lucky.

OLIVIA: Luck had nothing to do with it, Jon. (looks at interviewer) My husband came from *nothing*. He grew up on a council estate where most of his friends were either in jail or dead before they turned eighteen. His mother was an alcoholic, his father left before Jonny was even born. Nothing was handed to him, like this younger generation seems to expect. He never looked for handouts, did you, darling? Pulled himself up by his bootstraps.

JONATHAN: Yes, well, I was lucky in other ways. I met Robert.

INTERVIEWER: You're referring to Robert Calloway of the Calloway London Group?

JONATHAN: Yes. By the time I met Robert, I'd been working at Calloway London for about five years. I'd worked my way up from kitchen staff to restaurant manager and I guess Mr Calloway saw something in me. I didn't drink – couldn't stand the stuff, not after what it had done to my mother – and that marked me out as different in this industry, more serious, I suppose. Reliable. But that'll only get you so far – you still need someone to believe in you. And Robert did. He took a punt on me when no one else would. And when I found the right property –the place was cheap, it was falling down and infested with rats, but it was near the King's Road. That was where all the cool people were, the artists and—

OLIVIA: Mary Quant opened her first store there! London was so much fun in the sixties.

JONATHAN: It was the right place to be, if you wanted to get that crowd, and I did. I knew I couldn't get their parents – and those kids wouldn't want to hang out anywhere their folks approved of at any rate. But the banks wouldn't lend me the money; they said I was an 'unproven entity'. It was Robert who backed me. If it wasn't for him, I wouldn't be sitting here talking to you.

OLIVIA: You paid Robert Calloway back within three years. The full loan, with interest. That man had nothing to complain about.

JONATHAN: Then I opened the second Kinsella Hotel in 1964—

OLIVIA: 1965, darling.

JONATHAN: Sorry, 1965.

INTERVIEWER: And you were a receptionist at the hotel, is that correct, Olivia?

OLIVIA: Yes. I wasn't the usual type for a job like that – I was Irish, I didn't have the right accent, I didn't go to the right schools. But I went for the interview anyway, because word on the street was the man who owned the hotel wasn't the usual type either – his surname was Kinsella, for heaven's sake! I presumed he was Irish too, thought it might help my case. And it must have done, because I got the job.

JONATHAN: It helped that she had a cracking pair of legs. She still does.

OLIVIA: Jon, *really*.

INTERVIEWER: And was it love at first sight?

JONATHAN: It was for me. I was thirty at the time—

OLIVIA: And unmarried, and never seemed to date anyone. People were beginning to *talk*.

JONATHAN: Who was 'talking'? No one cared about that stuff in those days.

OLIVIA: None of the kids on the King's Road cared, darling. But others did, including the bank managers you were so desperately trying to charm. Here was this man in his early thirties, successful, but permanently single. You can *imagine* what people thought.

JONATHAN: I didn't have time to date! I was trying to get a business off the ground.

OLIVIA: You mean you were waiting for the right person, darling.

JONATHAN: Sorry, yes. And then I found her. This beautiful redhead at the front desk who was completely indifferent to me. She barely gave me the time of day. *Good morning, Mr Kinsella. No messages today, Mr Kinsella.* It took me weeks to even get a smile out of her.

OLIVIA: I knew what I was doing. I saw the way the other girls were, fawning all over him. I knew I'd have to play it smarter to get what I wanted.

INTERVIEWER: You married quickly; it was a whirlwind romance.

OLIVIA: Married in '66, and we had Charlie in '67. He was a honeymoon baby, nine months to the day after our wedding. We hadn't expected to have children quite so quickly, did we, Jonny? But Charlie was such a blessing.

JONATHAN: We had our second son in 1970.

INTERVIEWER: Henry, who is, of course, dating the model Greta Ainsworth.

JONATHAN: Yes, that's it.

OLIVIA: We adore Greta, don't we, darling? Brings a dash of glamour to the place, and, let me tell you, artists, especially the serious ones, absolutely *love* some glamour.

INTERVIEWER: I think our viewers will be interested in what brought you to Inish . . . I'm sorry, I'm afraid I'm going to make a terrible hash of this pronunciation.

OLIVIA: It's Inish-roon. I was born here. My mother was an islander, but she died when I was a baby. My father never settled after that; he was from Dublin originally, and when the war ended he brought me and my older siblings back to the city. I went to England when I was sixteen, I even changed my name – Olivia Walsh seemed far more cosmopolitan, more *London* than Orlaith Breathnach, I thought. And that was that. There was nothing left for me in Ireland any more. (pause) But after Charlie was born, I suppose it was only natural that I started to wonder about my roots.

179

JONATHAN: And my great-grandfather was born in the west of Ireland, a little village in Mayo, but he went to England during the famine. I had grown up listening to stories about the Old Country, but I'd never actually been to Ireland before our first trip in '69. I must admit, I was shocked by the place. The island didn't have power, they used these things called tilley lamps, that's all they had for light. And the people here were so poor, those who were left anyway. I remember one man telling me that he had forty-two first cousins living in Chicago. Forty-two! And more people emigrating every day.

OLIVIA: But we fell in love with it all the same. How could you not? Look at that view! Have you ever seen anything quite so spectacular in your life?

INTERVIEWER: It's breathtaking.

OLIVIA: Thank you. We came for day visits for the first few years, usually without the children, just to get a feel for the place. Jonathan lobbied a friend of his, a man who had the ear of the Irish Prime Minister, and he suggested that perhaps Inisrún could benefit from a little more attention. We waited until the place had electricity before we built the house on the far side of the island, and we came here every summer after that.

JONATHAN: It was in the early nineties that I could sense things were changing for Ireland. It was like how London felt in the sixties. Like . . . youth. Or excitement, or something. I can't explain it. Livvy is the smart one, not me. But

180

whatever it was, I knew I wanted in. I bought a building in Dublin and a castle in Laois – it was the first luxury Kinsella Hotel and I brought American investors in on that one, the Yanks love a good castle – but Inisrún had our hearts. We wanted to do something to help the people here; we didn't think it was right that all this new money should stay in Dublin. The islanders deserved to have a piece of the pie as well.

INTERVIEWER: That being said, the decision to buy up the houses on the island to build the Misty Hill retreat hasn't been welcomed by all, has it? Initially some locals referred to the area where you rehomed them as a 'ghetto'.

OLIVIA: That's ridiculous. Those old houses were decaying, and the damp, my God, I'm surprised a child survived a night there, they were like *tenements*. And we still paid well over market price for them. The new homes are warm and have double glazing and central heating and—

JONATHAN: It's OK, Livvy. Listen, I'm not going to lie to you. Naturally it upsets me to hear some of the islanders were dissatisfied with their new homes. But we saw what life was like here in the seventies and eighties – those people were living hand to mouth. They'd nothing, and I know what it's like to have nothing. I think if you asked them today, their answers would be different. Things have changed here because of Misty Hill, and for the better.

OLIVIA: They most certainly have. Misty Hill put Inisrún on the map. Because of the centre, emigration has been almost halved; young people don't have to go to Liverpool or Boston or wherever to find work. Families are able to stay, bring up their children here. Misty Hill has been a rebirth for the entire island.

Note: Jonathan and Olivia Kinsella declined to be interviewed for The Crowley Girl *documentary.*

CHAPTER TWENTY-FOUR

'I'd just moved back to the island when Misty Hill was being built,' Keelin said, leaning over to look at what Jake was adding to the pot of cold water. 'What are you getting up to here, now?'

'You have your pineapple,' he said, throwing large chunks of the fruit into the mix. 'Your onion, your lemongrass, your ginger, your chicken bouillon.' He stirred the ingredients together. 'And a dash of this smoked sea salt – in you go, you beauty – and some sugar. Perfect food for a cold November night.'

'It smells incredible,' she said. They were in the kitchen of Marigold Cottage. Jake was wearing loose tracksuit pants in a grey marl, his feet bare on the slate tiles warmed by underfloor heating. His MacBook was open on the counter, playing some sort of easy jazz, both of them ignoring the exaggerated sighs coming from Noah's bedroom as he packed his suitcase. Call to the cottage for dinner, Jake had texted earlier. Noah is heading to the mainland for a couple of days so we should have the place to ourselves. I'll teach you how to make Bún bò Huế, my ma's recipe. Henry had picked up her phone when it beeped, reading the message silently. Happy cooking, darling, he'd said, and he left the room without another word.

'I think that's the smell of the pork blood,' Jake teased, pointing his knife at the other pot on the stove.

'Don't mention it.' She pretended to gag, Jake laughing, nudging her over to the counter and instructing her on how to prepare the meatballs.

'You were telling me about when Misty Hill was set up,' Jake said, turning the heat down once the water started to boil. He checked his phone. 'We have approximately two and a half hours until that's ready so you can take your time.'

'Lord above,' Keelin said, handing him the mixing bowl. Jake covered it and put in the fridge while she washed her hands. 'Vietnamese cuisine is intense.'

He lightly whipped at her knees with the tea towel. 'Stop avoiding the subject.'

'I'm not,' she said, grabbing the towel from him to dry her hands. 'It was '94, and Daddy had just died. Mam and I barely knew whether we were coming or going – we were in such a state. There'd been a letter from the Kinsella Group, informing us the family wanted to buy our house.

All the islanders were given the same offer, and it was the sort of money that seemed impossible in those days, more than any of us had ever seen on Rún. Not that it lasted long, unfortunately. Between taxes and paying the solicitor to sort out the custody agreements with Mark and my college fees, and then Mam got some bad financial advice I only found out about after she died – sure, the money was as good as gone before we even had it.' Keelin took a bottle of white wine from the fridge and poured herself a glass, offering some to Jake but he refused. 'Jonathan Kinsella – that's Henry's father – he had the idea that he wanted Inisrún to look deserted when you approached by ferry or helicopter, like it was a private island belonging to the artists alone. He hated the old houses and, to be fair to him, there was neither rhyme nor reason to the way they were built. Thrown up, they were.'

'How did the islanders react to this plan?'

'Ah, a few of the older ones refused to go, as you can imagine. They'd been born in those houses and they planned to die in them too. But some were only delighted to move. The new houses were given to us for free, on top of the money we got, and it all happened so fast. We didn't have time to think.' She took a sip of her wine, remembering the excitement as Misty Hill was being built, the rumours flying around the island about what was going to be there – swimming pools and tennis courts and maybe even a cinema, the local kids whispered, delirious with joy at the very thought. In the end, it had been a circle of cottages that had been created, like a ring fort, a village within a village. The Kinsellas knew they would have to provide the sort of services the artists were accustomed to in their lives in New York and LA; they hired a yoga instructor, an on-site psychoanalyst, an energy healer who was proficient in aura readings and past-life regressions, but they wanted Misty Hill to have a distinctly Celtic feel as well. There was a craft shop selling pottery and hand-knitted woollen jumpers, and a communal space in the centre, a round cottage with glass walls and a thatched roof, where the artists would come together to eat their evening meal. A chef had been hired from London, one who was used to dealing with nutritional requirements from veganism to a macrobiotic diet, and after dinner the staff would clear the tables and prepare the room for the entertainment: sean-nós dancing, fiddles and harps, the oldest man on the island introduced as the local seanchaí with hushed reverence. Ireland was the land of saints and scholars, the prospectus said, the homeplace of Oscar Wilde and James Joyce. Come to Misty Hill and be inspired.

'The state of the place,' Keelin said, shaking her head. 'It was like a Disney version of an island. The Kinsellas even built a pretend ruin, over by the fulacht fiadh, and they hired some of us to give tours and talk about its "ancient provenance", when the thing wasn't up a wet week.' She froze, putting the glass down. 'But Misty Hill brought money to the area, we were –'

'It's fine,' Jake said. 'He's not here. He can't hear you.' The younger man didn't look at her, staring at Spotify on his laptop, and she let out a long breath. She hopped up onto the counter, taking the MacBook from him and cradling it in her lap, scanning through the other playlists. All Out 80s, she decided, shimmying her shoulders as Tiffany started to sing 'I Think We're Alone Now', ignoring Jake's groan.

'Do we have to listen to this?'

'Yes, we do,' she said, ruffling his hair. 'You will listen to Tiffany and you will enjoy it.'

'Well, well,' a voice said from behind them. 'Isn't this cosy?' It was Noah, wearing a Barbour rain jacket and carrying a canvas backpack. 'Keelin,' he said, 'I'm beginning to feel like you've moved in with us these days, you're here so often.'

'All right, mate,' Jake said warily. 'Take it easy. I'm cooking my ma's Bún bò Huế, if you're interested. It won't be ready for a while but there's plenty to go around.'

'Yeah nah, *mate*,' Noah replied. 'Nan will have something for me. I'll see you in Cork on Monday to go over next week's schedule. Not that there's much point in any of it any more, is there?' He slammed the half-door behind him, causing the tea lights on the windowsill to tremor. One fell to the ground, the flame dying immediately. Neither she nor Jake said anything, George Michael's 'Faith' floating from the laptop.

'Well,' Jake said, rubbing the patch of skin between his

eyes. He had a tendency to do that when he was anxious, she had noticed, the flesh there was often pink, tender. 'That was awkward.' He glanced at her, then down at the floor. 'I'm sorry about that, Keelin. He's annoyed because . . .' He trailed off. He didn't need to explain. They both knew the reason Noah was annoyed. She slid off the counter, walking over to the sink and stood next to him. She looked at his reflection in the glass of the window.

'I'll talk to Henry,' she said.

'I can't ask you to do that.'

'I'll talk to him,' she said again, and this time he didn't refuse. 'Thank you,' he said quietly, and the way he looked at her, Keelin felt a steady warmth spreading across her chest, licking at her ribs. Jake thought she was capable. He didn't view her as broken, or damaged, the way everyone else seemed to do. It was a long time since anyone had seen her the way this man did and she found that she liked it.

'Anything for a friend.' She touched the tattoo on his left arm. 'I've been meaning to ask you about this. What does it signify?'

'I remember the first day we arrived on the island,' Jake said. 'In the kitchen in Hawthorn House. You were staring at it, and you looked so embarrassed when I caught you. Isn't it funny to think of that day now? We didn't even know each other.' He sounded amazed, like he couldn't imagine a time in which he did not know Keelin Kinsella. 'Would you ever get one?'

'Get what?' she said, moving her hand away, the warmth of his skin still on her fingertips.

'A tattoo.'

'No,' she replied, leaning against the countertop, light-headed. 'Jake, I need some . . . some water. Please.'

'Are you all right?' he asked, grabbing a pint glass from the cupboard.

'I'm fine,' she said, taking it after he'd filled it from the tap. 'Sorry.' She waited until her breathing had settled, smiling at him. 'Sorry,' she said again. 'Low blood pressure. It looks more dramatic than what it is.' He didn't seem convinced but Keelin pushed on. 'Now, tell me. What does your tattoo mean?'

'It's just something my ma used to sketch for me when I was a kid. She said it was the Nguyen family design. It's probably not true, but . . .'

'Wait, I just thought of something. Why *are* you Jake Nguyen?' she asked, taking another sip of the water. 'Why not Jake Taylor? It's funny, I never put that together until now.'

'My father wouldn't give me and my sisters his name.'

'What? How do you mean?'

'He refused to allow Ma to take his surname when they got married. And he said we couldn't have it either, we would have to work for the "honour" of being called a Taylor. Charming man, my father.' He held out his arm, inspecting the tattoo. His face softened, and Keelin wondered if her son looked this gentle when he talked about her. She doubted it, somehow. Maybe she would have to die too. Maybe then he would forgive her for what she had done.

'Every time I see it, I think of my mother,' Jake said, his fingers tracing the swirls of ink. 'I like to think of her.'

CHAPTER TWENTY-FIVE

The Crowley Girl

When Henry and Keelin were first married, she had been relieved to discover that, unlike her first husband, Henry wasn't the jealous type. He didn't look at her text messages or demand access to her emails, he didn't expect her to hand over the password to her Facebook account for the sake of 'transparency'. There was a level of respect there from the very beginning, a mutual understanding that they were both entitled to some privacy.

So, when Keelin went into Henry's study that day, she hadn't intended to look at his computer. She was searching for a book on transcendental meditation her father-in-law had given Henry the previous Christmas. Jonathan had been meditating for years; everyone was doing it in the seventies, he said, everyone cool anyway. Keelin loved it when Jonathan told stories about London at that time, the parties he and Olivia had thrown in their Kensington townhouse. Mick Jagger would come with Bianca, he said, Edna O'Brien was a staple and even Princess Margaret would sometimes arrive, accompanied by her sullen protection officer, who would eye the inebriated guests with suspicion. It had been one of the Beatles who'd turned Jonathan on to TM – Ringo, or maybe Paul, he couldn't remember, but he promised Keelin the practice would transform her life. My life could do with some transforming, she joked, hugging Jonathan and Olivia goodbye. What's wrong with your life, exactly? Henry asked in the car as they drove away, both of them still waving at his parents through the windscreen. I'm trying so hard here, Keelin, to make things perfect for you and the kids. What more do you want from me? She apologised. It was a flippant remark, she hadn't meant anything by it, she said, but he refused to talk to her for the rest of the journey to Inverness airport, Evie dozing in the back seat.

She couldn't see the book on the shelves or in Henry's desk drawers. Maybe her husband had thrown it away. It wasn't his thing, too 'woo-woo', he had said when he'd unwrapped it. She sat on the cushy leather seat, twirling it around once, twice, before coming to a standstill. His desk was perfectly neat, as always; it was just the PC, a leather-bound jotter and a Montblanc fountain pen, engraved with his full name in a cursive print, *Henry Thomas Kinsella*. Her eyes began to follow the movement of the computer's screensaver, hypnotised by the cosmos of writhing stars. For some reason – she couldn't explain it to herself, although later she would wonder if she'd been led by instinct, a sixth sense which had compelled her to do it – she put her hand out and shook the mouse, pausing when the computer asked for Henry's password. She typed in Evie's date of birth, putting a hand on her heart with an 'awww' when it worked on the first try. Henry could be so sweet sometimes. She scanned the folders on the desktop, *boring, boring, boring.* It was all work related, Misty Hill accounts, nothing of any great interest. Then she saw one called 'Birdwatching'. When had Henry developed an interest in *birdwatching*? Oh, this was too good – she was already planning how best to mercilessly tease him for his new hobby as she clicked on the folder, finding a thumbnail of a photo inside. She clicked on that to enlarge it and—

'What are you doing, darling?' Henry's hands on the chair, spinning it around, smiling at her. He looked over her shoulder, his face paling at what he saw there. He reached around her and shut the computer down as quickly as he could.

'What was that?' she said, trying to see past him but the screen was blank. What had she just seen – long legs and fair skin and a delicate tattoo dancing across the ribs? It was the shape of a bird, the tattoo. A swallow, or a swift perhaps? 'Why do you have a photo of a naked girl on your computer, Henry?'

'Oh, please. It's rather rich you trying to take the moral high ground here, Keelin. This isn't the kind of relationship I presumed we had; we don't *snoop* around like this. I thought we trusted each other. I'm so disappointed.'

'Excuse me? You have porn on y—'

'For God's sake, lower your voice,' he said, pointing at the open door. 'Evie is in her playroom and I don't think she's quite old enough for us to explain pornography to her, do you?'

'You have a photo of a naked teenager on your computer. Jesus Christ, that girl looked barely legal,' Keelin whispered angrily. 'You can stop acting like the injured party, Henry.'

'I didn't realise you had such an issue with porn. You don't seem to mind when we watch it together, do you, darling?' he said with a half-smile. He knelt down, one hand on each of her knees, pulling them apart. 'You rather enjoy it then, I've always found.'

'That's different, that's for the two of us and not . . .' Keelin closed her eyes, her breath drawing shallow. She should tell him to stop, now. She should, she should . . . 'Evie . . .' she said weakly as Henry snaked his hand under her skirt, inching her knickers down her legs.

'She's playing with her new Crayola set,' he said. 'Barring an earthquake, we're not going to see her for at least half an hour.' Keelin pictured their daughter upstairs, sitting at the multicoloured table with legs that resembled sticks of crayon, her tongue lolling out the side of her mouth as she folded over the page, scribbling reds and blues and pinks within the lines of the colouring book. 'What about Alex?' she asked.

'He's gone for a walk with Nessa Crowley.'

Keelin tried to sit up, to push Henry away from her. They had to have a conversation about Alex's relationship with Nessa, it couldn't continue, they had to – 'Shh, darling,' her husband said, kissing his way up her inner thighs, and she gasped as he touched her clitoris with the tip of his tongue. 'Just relax.'

After she came, a hand over her mouth to silence herself in case her daughter heard her, Henry dropped to the floor, pretending to be exhausted. 'You'll be the death of me, Keelin Kinsella,' he said, as she shuffled her underwear back on, pulling her skirt down. She felt embarrassed suddenly, too exposed, and she wanted to cover herself.

'Henry,' she said cautiously, 'about that photo – I'm not trying to be prudish here, but I still feel weird about it. Don't yell at me, I can't help it.'

'I'm not going to yell at you. When have I ever yelled at you?' he said, propping himself up on his elbows. 'I'm sorry, darling. It was a stupid prank Miles was playing on me. It's nothing for you to worry about.'

'It's just that it looked so much like . . .'

It looked like Greta Ainsworth, Keelin wanted to say, the dead girl. The woman she was not allowed to mention in her husband's presence. She'd searched for Greta's name on the internet before, finding some old modelling photos, a couple of magazine covers from the nineties, but there was so little information about her. She had died in a car crash at the height of her career, a newspaper article said, only twenty-five years of age, but there were no other details. Did Henry still have old photos of his ex-girlfriend? Was Keelin even *allowed* to feel uneasy about that?

'You thought it looked like whom?' Henry asked, watching her.

'I thought it looked like someone I know,' she replied.

CHAPTER TWENTY-SIX

The Australians were away on the mainland until the end of November, setting up more interviews. They were hoping to talk to a journalist in Dublin who'd covered the Misty Hill case for *The Irish Times*, Jake told Keelin before they left, and a feminist activist who'd written extensively about how sexist the coverage of the case had been. He texted earlier that day – *We're back! Did you miss me?* – and asked her to go for a walk with him. Henry read the message aloud to Keelin. You should go, he said. Wear that green hoody and the Lululemon leggings. Your hair in a ponytail, nothing fussy. She did as she was told, kissing her husband goodbye at the front door. She walked down the garden path, past Marigold Cottage, and the road before her began to rise, a pleasant ache in the back of her legs as she climbed with it. Even on a dull November day like this one, the walk to Dún

Cholmchille was spectacular; the winding trail scaling the cliffs, the sheer drop to the sea below, shifting from grey to olive green. She found Jake at an inlet halfway up the hill, leaning against the back of a wooden bench engraved with the words, 'I gcuimhne Peadar Ó Súilleabháin'. *In memory of Peter O'Sullivan*, Keelin had explained hundreds of times, to foreigners who didn't speak Irish and wanted to know what was written on the fading plaque. She gave Jake a hug and told him she had indeed missed him while he was away. How had their trip been? she asked. Did you meet anyone interesting? It was then he told her about the interview with Alice Buckley.

'Alice Buckley,' Keelin repeated, picturing her old college housemate, a young woman in high-waisted jeans and platform trainers. They had lived together in their first year, that terrible house on Barrack Street with its damp rooms and wafer-thin walls, sharing with two other girls, Alice's best friends from Ballincollig. They were nice enough, but beyond some initial curiosity about the 'island girl' they didn't seem that bothered with her, and Keelin, who'd never had to make new friends in her adult life before, found she didn't know how to do so. She only knew how to be friends with Seán and Johanna, relationships that consisted of knowing the very bones of the other person, with a shared history and language, decades-old inside jokes only the three of them understood. These new kinds of friendships – casual coffee dates and running to the pharmacy to buy a new lipstick between lectures,

What do you think of this colour on me, Keelin? – felt vaguely intimidating, as if she was being tested, with no one ever telling her if she'd passed or not.

'I haven't seen Alice since –'

Carlow. The local Dunnes Stores. Keelin was heavily pregnant with Alex, maybe seven months gone. Mark was in the Toyota outside; he had given her ten minutes to get the shopping. I'll time you, he said, as if it was just a game. And there was Alice Buckley at the deli, like an apparition – Oh my God, Keelin! the woman said in her sing-song accent, reaching out to hug her. Look at the size of you! Are you having twins or what, girl? I can't believe this. What a coincidence! I'm up here for the day with Mam – my sister is getting married, and apparently there's a great boutique in town for mother-of-the-bride outfits, do you know it? – and on she continued, barely taking a breath. It was clear she was settling in for a proper chat, Alice had always loved to gossip, but all Keelin could think about was how Mark was waiting for her. She backed away, dropping her basket of groceries to the ground. Ignoring the look of surprise on the other woman's face, Keelin turned on her heel and ran. I'm sorry, I'm sorry, I didn't mean to be so long, she stammered as she climbed awkwardly into the car. Mark didn't say anything on the drive home, his jaw clenched and his knuckles white on the steering wheel. He walked ahead of her up the driveway, shutting the front door behind him. She tried the handle but it was locked. Please, Mark, she'd pleaded, banging her open palm against the wooden frame. Please let me in. She watched through the living-room window as he settled on the sofa, opening a can of Coke and turning on the television. Dusk settled around her, the light turning a dark blue, then navy, until it was so dark she could count the stars and then there were so many, she could not. She slept in the car that night, shivering, trying not to cry. You're OK, mo stoirín, she'd whispered, cradling her bump as the baby kicked inside her. I'm here. I'll always be here for you.

'I can't remember the last time I even *talked* to her, or any of the girls from college,' Keelin said now. 'Why on earth would ye want Alice Buckley for the documentary?

'Noah thinks she'll add some context, I guess,' Jake said. 'Since she knew you before all of this.'

'What . . . what did she say?'

That had been the worst part, over the last ten years. Picking up newspapers or turning on the news and seeing familiar faces – old colleagues and classmates and men she had dated briefly after her first marriage had broken down – telling anecdotes about the Keelin Kinsella they knew, but she could never recognise herself in their retellings. In their versions, Keelin was almost debilitatingly shy, she could be aloof, she wasn't the easiest person to get to know, she kept people at a distance. I always thought Keelin seemed quite a *sad* woman, a college tutor told a journalist. I would wager there's a great deal of unresolved trauma there, he continued, tapping the side of his nose. Keelin presumed she would have become hardened to it by now, this selling of stories, her trust broken anew, but every time it happened it felt like a fresh betrayal. You can't count on other people, Henry told her as she cried herself out. It's just you and me now, darling.

'Alice said she liked you a lot,' Jake said. 'She told us you could be really funny, in a way that was so dry that she would only realise it was funny a few minutes later. She said you came alive when Johanna visited from Limerick, that you surprised the other girls by how much "craic" you were that night, insisting everyone take another round of shots before you left the club, singing The Saw Doctors on the walk home. You got up early the next day, cooking a fry for everyone; she'd never seen you look that happy before. She said she wished you had given them more of a chance, that she would have liked to have been your friend, if you had let her . . .' He paused. 'I'm going to be completely honest with you, Keelin. We did ask about your relationship with your ex-husband, what it was like when you first got together. She said . . . She said Mark had seemed like a nice guy, but it was clear he was the one in charge. You would have done anything in order to keep him happy.'

Keelin turned to face the sea, the wind whipping through her hair. She had once told a supervisor on her counselling course that the greatest misconception about victims of domestic violence was that the women were weak, they wouldn't put up with this kind of behaviour if they were 'stronger'. But actually it took a huge amount of strength to get up every day, she had argued, to go out into the world and pretend like nothing was wrong. It took a rare kind of resilience to stay silent when you were screaming inside. Not everyone could do it.

'I hope I haven't upset you,' Jake said. 'People like Alice Buckley have very little understanding of what it's like to live in an abusive environment.'

'Yeah, I know. Thanks for telling me though.' She leaned against his shoulder. 'You've been really good to me, Jake. Our friendship means a lot to me.'

'And to me,' he said. His phone beeped and he reached into his pocket to pull it out. It was from Noah, she saw, Jake turning away from her to read the message.

'Everything OK?' she asked, pulling her foot onto the bench and pretending to re-tie her shoelace.

'It's fine.'

'OK,' she said after a moment. 'Listen, I'd better get back to the house – the boys will be waiting for me.' She hoped they would be anyway. She never could tell with Alex, these days. Her son had become an increasingly difficult person to track down.

'But I thought we were going for a walk,' Jake said, folding his arms across his chest. 'We haven't seen each other in two weeks. We have loads to catch up on.'

'I'm sorry, pet,' she said. 'It must have slipped my mind. I've been worrying about Alex, to tell you the truth. He's

202

going out a lot, which sounds grand in theory but it isn't like him. It's ju—'

'Alex isn't a child. He can do what he wants.'

'You think I don't know that?' Her words were sharper than she'd intended and Jake flinched. He didn't like sudden noises, Keelin had noticed; he was on edge if anyone raised their voice around him, shrinking in his seat as if to hide. 'I'm sorry.' She softened her tone. 'It's just that you never stop worrying about your children, no matter what age they are.' He bit his lip, no doubt thinking of his own family, how he had no one left to worry about him now. *Shit.* She shouldn't have said that. 'We can have dinner tomorrow night,' she rushed on. 'What about if I come over to the cottage early and help you cook? That'll be fun, won't it?' He nodded reluctantly. 'Now –' she pointed at the pathway winding past them – 'go up to Dún Cholmchille anyway. It'll clear your head.'

The wind beat against her face and roared in her ears as she walked back down the hill. Keelin turned her head to the side for momentary relief, and she was outside the Steins' old house, a stone bungalow with a polytunnel and a wire chicken coop out the back. The lilac door was opening and Keelin's heart tightened in her chest, with hope, maybe, that she had found a portal back in time, that it would be 1987 again and a teenage Johanna would walk towards her, proudly waving the latest copy of *Jackie* magazine.

But it was Noah who was leaving the Steins' house, his

camera bag in hand, calling goodbye over his shoulder to either Lena or Oskar; Keelin couldn't see which one of Johanna's parents it was. He adjusted the bag on his shoulder, stopping in his tracks when he spotted Keelin.

'Hi, Noah.'

'Hey,' he replied. He paused, clearly hoping she would walk ahead and he wouldn't be obliged to make conversation with her. But she stood still, and irritation flashed across the young man's face. He brushed past her, apologising when the edge of his camera bag jammed against her hip, but he kept moving as fast as he could.

'What were you doing in the Steins'?' she called after him. Noah spun around, taking down his bun and shaking out his hair. 'Johanna hasn't lived there in years.'

'She's home for the weekend,' he said. Keelin instinctively turned towards the house, and she thought she saw the twitch of a curtain, someone ducking out of sight – *a woman. Jo* – and she felt the loss of her friend like a physical pain, a bruise beneath her chest bone, still tender after all these years.

'It wasn't her I wanted to see – not this time, anyway,' Noah said. 'But don't worry, her old pair refused to talk about you on camera. They gave me heaps of tea and a *disgusting* piece of bread and sent me on my way.'

Johanna's father had tormented himself for years trying to perfect his recipe for soda bread, but it invariably turned out rock hard and practically inedible. Keelin had been the only one who ever ate it, smothering it in butter and blackberry jam, lying to Oskar that it was delicious. The way he looked at her when she said that, the grin almost breaking his tanned face in two. *Danke, meine Liebling*, he would say, ruffling her hair. Sometimes Keelin missed Oskar and Lena as much as she did Johanna.

'I see,' was all she managed to say in reply. What did Noah mean, 'this time'? Had they already interviewed Jo for the documentary? Surely her friend wouldn't have broken her silence after all these years? And why hadn't Jake told Keelin if she had? 'But why are you by yourself?' she asked. 'I just met Jake and he's—'

'I know where he is,' Noah said. 'But it's pretty clear his loyalties are divided right now and I, for one, still care about journalistic ethics. It's important to remain impartial, you know? I'll have to do some of this work alone. Keep asking the questions, try to find *real* answers.'

'But the two of you are a team,' Keelin said, an unpleasant dip in her stomach at the thought of Noah out there, searching for 'real answers'.

'We're still a team. But unlike Jake, I'm not looking for a replacement mammy wherever I can find one.'

'I don't know why you're being so mean ,' she said, taken aback. 'I've never been anything but nice to you, Noah. I don't deserve to be treated like this.'

'This isn't about you, Keelin. I have a job to do. A woman *died* on this island. Have you forgotten that?'

He walked away, taking tentative steps as the hill dropped

in a steep decline, careful in case he might stumble. How could she forget? she wanted to scream after him. No one would allow her to think about anything else except the dead Crowley Girl in the last ten years.

When she got home, she called her son's name. 'Alex? Alex, where are you?' She looked in the attic, in the television room, in the kitchen, but there was no sign of him. In the dining room she found Henry, sitting alone in the dim light. 'Do you know where Alex is?' she asked her husband, turning on the overhead chandelier so she could see properly. 'I can't find him anywhere. Surely he's not gone out, again! That's every night this week. What are we going to do about this, Henry?' It was only then Keelin noticed the candles, the fresh flowers in the vase and the two plates of food on the table, untouched.

'Oh God, were you waiting for me? I'm so sorry.'

'I thought it would be rude to start without you. You know how important I consider good manners to be,' he said. He stood up, taking his plate with him. Keelin followed him to the kitchen, watching as he swept the chilli con carne into the bin, his knife scraping against the china. 'I thought we were having cod for dinner tonight,' he said. 'At least that's what I asked you to tell the housekeeper to prepare.'

'But you like chilli, don't you? It's almost December, I thought you might prefer something more warming than fish at this time of year.'

'The table wasn't set properly either,' he continued. 'She

used that cheap cutlery you bought in Dunnes ages ago. I don't know why you insist on keeping it; you should throw it away or, better yet, give it to the boys down in Marigold Cottage. They're practically family at this stage, aren't they, Keelin? You'd probably offer one of them a kidney if it was needed.'

'I'll remind Gosia tomorrow, I promise. I'll tell her that she—'

'Forget it,' he said, throwing the dishes into the sink with such force that Keelin jumped back, her heart beating against her ribcage. 'Why do you look so anxious?' he said, reaching for her. His hands on her hipbones, pulling her closer to him. 'What's wrong with you?'

'I . . .' She willed herself not to cry. 'I hate when you're angry with me.'

'I'm not angry,' he said, leaning in to kiss her. 'Why would you think that, silly? I'm just expressing my feelings. That's important in a relationship, isn't it? You're the one who always says communication is the cornerstone of a healthy marriage.' He backed her into the cupboard behind her, a round knob twisting into her spine. 'I'm grateful we can talk about these things openly. Aren't you?' His hands nestled around her neck, caressing her skin gently. 'How was your date with our Australian friend?'

'It was fine,' she said, looking over his shoulder. Her eyes on the open door. 'Jake trusts me.'

'I would hope he does, for both our sakes,' Henry said,

kissing her again, slipping his tongue into her mouth. His fingers were against her throat and she coughed as he increased the pressure. She coughed again, starting to choke, silently pleading with him to stop, *I can't breathe, please, please* . . . 'I love you,' he whispered, and he loosened his grip on her neck, touching his lips to the place where his hands had been, covering her with delicate kisses. Later Keelin examined herself in the mirror, trying to see if he had left any trace. She was searching for bruises, she thought, for evidence. But there was nothing, her skin was perfect, flawless. And she wondered if it had really happened, or if she had imagined it all.

CHAPTER TWENTY-SEVEN

The Crowley Girl

'I'm sorry – what?' Keelin was about to place a bauble on the Christmas tree but she stopped, staring at her husband. 'You want to invite *Nessa Crowley* to the Christmas Eve drinks party?'

It was the eighth of December, and most of the island had decamped to the mainland, as was customary on the Feast of the Immaculate Conception. Culchie shopping day, her housemates in college used to call it, shuddering at the prospect of 'those farmers' arriving to the city en masse to get their last 'bits' for the season. Henry couldn't bear the ferry on a day like today, it would be far too crowded for his liking, so he suggested they put up the Christmas tree that afternoon in an attempt to distract Evie. Their daughter had soon grown bored, demanding to watch a DVD before bed-time, and Keelin didn't have the patience to argue with the girl when she was in one of her moods. She thought of other Christmases, years before, when it was just her and Alex and her mother. Standing on the rickety stepladder and hoisting herself into the attic, sneezing at the dust, stepping from one ceiling beam to the other to find the cardboard boxes stuffed full of garlands and fairy lights. Her mam calling up from the kitchen. Bí cúramach, Keelin, you'll come through the ceiling if you're not careful. Her son's delighted face as the old tree was reassembled, branch by branch; singing along to 'Jingle Bells' as he threw tinsel on it with abandon, begging to be the one to place the star on top. I love Christmas, he said as she tucked him into bed and she bent down to kiss him on the forehead. I love Christmas too, she whispered, but not as much as I love you, mo stoirín.

Things were different now. Henry had always had particular ideas about how he thought a home should be decorated for the festivities; tinsel was 'tacky', artificial trees were an 'abomination', fake snow was 'preposterous' – we don't live in California, darling. We had a real tree in Kensington every year, he told her. Mum says it isn't Christmas unless there's a smell of a fir about the house. Her husband preferred orna-ments bought at Brown Thomas – Oh, aren't we fancy? Keelin teased him when she heard this; she'd never stepped foot in the luxury department store before she starting dating Henry – in coordinating shades of creams and golds, and he was amused when Keelin produced the keepsakes she had brought from her parents' old house – an angel with a splintered wing, the snowman hanging from a glittery gold loop, half his plastic face worn off, a busted Santa with one leg – and he told Keelin to hang them on the back of the tree, where no one could see them. You're an awful snob, do you know that, Henry Kinsella? she'd said. But you love me anyway? he asked, and she had laughed because it was true.

'I hardly invited Nessa, now, did I? Alex did – he told me this morning,' Henry said, standing back from the tree to check the lights were symmetrical. 'But what's the problem? It's only one more person.'

'For one thing, it's just family on Christmas Eve. It's always been family,' Keelin said, sitting on the sofa, suddenly feeling very tired. 'And you know my concerns about Alex and Nessa. It's not going to end well, mark my words. She's too old for him – he's still a child, for God's sake.'

'He's seventeen,' Henry began, but she zoned out as he spoke, a creeping uneasiness moving through her at the thought of Nessa Crowley coming to the party. She was already dreading it, this get-together Henry insisted they throw every year. The housekeeper would be relieved of her duties for the evening, unable to create the kind of hors d'oeuvres Henry's parents expected, the dates stuffed with honeyed goat's cheese and walnuts, seared scallops on pea puree, cumin-scented lamb koftas with mint yogurt. Her husband would try on ten different shirts, asking Keelin what she

211

thought of each one, his face falling when the first thing his mother said when she walked through the door was, Goodness, Henry, what an *interesting* shirt you're wearing. That would be the start of it, a night where Henry would try to win his mother's approval, or at least her attention, but Olivia Kinsella would be, as ever, totally fixated on her first-born – what Charlie was up to, what important charities Charlie's wife was supporting, how marvellously well Charlie's children were doing in school – while the much-loved Charlie steadfastly ignored her, instead talking to his father about what the hotel industry would be like in a post-Lehman Brothers world, the challenges that lay ahead. Charlie looked similar to Henry, the same dark red hair and strong features, but he was a much more serious man, almost dour at times, and altogether too keen to assert his dominance as the eldest son in the family business. Keelin liked Charlie's wife, Rebecca, a quietly determined woman who wasn't averse to sneaking off with her sister-in-law for a sly cigarette and a bitch about Olivia, and their two daughters were lovely, well-behaved girls, but the overall effect of having the entire Kinsella clan under the one roof could be overwhelming. Keelin didn't want to have to deal with Nessa Crowley making eyes at her teenage son at the same time.

'Keels?'

Henry was staring at her, waiting for an answer to a question she hadn't heard him ask. She pushed herself off the couch, bending down to grab another decoration from the hand-carved wooden box. 'Put that star there,' he said, nodding at an empty space in the middle of the Christmas tree. 'And we can't control Alex or whom he wants to spend time with. We want him to fit in on Inisrún, don't we? That was partly why we agreed to let him leave boarding school, because he didn't have any friends.'

'But won't Nessa want to be with her own people?' she tried. 'She must have friends her own age.'

Keelin remembered Christmas Eves from when she was young – pints of Guinness and toasted cheese sandwiches for lunch in O'Shea's, shouts of 'noble call' later, a shiver running down her spine as Gráinne Breathnach, the best singer on Rún, gave a haunting rendition of 'Oíche Chiúin'. Swaying in the wooden pews at Midnight Mass, cursing that last glass of whiskey forced upon her by a neighbour with a Nollaig shona! She and Seán and Johanna marching back to the Crowley house, arms linked and singing carols, tumbling into the front living room and demanding Seán's mother provide them with slices of spiced beef on her home-made soda bread. At three a.m. Keelin said she'd better be heading, her parents would kill her if she wasn't home soon, and Padraig, one of Seán's older brothers, went to follow her, grabbing his rain jacket from the coat stand. Where do you think you're going? Johanna asked, laughing as Padraig said that he wasn't going to let a girl walk home by herself, especially . . . He trailed off, embarrassed, but Keelin had an idea of what he was going to say. *Especially not a girl as timid as Keelin Ní Mhordha, this little mouse, this shadow of a human being.* Keels doesn't need any minding, Jo said, raising her cup of cheap wine in toast to her friend. She's the bravest person I know.

'What self-respecting twenty-something-year-old is going to want to spend her night hanging out with people twice her age?' Keelin said now. 'Nessa Crowley will have better things to do than making small talk with your parents, surely.'

'Apparently Alex has already mentioned it to her,' Henry said, bending down to check how many baubles were left in the box. 'And she said she'd love to come. Look, better they be here where we can keep an eye on them. Although Nessa is twenty, so I'm not exactly sure what—'

'What about Nessie?' a small voice piped up behind them. Evie, balancing on one leg, using the toes of her other foot to scratch her calf. She was in her pyjamas, brushed cotton in a pink polka dot, her red curls mussed.

'Evie, what are you doing still up?' Keelin said. 'You're supposed to be in bed.'

'I need water. I'm thirsty, Mummy.' She touched her throat to demonstrate how parched she was, giving a cough for extra emphasis.

'OK,' Keelin sighed, taking her hand. 'Let's go, madam.'

'Mummy,' her daughter said, looking up at her, 'did you know Daddy and Nessie have the same birthday? Christmas Day, like the baby Jesus.'

'Like the baby Jesus, is it?' She smirked at her husband;

214

he could be so pretentious sometimes. 'What a coincidence. Who told you that, lovey?'

'It was—'

'I was just telling Mummy that Nessa is coming to our Christmas Eve dinner – isn't that nice?' Henry cut across her, smiling as the girl clapped her hands, jumping up and down on the spot in excitement.

'For God's sake, Henry,' Keelin hissed under her breath. 'She'll never go back to sleep now.'

'Nessie is coming to the party!' Evie chanted, sticking her little bum out and wiggling it in their faces. 'Nessie is coming to the party!' She weaved her way around the Christmas tree, waving her arms overhead. 'Nessie is coming to the party! Nessie! Coming! Party!'

Keelin gathered her daughter up in her arms, ignoring Evie's flailing limbs as she demanded to be put down again, Stop it, Mummy, you're a meanie. 'Bedtime,' she said, glaring at Henry over her daughter's head.

'Nessie is coming to the party!' Evie bellowed into her ear, causing Keelin to flinch. Yes, she thought, as she carried her daughter upstairs. Nessa Crowley was coming to the party, whether she liked it or not.

CHAPTER TWENTY-EIGHT

Professor Linda Kaplan-Greene, former State Pathologist of Ireland

LINDA: It took us two days before we could get out to the island after the body was found.

NOAH: Because of Storm Ida?

LINDA: Yes, there was no way we could chance the journey until the wind calmed down.

NOAH: What impact did that have on your investigation? We know that Nessa was left outside and the party guests were trampling the scene, walking up to and around the body. She had been picked up; her father tried to move her at one point. The scene must have been in a state of disarray when you arrived, Professor.

LINDA: It affected the forensics. If left exposed for that period of time, some trace evidence on a weapon can be lost; you wouldn't get the same sort of results that you'd get if the scene was in pristine condition. But it doesn't necessarily impact the pathology, which is my job. It just made it harder to determine the time of death, and that isn't an exact science anyway. Ultimately, it came down to the last time Nessa Crowley was seen alive and the time at which the body was found; we called her time of death somewhere between those two points.

JAKE: Did you know immediately this was a murder?

LINDA: Any death like this, which involves a young, healthy woman found in unusual circumstances with a wound to the head, is going to be treated as suspicious. She had *two* sites of impact on the skull, which would have been unusual if she had simply fallen and hit her head. One of the wounds was, to my mind, very irregular; it left a laceration on the scalp that suggested she'd been hit with a blunt object. But head wounds are never as straight forward as, let's say, a stabbing or a shooting. All pathologists have seen cases where a head injury is complicated but it does turn out to be an accident in the end. We're always cautious in these cases. We have to be.

NOAH: What did you do next? After attending to the body.

LINDA: I told the gardaí I wasn't happy with the two blows to the head. Even if the victim had fallen in an area that was rough, as this was – if I recall, the body was found in some sort of ornamental rock garden outside the Kinsella

217

house – I still couldn't see how the fall would cause two sites of injury. The body was held in the hospital morgue for five working days, but her parents wanted her back, they wanted to bury their daughter. You need to be sensitive in situations like this; no one wants to make it any worse for the family than it already is. But we still had some analysis that needed to be done. That was when the decision was made to release the body but the brain was retained for our purposes.

JAKE: Sorry, can you elaborate on that?

LINDA: It probably sounds a bit gruesome but it does happen. The brain was retained at the neuro-pathology centre in Cork University Hospital for further examination.

NOAH: How long did that take?

LINDA: Around six weeks. When I received the neuro-pathologist's report, it confirmed my suspicions that this was a homicide.

NOAH: And that was when the Misty Hill case became a murder investigation?

LINDA: Precisely.

CHAPTER TWENTY-NINE

Keelin had long been accustomed to watching the men in her life. Every morning she watched Henry, trying to measure the temperature of his mood, twisting her spine so she could mould herself into whatever shape he needed her to take that day. She was always conscious of where her husband was in the room at any given time, counting how many steps he was away from her, estimating how long it would take her to reach the nearest door. She even slept facing him, a trick she had learned during her first marriage, to give herself a head start if she needed to run in the middle of the night.

But she had watched Alex too, from the moment he was born. She would stare at him for hours, looking to see whose face was forming out of his bones, if she would see herself reflected there or Mark. She had been afraid she would find his father in him, that he would become prone to fits of rage, lashing out with his fists. But he did neither. He could be needy, clingy, he was often possessive of Keelin, but he was a gentle boy, most of the time. Ná bíodh imní ort, Cáit would say to her, but Keelin couldn't help but worry about Alex. He was twenty-seven years of age now, an adult, and still she watched him. Still she worried.

'Did you order something from . . . ASOS?' Henry asked her. Keelin was sitting in bed, listening to a podcast called *Indestructible*, first-person stories about women thriving after domestic abuse, something she would have gladly recommended to her clients, if she had any left. She pressed pause, waiting for her husband to repeat his question. 'There's a charge here from a website called ASOS,' he said, holding up a credit-card statement. 'We didn't discuss you buying anything online, did we? I don't remember giving you my Visa card.'

'I don't know what you're on about,' she said, taking out her earbuds. 'Could it have been Evie? She probably wanted something new for the Christmas disco at school.'

'Evie wouldn't wear anything like that,' he said. 'You know she believes fast fashion is killing the planet. 'Keelin suspected this altrusim was merely a ploy on her daughter's behalf to persuade Henry to buy her clothes from Stella McCartney, but she said nothing. He wouldn't hear any criticism of their daughter, not from her.

'Anyway,' he continued, 'I contacted their customer services and they said the package was delivered on 6th December. Here to the island.'

'Well, I'm sorry, Henry but it wasn't –' She stopped. *Alex*. 'Maybe it was a mistake?' she tried, but her husband pulled a sceptical face. He turned to leave, still clutching the statement. 'Don't worry about it,' she called after him. 'I'll get it sorted out.'

She had given up trying to talk to him about her concerns over Alex. You told me you'd find out where he was going, she said. You *promised*, Henry. But her husband swore there was nothing to 'find out', she was just being paranoid. But what then was the reason for the changes in her son – the new clothes in the laundry basket and the haircare products in his bathroom cabinet, his cheery demeanour when she bumped into him in their small gym. 'Fancy meeting you here,' Alex joked when she came in, climbing off the exercise bike, grabbing a hand towel from the wicker basket to dab sweat away from his face. 'Do you want me to adjust the seat for you?' he asked as Keelin glanced at the screen – he had cycled twenty miles, she saw. Alex, who for so long could barely manage to walk from here to Marigold Cottage, had somehow, without her noticing, built up enough stamina to cycle twenty miles.

'I think Alex might be seeing someone,' she confided in Jake later that day. He'd asked Keelin to meet her in Cupán Tae, waving away her objections that her presence might put the other customers off their food. People hate

Henry, Jake argued, but you're *from* here, you're one of them. Keelin didn't know how to explain that sometimes that meant the islanders hated her even more. She took a sip of her coffee, tasting something sour, but she decided against mentioning it to Cormac, who was glaring at her from behind the counter, half-heartedly wiping the display with a grotty rag. At least it was quiet in the coffee shop today, no one to point at her, whispering, There's your wan from the Big House, where that poor girl was found. That's Henry Kinsella's wife.

'Hey,' she said, nudging Jake's foot under the table. 'Are you listening to me? I said, I think Alex might have a girl-friend.' A woman had to be the reason for her son's behaviour. The last time he'd started taking this kind of care with his appearance had been the day Nessa Crowley had arrived at Hawthorn House, schoolbooks in hand.

'Oh yeah?' Jake said, picking up the jug of milk and finding it empty. He half stood, raising his hand to get Cormac's attention, and his T-shirt pulled up to show a flash of taut abs. Keelin saw the two women at the other table looking at him and she had the sudden urge to reach across and yank his shirt down.

'Thanks, mate,' he said to Cormac when he brought over a new jug. Keelin smiled hopefully at the older man, but he avoided eye contact with her, retreating to his beloved counter-top as quickly as possible.

'Have you heard anything?' she asked, shaking off the snub as best she could.

'Heard anything about what?'

'About Alex.'

'Yeah, nah.' Jake shrugged. 'Hey, Noah told me Henry is off to Scotland this arvo.' *What?* Keelin's head snapped up in surprise. This was news to her. Why would Henry be going to Scotland? Was he visiting his parents? Evie? 'While he's gone,' Jake continued, 'do you want to do the lighthouse trail? I can't believe I've been here over six months and I still haven't completed the full thing.'

'I don't know.' Why hadn't Henry said anything to her about leaving the island? He hadn't gone away since the miserable expedition to London at the end of August. 'When was Noah talking to him?' she asked, attempting to sound casual.

'Yesterday. Noah's done a couple of interviews with him since, well, you know . . . Henry still refuses to talk to me.' He grimaced. 'Makes things a bit awkward.'

'But you said you weren't filming as much this week. I thought you were winding down in the run-up to Christmas.'

'We've a few things we need to get done if we're going to meet our deadline. We're flying to England next week because we finally got a hold of Miles Darcy – he's a tough man to pin down,' Jake said with a laugh. Keelin nodded, trying not to look panicked at the mention of Miles, Henry's friend from school. Gorgeous, irresistible Miles. What would he have to say about the night of the party? 'But don't worry,' Jake reassured her. 'I'll be reviewing all the footage. You won't be surprised by anything, OK? I've got you, Keelin.'

'Thanks.' She almost asked him about Johanna then, if her best friend had spoken to them on camera, but she wasn't sure she wanted to hear the answer. Instead she took her fork and sliced down into the mince pie. It was cold and she looked at Cormac, wavering, but decided against asking him to heat it up, maybe add a dollop of brandy cream. He looked as if he was waiting for any excuse to throw her off the premises, and Keelin wasn't supposed to eat pastry, not when tomorrow was weigh-in day. *What the actual fuck?* she imagined Johanna saying if she heard about this, but Jo wouldn't understand, she'd always been so thin, able to eat whatever she wanted without gaining weight. Keelin was different – she *needed* Henry's support with her diet. She couldn't do this without him. She pictured his face when he jotted down the day's number on the chart he kept tacked inside her closet, and how proud he would be if she maintained her weight. How good that would feel. 'To be honest,' she said, pushing the uneaten mince pie away, 'this mystery with Alex is keeping me too occupied to think about much else. He keeps sneaking out at night-time and he's . . . *happy.*' It had been a long time since anyone had been happy in their house. 'Are you sure you haven't heard anything around the island? You must have interviewed every man, woman and child at this stage.'

The door to the cafe opened, a tinny bell tinkling overhead, and Jake shivered as a gust of wind snuck in, a lick of frost in the air. 'This weather can do one,' he said, taking his coat from the back of his chair and pulling it on again. 'I knew Ireland was going to be cold, but it's the damp that kills me. It gets into your bones, doesn't it?'

'Jake?'

'And where is the snow? It's December – surely there should be snow.'

'*Jake.*'

'I've never seen snow before,' he said. He took a bite of his pastry, the steam rising out of it. She cut a resentful glance at Cormac, smirking behind the counter. 'I'm going to be upset if it doesn't snow while I'm here.'

'Jake,' she said again, 'why are you avoiding the question? Do you know something that I don't?'

'No, I don't,' he replied, slamming his tea cup down on the saucer, the teaspoon rattling. 'I just don't feel like talking about Alex right now, if that's OK with you. We're *always* talking about him.'

'Are we?' she asked in surprise. She couldn't recall talking about Alex any more than any other subject, but he was her son; it was only natural she mention him occasionally.

'Fucking oath we are. Alex, Alex, Alex . . . I'm sick of hearing about him.' Jake's voice spiked and the other customers looked over, startled. That was the last thing she needed, people taking note that Keelin Kinsella was having an argument with a man who was not her husband. What would Henry say if he heard about this? She was supposed to be keeping Jake onside; it was her one job.

'There's no need to raise your voice.'

'I'm not raising my voice,' he snapped. 'But I don't want to sit here with someone who is supposed to be my friend –'

'I *am* your friend,' she said, her own voice higher too. She didn't want to fight with Jake. He wasn't supposed to get angry with her, the way Henry and Alex did, constantly competing for her love and attention, neither man ever feeling he had gotten his fair due in the end. She couldn't seem to keep them both happy, no matter how hard she tried.

'– and then I'm forced to spend hours talking about some ungrateful idiot who doesn't deserve your—'

'Hey,' Keelin said, sitting up straight. 'Less of the "ungrateful idiot" business, please. That's my *son* you're talking about. And Alex has been through a lot, I thought you of all people would understand that.'

He stared at her incredulously. 'Are you actually comparing the two situations?'

'Alex's father was abusive as well, wasn't he?'

'You brought him back to the island when he was a toddler – he can't even remember any of that. His life was a piece of piss compared to mine.'

'He might not have been consciously aware,' she said. 'But it's still an adverse childhood experience, and the research shows that—'

'I don't care what the research shows,' Jake said. 'That's

226

just an excuse for Alex to not get off his arse and make something of his life. He was allowed to stay on the island, living in a cottage he doesn't pay a dollar for. He doesn't need to worry about rent or bills or food. He—'

'That's not fair. He was *traumatised*. He found his grandmother dead in her bed. And . . . and he . . .' She could hardly say the words. 'Alex loved Nessa,' she whispered. 'What happened to her broke him. He's never been the same since.'

'Let me get this straight.' Jake pinched the bridge of his nose. 'Are you asking me to feel sorry for Alex? A teenage boy tried to root some chick way out of his league and he got burnt. Boo-fucking-hoo.'

'Nessa Crowley is dead, isn't she? It's not quite your usual teen drama.'

'You know what else isn't quite your usual teen drama, Keelin?' he said her name very deliberately, his eyes narrowed, furious. 'Waking up for school on a Tuesday morning and being told by your grandpa that he has some bad news, although "bad news" doesn't quite cover hearing that your mother is dead and it was your father who did it, just like you were always afraid he would. He murdered your two sisters too, but in a more "humane" way, according to the media, by giving them a massive dose of sedatives before slitting their throats. That the reason your father sent you to stay with your grandparents wasn't because he was worried about your grandma's dementia, like he told you, but because he had been planning this fucking *massacre* for months, and

227

he didn't want his "only son" to be involved, at least that's what he wrote in the suicide note. And then I had to sit back and watch the tabloids scramble to find a reason for Lucas Taylor's actions. He had mental-health issues! He was depressed! He'd lost his job and his sense of manhood was threatened! Anything rather than just admitting the man was an evil, misogynistic piece of shit who thought his family were his fucking property and he could do what he wanted with us.' Jake's hands were trembling now, but when she went to take them in her own he pulled back from her, curling them into fists in his lap. 'You can't expect me to feel sorry for *Alex*,' he said. 'Alex who still has his mother and doesn't even appreciate her. Alex doesn't know how lucky he is.'

Keelin could feel her eyes well up. 'I'm sorry. I shouldn't have compared you two – that was wrong of me. I don't know what I was thinking.'

'Just leave it,' he said, pulling the sleeve of his jacket over the back of his hand and wiping his nose. 'It's just been . . . Noah says I should go home to Sydney, that this is bringing up too much stuff for me. But this is why I wanted to become a journalist in the first place. I wanted to tell these stories in the way they should be told, in a *responsible* way, not like what happened to my family. And the last doc was explicitly about domestic violence, much more than this one. I don't know why it's getting to me.' He shifted in his chair. 'Although,' he said, not looking at Keelin, 'I think it could be because you remind me a little of her.'

'Of your mother?' she said, surprised at how pleased she was by this. It made Jake's protectiveness of her easier to understand, as well as his dislike of Henry, his barely concealed jealousy of her son. But she had to admit that she hadn't done anything to discourage Jake's growing attachment to her, ordering books from Amazon she thought he would enjoy, sending him recipes she found online, quizzing him about his love life over too many glasses of wine at Marigold Cottage, the way she wished she could with her own son. She'd always assumed Alex would bring girlfriends home, cute, smart girls who would address her as Mrs Kinsella no matter how many times she insisted they call her Keelin – *Please, Mrs Kinsella reminds me of my mother-in-law.* Girls who would make small talk with her until Alex said, Enough, Mam, we're heading out now. But her son had never been like that. He'd refused to talk to her about his feelings for Nessa, the pages of his diary the only insight she'd ever received into their relationship, and that had been something she had stolen from him; it wasn't a confidence freely given. Even today, when she suspected there was a new romance in his life, she was afraid to ask Alex outright in case she scared him off. Instead it was Jake she asked questions of, Jake she teased, all the while pretending it was her son to whom she was talking.

'What a compliment,' Keelin said. 'Your mother sounded like an amazing woman.'

'She was.'

He looked like he needed her to say something else, *do* something, but she wasn't sure what it could be. Did he want Keelin to hug him? Would that be inappropriate? She took another sip of her tea, stalling.

'After all that, I'll take it you *don't* know anything about Alex having a girlfriend,' she joked, expecting Jake to laugh and change the subject. He would give out about how annoying Noah was, the other man's refusal to cook, perhaps, or his inability to clean up after himself despite being almost thirty years of age. Or he might tell her about a new documentary he had watched on Netflix, his eyes shining as he explained how brilliant the director was, how provocative the storytelling, how important the subject matter, *You have to watch it, Keelin – promise me you will.* But he didn't do any of those things. Instead he stood up, took out his wallet and threw a five-euro note onto the table, and he left without saying another word.

'Jake,' she called after him. 'Jake, come on. I was only messing. I'm sor—' But the door slammed shut, and he walked away, hunching his shoulders against the gusts of wind.

'Fuck,' she swore under her breath. She leaned her forehead against the window, listening to the patter of rain hitting the glass. Why did she always have to say the wrong thing?

Someone was beside her now, clearing his throat. Cormac, cloth in hand, wanting to get rid of her. She ignored him and sat up straight, pulling the ends of her geansaí over her hands to wipe away the condensation on the window, and it was then she saw Noah. It couldn't have been anyone else. His rain jacket was a wine-and-yellow paisley print, his skinny jeans tucked into wine Doc Martens; there was no other man on Inisrún who would possess such clothes, let alone go outside where the neighbours could see them. He was at the pier, flanked by three islanders, helping a stooped elderly woman with a walking stick down the steps, his Nikon bag slung over his shoulder. Where was Noah Wilson going with that camera of his? Jake said they weren't going back to the mainland until next week. Cormac coughed again and she stood up, placing a twenty-euro note on top of what Jake had left already. 'Keep the change,' she said, knowing full well it would infuriate the man. He would tell the next customer who came into the cafe that Keelin Ní Mhordha was in earlier, *bold as brass she was*, and she left twenty-five euro for a ten-euro bill. Isn't it fine for some, she imagined him saying to anyone who would listen, all the money in the world and Brendan and Bríd left in that house, their hearts broken, only two of the Crowley Girls left in this world?

For once, Keelin didn't care. Let them say what they wanted about her. None of them knew the truth anyway. There were so few people who knew exactly what had happened that night, and one of them was dead.

CHAPTER THIRTY

Róisín Crowley, Nessa's sister

RÓISÍN: I dream of her, still. The same dream every time. We're dancing in a circle, Nessa and Sinéad and me, holding hands. We're wearing white dresses, and we've red flowers in our hair, peonies, I think. They were Nessa's favourite. *Rock-a-bye baby,* someone is singing, but it's not one of us. It's eerie, that voice is, like a tape stuck in the cassette player, warping. And then we all fall down, and when we get up, it's only me and Sinéad left. At first I think Nessa is hiding, and it's a game. Sinéad and I are laughing as we go look for her, but we can never find her. That's when I wake up, crying. (pause) I must have Kyle driven demented.

NOAH: Kyle is your husband?

RÓISÍN: Yeah. I met him six months after I arrived here in Auckland. He'd never even been to Ireland, let alone heard of Inisrún.

NOAH: Was that a good thing?

RÓISÍN: You could say that.

JAKE: And Cooper – that's your little boy, isn't it? He's a cute-looking kid.

RÓISÍN: Please don't say that.

JAKE: I didn't mean—

RÓISÍN: I just . . . I don't want him to grow up hearing that stuff. It didn't do any of us any good.

NOAH: Did Nessa grow up hearing things like that? (silence) OK, Róisín, do you want to tell us about your childhood? A lot of the reports from the Misty Hill story mentioned your relationship with your sisters. The three of you were extraordinarily close, locals said.

RÓISÍN: 'Extraordinarily close' – they always make it sound so *weird*, like we were in a cult or something. What other choice did we have? The boys at school would just stare at us like we were animals in the zoo, and the girls hated us, accusing us of trying to steal their boyfriends if we so much as said hello to them. As if we would have looked at them, Nessa would say. They were pathetic, the lot of them. No ambition, she said. I think that's why she was drawn to Alex Delaney in the first place, he had plans to study in Dublin. Nessa liked that. (pause) I found it hard enough when she started at college, and then

233

suddenly she was spending every weekend up in the Big House too, leaving me and Sinéad behind. We'd always been the Crowley Girls, the three of us together, and now she was . . .

NOAH: What was she doing?

RÓISÍN: It was like she was different to us, for the first time ever. It's funny – it wasn't until I came to New Zealand that I started to think about the idea of the 'Crowley Girls', and what that had meant for us, for me. It had become a sort of identity, in a way.

NOAH: How had it been your identity?

RÓISÍN: I don't know, like. I'd always been the middle Crowley Girl and then, overnight, I was the eldest. On my twenty-second birthday I remember thinking that for the first time in my life I was older than Nessa, and that broke me. It felt like I'd stolen something from her.

JAKE: I'm sorry, Róisín.

RÓISÍN: When I moved to New Zealand, I thought I'd be glad of the anonymity here. I was so tired of being asked about Nessa and Misty Hill and the fecking Kinsellas, I couldn't wait to be done with all of it. But after a while, I found myself wanting to tell people, 'I'm a Crowley Girl, you know,' like they would get it, or even care . . . The Crowley Girls of Inisrún island. We really thought that meant something.

NOAH: (coughs) We're leaving for Ireland next week, you know. Do you have any tips for us?

234

RÓISÍN: Yeah, I have a tip for you all right.

JAKE: What's that?

RÓISÍN: Don't believe a word Keelin Kinsella tells you.

CHAPTER THIRTY-ONE

Keelin had been bewildered when she and Henry had started dating; she could see that now. Her parents were dead – I am nobody's daughter now, she whispered to herself as she tried to fall asleep, I am alone in this world – and she was a single mother with a small child to care for, a boy who had become as silent as if Keelin had cut out his tongue. She kept looking around for someone to come and fix this mess; an adult had to be on their way, surely. It took Keelin longer than it should have to grasp that *she* was the adult now. Seán and Johanna tried to help; they would come over to the house and find Keelin still in her dressing gown at four in the afternoon, lying prone on the sofa. Come on, they said. Up you get, a chailín. They insisted she shower, dragging her for a walk on the cliffs before accompanying her to pick up Alex from school, Johanna asking the teacher for updates on her son's progress, whether he was mixing with the other kids more, if he was talking at all during class. Her friends cooked dinner, helped Alex with his homework, filled her cupboards with groceries, stayed until the early hours of the morning, drinking red wine and crying with her, for they had loved Tomás and Cáit too, they were also grieving the loss of her parents. But soon enough they had to return to their own lives. Johanna was teaching in the primary school in Schull by then – it wasn't feasible for her to come to the island every afternoon to check on Keelin – and Seán had to go back out fishing. Jobs on the bigger boats were hard to come by; he couldn't afford to put his spot in jeopardy. I'll be back in eight weeks, he said, and he was. Seán had always been a man of his word. But a lot had changed in those eight weeks.

Henry Kinsella? he asked in disbelief when he got in from Castletownbere port. You're with one of the *Kinsella* brothers?

Why not? she wanted to ask him. Why shouldn't Keelin date one of the Kinsellas? He was making her life so much better. It was Henry paying for the child psychologist who had made such a difference to Alex's behaviour; Keelin couldn't have afforded the eye-wateringly expensive consultancy fees by herself. She'd confided in Henry that her ex-husband was kicking up a fuss again – Mark Delaney had long since married his second wife, but he was still determined to make Keelin's life as difficult as possible, filing police reports saying she had stolen property from the house in Carlow, that she had physically assaulted his sister's children on numerous occasions, that she'd a well-known paedophile minding Alex while she was off with strange men. Mark was also accusing Keelin of parental alienation because Alex was reluctant to spend time with his father, as well as demanding increased visitation rights despite paying little to no maintenance. There was a social worker involved, a middle-aged woman called Sandra, who repeatedly reminded Keelin that her ex-husband was a reformed character, he had a new family and two little girls who adored him, it wouldn't be fair to deny Alex the same sort of relationship because of his mother's 'issues'. Sandra said Mark was a 'broken man' after what Keelin had done, taking his child away and abandoning the family home. Keelin had been tempted to tell Sandra to check the doctor's reports to see what 'broken' actually looked like, but she knew there was no point. The courts didn't care about that. Mark had never beaten Alex, and 'a boy needs his father', the social worker admonished her. Henry had listened to this and he told Keelin he would deal with the situation. A few phone calls later – and a substantial cheque, Keelin suspected but didn't dare ask – Mark was much more amenable about custody arrangements. There's no point in making this nasty, is there? he said. Let bygones be bygones. The weekly visits every Saturday became monthly visits became twice-yearly, and then it was just a phone call on Alex's birthday, a card arriving in the post every Christmas, the handwriting on the envelope that of Mark's new wife.

After a few month's of dating, Keelin began to see that Henry understood her in ways she could never have imagined. He'd lost someone too, he told her, a girlfriend. Greta Ainsworth. A terrible car crash, he said, although he didn't want to talk about it, it was too painful. But he knew what grief tasted like, how it seeped into everything, turning the world grey, like a mouthful of broken teeth. After Greta's death, it was hard for him to open up, Henry said, he'd never thought he would feel this happy again, he couldn't believe how lucky he was to have met someone like Keelin. He was good with her son too, patient and kind despite Alex's obvious resentment of this man he saw as an interloper trying to steal his mother away. Henry read books about bereavement, the long shadows cast by trauma, and selective mutism in children, sharing them with Keelin and discussing what techniques they might use to help Alex recover. But he never put any pressure on the boy to speak, not until he was ready. Instead, Henry took her son to the mainland to see the latest Pixar movie or walked with him on the beach to collect seashells. He always arrived to the house with plates of delicious food wrapped in tinfoil, courtesy of the chefs at Misty Hill, to save Keelin from having to cook, and the two of them would stay up for hours, talking. Henry wanted to know everything about her. Not just about Mark – although she was comforted by Henry's hissed revulsion when she told him what her first husband had done to her – but also Keelin's likes and dislikes, her hobbies, what kind of music she was partial to, the movies she enjoyed. He really listened too, arriving with presents on their subsequent dates, small, thoughtful gifts, and they were exactly what she would have chosen for herself. A print by an artist she'd mentioned in passing, a pleated skirt with a cherry pattern, the fruit Keelin said she was particularly craving that summer, the latest Marian Keyes novel which had received rave reviews in the Sunday papers. I love traditional Irish music too, Henry said when he came to the house and found Keelin listening to Stockton's Wing on the radio. He took her by the hand and they danced around the kitchen, Keelin leaning her head against his shoulder and biting her lip to stop herself from laughing out loud with the sheer, unexpected joy of it all. We'll have to go fishing together, he said, when she told him she used to go out on her father's boat as a child and that, to her, happiness smelled of oilskins and salt. There's nothing better than fresh mackerel you've caught yourself, he said, and Keelin said yes, *yes*, for that was exactly how she felt herself. Henry seemed to see her so clearly and he accepted her unconditionally, and in doing so he made her feel truly loved and, for the first time in a long time, she felt safe.

He's perfect, she told Johanna, and her friend hesitated. What is it? Keelin asked her. You know I think Henry is great, Jo said, but . . . just be careful, OK? It's so soon after— Keelin cut her friend off. She didn't want to talk about her mother's death, not now. She just wanted to be happy. Ten months later, when Henry was kneeling in front of her holding the biggest diamond ring she'd ever seen in real life, she ignored the voice inside her wondering if this might be going too quickly and she said the only thing she could say in that moment – yes, Henry. Yes, I will marry you.

The wedding had been held in a Kinsella Hotel in Dublin, a large, ostentatious affair, and not really what Keelin would have wanted for herself, if she'd been given the choice, but she didn't mind. Her parents were dead, and Olivia and Jonathan were paying for everything; it made sense that they would want to invite their friends, some important business associates too. All that mattered was that she and Henry were married, they belonged to each other now. She wasn't alone any more. I'm the happiest man in the world, he said when they fell into the Presidential suite that night, half tipsy, and they made love slowly, gazing into one another's eyes.

It was only after the honeymoon that Keelin noticed tiny cracks in Henry's façade appearing. They were minor things, nothing she couldn't forgive, and God knows it wasn't as if she was an angel herself. She'd come into this marriage with enough baggage for the two of them, and Henry had shown her nothing but love and support – wasn't it only fair that she do the same for him in return? When they were driving home from the airport, she popped her favourite Planxty cassette into the tape deck, and Henry had baulked. I can't bear all that diddley-eye rubbish, he said, turning the radio dial until he found a classical-music station. I only told you I liked it to impress you, he said. Isn't that what everyone does when they're first dating? And Keelin supposed he was right; there was no point in making a fuss about it anyway. Then, he wanted to spend all his time with her, but it was the honeymoon period, it was only natural; she wanted to spend time with him as well; it was a two-way thing. But it didn't take long for her to worry that her circle of friends was shrinking. It started with Seán Crowley – Henry wasn't overly keen on him, but Keelin was sure she would have felt the same about the mysterious Greta Ainsworth, if she were still alive and calling herself Henry's closest friend. And there'd been that awful incident with Helen, her therapist pal from Clonakilty, who made a pass at Henry after a particularly raucous party in Hawthorn House. He hadn't wanted to tell Keelin – 'But I hated the idea of keeping a secret from you, darling. It was nothing, the poor woman was blotto, she'll be mortified if you bring it up' – and Helen herself had been too drunk to remember the details of what had happened, just saying she was so, so sorry, and could Keelin ever forgive her? Keelin had said, Of course, let's just forget it, but she found herself phoning Helen less and less, until their friendship was reduced to exchanging Christmas cards, the odd text on her birthday. That had left only Johanna, and Henry always suggested they meet Jo and her partner, Susan, in their favourite seafood restaurant in Ballydehob, rather than hosting dinner parties at home on the island, as Keelin would have preferred. Her husband would be as charming as ever, making the three women scream with laughter at his impressions of the celebrities who'd stayed at Misty Hill over the years, and Keelin would flush with pride when other people in the restaurant glanced over, wanting to know what the joke was. But dinner would be over too quickly, Henry insisting they go home to Inisrún that evening rather than crash in Jo's spare bedroom. (I have a ferry chartered, he would say, resting his hands on her hips, grazing his thumbs against her hipbones in the way she liked. Let's go home, darling.) It made sense, and Keelin was inevitably relieved when she woke up the next morning in her own bed, but it bothered her when evenings out with Henry's friends turned into all-night affairs, yet another bottle of wine opened at four a.m. She couldn't figure out a way to have this conversation with her husband without sounding petty, as if she was counting up the hours they spent with his friends versus hers, so she just decided to see Johanna on her own more often; what was stopping her from getting the ferry to the mainland on a Friday night? Yet whenever she was about to leave the house, red lipstick and high heels on, Henry would appear with champagne, saying he had forgotten she was supposed to go out and he'd planned a romantic night in, just the two of them. Jo will understand, he said, uncorking the Pol Roger. We're newly-weds after all. The next time Keelin was due to meet Jo for dinner, it was a successful deal for Misty Hill that Henry wanted to celebrate; the time after that, he had a throat infection, although he begged her to go out anyway. You need to see your friends, Keelin. I don't want to ruin your night. But what kind of a wife would she be if she abandoned him on his sick bed? Johanna's voice on the phone when Keelin called her to cancel plans, again, her friend's terse *Fine*.

If it had been a client telling Keelin this, alarm bells would have rung immediately. These are all the classic signs of a controlling partner, she'd have said, you need to be careful here. But somehow that description didn't quite fit Henry. He was an inherently good man. He phoned his mother every day, sending presents for her birthday without expecting Keelin to remind him of the date. He was respectful to the Misty Hill employees, kicking any artists out of the centre if they were rude to the staff, and their Christmas bonuses were legendary. He made her laugh more than anyone else in the world, and the sex was a revelation; Keelin hadn't known it was possible for her to feel pleasure like this. Their connection was electric, Henry knowing exactly what she wanted him to do to her without having to say a word. And, although she was ashamed to admit this, she found that she *did* enjoy the Kinsella money. After her mother had died, Keelin had been shocked to learn of the state of the family finances. All that's left is the house, the solicitor told her, and the contract with the Kinsella Group stipulates it can't be sold on to anyone who's not currently living on Inisrún. She was broke, staring at the diminishing figure on her bank statements with a rising

244

panic, wondering how she and Alex were going to survive until the next social welfare payment came in, attempting to eke out their meals as best she could to the end of the week. How could any woman who had ever been afraid she would have to choose between paying the heating bill and feeding her child not be dazzled by this new life that was somehow, inexplicably, now hers? The first-class flights to far-flung destinations, sipping champagne and snuggling under cashmere blankets to sleep in her private cabin until the airplane touched down. The luxurious suites in five-star hotels, the clothes from boutiques that she couldn't have imagined she would ever step inside, the wardrobe full of designer labels she'd only seen in magazines. Her hair, expertly cut and coloured in the most exclusive salon in London, a swish of silk as she skipped out the door, leaving a generous tip behind her, because that's what rich women did, she had learned. The Michelin-starred restaurants, heavy napkins placed on her lap by obsequious waiters, trying not to gasp when she saw the price of the wine that Henry had chosen; that was two social welfare payments, she thought. (For years, she would relate everything back to those payments. A Fendi handbag was seven welfare cheques, a romantic getaway to the Royal Mansour in Marrakech thirty-eight. It was a compulsion; she couldn't seem to stop.) And then, of course, there was Hawthorn House. A mansion cut from glass and steel, a lighthouse of its own kind, and a reminder to every islander who saw it that Keelin Ní Mhordha had made a success of her life. It didn't matter that her first marriage had fallen apart, leaving her a single parent, forced to limp back to Inisrún to her mother's home for sanctuary. She was loved now, and by one of the Kinsella brothers no less.

There was only one more thing required to make their marriage complete, but it continued to allude them. For nearly a year after the wedding, Keelin's period would arrive like clockwork, the stains on her underwear a punishment of sorts. She began counting the months by the blood moons and the new loss each one brought, Henry whispering to her, It's OK, we'll try again, I love you. But then, one month, her period did not come. I'm pregnant, she told him, and he fell to his knees, wrapping his arms around her waist and kissing her stomach. Hello, little one, he said. I'm your daddy.

When she started to bleed ten weeks later, she phoned him, screaming at him to come home, to help her, to make it stop. But this was the only thing Henry could not do; it was something not even the Kinsella money could fix. When it was over, he held Keelin while she cried herself to sleep. Please don't leave me, she begged him, for what if she was damaged in some way? What if it had been more than her ribs that Mark Delaney had broken that day she lay on the kitchen floor in Carlow, the metallic tang of blood on her tongue? She knew Henry wanted children of his own but what if she couldn't give them to him? Would he still love her, in spite of it all?

I wouldn't know, Henry said, lying down on the bed beside her, one hand on her lower belly. You are my North Star, he said. You are my forever. I couldn't live without you, Keelin.

CHAPTER THIRTY-TWO

Alex Delaney, Keelin's son

ALEX: She was an amazing mother. She was younger than all the other mams and she was just *fun,* you know? She always said yes when I asked her to play catch, or hide and seek, or just to lie on the grass and find shapes in the clouds – she was never too busy to spend time with me. When I was eight, I went through this phase of being obsessed with the Famous Five books, they were the only thing I read that summer, so one day she made a picnic for the two of us, jam tarts and sausages and 'lashings' of ginger ale because she couldn't find ginger beer. (laughs) Sometimes it seemed like she was enjoying it more than I was.

NOAH: Does your mother know you're here today? She was

adamant she didn't want you involved in the doc when we first spoke to her.

ALEX: No, she doesn't know. Neither does Henry. (pause) But it'll be fine.

NOAH: It must have been hard for Keelin, coming back to the island after her first marriage broke down. What was your relationship with your father like after the divorce?

ALEX: What relationship? Do you want to know what my first memory is? I was about three and my father was standing in the garden, shouting he was going to burn the house down with all of us in it. I heard Mam and my grandmother in the hall, and Mam started crying. I was scared then. Mams weren't supposed to cry, you know? After the social worker got involved, she would take me to the mainland every Saturday, and she'd drop me at McDonald's on Patrick's Street to meet him. I'll never forget her expression when she saw me walking towards her afterwards . . . The relief was written across her face. It was like she was afraid I wouldn't come back at all.

NOAH: How did the visits themselves go?

ALEX: Ah, look. It was pretty obvious the man had no real interest in me, he just wanted to hurt Mam in whatever way he could. He hadn't a notion how to talk to a kid – he'd get competitive with me over the stupidest shit. Like, if I said we'd painted leaves in school that week, he'd have to tell me that he was a brilliant artist, actually, his art teacher told him he could go professional if he wanted, but he'd never

249

had enough support from his own father. And then he'd be off on a rant about how unfair his life had been, how he'd never had enough chances, how everyone had always been against him. Of course he was totally different when the social worker was there, even I could see that; he had that woman wrapped around his little finger. He'd be totally engaged then, down on the floor playing with me, there'd be no television, no fast food. She thought the sun shone out of his arse. (pause) It all dwindled after a while anyway. He didn't even get in contact after everything with . . . I haven't spoken to him since I was fourteen or fifteen.

NOAH: How did you take it when Keelin married Henry? It must have been tough, having your family change so dramatically in such a short space of time. Your grandmother dying, a new stepfather, new house, new baby sister. How did you cope with that?

ALEX: It was grand. Like, it was weird at the start, obviously. It had always been just me and Mam and I didn't want to share her, I guess. But Henry made her happy. And I loved Evie from the minute she was born.

NOAH: Alex, I'd like to ask you a few questions about the night of Nessa Crowley's death, if that's OK? Witnesses say you were drunk at the party . . . ?

ALEX: I was seventeen, my tolerance for alcohol wasn't exactly high. I'd been mixing drinks and I was puking my ring up by eleven o'clock. Mam had to put me to bed. I can't remember anything after that.

NOAH: The next day must have been rough. A blinding hangover and then you hear that your friend has died. Do you want to tell me about that? (silence) Some of the islanders say you were in love with Nessa Crowley. Were you?

ALEX: I cared about her.

NOAH: Was that all? (silence) OK, Alex. What do you think happened to Nessa the night of the party?

ALEX: I don't know.

NOAH: Do you think your stepfather was involved?

ALEX: Come on. Henry is the obvious choice, isn't he? People just want to believe he's the villain because it's more palatable than it being an islander who did this.

NOAH: Well, I don't think that's the *only* reason why people decided Henry is the—

ALEX: I don't want to talk about that.

NOAH: I understand it's difficult, mate, but we have to discuss the facts, and the facts are—

ALEX: I don't have to discuss anything with you, 'mate'. You could *never* understand what it's been like for me, these last ten years. I tried to go to college, I tried to get on with things, I tried to be normal and I just . . . I couldn't do it.

NOAH: And what about now? Are you 'normal' now, Alex?

ALEX: I don't know. I'd like to be. Nothing will bring Nessa back and we all have to live with that for the rest of our lives. But I want to be happy again. (looks into camera) Do you think that's possible?

CHAPTER THIRTY-THREE

Christmas comes earlier and earlier every year, doesn't it? the women on the island said to one another as they baked their plum puddings and ordered their turkeys and spiced beef from the butcher, deliberating over how many boxes of Quality Street they would need to keep the family satisfied until the siopa re-opened again. Her mother had never liked Christmas very much, and it was only now, as an adult, that Keelin could understand why. It was so much work, particularly if you were a woman. The perfect tree to be chosen and hauled into the house, decorations to be located in the attic, dozens of cards to be sent, the exact right shade of silver bows to be placed on top of perfectly wrapped gifts. She made a new to-do list every morning: presents which still needed to be ordered online, phone calls to be made to her daughter, begging her to come to Inisrún for the holidays rather than staying at her grandparents' estate. It was a protest, Evie said, for her parents' cooperation with this 'travesty'; she would not set foot on the island while the Australians were still here, and that was final.

'Jake told me Alex did an interview for the documentary,' Keelin said in a low voice as her son left the dining room after breakfast, whistling happily. Her husband was reading the *Financial Times*, half the paper disguising his face, but he folded it and slapped it on the table next to his side plate as soon as she spoke. 'Did Alex say anything to you about this beforehand?' he asked. 'I thought we agreed an interview wasn't the best idea.' 'Jake said it went OK,' she reassured him, putting down her spoon. She couldn't bear to eat any more of this semolina porridge Henry had decided they should try. It's rich in protein and vitamin B, and only 147 calories per serving, he claimed. And all of them revolting, Keelin wanted to reply.

'Well, then,' her husband said, cutting his grapefruit in half with a sharp knife, 'nothing to fret about. You can be such a worrywart, darling.'

'Can I?'

Keelin didn't like it when Henry was like this, when he sank into this very deliberate composure, holding on to the sides of his temper with a white-knuckled grip. In a strange way, it reminded her of her previous marriage. Mark Delaney would have periods of serenity too, usually after he had hit her so badly that she would smell the blood seeping

253

between her teeth. He would say he was sorry and there would be kisses and sweet talk, talks of trips to the island to visit her parents, excursions to the playground with his sister's children arranged. Keelin forgave him and she stayed with him because that's what marriages were about – you didn't just run away when things got uncomfortable. She wasn't a quitter, she told herself. She didn't want to leave Mark; she never dreamed she would raise her son in a broken home. But she came to realise that there were more ways than one for a home to be broken. She remembered an article she had read once, where a survivor said it wasn't 'learned helplessness' which kept women trapped in abusive relationships, but rather it was a learned *hopefulness*, and certainly that had been true for her. Keelin would have so much hope in that peace between beatings, she grew fat on it. She'd begin to imagine a life for her and Mark and Alex, one where they would be happy, the perfect family. But it never lasted. The day would come when she could feel the tension build in the house, as if the windows were jammed shut, the air turning stale and catching in the back of her throat. Everything she did would start to annoy Mark, everything she wore was unflattering, the way she ate was too loud, her laugh too grating. She found she was anticipating the moment he would lose his temper again, almost looking forward to it, in fact, because at least then it would be over until the next time, and she could begin to hope again.

'I'm heading out for a walk,' Henry said, popping the last

segment of grapefruit into his mouth. He patted down his shirt and blazer until he found his AirPods. He tapped at the screen of his iPhone, scrolling through the apps to find Spotify. 'It's such a gorgeous morning. I do love the weather at this time of year. It's deliciously crisp, isn't it?'

'I was listening to a good podcast the other day, if you're interested,' Keelin offered, stacking her plates on top of his, gathering the dirty cutlery together. 'It was about the history of Christmas songs, it was so cheery. I think it was called—'

'Honestly,' her husband said, gesturing at her to hand over his leather gloves, 'the *rubbish* you listen to at times. Do you know what's happening in Syria? In Myanmar? You really ought to pay more attention to current affairs – the world is a great deal larger than Inisrún island. You don't want to become completely uninformed, do you, darling?' He bent to kiss her goodbye, then left, closing the door to the dining room behind him.

Keelin sat back down, staring at the dirty plates, the semolina congealing at the edges of her bowl. The truth was, she'd made a conscious decision to avoid such programmes a long time ago, fearful of hearing her own name. Continuing to listen was like receiving an accidental phone call, and instead of hanging up immediately, she pressed the phone against her ear, eavesdropping on a conversation she should not have been privy to. She'd never told her husband about what had happened a year before, when she'd turned on the radio in the middle of a lively discussion of the Misty Hill story and, taken by surprise, she made the mistake of listening to the whole thing.

'One simply *cannot* discount the role post-colonialism played in this case,' a woman with a nasal voice had declared. 'The relationship between the islands and the mainland has *always* been a metaphor for Ireland's relationship with England, this uneasy symbiosis where the oppressed still relies on its oppressor for trade, employment opportunities, et cetera. The islanders would prefer to be independent and t—'

'I doubt the people of Inisrún think they're oppressed by the mainland, Iseult.'

'Of course not, Fintan. If you would allow me to finish my point? *Thank you.* As I was saying, it's obvious how post-colonialism manifested itself in the Misty Hill case. Henry Kinsella becomes the human embodiment of Albion itself; we project all of our, er, *congenital* resentment of the English onto this one man, the dreaded Sasanach, as it were, as if our collective fury will somehow *undo* eight hundred years of oppression.'

'Jennie? Do you want to jump in here?'

'Thank you, Fintan. I think Iseult's point is . . . very interesting, as always, but we can't go any further without acknowledging how class played into this. And not just because of the Kinsellas' wealth, even though there's no doubt in my mind that it protected them in ways it wouldn't have done for working class people like me. The media likes to pretend we don't have a class system in this country but come on. Look at Nessa Crowley herself – women go missing in Ireland all the time; why is this particular case *still* receiving this amount of attention? If she wasn't a conventionally attractive white woman from a "good" family, whatever that means, would we care nearly as much?'

'She *was* beautiful, wasn't she?' the other woman sighed. 'I don't know what Keelin Kinsella was thinking; I wouldn't have allowed a woman who looked like that anywhere near *my* house, not with my husband and teenage son there. I can tell you that much for nothing.'

'Ah, here, Iseult, you're veering dangerously into victim-blaming territory. Before you say it, yes, Keelin Kinsella was a victim too. And at the end of the day, she's always said she doesn't know what happened on Inisrún that night. If we've decided we need to believe women, surely that means we must believe *all* women, not just the ones we've decided are worthy of our support?'

Keelin had sat in her kitchen that day, listening to the debate rage on, a cup of coffee turning cold in her hands. I am not a victim, she thought. She had been a *real* victim before and she knew what that felt like – the powerlessness of it, the grinding despair, the realisation she could be so easily destroyed by the person she loved most in the world, and she was incapable of making him stop. She had made a decision on the night she'd run barefoot from the house in Carlow, Alex asleep in her arms, only the clothes on her back to call her own. She had promised herself she would never be a victim again.

CHAPTER THIRTY-FOUR

The Crowley Girl

'I must of been an extra-good girl this year, Mummy,' Evie said as Keelin picked up the wrapping paper on the floor and shoved it into a black plastic bag for recycling. 'Santa brung me so many toys. Alannah said Santa was only getting her *one* present and a small surprise. I got loads more things, didn't I?'

'That's not quite how it works, pet,' Keelin said. She looked around the room, at the beautifully decorated seven-foot tree and the stacks of presents piled up beneath it – the books and clothes and CDs for Alex, the Cartier watch and Proenza Schouler handbag for her, the countless toys Evie had received – and she felt somehow repulsed by it all. There had been far less fuss when Keelin was a child, although her parents always made an effort to find something she would love, saving their money for months beforehand in order to afford it. But things were different in the Kinsella household. The first few presents were fun to open, she had to admit, her sharp inhale of breath when she unwrapped the box and saw the watch, glittering and hard (It's a Tank Française, Henry said, fastening it on her wrist. Like Princess Diana wore), but then she had become greedy, tearing open each new gift, barely seeing what was underneath before she moved to the next and the next and the next, each time becoming more dissatisfied. Now that it was over, she wanted to sweep all the presents out of sight, hide the evidence of her family's grotesque materialism.

'You're not to be telling Alannah about everything you got from Santy,' Keelin warned Evie. 2008 had been a difficult year for everyone, and she knew many of the islanders were concerned about what the recession would bring in the months ahead. 'No one likes a show-off.'

'Who's calling my darling daughter a show-off?' Henry said, picking Evie up and swinging her around, almost knocking a Waterford crystal vase off the mantlepiece. 'And it's Father Christmas *brought* me, not "brung" me. Grammar is important, Evie Diva.'

'Can we use our indoor voices, please?' Keelin's head was throbbing from the mulled wine she'd drunk the night before; Henry always did make the mix too potent. But she'd needed the extra fortification after Nessa had arrived in a tartan skirt and knee-length boots, everyone oohing and aahing over how stunning she was, Henry's parents commenting on what a lovely couple she and Alex made. Alex stammering, his face turning red, insisting they were only friends. Nessa saying nothing, which was even more disconcerting. Why was Keelin the only one who could see this relationship was headed for disaster? She felt like Cassandra, destined to see the truth but forever doubted when she spoke it.

'Where's Alex?' she asked. 'We need to get going; we'll be late for Mass if we're not careful.'

'Is that what you're wearing?' Henry asked, putting Evie down, and the little girl stumbled, still dizzy. He touched the fabric of Keelin's dress, the cerise shift she'd paired with opaque tights and a black belt to cinch her waist. 'It's very . . .'

'It's very what, Henry?'

'I didn't say anything. I don't know why you're getting defensive, darling.'

'I'm not getting defensive. You clearly have an issue with my outfit and—'

'I never said that. There's no need to take my bloody head off.'

'Don't be cross at Daddy,' Evie said, curling around Henry's legs and looking up at her mother forlornly. 'That's not nice.'

'Exactly, Mummy,' Henry said. 'It's Christmas. And it's my *birthday*. She's not allowed be cross with me on my birthday, is she, Evie?'

Keelin couldn't help but laugh. 'You're some chancer, Kinsella,' she said, relenting. She never could stay mad at her husband for long. 'Up off the floor, now, and get your coat on,' she said to Evie. 'And tell your brother to hurry on, will you?'

'It's showtime, children,' Henry said, clapping his hands together as Evie ran upstairs. 'Showtime!'

It was crisp outside, their breath smoking in the cold air. Like dragons, Keelin thought as she linked arms with Alex, watching Henry stride before her, carrying Evie on his shoulders. They always walked to Christmas Mass together, it was tradition, taking the road that snaked down from Hawthorn House, around the sea cliffs and into the village itself. 'We'll visit your mamó and daideo later,' she said to Alex as they passed the small graveyard where her parents were buried, not even a hundred headstones there, sticking out of the earth like jagged teeth. She gave his arm a squeeze – she knew how much he missed his grandmother. Evie had always been too little to join them on their annual expedition, even if she had wanted to, which she did not. Jonathan and Olivia Kinsella were the only grandparents Evie had ever known and they doted on her, bought her sweets and expensive toys, told her she was pretty and clever, the best girl. A gravestone and the handful of stories about Keelin's own childhood on Rún were a poor substitute for that.

A few people were standing outside the church door, exchanging kisses and handshakes, wishing Nollaig shona to each other. They turned to look at the Kinsellas as they approached, and Keelin imagined what it must look like – the handsome husband, the beautifully dressed children, and there was she, Keelin Ní Mhordha, right in the middle of them all. Not bad for an island girl. She let go of Alex, hurrying forward to take Henry's arm instead, smiling as they approached the other islanders.

'There's the man himself,' an old friend of Keelin's father said, reaching out to shake Henry's hand. Her husband greeted the elderly man by name, something he repeated for every other person there. He was like the consummate politician, remembering life stories and kissing babies, looking each islander in the eye as if they were the most fascinating person he'd ever met. There were many on the island who were suspicious of Henry, Keelin knew, wary of his money and his accent and his slick charm, those who were uncomfortable with the changes Henry's family had brought to Inisrún, whether the locals had wanted them or not. But these people needed him too. They had grown dependent upon the Kinsellas over the years, and now, when the world was limping away from the jaws of an economic collapse, the island's very survival could rest upon Henry's shoulders.

'Where is she?' Evie whined, tugging at Keelin's hand. 'You said she'd be here!'

'Alannah went to Midnight Mass,' Keelin fibbed. 'You'll see her at the charity walk tomorrow, OK? Now remember, it's Jesus's birthday and he wants you to be good while we're in his house.'

'But I want to show her my new dress, Mummy! You said she—'

'Evie –' she bent down so she was eye level with her daughter – 'if you don't behave, Santy will come and take all your presents away and leave a big lump of coal instead. Is that what you want?' Evie's jaw jutted out, the way it always did before she threw a tantrum, but she stayed quiet. 'That's a good girl,' Keelin said, adjusting her daughter's sequinned beret.

She waved at the Steins as she walked into the church, the dark oak pews gleaming, the scent of furniture wax and incense hanging heavy in the air. 'The stollen was delicious,' she mouthed at Lena, who blew her a kiss in return. Johanna wasn't on Rún this Christmas; she was spending the day with Susan's family. (Isn't having Christmas together serious? Keelin asked as she watched her friend pack for the week in Adare, and Jo had laughed. We've been dating five years, she replied. It would want to be getting serious at this stage.)

'Up the top,' Henry murmured to Keelin, like he always did. He wasn't religious; he hadn't even been baptised. His parents were long-lapsed Catholics, and Rebecca had texted Keelin that morning to let her know they wouldn't be there either. Charlie was dying after all the mulled wine, her sister-in-law said, and the girls were refusing to get out of bed. But Henry insisted on attending Mass every Christmas morning, no matter how bad the hangover, claiming one of the front pews so his family were in full sight of the congregation, ready to be admired. The church was filling up quickly, but she saw some empty spots in front of the nativity scene. She pointed at the third row, ushering the kids in before her.

'Oh,' she said, when she realised who was in the pew behind them. 'Hello! Nollaig shona.' She leaned back to embrace Bríd Crowley, then Brendan. 'I haven't seen the two of you in ages.' Their cheerful smiles froze slightly when they saw Henry beside her, reaching out his hand to shake theirs. 'Nollaig shona,' he said, butchering the pronunciation, his English accent flattening the shape of the words. 'Season's greetings, et cetera.' He unwound the houndstooth scarf from around his neck. 'We were just talking about you last night, Brendan, your ears must have been burning. My father was telling me about the new plans for the school. I'm glad to hear you'll finally be getting rid of that ghastly prefab – it was an eyesore.'

'Hmm,' Brendan said. Bríd rested a hand on his knee, gently, and her husband cleared his throat. 'It was very generous of the Kinsella Group to make that donation,' he said. 'I hope your parents know how grateful we are.'

'Oh,' Henry said, and Keelin could tell he was embarrassed, his cheeks colouring. 'I didn't mean it like—'

'And a happy Christmas, ladies,' Keelin interrupted him, smiling at the Crowley sisters. 'I trust Santy was kind to you?'

The youngest girl, Sinéad, laughed – as if to say, Excuse

265

me, I am a teenager, how dare you think I still believe in Santa Claus? – but she shut up when Nessa elbowed her, jerking her head in Evie's direction. The little girl was gazing up at them, her bright eyes moving from one sister to the next, as if she'd never seen such glamour in her life. They did make a pretty sight, Keelin had to admit, all three dressed in fitted sweaters and pleated miniskirts, seemingly oblivious to the hungry eyes of the young men in the congregation, staring at them openly.

'Hi, Alex,' Sinéad said, flushing. 'Hey,' he replied, not even looking at the younger girl, his gaze firmly on Nessa. Keelin studied the girl with more interest. *What was this?* Did Nessa's sister have a crush on her son?

'Happy birthday, Nessa,' Henry said, kissing her on the cheek. 'What are the chances? Two Christmas babies. Let the Lord save us from "joint" presents, am I right?' he said, pretending to bless himself, the three girls giggling easily.

'Happy birthday to you too, Henry,' Nessa replied, fiddling with a delicate gold charm on a fine chain. 'I can't believe I'm twenty-one, it's mad. I'm a proper grown-up now.'

'That's a lovely necklace, Nessa,' Keelin said, looking more closely at it. 'Is that a—'

'It's a swallow,' Sinéad piped up. 'It was a birthday present from Alex. Isn't that cool?' Her voice was strained but she kept smiling anyway, as if determined to show she was happy for Nessa and didn't mind that Alex Delaney was buying jewellery for her sister rather than for her.

'Oh,' Keelin said. 'Of course. How nice.'

Her son had come to her at the beginning of the month and asked for three hundred euro. That's a lot of money, she said, taken aback. What do you need it for? And he told her he had a special present to buy this year. Keelin had foolishly assumed he'd meant a present for *her*, to thank his mother for rescuing him from the boarding school where he had been so miserable. She'd been surprised, that morning, to open the box Alex had handed her and find a romance novel and a Lush bath bomb nestled in candy-pink crêpe paper. But now, looking at the beautiful necklace hanging around the Crowley girl's neck, she knew where her money had gone. Was she actually jealous that Alex had bought jewellery for Nessa instead of her? *Jesus Christ.* If that was true, then she was behaving like a deranged harridan from a Hitchcock movie and she needed to get a grip before it was too late.

'It was so nice of him,' Nessa said, tucking the necklace underneath her jumper, hidden away from sight. 'I love it so much. Did you help him pick it out, Keelin? You have great taste.'

Keelin smiled tightly in response as the organist started to play 'Hark! The Herald Angels Sing', the priest walking on to the altar, flanked by a small, chubby altar boy. 'In the name of the Father . . .' he began, and it was then she heard Sinéad Crowley say one more thing.

'It's to match her tattoo.'

'What?' Keelin turned around to make sure she had heard the girl correctly. 'What did you say?'

'The swallow tattoo Nessa got at college. It's here.' Sinéad gestured in the direction of her own ribs. Her guileless smile sliding off her face at Brendan Crowley's stern *excuse me* followed by Nessa's protestations that Sinéad was lying, she swore on Granny Crowley's grave it wasn't true, she didn't know what her sister was on about.

'A tattoo?' Keelin asked, her voice sounding very far away. 'Did you say that Nessa has a swallow tattoo?'

CHAPTER THIRTY-FIVE

Bríd Crowley, Nessa's mother

BRÍD: I'll always remember the day Nessa was born. I wasn't due till the end of January, and everyone knew you went over with your first. I'd loads of time, I thought. It wasn't until the afternoon that I started to have a bit of pain. We'd just finished our Christmas dinner so I didn't pay much attention, it was probably indigestion, I said. But then my waters broke and it was all systems go – we were in such a tizzy, wondering if we should call Liam Óg, he was the ferryman then, and tell him we needed to go to the mainland but the baby was coming in such a hurry – which was pure Nessa, as it turned out; always in a hurry to be part of everything – so we had to phone the public health nurse, and, thank God, the woman was on the island

269

for Christmas. Nessa Bláthnaid Crowley was born at six thirty-five on the 25th of December, and she was beautiful. I know everyone thinks that about their own child and, really, all you want is for them to have ten fingers and ten toes, but Nessa was something special.

NOAH: What was she like as a child?

BRÍD: She was a pure daddy's girl, following him around, hanging on his every word. Whenever you looked at the two of them, Nessa would be sitting on Brendan's knee, and he was so patient with her. People used to ask him if he was disappointed that we had the three girls, did he want a son, you know, and it annoyed Brendan because he loved those girls so much. He said he had everything he needed on this island. He had the school and me and Nessa and Róisín and Sinéad. What else could he want for?

NOAH: I'm sorry Brendan couldn't be with us today.

BRÍD: Ah, he wouldn't be able for this at all, at all. Not any more. He's . . . he's not been the same since everything happened.

NOAH: How do you mean?

BRÍD: It's not my place to speak for my husband. I wouldn't normally talk about this at all, we're private people. We haven't agreed to many interviews since Nessa died, but it's ten years on and we still don't have any kind of resolution. We still don't know what happened and . . .

NOAH: It's OK, Bríd. Take your time.

BRÍD: Thanks. (pause) It was Sunday before we heard

anything. The electricity was gone but the landline was still working grand. Brendan picked it up when it rang, he was half asleep. Then he sat upright in the bed and I could hear him say, Just tell me she's all right. Will you just tell me that for fuck's sake? He turned to me then and he said there's been an accident in the Big House, it's Nessa. And he left to . . . I should have gone too – it wasn't right to let him face that alone – but I just couldn't. I *couldn't*. I sat on that bed and I prayed harder than I ever had in my life. I begged God to make sure my daughter was safe. I would do anything, if only she would walk in that door alive.

NOAH: There are some tissues beside you, Bríd. On the table there.

BRÍD: Sorry. (sniffs) Yes. I . . . It all happened so fast after that. It was hard to understand what was going on – it felt as if someone had ripped my heart out with their bare hands, I couldn't *breathe* with the pain. No one should have to bury their child, it's not natural. A part of you dies and it never heals again, no matter how much time passes. It's just . . . your twenty-one-year-old daughter goes to a party and you expect her to come home. She was supposed to come home.

NOAH: Did Nessa tell you she was going to the Kinsellas' party?

BRÍD: Yes. I wasn't delighted at the idea – those parties were always wild – but she was an adult. I couldn't be telling her what to do any more.

271

NOAH: How did you feel about her spending so much time in Hawthorn House before that?

BRÍD: It was a bit awkward in the beginning. I didn't have any issues with the Kinsellas myself, but Brendan had never liked Henry, said he was too smooth for his own good. It didn't help that my husband never really settled into our new house either and he blamed the Kinsellas for that too.

NOAH: This was the house you'd moved into when Misty Hill was set up?

BRÍD: Yeah. The new houses were built on the far side of Rún, about fifty of them. It was the only part of the island with no sea views so they were of no use to the Kinsellas. The houses were comfortable – they had all the newest mod cons: a dishwasher and microwave and whatnot – but Brendan was heartbroken to see the old farmhouse knocked down. It had been our first house as a married couple, the place where we brought our babies home to, but I told him we couldn't say no, not with the sort of money the Kinsellas were offering, and us with three girls to send to college. I think as well, Brendan felt he couldn't complain, not with the support Jonathan Kinsella was giving the school and he the principal. He was against Nessa going to the Big House, but I said what was the harm? The Kinsellas would pay her well, and we trusted Keelin, she was practically family. (pause) Wasn't I the bigger fool?

NOAH: How has this affected *your* family?

BRÍD: How do you think it's affected us? We're broken. Sinéad tried to go to college but the first thing people asked when they heard she was from Inisrún was, *Did you know Nessa Crowley?* Everyone was fixated on the story, the way they are now with all these true-crime shows or what have you. Salivating over the details, play-acting like a bunch of Nancy Drews, as if there's not real people involved, real families torn apart . . .

NOAH: Did Sinéad ever try and go back to university?

BRÍD: No. We should have encouraged her, but every time she went out the front door I was frightened she'd never come home. She's all we have now. You've already interviewed Róisín in New Zealand, so you know she's not likely to return any time soon, or bring Cooper to visit us. Isn't that funny? You've met my grandson and I haven't. We've never seen that baby outside of Skype. Ró keeps asking me to visit, but I can't leave Brendan, not the way he is now. (pause) Sometimes I think about when we first met. He was one of the only men at the teaching college and he was so handsome, we were all swooning over him. I couldn't believe it when he asked *me* to dance, of all the girls there. And then he asked me to marry him and he told me about this island. It was the perfect place to raise a family, he said.

NOAH: You're very brave, Bríd.

BRÍD: People always tell me that and I hate it. What other choice do I have now? We can't both . . . Well, one of us has to get on with things.

273

NOAH: Do you think Henry Kinsella was responsible for what happened to your daughter?

BRÍD: Let me put it this way – I can understand why the other islanders think he was. The scratches on his face, throwing things on the bonfire, the way he disappeared after the power cut and neither he nor Nessa was seen again that night, or Keelin for that matter. It doesn't look good, does it?

NOAH: But do *you* believe it was him?

BRÍD: I'm not sure, if I'm being honest. Brendan is convinced he did it, and Róisín too. It used to kill her seeing him around the place, brushing up against her in the siopa, acting like everything was fine. Why does *he* get to be happy? she'd ask me. When our lives have been destroyed? But people like the Kinsellas, they think their money gives them immunity, that they never have to take responsibility for their actions, and they're right in a way, I suppose. Justice is only for the poor, my husband keeps saying. (snorts) We even got a cheque from Keelin for Nessa's Memorial Fund, when we first set it up. Ten thousand euro. Can you believe that? The cheek of her.

NOAH: What did you do with the cheque?

BRÍD: I posted it right back. Along with every family photo she had been in over the years, and there were plenty. I couldn't bear the sight of them.

NOAH: Have you considered moving? I'm sure a lot of people would have left Inisrún by now.

BRÍD: Nessa is buried here. She died alone – I can't leave her in that graveyard alone too. (silence) You know what's strange? A part of me hopes that it's true, that it was Henry Kinsella who did it.

NOAH: Why would you hope that, Bríd?

BRÍD: Because no one could get onto the island that night, and no one could get off it either. It was someone *here* who did this, someone on Inisrún. If it wasn't Henry Kinsella who killed my daughter, then who did?

CHAPTER THIRTY-SIX

Henry was at the bottom of the stairs, waiting for Keelin to join him. '*Très chic*,' he said as she walked towards him, with an overly enunciated French accent, the same as he did when he bought *croissants* or *macarons*, something Keelin used to mock him about, before, when she and Henry still had fun together. Holy be to God, she would say, deliberately thickening her Cork brogue to amuse her husband. Did ya go to a fancy school or what, mister?

'Thank you,' she said, as he picked a piece of lint off her coat. It was the outfit he'd selected for her, a fur-trimmed parka from Mr&Mrs Italy, a maxi skirt from Margiela, Saint Laurent slouched suede boots, all in black; Henry thought women who dressed in black were more stylish. Sometimes she dreamed of the clothes she would buy if she was allowed use of her own credit card again, scarlet red and iris blue and buttercup yellow, clashing prints and patterns, shoes with diamanté adornment, all a-glitter. She would be a vision, she thought. 'Where's Alex?'

'Táim anseo,' her son said, standing in the doorway to the kitchen. It had been many years since Alex had come to the church with them on Christmas morning, ten to be exact. That last, awful Christmas before Nessa died. *It's to match her tattoo.* The four of them walking back home after Mass that day, she and Henry and the children, Keelin talking too loudly, her voice trembling into the wind, trying to act as if nothing had happened. The words *swallow tattoo, Nessa has a swallow tattoo*, circling around her skull, nicking slivers of bone as it took the corners too sharply. I feel sick, she told Evie and Alex when they were back at the house, and she went straight to bed. Keelin, her husband said, turning the doorknob and finding she had locked herself inside their bedroom. Open the door, darling. My parents will be here any minute, and Charlie and the girls too. They'll be expecting you for dinner. Please, Keels, don't be like this. There's a perfectly good explanation, I swear.

She had laid down on the bed, crying as quietly as she could so the children wouldn't hear her. She would have to leave Henry, she supposed. She couldn't stay with him now, not knowing what she did. The very thought made her heart crack inside her chest. She didn't want to lose Henry. She loved him too much.

And yet here they were, ten years later. Still married, still walking to Mass together on Christmas morning. Who would have thought it? 'You look handsome,' she said to Alex now, pulling out her phone to take a photo of him, ignoring his protests. Twenty-seven, she thought as she looked at him. How was it possible she had a son who was twenty-seven? 'I'm glad you're coming with us today,' she whispered into his ear as she hugged him. 'Things are getting better,' he said. '*I'm* getting better, Mam.'

'We need to get moving,' Henry said, checking his watch, steering them towards the front door. 'It's a pity Evie isn't here,' he sighed as they walked down the hill towards the village. 'It doesn't feel like Christmas without her.' He had phoned their daughter when he'd heard of her plans to spend the holidays with her grandparents in Scotland, first asking her to come home, promising her increasingly lavish presents, then insisting Evie couldn't possibly impose on his parents for much longer, her grandfather was eighty-four now, for God's sake, and then, finally, he booked her a flight to Cork on Christmas Eve and told her she'd better be on it if she knew what was good for her. He was shocked when his daughter steadfastly refused to comply. Not while *those men* are still on the island, she'd said. Henry raged for hours, telling Keelin that 'her daughter' was a brat, a spoilt little princess, and he couldn't believe her impudence, he would *never* have treated his own parents like this, his generation had some *respect* for their elders. She waited until her husband calmed down, like a wind-up toy running out of steam, and then he sat on

278

the bed, his head in his hands. I don't want to lose Evie, he said. Like I've lost everyone else. Keelin sat next to him. You haven't lost me, she said. I'm still here. I'll always be here.

They passed the graveyard on the walk to the church, Keelin mouthing, *Nollaig shona*. She would go to the grave later, lay down the wreath made of holly and red ribbons, the one she knew her mother would have liked. Hopefully the ritual would be of some comfort to her. 'Here we go,' Alex muttered as they approached the church. She tightened her grip on Henry's arm, telling herself to be brave. As always, there were a few people chatting outside, women in well-cut coats, men in woollen scarfs, a little girl in a pinafore dress and red loafers. Keelin counted – a DeBurca, two Ó Gríofas, a few Breathnachs, and the little girl had to be another deBurca, there was no mistaking that ginger hair – but no Crowleys that she could see. She let out a shaky breath, adrenaline skewering her legs like pins and needles. She didn't want to see Bríd or Brendan Crowley. She didn't want to bear witness to their despair, to see what ten years of grief had done to them.

'A very merry Christmas to you all,' Henry said. The group turned to face them, tight-lipped at the sight of the Kinsella family. One of the women took the child's hand, pulling her inside the church. The others stood there, silent, their faces blank. Seóirse Breathnach, an emaciated man with a tarnished silver buckle on his belt, took a final drag of his cigarette, scrubbing it out underneath his boot. 'Come on,' he grunted at his wife, jerking his head towards the building, and the others followed close behind.

'Oh, do hurry,' Henry snapped when neither Keelin nor Alex moved. It was as if her husband had forgotten whose idea was this. She hadn't wanted to go to Mass today; she would be happy if she never stepped foot inside that church for the rest of her life. But if we don't go, Henry reminded her last night, it'll look as if we have something to hide. 'Let's get this charade over and done with,' he said grimly, pointing at the church door.

Mass was fine, after all that. They crept in behind Henry, who walked to the top of the church, his head held high. 'Excuse me,' he said, as he brushed past an elderly couple sitting together, gesturing at Alex and Keelin to follow him into the pew. He ignored the whispers, *the nerve of him*, the refusal of anyone to shake their hands during the sign of peace. After his sermon, the priest announced that the proceeds from the annual Saint Stephen's Day charity walk would be going to the Nessa Crowley Memorial Fund, and there was a spontaneous round of applause in the church. Keelin stared at the ground, pretending she couldn't feel dozens of eyes on her, watching to see if she flinched at the mention of the dead girl's name.

Back at Hawthorn House, Alex went upstairs for a 'rest'. 'I'm sorry, Mam,' he said, his face pale. 'I just need some time to myself.' She and Henry opened their presents alone, exchanging polite *thank yous*. Henry bought Keelin things that Henry wanted his wife to have – Gucci trainers, a velvet Balenciaga dress better suited to their old life, when Keelin actually had a social life, parties to go to, friends to see – rather than anything she would have wanted for herself. She forced herself to smile as he unwrapped his present from Evie, a photo their daughter had taken in the gardens at his parents' estate, stripped trees stark against the twilight sky, the river gleaming silver. A peace offering, Keelin knew, for her refusal to come home. Evie had never refused her father anything before. He turned the gilt frame around and read out what his daughter had written on the back. '"Merry Christmas to the best daddy in the world. With all my love, Evie Diva." Isn't that sweet?' he said. 'How thoughtful.'

'Very thoughtful,' Keelin said, pushing the cheap eyeshadow palette Evie had given her back in the gift bag. This was a recurring theme; Henry receiving delightful, considerate gifts, while she was given second-hand pieces of tat that Evie wouldn't deign to use herself. There was no point in confronting her daughter about it. Evie would just smirk and say, What does it matter? Daddy pays for everything anyway.

Keelin wasn't sure exactly when Evie had begun to hate her so much. She'd tried to protect her daughter from the worst of the news coverage, telling her it was lies, that her father was a good man. You mustn't believe the rumours, pet, she'd said. Maybe she had done too good a job because here they were, a decade later, and Evie could barely stand

281

to be in the same room as her, whereas Henry was adored, the perfect daddy who could do no wrong. She wished she had someone to talk to about this, preferably another woman whose teenager was equally vile to her. They could share stories of their daughters' casual cruelty, the dreadful mood swings, the screams of *I hate you* and *I never asked to be born*. Keelin and this imaginary friend would talk about Instagram, TikTok and Snapchat, worry about how revealing their girls' clothing was, and worry even more whether their noticing the revealing clothes meant they were shaming their daughters, making them conscious of their bodies and their sexuality, in the same way their own mothers had done to them in the eighties. Whenever Evie posted a photo on social media, it took all of Keelin's willpower not to phone her daughter and tell her to be careful, to wear more clothes, to drink sensibly, to get a taxi home, to save her virginity for someone she trusted. Wait for a boy who will be kind to you, she wanted to tell her daughter, one who will still respect you the morning after. Keelin knew she shouldn't think such things, it was old-fashioned; Attitudes like that perpetuate rape culture, Mum, Evie would tell her heatedly. But Keelin knew, too, that sometimes girls went to parties and they never came home again.

In the afternoon, Alex trudged downstairs from his bedroom and the three of them ate dinner together. They pulled the crackers she had bought online, recited the terrible jokes aloud. 'Ha,' Keelin said, after each punchline. 'That's not bad, is it?' The dining room was too big, really, for just the three of them. It was designed for a large family, for her and Henry and their parents and Alex and Evie and their prospective partners, maybe a handful of grandchildren, when the time was right. It was a room for the family that the Kinsellas could have been, if Nessa Crowley had not died. She took a nap after the Christmas pudding, gratefully accepting Alex's offer to clean up the table – You worked so hard today, Mam, let me help you, he said – and when she woke hours later, she was groggy and disorientated, a sourness congealing on her tongue. She grabbed her phone to check the time. It was gone ten p.m.; she had been asleep for three hours. She still had to visit the grave, so she dragged herself out of bed with a groan, changing into runners and an old hoodie. She hoped that Henry wouldn't object to her going out so late. It's dark out there, he would say. I only want you to be safe, my darling. Her safety – that was the reason for her husband's determination to keep her locked in this house. Keelin would die here, and Henry would dig her grave, oh so slowly, all the while telling her he did it because he loved her.

'Where's Alex?' she asked when she walked in on Henry in the lounge. It was a spacious room with high ceilings, two plush grey sofas with cream scatter cushions, and grey lattice window frames. A low coffee table in a dark wood held a sterling-silver candle holder, a Diptyque scented candle in Figuier cradled in its heart. 'He's gone out,' her husband said.

'*Out?* It's ten o'clock on Christmas night – where's he gone "out" to? This has gone on for long enough; we can't allow him to run around the place like this.'

'He's fine,' Henry said, holding up a bottle of Bordeaux and tilting his head towards the antique cabinet behind him which held the wine glasses. 'Care to join me?'

'I thought I might go down to the grave,' she said, gesturing at her tracksuit. 'Is that OK? I'll be quick, I promise.'

'Why are you asking for my permission?' he said, turning the TV back on. 'You can do whatever you want.'

She shivered as she stepped onto the front porch, the sharp wind cutting through her. She wrapped the cashmere scarf tighter around her neck, testing the ground ahead of her with the tip of her toe for patches of ice before she took each step. She was like one of Seán Crowley's cousins, the boys who would arrive from the mainland every summer, pale-faced and thin, squatting to scoot down the hills when they felt nervous of their footing. Invariably, one of the boys would step in a puddle or fall over and scrape their knee, and instead of jumping up, like Seán or Keelin or Johanna would have done, blinking back tears and insisting that it didn't hurt, not one bit, the cousins would race home to the Crowley house to be minded and petted by Seán's mother. That was what she was reduced to, Keelin thought wryly, a mollycoddled city slicker who couldn't cope with the island's moods. She wondered where Seán was spending his Christmas this year; she hadn't seen him or Johanna for such a long time. They'd

284

tried so hard, in the beginning, begging her to leave Henry; how could she bear to stay with him, after everything he had done? You don't have to be afraid of him any more, they told her, and they didn't believe Keelin when she said she *wanted* to stay, that she needed her husband in ways they could never understand.

Something rustled in the grass and she recoiled, laughing at her reaction when she realised it was just a rabbit. She'd always found Christmas night on Inisrún eerie; it was too quiet, all the islanders sequestered in their houses. She peeked through windows as she passed, taking in the fat candles flickering on windowsills, rows of multicoloured fairy lights strung over blazing fireplaces, and she could see people too, in pastel paper crowns, miming for a rowdy game of charades or dozing in front of the television, watching the Christmas special of *Father Ted* yet again. She hurried a little through the village, past the siopa and the pier, until she came to the graveyard, weaving her way around the headstones. She was deliberately avoiding a particular grave, the one marked by a three-foot-tall angel in shining white marble. That one was always brimming with flowers, gifts and cards from islanders and from mawkish tourists, all come to pay their respects to the Crowley Girl, taken too soon from this world.

'Nollaig shona,' she said when she was standing in front of her parents' final resting place. The small, square corner the Ó Mordhas had claimed for their own was covered in chips of quartz stone, a narrow flower trough running along the top, choked with weeds. Her father would have hated that – he was always so fussy about their rose garden, heading out on a Saturday morning with his trowel and bag of soil, Cáit calling after him to remember his hat. Keelin squatted down, tracing her fingers along the inscription in the grey-flecked marble. She had been fascinated by this place when she was younger, counting off the familiar family names of the island – Murphy, Breathnach, Ó Súilleabháin, deBurca, Ó Gríofa. Ó Mordha. Crowley – and yet these people were strangers to her, their memories as faded as the half-chipped names on broken-down stones. Would she be buried here one day? Would future children skip over her grave and recite her name out loud? What would they think of her, and what she had done?

She said a few prayers; they meant nothing to her now, just empty words, but Cáit would have appreciated the gesture; her faith had always been strong. When Keelin was a child, her mother would kneel down beside her single bed every night, sprinkling her with the holy water brought back from Lourdes, and make the sign of the cross. *Now I lay me down to sleep*, she would mouth along with her mother, her small hands clasped together in prayer, *I pray the Lord my soul to keep.*

'Braithim uaim sibh,' she whispered, covering her face with her hands.

I miss you, Daddy. And you, Mam.

I hope you can forgive me.

'Tá sé fuar anocht,' a man said. 'It's bitter.'

Keelin heard the voice and she looked up to see where it was coming from. It was so dark she couldn't quite make out who it was – two shadowy figures at the entrance to the graveyard. She squinted, peering into the gloom, until their features began to emerge, picked out of flesh, and her throat closed over when she realised who was coming towards her.

'We're nearly there now, a ghrá,' Bríd Crowley said to her husband, one hand on his back, the other holding his upper arm.

Keelin shrunk away; for one, absurd moment, she wondered if she could hide behind the headstone until they passed. She had been so careful in her efforts to avoid them, sneaking around the island whenever she left Hawthorn House, trying to fade into the shadows to avoid a moment like this one. But there they were, after all this time. Nessa's parents.

The last decade had taken its toll on the Crowleys. Bríd had been considered an attractive woman for her age; she was forty-eight when Nessa had died – almost the same age that Keelin herself was now, she thought with a jolt – but Bríd had gotten so thin, almost skeletal, her greying hair pulled off her bare face in a tight ponytail, and she was wearing a man's woolly jumper over threadbare leggings and lace-up boots. However, it was Brendan that Keelin could hardly take her eyes off. Gone was the handsome, strapping man from whom the Crowley Girls had inherited their long legs

287

and green eyes, and in his place was this elderly *créatúr*. That was the only word she could use to describe him as he hobbled down the footpath, leaning on his wife as if he was unable to support himself unaided. He was only in his late fifties, but he could have been many years older, and he was bloated, his face a swollen moon. From medication, Keelin had to presume; the papers had reported on his depression, the multiple suicide attempts. Yet another thing to blame the Kinsellas for. Brendan was the first to see her and he stopped in his tracks, stumbling.

'Are you OK?' Bríd asked, steadying him. 'Bí cúramach, a ghrá.'

Brendan didn't reply, just held out his hand, pointing at Keelin. 'What's that?' Bríd said, looking across the graveyard. 'Hello? Who's there?'

Keelin stood up, unfolding her body out of the darkness, and Bríd froze at the sight of her. They stared at one another for a heartbeat, neither of them moving. Her mouth went dry. *Go,* she screamed at herself silently. *Get out of here, Keelin.* Until, finally, her limbs cooperated and she walked away as fast as she could, dashing past the couple. She tried not to look at them or touch them, and although she heard one of them say something to her, she did not stop. What had she been thinking, coming to the graveyard? Of course the Crowleys would want to visit Nessa on Christmas Day, but she hadn't imagined they would come so late; they never had before. She could hear footsteps behind her then, gaining

288

ground. Bríd and Brendan chasing her, they were coming to claim the price for the loss of their daughter. Keelin broke into a run, a queasy terror ripping through her. What would the Crowleys do when they caught her? What would they say to her? 'Fuck,' she hissed as she hit uneven ground, a pothole left unfilled after a bad storm last winter, and she turned over on her ankle, crying out in pain.

'Mam. Mam, it's me. Are you all right?'

She looked up to see Alex standing over her, his face concerned. 'Why were you running away like that?' he asked, holding his hands out and helping his mother up to standing. 'Are you OK?'

'I was at the graveyard. I was going to the grave, like we used to, remember? I thought maybe this year you'd be well enough to come with me, but you weren't there when I was leaving the house; Henry said you'd gone out – where did you go? I came down here by myself and then I saw them, and I—'

'Mam.' Her son motioned at her to slow down. 'Mam, you're babbling. Try to calm yourself.'

'The Crowleys were in the graveyard – Bríd and Brendan. They looked so old, they looked—'

'My mam and dad?' another voice said, and when Keelin saw who was standing there, she lost her breath; it was whipped clean out of her throat, leaving her gasping for air. *The Crowley Girl.* Keelin felt something twisting in her stomach, dread, or hatred maybe, she couldn't tell. *I thought we were finished with you, girl.* Her heart was screaming, tearing its way out of her chest, and she could taste vomit at the back of her throat. But she looked again, blinking rapidly, and she saw that it wasn't Nessa, of course it wasn't. This girl's hair was curlier, falling to her shoulders in twisted coils, and her legs weren't quite as coltish as Nessa's, she was a little shorter, carrying more weight on her hips. Alex took the girl's hand, this shadow of Nessa Crowley made flesh. This girl who was very much alive, and breathing. Staring at Keelin like she knew her.

'Sinéad?'

Bríd and Brendan were behind them, their gaze darting between Alex and their daughter, foreheads creased in confusion. Brendan glanced down, paling when he saw their intertwined fingers. He stood up straight, grimacing as the bones cracked in his spine. 'Go home, Sinéad,' he said. 'Go home right now.'

Bríd was shaking her head, saying, 'No, no . . .' under her breath, and Brendan turned to his wife and said, 'You go home too. I'll deal with this.'

'Dad,' Sinéad said, moving closer to Alex. 'I didn't want you and Mam to find out this way, but Alex and me, we're—'

'No,' her father cut her off. 'I don't want to hear this.'

'Dad, please. I'm trying to—'

'Sinéad,' he roared, and Bríd started to cry then, tears rolling down her face. Keelin wasn't sure if the older woman even knew she was crying, she just stood there, staring at her daughter open-mouthed. 'Get home now, I said,' Brendan repeated. 'I don't know what exactly is happening here, but I can tell you one thing for nothing: it stops right now, a chailín. An gcloiseann tú mé?'

'I love him,' Sinéad said simply. Alex nodded, confirming her words. He squared his shoulders, and the look on his face gave Keelin pause. *Love?* If it was love, why had her son not told her? Why hadn't he confided in her about any of this? And, the sly thought slithering through her before she could stop it, why did it always have to be one of the Crowleys who took Alex away from her? What would she have to do to be rid of these girls for good?

Brendan laughed, a harsh, ugly sound. 'And what about Nessa? Did you ever love her, ha?'

'Dad!' The girl was winded by this. 'How could you ask me that? Of course I loved Nessa. I still . . .' She swallowed. 'Nessa is dead,' she continued in a clear voice. 'And it's not fair to blame Alex, he didn't do anything wrong and he—'

Her father lunged forward, grabbing hold of her arm and yanking her away from Alex. He shoved his daughter in Bríd's direction, and the girl tripped, half falling to the ground. Alex rushed to help her but Brendan moved in front of him, one hand on the younger man's chest, holding him back. 'Take her home,' he said, and Bríd snapped out of her stupor, dragging Sinéad to her feet.

'Sinéad,' Alex called after her. 'Sinéad!'

'Don't you dare,' Brendan said. He moved closer to Alex

until their noses were practically touching. 'You will never speak to my daughter again; do you hear me? You won't contact her; you won't see her. You will forget she even exists. She's *dead* to you now.' He turned to spit on the ground beside them. 'You get that, don't you, boy? You Kinsellas should understand what it means to have a Crowley Girl dead to you.'

'I can't do that,' Alex said. 'I love your daughter.'

With that, all the energy seemed to leach out of Brendan's body, his limbs sagging. He looked something more than merely old in that moment, he looked *destroyed*, as if he was barely alive, rotting from the inside out. 'Why?' he said, and his voice cracked in half. 'Why can't you just leave my family alone?' He tried to control his tears, desperate to retain some dignity, but he couldn't stop himself. The man stood in front of them and he wept. 'You people took her from us,' he said, wiping his eyes. 'You took my Nessa. Wasn't that enough for ye? You want Sinéad now too?'

'I'm sorry,' Keelin whispered as the man turned away, limping, fading into the shadows like a ghost. 'I'm so sorry.'

CHAPTER THIRTY-SEVEN

'You have to talk to him, Henry. You have to put a stop to this madness,' Keelin demanded, throwing the door of the lounge open.

Her husband, still on the couch, picking at a box of Butler's chocolates, looked up at her in surprise. 'Put a stop to what?' he asked, pushing the herringbone blanket away from him. 'Darling, are you *crying*? I'm aware it's Christmas Day, but your parents have been dead for almost two decades. It's hardly what one would call a fresh wound.' She narrowed her eyes at him. 'I was only joking,' he said. 'I didn't—'

'Shut up,' she shouted, and she wasn't sure which of them was more astonished at her outburst. They didn't behave like this, she and Henry. They had agreed when they married that they wouldn't be the sort of couple who raised their voices; such behaviour was beneath them, they decided. Our house will be calm, Henry said. We will always be so kind to one another, won't we, darling?

'I'm sorry,' she said quickly. 'I was upset, I didn't mean to talk to you like that.'

'Mam!' Alex, close behind her. 'Mam, I can explain.' He went to hug her, but she pushed him away. She couldn't even look at him.

'Alex has been—'

'Dating one of the Crowley Girls?' Henry said, folding the blanket up neatly. He put the lid on the box of chocolates and placed it on the coffee table, bending down to blow out the candle.

'You knew?' Keelin gaped at him. 'Who else on the island knows about this? We have to keep this a secret; if it gets out, there will be—'

'Surely that's not all you care about, Mam?' her son asked. 'What the islanders think?'

'Don't start with me, Alex.' She turned back to her husband. 'You knew about this and you did *nothing*?'

'Of course I did something,' he said. '*I* always have to be the one to do something, don't I? I went to Alex as soon as I saw the two of them together, sitting up at the lighthouse holding hands. Rather indiscreet, I thought, but we discussed the matter, man to man. Alex promised he would be more careful in future. He said he was well enough to handle this relationship, that he wasn't going to do anything stupid. And that was that, really.'

'How could you not have told me? I'm your *wife* – we're supposed to talk about things like this.'

'Alex wanted to tell you in his own time.' Henry picked up his wine again. 'He is an adult, as I keep reminding you, and the Crowley Girls have always been very attractive.' He watched her son, waiting for his reaction. 'I think we can all agree on that.'

'Henry,' Alex said, his hands at the side of his body, clenching into fists, 'don't talk about Sinéad like that, I'm warning you.'

'What did I say? I thought you'd agree with me, considering how you felt about Nessa. I must admit, the resemblance is uncanny. Almost *unnerving*, one might say.' Henry poured more red wine into his glass. 'Does she know?' he asked Alex conversationally. 'About what happened between you and her sister.'

'Shut up,' Alex said. 'I mean it.'

'The Crowley Girls are not like, er, *Pokémon*,' Henry said, his mouth twitching with amusement at his own joke. 'You don't have to "catch 'em all".'

'I said, shut up!' Alex screamed, his face contorting in rage. He tore Henry's wine glass out of his hand and smashed it to the floor, shards of crystal exploding in a white fire. 'I'll kill you,' he shouted, swinging for the older man. 'I'll fucking kill you.' Her husband jumped up, crunching glass beneath his bare feet. He was bleeding, but he didn't appear to feel any pain, pinning Alex against the Murano glass accent wall that separated the lounge from the kitchen, banging her son's skull against its shell with a sickening snapping sound. Keelin stood there, too paralysed with fear to move, watching as her son's body went limp.

'I'm disappointed in you,' Henry said, letting go of Alex's shirt. The younger man slumped to the floor, pulling his knees into his chest and burying his face between them 'This sort of behaviour isn't becoming of a Kinsella.'

'I'm a Delaney,' Alex choked. He felt the back of his head, moaning when his fingers came away damp with blood.

'Oh, but you're a Kinsella when it suits you,' her husband said. 'You're a Kinsella when you need to be, aren't you?'

Henry balanced on the side of the claw-foot bathtub, removing pieces of broken glass with a pair of tweezers. The bathroom's floor was tiled in squares of green and white, now spattered with blood, oozing into the immaculate grouting. She would have to clean that up before the housekeeper returned after Christmas; they couldn't afford any more rumours about blood being shed in Hawthorn House.

'Where's Alex?' her husband asked, hissing as he pulled out a shard of crystal from between his toes.

'He's upstairs. I don't think we need to worry about him sneaking out tonight; the Crowleys must have Sinéad under lock and key.' Keelin wished she could do the same. She imagined herself going to the attic and attaching a padlock to her son's door, making sure he couldn't escape. 'How long have you known about him and that girl?'

'Not long.'

'How can you be so calm?' she cried. 'We could be in serious danger here, Henry.'

'You think I don't know that? I have just as much to lose here as you do, don't forget that. But what exactly would you have had me do in this situation?'

She put the toilet lid down and sat down, her legs shaking. 'Why didn't you tell me?'

'I was hoping it would burn itself out before you had to hear.'

'So you would have kept lying to me?' She stared at him incredulously. 'You would have never told me about this?'

'You wouldn't have been able to cope with it. You know that as well as I do.'

'That wasn't your decision to make.' She put her fingers to her eyes, feeling the beginnings of a migraine forming behind them. 'I'm not a child.'

'You get so overwhelmed, Keelin, and as I said already, I presumed it would fizzle out on its own. What was the point in you getting upset over nothing?'

'But what if Alex tells—'

'Darling, let's be realistic. Alex hasn't had much luck in his relationships with Crowley Girls up until this point, has he? Why should this one be any different? No –' her husband took out the last piece of glass from his foot, placing it carefully on a bloodstained towel – 'it was better for you to have some peace of mind until there was any real reason to think this dalliance might last.'

'But . . .' She wanted to explain why she was upset, why she felt betrayed by his decision to keep this secret from her, but it seemed silly when Henry put it in those terms. Wasn't this what she had always wanted, after all? A husband who would do anything to ensure her happiness? 'I still think you should have told me,' she said, rubbing at the edges of her wedding ring.

'Come on, darling. You must agree I did the right thing here.' There was silence and her husband frowned at her. 'Keelin. You agree that I did the right thing, don't you?'

She hesitated just a second before nodding. It was easier to agree with him. He had always been too smart to argue with; it was like his words were coated in oil, slipping through her fingers before she could grab hold of them and make sense of what he was saying. He stood, wincing as he put weight on his injured feet. 'And how exactly are you going to thank me, darling?' he asked.

She dropped her head and pulled her hoodie off, shucking her leggings down, removing her underwear quickly. She didn't want to give herself too much time to think about this. Henry traced his fingertips across her collarbones, her ribs. 'You're so thin,' he said, his voice admiring. He liked her this way, liked how pure she looked. He pushed her down on the floor, the marble tiles cold against her naked back, and he spread her legs. She turned her head away while he entered her, a tear trickling down her face, salt on her lips, but he didn't seem to notice. And why would he? She'd always wanted Henry; she had never said no to him. He wouldn't even think to ask Keelin for her yes, a yes that was automatically assumed. *I love this man, I love this man . . .* she repeated silently, like an incantation. And she waited for it to be over.

When he was done, he rolled off, zipping his trousers up. She lay there, her legs apart and a stickiness between her thighs, unable to move. Her husband kissed her on the side of the jaw and he told her he loved her. 'You are my North Star, Keelin.' He whispered. 'You are my forever.'

CHAPTER THIRTY-EIGHT

The Crowley Girl

'I saw Henry's post on Facebook,' a woman said to Keelin in the siopa that afternoon. 'Looks like he went all out for Valentine's Day! That man has you spoilt rotten, so he does.'

Keelin smiled, handing over a twenty-euro note to pay for the sliced pan and bottle of white wine. Stuffing them in a cotton shopping bag, she hurried up the hill to Hawthorn House. In the study she sat at the computer – the Birdwatching folder was gone, she couldn't help but notice, long since deleted – and she typed Facebook into the search bar. Henry had uploaded a photo of the enormous bouquet of flowers he'd had specially delivered from the mainland that morning, and the homemade pavlova in the shape of a heart, adorned with strawberries. *Happy Wife, Happy Life,* he had written underneath, adding a *PS – Credit to our lovely housekeeper for helping me with pudding!* There were dozens of gushing comments already, telling Henry how impressed they were, what a 'lucky girl' Keelin was to have a husband as thoughtful as he was. He often did this with social media, posting regularly about his 'incredible' wife, how wonderful his children were, how fortunate he was to live on Inisrún, and to be surrounded by such gifted artists at the Misty Hill retreat. They were like pieces of a jigsaw, she and the children and this house, slotting neatly in place to make a picture of perfection to present to the world.

Keelin took a deep breath and shut down the computer. It was 2009 now; a new year, a fresh start, and she had promised herself – and Henry – she would put all that *unpleasantness* from Christmas behind them. Nessa Crowley was back at UCC, Seán told her when she bumped into him while walking past Peadar Ó Súilleabháin's bench the other day – 'Keels!' he said, embracing her. 'I've been trying to phone you for weeks. Where've you been hiding, girl?' – and, according to Seán, his neice wouldn't be back on the island until Easter at least. Needs to buckle down, apparently. You know what students are like, he laughed.

Not that any of this was Nessa's fault, Henry explained to her. Alex had been using his stepfather's computer for a school project – that naked photo of Nessa had been sent to *Alex's* email account, not his. I don't know what he was thinking, saving it to the desktop, Henry said, Evie could have seen it, for goodness' sake. But I didn't know what to do, I'm not the boy's father, I didn't want to overstep my boundaries. I panicked, and I made an error in judgement, I admit that. But how could you think I would cheat on you, Keelin? Especially with Alex's girlfriend? Do you think I'm capable of doing something like that to you?

Henry kept talking, reiterating everything he had already said until Keelin felt like he was carving the letters into her bones. Nessa Crowley is a child, he said. Why on earth would I be interested in her? I love you, Keelin. Do you honestly believe I would do this to you?

She didn't know what to believe. She could have asked Alex to confirm the photo was his, that was the most obvious solution, but the thought of doing so made her squirm with embarrassment. (And what if her son said, *What photo? What are you talking about, Mam?* What would she do then?) She was exhausted, trying to pretend for the children that everything was fine; Evie already demanding to know when she would next see her beloved Nessie. Keelin would smile, tell the little girl that Nessa was busy with college but she'd be back soon, avoiding her husband's eye as she told the lie. If she divorced Henry, she'd have two failed marriages under her belt at the age of thirty-six, two children by two different men. Who would have her then? And where would she even go if she did leave? She kept waking in the early hours of the morning, her nightgown damp with sweat, but instead of counting sheep to help her fall back asleep, Keelin began to count numbers. She spent hours calculating different budgets in her head, trying to figure out how much money she would need to support herself, Alex, and Evie without the Kinsella safety net, but the figures never seemed to add up correctly. It was impossible.

'What are you going to do?' Henry asked her when he came home that evening, and somehow she knew her husband wasn't asking about Valentine's Day dinner or what television programme she wanted to watch for the night. It was time for Keelin to make a decision about the future of their relationship.

'I'm not sure,' she said.

'I love you. You must know that.'

'I love you too,' she said, and for the first time in their marriage, she wished it wasn't true.

'Let's have a party.' He sat next to her on the sofa. 'It's your birthday next month – that's the perfect excuse to throw a bash.'

'My thirty-seventh,' she said. 'Not exactly an important one.'

'I think all of your birthdays are important, darling,' he said, and he kissed the inside of her wrist. She recognised that look on his face. He would want to have sex with her tonight. They hadn't fucked since Christmas Eve, since before she found out about Nessa Crowley's swallow tattoo. She thought of a client she'd worked with, years ago, an anxious woman with mottled hands who started every sentence with 'I know this is going to sound crazy but . . .'; the same phrase all her clients used when they described how their partners had terrorised them until the victims were convinced *they* were the ones who were insane. There were rules in my house, this woman had told Keelin. You did not say no to my husband. You did not answer back. You did not keep him waiting, if you knew what was good for you. What about sex? Keelin asked her. The woman had looked away, flushed. First job of the morning, last job at night, she said, her voice so low that Keelin had to strain to hear her. Whenever, wherever, however he wanted. And in that moment, Keelin had felt so sorry for the woman, but she'd felt grateful too, grateful she had Henry, who had awakened something in her that she hadn't even known was there. How could she have known, before him, that her body would respond so intensely to being called a whore, a dirty little slut, until she was crying out, begging him for more. She had thought what they shared was special, but when Keelin closed her eyes now, all she could see was that photograph. How slim the body was, how spare the flesh covering its bones. The black ink against the pale skin, a bird flying across snow. The legs spread, proudly; there was no shame there. Nessa was a girl born in a different time to Keelin, a different Ireland, a country that sold condoms in pub toilets and *Playboy* magazines displayed in plain sight in village newsagents. Nessa didn't see her body as something that she should cover up or hide away for fear of what might happen to it. Nessa saw her body as something to be proud of.

304

'A party?' she said. The Kinsella parties were notorious. Champagne, nudity, cocaine, ketamine and weed. Burning turf and fire bright, everyone coming up as one, like they were made of shooting stars. She would look around and think how beautiful the guests were, how lucky she was to be among them. The chosen ones.

'We can invite your friends,' he said. 'Johanna, obviously, and Susan. Seán Crowley too, if you'd like.'

'No,' she said. She had been avoiding their phone calls, instructing her husband to tell Johanna she was at the shop or out for a walk whenever her friend called. She couldn't bear the idea of them seeing her like this, of knowing what a mess she had made of her life, again. If they got close enough, they would see how broken she was; they knew her too well; they would be able to smell the pain coming off her. Her friends would try to fix her, and some things, Keelin was beginning to understand, could not be fixed.

'What do you say, Keels? A party for your birthday?'

'Do whatever you want, Henry,' she replied, pushing his hands away from her. Suddenly she couldn't bear to have him touch her. 'You always do.'

CHAPTER THIRTY-NINE

It was impossible to keep a secret on Inisrún. We had learned that as children, arriving home from a day running free across the island's skin, and our mothers would be waiting for us, recounting a list of our wrongdoings, as if they had been there to see them first-hand. It was a form of magic, we thought; the women of Rún must be witches. We didn't yet understand this was simply the way of the island. Words skipping from mouth to ear, like pebbles skimming the water's flesh, leaving ripples behind. We traded stories like we were bartering goods, for information was vital in a place such as this. We could not live so close to one another if we did not know each other's secrets. The knowing kept us safe.

It was after Christmas when we began to hear the whispers of trouble from up in Hawthorn House. Tension between the Kinsella man and the Delaney boy, all grown up now. Words that could not be unsaid and fists flying. More blood spilled on this land because of that family.

We did not know yet what had been the cause of this fight, but we did not mind. We knew all we had to do was be patient and the island would reveal the truth to us, like it always did.

And so we waited.

CHAPTER FORTY

'The Australians are back, I see,' Henry said. He was looking down at Marigold Cottage, squinting in the harsh January light. 'They didn't take very long for their Christmas break, did they?'

'Hmm.' Keelin put down the secateurs she was using to prune the wisteria, standing to stretch out her legs and rubbing away the dull ache in her thighs.

'I didn't get a text from the man at Baltimore pier. Did you know they were on their way?' he asked, sitting on the old wooden school bench that Keelin had brought with her from her parents' home. Her mother used to sit on that bench when the weather was fine, raising her face to the sun dappling through the two towering monkey-puzzle trees in the back garden. She would stay there for hours, drowsy with the heat and the heady scent of roses and the buzzing of bees. Sure, amn't I happy out here? Cáit would say, when Tomás asked if she was ever coming inside again. Lig dom agus imigh leat.

'I . . .' Keelin hesitated. She wasn't quite sure what the question had been. She'd barely slept in the two weeks since the revelation about Alex and Sinéad Crowley's relationship, the fear thick as smoke in her chest. Alex refused to speak to her, claiming she had taken Henry's side, as always, and the tension between him and her husband felt combustible, as if the two men were seconds away from setting off an explosion which would destroy them all. When she did manage to sleep, the nightmares were always there, waiting for her. They were the same ones she'd had for years – Nessa Crowley begging for mercy and Keelin with a bloodied rock in her hand, hitting the young woman across the skull and screaming, *I'll kill you.* Henry's hands around her waist, pulling her away. A body in the grass, lifeless. *What have you done?* a voice said. *What have you done?* – and when she woke, the sobs breaking like waves in her chest, her husband would be in bed beside her, watching her. He put his finger to her mouth, whispering *Stop that. You need to stay quiet, remember?* She blinked, and there was Henry again, but he was snoring, unconscious. She couldn't decide if that had been real or just part of the dream too.

'I'm sorry,' she said now. 'I didn't hear you.'

'I was just saying that the Australians are back.' Henry waved in the direction of the cottage. 'There's smoke coming

309

from the chimney at Marigold anyway, so unless we have ghosts, I'm going to presume it's them.' He laughed, for Henry didn't believe in the island's spirits, he hadn't been reared on the taibhseoir's stories of the púca and the bean sí, like Keelin had. He was far too sensible for such things, 'too English, I'm afraid,' he claimed.

'You should call down,' he said, picking up her secateurs and neatly slotting it into her garden-tools belt. 'Say hello. They're leaving at the end of this month, aren't they? You're running out of time, darling.'

'Come in, come in,' Jake said, breaking into a wide smile when he saw her, dimples forming in the corners of his mouth. He welcomed her into the warm cottage, where the stove was lighting, as Henry had guessed. 'Happy New Year!' he said. The artificial Christmas tree was still standing in the corner, the fairy lights blinking forlornly. 'The decorations always look sad in January, don't they?' she said, fingering a piece of wilting tinsel. They asked about each other's Christmases. Uneventful, Keelin lied, very quiet altogether. Jake told her about the Wilsons' ramshackle farmhouse in Beara and Noah's grandparents – his nan does nothing but read the death notices in the paper, Jake said, and his grandfather wouldn't stop complimenting me on how good my English was. The endless days of turkey and stuffing sandwiches, tins of Roses opened and the fighting over who got to highlight the television listings in the *RTÉ Guide*. Drinking tinnies in the front room with Noah's cousins before going to the local nightclub, a crush of a queue to get in before midnight. The DJ who played 'Wagon Wheel' five times while young men in checked shirts watched young women in tight dresses dance. 'You had fun then?' she asked, and Jake laughed. 'I did,' he said. 'It was nice to spend Christmas with a proper family again.'

He put the kettle on to boil, asking Keelin what kind of tea she would like. 'Chamomile, please,' she said; she needed something to settle her nerves. He unwrapped a cake from tinfoil, an apple tart that Noah's grandmother had insisted the boys bring back to the island with them. 'Are you sure?' he said, when she shook her head. 'It's fresh out of the oven this morning.'

'I'm not hungry.'

'You . . .' He hesitated, cutting a slice for himself and grabbing a fork from the cutlery drawer. 'You look thin, Keelin. You're not crook, are you?'

'Crook?'

'Sick, I mean.'

'I'm fine,' she said. She knew she had lost weight since she last saw Jake, and this time it wasn't because of Henry's careful efforts, weighing her twice weekly and doling out smaller and smaller portions of food, checking her Fitbit every night to make sure she'd exercised enough that day. (Exercise is essential in fighting depression, he explained, and fasting can help reduce the risk of disease – the studies are

311

fascinating, darling.) No, Keelin had simply lost her appetite – fear would do that to a person, and God knows she
was scared right now. Please, she'd implored her son every
day since Christmas. You can't do this. It's not safe, for you
or Sinéad, for that matter. Of all the people you could have
chosen, why did it have to be one of the Crowley Girls? But
her son wasn't for turning. This was a chance for him to be
happy, he said. Didn't his own mam want him to be happy?
Of course she did, she said, but not like this, not with *Nessa's*
sister. They needed to end this before the rest of the island
had the story; it was impossible to keep a secret here for
long, he should know that by now. Keelin kept insisting he
had to break up with Sinéad, and her son was disappointed
with his mother at first, but then he went cold. He locked his
bedroom door, turning his music up to drown out her pleas
as she begged to talk with him. She'd even contemplated
going to Bríd and Brendan, appealing to them for help, but
she wasn't sure she had the stomach to see them again, not
after what had happened on Christmas night.

'It's been a mad couple of weeks,' she said, blowing gently
on the tea to cool it down.

Jake swallowed a piece of the tart. 'Yeah,' he said. 'I heard.'

'What did you hear?'

'About Alex . . .' He paused. 'And Nessa's sister.'

'You . . . you can't put this in the documentary,' she said,
her mouth dry. 'Jake, please. Promise me.'

'I promise,' he said. 'And don't worry –' he put his hand

312

on hers as Keelin looked towards the other room in panic – 'Noah doesn't know anything about it. He's still on the mainland. He had to interview someone; I'm not sure who.'

'For God's sake, Jake. What do you mean, you're not sure who?'

'It's probably just a few re-shots – we've all the main interviews in the can.' He raised his hands as if in surrender. 'Calm down.'

'Funny, there's nothing that annoys me more than people telling me to calm down,' she said. She took a gulp of the tea, barely registering when it scalded the roof of her mouth. 'How did you find out about Alex and Sinéad?'

'Seán told me.'

'My Seán? Seán Crowley?'

'Yeah,' Jake said. 'He got the ferry this arvo – he'll be on the mainland by now, I reckon.' He walked into his bedroom, leaving the door open behind him. It was immaculate, she saw, the bed neatly made, his unpacked suitcase in the corner. He unzipped his laptop bag and pulled out a white envelope.

'Here,' he said, holding it out towards her. 'He left this for you.'

Seán used to write her letters all the time when they were younger. He would stuff notes into her school bag, leave them under her pillow for her to find when she went to bed. Keelin had kept them in an old shoebox, tucked away in a cupboard in her parents' house, the letters and cards and the pieces of cheap jewellery Seán had given her when they

313

were teenagers. She had forgotten all about it until she and Henry were clearing the place out, a few months after he'd proposed. Look at this! she exclaimed, riffling through the random trinkets. Mam must have brought it with her when we moved to this side of the island. This is so sweet, Henry said, reading one of the letters. We were babies, Keelin said, shaking her head. When she came back to the cottage the next day to pick up the cardboard boxes full of keepsakes she had set aside – her father's gardening tools, the family photo albums, an Estée Lauder perfume her mother kept for 'good wear' – Seán's letters had disappeared. Shit, Henry said. I wonder if the removers threw the box into the skip by accident? They rang the company to check but it was too late, everything had already been sent to the dump. I'm so sorry, her husband said. I'll make this up to you, I swear. I will spend my life writing you love letters.

'For me?' Keelin repeated, taking it from Jake.

'Yeah,' he replied. 'He said he didn't want to phone you in case Henry answered, and he said he wasn't going to text or email because he had a suspicion Henry read all of those.' Jake looked at her nervously. 'He doesn't actually do that, does he?'

She didn't reply, tearing the envelope open and unfolding the single page that was inside. Seán's handwriting, as messy as ever, words scribbled out and hastily drawn arrows pointing to the corrections above the line. It had been written in a hurry; she could tell.

Keelin,

I heard from Brendan after Christmas. He's beside himself, Bríd too, and Róisín isn't much better, she's calling me every night from New Zealand in an awful state. This whole thing has been a shock to them, as you can well imagine.

We were friends for a long time, Keelin, and I never asked you for anything, but I'm asking you now. Keep Alex away from Sinéad. No good will come of this. The two of you have always been so close, he'll listen to you.

Please, Keelin. My family has been through enough.

Seán.

She put the letter down on the table, pressing her lips together as hard as she could to stop herself from crying. She wanted to scream, but it was as if her throat had been slit open, her voice seeping from the wound. She had to stand there, silently, watching it all unravel before her.

'Oh, Keelin,' Jake said. 'Please don't cry.' He crouched beside her, a hand on the small of her back. 'You didn't do anything wrong. This isn't your fault. This is so common with wives of abusers, blaming themselves,' he said. 'I saw it with my own ma. It didn't matter how often my father beat her, he always told her it was her fault because she provoked him, and in the end she was so worn down that she believed him. "If I hadn't said that to him . . . if I hadn't had that last glass of wine . . . I tipped him over the edge . . ." She just needed to try harder, she said. She kept trying, she . . .' He swallowed hard. 'But that's not how it works with domestic violence, Keelin.'

'I have a little experience in the matter too,' she said. 'I left my first husband because I was afraid he was going to kill me. I spent years in the field, working with women whose partners had broken all the bones in their bodies. I know what domestic violence looks like, and my relationship with Henry is *nothing* like that.'

'We both know there's more ways to be abusive than just physically.' He rubbed the base of her spine in small circles, attempting to soothe her. 'I imagine Greta Ainsworth felt the same way as you do.'

'Don't,' she said, pulling away from him. 'Don't touch me. And don't talk about Greta – you don't know what you're on about.'

'I'm only trying to help. That's what I've been doing all along, Keelin. I've—'

'Did you interview Johanna?' she cut across him.

'What?'

'You heard me. Did you talk to Johanna Stein for the documentary? If you're trying to help me so much, why didn't you tell me that you interviewed my best friend?'

'I . . .' He stopped, his face guilty. 'You never asked. And that was before we became mates,' he said. 'I've been completely honest with you ever since. All I want is to—'

'To what?' she asked. 'To save me, is it? Who told you I needed saving?' She crumpled the letter up, opened the door

316

of the stove and fed it to the fire, watching as it turned to ash. 'I'm not your mother, Jake, as difficult a concept as that seems to be for you to grasp.'

'What the fuck?' he gasped. 'You're way out of line, Keelin. That was uncalled for.'

But she didn't care any more. She didn't care about Jake or Noah or this godforsaken documentary. She had spent the last ten years holding on to her secrets as best as she could, and for what? For her son to fall for the only person he was forbidden to love, yet again choosing one of the Crowley Girls over his own mother. Maybe it was better if the truth did come out, she thought. Maybe it was time that it did.

'I'm sick of you,' she said, the words clipped. 'I'm sick of listening to you talk about your childhood and your trauma and your dead mother. I'm sorry that happened to you, I am, but we've all been through shit, we've all seen things we wish we hadn't, and I'm trying to, I'm trying to . . . Jake, I need you to leave me alone.'

'No,' he said, and he was crying now. His face blurred before her, morphing into Alex, then Seán, Henry, then Alex again. Alex as a little boy, his eyelids fluttering as he fought sleep. Asking Keelin to hold him, to sing him a lullaby, to make everything better. These men, always wanting something from her. But she had nothing left to give them.

'I'm sorry,' she said. She had her fingers on the door handle, ready to leave this cottage once and for all. 'I shouldn't have said that. And I was wrong to spend so much time with you

317

over the last few months; it wasn't fair on you. I just . . . I needed *someone*. I haven't had a friend in so long.'

'Where are you going?'

'Home,' she said. 'To my husband, where I belong.'

'You can't stay with that man,' he pleaded with her. 'He'll kill you. I've been looking into what happened to Greta Ainsworth, and the police reports are shady, there's something not quite right about them. I'm telling you.'

'Stop it.'

'I can't just "stop it". I think your husband killed his ex-girlfriend and I'm almost sure he murdered Nessa Crowley which means you're in danger, Keelin. I can't stand by and watch another woman die. I can't, I –' he broke off, panting.

She opened the door, looking at the sky, a glowing haze of blue-purple settling on the hills. How beautiful the island was at this time of the evening, she thought. How lucky she was to live in a place like this. 'Don't follow me,' she said to him. 'Make your documentary, tell the story as you think it needs to be told. Do what you have to do. But I'm done.'

'Henry is a murderer,' he said, still sitting on the wooden stool and looking up at her.

'No,' she said, and there was a note of pity in her voice, for there was so little that Jake understood, in the end. 'No, he's not.'

CHAPTER FORTY-ONE

When they were building Hawthorn House, Henry showed his wife the sketches the architect had created for them – glass and steel, windows from ceiling to floor to take advantage of the way the light shifted on the island, splintering into hundreds of shades of blue, filtered through the sea and the sky. Keelin thought the plans were stunning, but she hadn't been able to conceive of the full scale of it at first, becoming increasingly uneasy as the foundations were laid and the building began to climb, brick by brick, as if trying to reach the sun. There had never been anything like it built on Inisrún before, and secretly she wondered what the rest of the islanders would make of it. But she smiled and said, Whatever you think is best, my love, to her husband. She asked for one room – just one, she hadn't wanted to seem greedy then, especially when it was Kinsella money paying for everything – which she could decorate herself. Wasn't it supposed to be the husband who got a man cave? Henry had laughed. But she didn't care about those things as much as he did, he fretted over fabric and wallpaper and tiles, wanting to ensure his choices were the 'correct' ones, which meant the choices his mother would approve of. Once the house was built and they invited the Kinsellas to visit, all Olivia could say was, Goodness, it's rather large, isn't it? Henry's face falling, looking to Keelin as if it say, *Is it? Is it too big? Did I make a mistake?* And she had stood beside her husband, and she said loudly, Well, I think it's perfect, Olivia. I feel blessed to live in a house like this.

Henry said she could take the upstairs living room as her own, telling his wife to do her worst. She ordered a paint in a dark blue, a large, squishy couch in wine velvet upon which she could curl up and read, and she laid an Aztec-print rug on the unvarnished wooden floor. She asked the architect to put an open fire in there, exposed red brick, and covered the walls in prints she had found in flea markets in Berlin and Paris, refilling a vintage brass jug with wild flowers she picked on her daily walk. It was in this room that Keelin stood now, staring out the circular window which overlooked where Misty Hill had once been, and she watched Jake Nguyen and Noah Wilson leave Marigold Cottage for the last time. Noah bent down to tuck the key under the mat, as Henry had instructed, then clapped his friend on the shoulder. Adjusting his backpack, Jake looked up at Hawthorn House and she moved into the shadows before he could spot her. She waited a few seconds before creeping back, but all she could see was the back of their heads as they walked down the hill to the pier to catch the ferry. It was the end of January, it was time for the Australians to go home, but she was sorry she hadn't said a proper goodbye to Jake. She regretted the way she had spoken to him that night in the cottage, and for the way she'd treated him for the entirety of their friendship really. She'd used him, and not just in an attempt to influence the direction the documentary took, to make sure he cast the Kinsella family in a flattering light, as Henry had asked her to do. It was more than that. Keelin had liked the way Jake made her feel, as if she were still an interesting woman, good company, a decent friend. She would miss feeling that way, as she would miss him. But Jake would be fine without her. He would find another woman to rescue, another broken doll to fix, lovingly gluing the shattered pieces of china back together. He would forget all about Keelin Kinsella then; she would just be some woman on an island he had once known.

A floorboard on the stairs creaked – *Henry?* she thought, holding her breath – but when she turned around, it was Alex she found there. He was dressed smartly, a forest-green shirt under a fitted black sweater, an overnight bag in his hands, tiptoeing past her with the exaggerated movements of a cartoon cat burglar.

'Where are you going?' she asked. Her son flinched but he didn't look at her. 'Alex,' she said. 'I asked you a question.

Where are you going? Why have you got that bag with you?'
He ignored her, hurrying his step. 'Are you going to see *her*?
After everything we talked about?' Keelin followed him, her
socks slipping on the polished stairs and she grabbed at the
handrail to steady herself. 'You can't do this.'

'And what would you rather happen to me?' He leaned
against the banister, looking up at her. 'Should I rot away in
the attic, like the proverbial madwoman? I can't stay here,
Mam. I can't be around Henry any more. Not after what he
did to me on Christmas Day.' His hands went up to touch
the back of his head, the wound still healing over. 'He could
have *killed* me, Mam, and you did nothing to stop him. You
just stood there, exactly like you did when—'

'That's not fair.' She didn't want to talk about that night,
about what she had or hadn't done, all the ways she had failed
her son. 'Your stepfather is trying to protect you.'

'*Protect* me?' He stared at her. 'You saw what he did, Mam.
I was lucky I didn't need stitches.' He gripped the banister
tightly. 'I don't know how you can stand it either,' he said.
'After what he did, I don't know you can bear to be in the
same room as that man.'

'That was a long time ago.'

'Maybe for you it was. But I . . .' His voice was so sad it
hurt her to hear him. 'I don't want to end up like you, Mam.
I don't want to be trapped here, on this island, surrounded
by ghosts. Sinéad makes me happy, she's—'

'She's Nessa's sister!' Keelin shouted. 'You're putting us all in danger. You're putting *me* in danger, Alex. Don't you care about what will happen to me, after everything I've done?'

'Don't put that on me,' he said, switching the bag from his left hand to his right. 'That was your decision, yours and Henry's. I didn't get much say in the matter, did I?'

'I just . . . don't want you to get hurt,' she whispered. 'Not again.'

'No one is going to get hurt. It'll be different this time.'

'Are you trying to convince me of that?' she asked, walking downstairs until she was beside him. She stood up on her tippy-toes and touched a hand to his cheek. 'Or yourself, mo stoirín?'

CHAPTER FORTY-TWO

Keelin rarely went on Facebook any more. She'd been forced to tighten her security settings when her page was hacked after the murder, photos of her family copied and shared on social media, *This is what a murderer looks like!!!* captioned beneath. Her account was now under her maiden name, her profile photo a generic shot of a sunset and her friend list kept barebones small, but she still avoided the site as much as possible. She was protecting herself from the inevitable agony she would feel when confronted with a photo of Johanna and Susan and their adopted sons, twin boys she knew she should have been godmother to, rather than Susan's older sister, or an update popping up to tell her Seán Crowley was 'in a relationship' with someone Keelin didn't know, an olive-skinned woman with a Spanish surname. She should be grateful, she thought, that Seán and Jo hadn't simply unfriended her, severing the final link between them all, but it still stung, these reminders of how far they had drifted from her. But she had to log on today; she needed to find Sinéad Crowley and she couldn't just ring the house phone and ask Bríd if she could speak with her daughter, so she was reduced to searching for the girl on social media. She was surprisingly easy to find – young people, Keelin thought, no understanding of privacy – and she sent her a short message, telling the woman that she needed to speak with her urgently. She pressed send, then sat in front of the computer for the next hour, waiting for a response. The screen went black, and for some reason she found herself thinking of a summer's day, many years before. It was during a heatwave and everyone on the island was complaining about the weather, how clammy they felt, how sticky the air was. Keelin had been sitting at the picnic tables down by the pier, the one marginally less covered in dried bird shit than the other, an ice lolly sweating onto the back of her hand. Alex was sitting next to her, turning the pages of his comic book, and as she looked down at her son she had the rare sensation of being utterly content, a lightness unfolding in her chest. There were children on the beach, running to the edge of the water and shrieking at how cold it was, their mothers calling, Stay where I can see you. Keelin's eye was drawn to a blonde girl, maybe eight or nine years of age, and it took her a few seconds to recognise who it was. Nessa Crowley. She was picking something up from the shallows of the shore, pulling her arm back with as

325

much force as she could manage, and throwing it back out to sea. Keelin tossed her ice pop into a nearby bin, wishing she had something to clean her hands with. She asked her son if he wanted to come for a paddle but he said, No, Mammy, I'm reading my book. Keelin said she would only be a few minutes and she walked down the uneven stone steps to the sand below, picking her way through seaweed and driftwood and cigarette butts, the odd Coke can crushed beneath them. Hello, she said as she approached the girl. What are you up to, Nessa? The girl held out her cupped palms for Keelin to see, and nestled in the heart of them was a round jellyfish, a translucent, quivering disc threaded through with purple veins. I'm rescuing them, Nessa said. I'm sending them home.

Facebook Messenger dinged and Keelin shook the computer mouse quickly, re-awakening the screen.

SINÉAD CROWLEY: Hi Keelin.

KEELIN NÍ MHORDHA: Is Alex with you?

SINÉAD CROWLEY: Yeah.

SINÉAD CROWLEY: He's here.

KEELIN NÍ MHORDHA: Are your parents there?

SINÉAD CROWLEY: No.

SINÉAD CROWLEY: Dad had to go to the doctor so Mam took him to the mainland yesterday. They're staying in my aunt Áine's for the night, she still has the place on Model Farm Road.

KEELIN NÍ MHORDHA: Can I come over?

Keelin Ní Mhordha: It's important.

Keelin Ní Mhordha: Please Sinéad.

Henry would check the search history on the computer later. He often did that, just to make sure Keelin wasn't googling the Misty Hill case, it would only upset her, he said. Henry had her passwords now too – just so he could check her social-media accounts regularly, delete any threatening messages, get rid of friend requests from voyeuristic strangers – but he would be able to see that Keelin had been on Facebook without discussing it with him first. He'd see the messages she had written to Sinéad, and he would be disappointed that she hadn't listened to his advice, which was to leave this mess alone. Alex isn't going to do anything stupid, her husband said. Why would he? And really, darling, you need to remember what happened the last time you came between that boy and a Crowley Girl. We're still dealing with the aftermath of that disaster, aren't we?

The computer dinged again.

Sinéad Crowley: Sure. Come away over.

Alex opened the door to the Crowleys' house, his face reddening in frustration. 'Mam,' he said. 'I know you're upset, but you can't do this. It's not fair.'

Keelin didn't look at her son. 'Sinéad,' she said, peering over Alex's shoulder at the silhouette hovering at the end of

327

the hall. 'Can I talk to you?' Alex spluttered in annoyance but Keelin ignored him. 'Alone, please, Sinéad.'

'This is not OK,' Alex said. 'You can't control me like this. I'm not a child any more, Mam.'

But she kept her eyes on Sinéad, and she could see the younger woman relenting under her desperate gaze. 'Go for a walk,' the girl said to Alex, touching his arm with her small hands. They were delicate; thin fingers, nails painted a pale pink. Keelin thought of Nessa's hands when they found her, digging into the dirt as if searching there for something to save her. Life must seem so precious when it's about to be taken away from you. 'Up to the lighthouse, maybe,' Sinéad said. 'Give me and your mam a chance to talk properly.'

'I don't think—' he protested, but Sinéad wrapped her arms around his waist, pressing her face into his chest. 'It's fine, boo,' she said, and Keelin tried not to show how taken aback she was at the comfort they had with one another, the level of intimacy that 'boo' conveyed in one word.

Alex let out a loud sigh. 'I'm giving you twenty minutes,' he said to his mother, grabbing his jacket from a hook on the wall. When the door closed behind him, she and Sinéad stood there, neither sure what to say. 'Will you have a cup of tea?' Sinéad said. 'I will,' Keelin replied.

She sat at the pine table, its legs wobbling on the uneven lino. The room was a shrine to Nessa, photographs of her smiling face on every surface. Her eyes moved from the photos to the dozens of knick-knacks; Bríd Crowley had developed a taste for the sentimental since she'd last been here. There was a fridge magnet declaring 'Grief is the price we pay for love'; a pin cushion embroidered with 'The more beautiful the memories, the more difficult the parting'; and an etching of a broken heart with the words 'When a child dies, you bury the child in your heart', framed on the opposite wall.

'Do you want normal or herbal? We've lots of herbal teas,' Sinéad said, opening the cupboard and riffling through the boxes inside. 'Green tea, peppermint, we have chamomile, and I'm pretty sure we—'

'You know you can't keep seeing Alex, don't you?'

Sinéad stilled, her hands dropping to her side. 'But I love him,' she said, as if it were that easy.

'And you think that's a good enough reason to break your parents' hearts, do you? You're a smart girl, Sinéad. You must know your mam and dad will never accept him.'

'They might, in time.'

'They won't.' Keelin shook her head. 'You're not a mother – you don't understand how deep this goes. You bringing home a Kinsella is their worst nightmare.'

'Alex isn't a Kinsella,' Sinéad argued. 'And he was barely at the party that night; he passed out from the drink before the power cut.'

'Are we really going to argue over semantics here? Jesus Christ, girl. What were you *thinking*?'

'I wasn't thinking,' Sinéad said, sitting beside her. Keelin couldn't help but breathe in, wondering if this Crowley Girl would smell like apple shampoo too. 'For the first time since Nessa died, I wasn't thinking about her or Mam and Dad.' The girl dropped her head, a tear splashing against the table. It was filthy, toast crumbs and bits of food and a splodge of jam. When was the last time someone had cleaned in here? 'I'd fancied Alex for years. Ever since he arrived home from boarding school,' Sinéad said. 'He came to the house to drop back a maths book he'd borrowed from Nessa, and he seemed different to the island boys – less obnoxious, or something, although that wouldn't have been hard, the way they drooled all over us. None of them looked at us like we were real people, we were just a . . . a *trio* to them, a collection of bodies. The Crowley Girls. Alex wasn't like that.' She sniffed, touching her fingertip to her nose to stop it running. 'But he was clearly in love with Nessa, and she seemed mad about him too. It had always just been the three of us before that. The three musketeers, my dad called us, like peas in a pod. But all of a sudden, the only thing she wanted to do was spend her weekends with Alex Delaney. Ró used to give out about it, say Nessa was being selfish, but I understood. I'd want to spend all my time with Alex too, if I could. But he wouldn't have me, not while Nessa was around. The nights I spent crying myself to sleep because I thought my heart was broken.' She tried to laugh. 'I'd find out soon enough what it was really like to have a broken heart.'

'I'm sorry.' That was all Keelin ever seemed to say these

days. *Sorry, sorry, sorry.* She had plenty to apologise for, after all.

'I didn't see Alex for years after Nessa died,' Sinéad continued. 'But when the documentary makers arrived to the island –' *That fucking documentary*, Keelin thought; of course it would have played a part in this debacle – 'and Mam and Dad were so het up about it. Hoping the Australians would solve the case, as if they'd be smarter than the guards. Dad keeps all the newspaper clippings, you know, he reads them every day. Every single one, as if he thinks he might find something this time, a clue we all missed. He didn't like it when he heard the Australians were staying in your cottage; he thought it might prejudice them. He wouldn't let it go –Will the documentary be fair, Sinéad, or do you think *that man* is paying them off? We need justice, Sinéad, *that man* can't get away with this – and I thought I was going insane. I started heading out during the day, I'd walk for hours, back and forth between the lighthouse and the fulacht fiadh until I could be sure my father would be asleep.'

'And it was there you met Alex,' Keelin said, leaning forward in her chair.

'Yes,' Sinéad said. 'At first I didn't talk to him. I pretended like he didn't exist. But after a while we were arriving at the lighthouse at the same time every day, and I couldn't keep pretending that it was a coincidence. He followed me on Instagram and I followed him back. It didn't seem . . . Well, it didn't seem like anything in the beginning.'

Did you talk about Nessa? Keelin wanted to ask. *Did Alex tell you it was her whom he loved, that it was Nessa who had been the girl of his dreams? Did he tell you what he wrote about your sister in his diary, the words he used to describe her, the things he wanted to do to her body? Did he talk to you about that photograph, pale legs, spread, and a tattoo dancing on her ribs, the one your sister sent so willingly?*

'We didn't plan to fall in love,' Sinéad said. 'You have to believe me. It just happened.'

'You have no idea what you're doing. Alex is . . .'

'Alex is what?'

'He's damaged,' Keelin said, the word searing, the shame of having to say such a thing about her own child. For it was her fault he had seen such terrible things. She had broken him herself, snapped him in two. He would never be the same again. 'He's been through so much, Sinéad. You don't understand.'

'Keelin –' the girl stared at her – 'are you honestly trying to imply that Alex is the only person who's had a hard time since the night of Nessa's murder? She was my *sister*. Do you know what my life has been like?' She took a breath. 'Róisín never comes home any more – she blames the cost of flights from New Zealand or the hassle of travelling with a toddler, but I know it's because she can't bear to be in this house. This *crypt*. All we're allowed to talk about here is Nessa. Perfect Nessa, who would have cured cancer and stopped climate change if she was still around, according to Mam and Dad. They seem to have forgotten they ever yelled at her for sleeping in late or for never tidying her bedroom. That she made –' She looked at Keelin, her face colouring in embarrassment. They both knew what else Nessa Crowley had done. 'And now we have to act like she was this *saint*,' the girl rushed on. 'The rest of us can't live up to it, and I don't even want to try any more. I'm suffocating, Keelin.' Her voice began to shake. 'All along, I've told myself that I can't leave the island because I'd be abandoning Mam here with Dad; Dad and his episodes and his medication and his conspiracy theories. I'm stuck here until one of them dies, and I'm praying it's my father first, because if it's Mam, I'll have to mind that man for the rest of his life and I'll never escape Inisrún. And I hate myself for even thinking like that but I've never been anywhere, I've never *seen* anything, I . . .' Sinéad was sobbing now, the garbled words falling from her mouth. 'I deserve to have my own life, don't I? I love Alex, and he loves me too, even after everything that's happened. Why can't you be happy for us?'

Keelin closed her eyes, praying for guidance. She blinked and for a second she thought it was Nessa sitting before her, watching her. Maybe Nessa would always be there when she closed her eyes. Maybe she was destined to see the Crowley Girls face in the shadows, waiting for her, for the rest of her days. She put one hand over her mouth, waiting for the nausea to recede – *it's not her, it's not her* – and when her heart rate slowed down, she spoke again.

'What age are you, Sinéad?' Keelin put her hands on the

table, spreading her fingers out, and she examined her rings. The large marquise diamond flanked by two trillion-cut stones, set in a platinum band, the simple silver wedding band that had belonged to her mother. And she remembered the day Henry had knelt before her, holding out a small velvet box containing this engagement ring, and he told her he would love her forever. How happy she had been.

'I'm twenty-five,' the young woman replied.

'You're so young,' Keelin said, meaning, you're too young. Meaning, you're just a child. You don't know what you're doing.

'I don't feel young,' Sinéad said. 'I haven't felt young in a very long time.'

CHAPTER FORTY-THREE

The Crowley Girl

Keelin sat in front of the dressing table, staring at her reflection in the vanity mirror. She forced a smile, and when her expression returned to neutral, she noticed that the tiny laughter lines at the corners of her mouth didn't disappear, like they would have before, but remained there, still creasing the skin. She was thirty-seven today and it felt like the end of something. She wasn't old, exactly, but she was no longer a young woman either, her future stretching out ahead of her, full of possibilities to be explored, diverging roads to be chosen between, each one leading to unknown destinations. She had decided upon her path – marriage, children, this island – and she had to be happy with that. You just have to get on with things, her father always said. Mar a chóirigh tú do leaba, caithfair luí innti.

From downstairs, she could hear the heartbeat of the party, frenetic, pulsating fast. The murmur of voices, the occasional shout of laughter, pounding music, bottles dropped and broken, a hissed *shit* as glass shattered against the tiled floor. A flash of light streaked across the room, and she pushed the window open, leaning out to get a better look at the storm knifing the sky apart. We should cancel the party, she had said when the weather warnings were put in place for the weekend. Nonsense, Henry replied. Where's your sense of adventure, darling? Maybe that was another thing she had left behind in her youth, her sense of adventure, along with her willingness to smile and stay silent when a man was making stupid plans.

'Keelin!' someone shouted from the room below. She couldn't hide in here all night; she would have to make an appearance at some point this evening. She was the guest of honour, after all.

As she walked downstairs, she passed people sitting in clusters on the steps, two men hanging out the large bay window, holding their phones up to the thunderous sky. 'Have you *anything*? Even one bar?' the shorter man asked his boyfriend, groaning when the answer was negative. 'Hi, Keelin,' they chorused. 'Happy birthday!' She smiled and kissed cheeks and asked about partners and children and 'Tell me, where did you get that dress, Jemima? It's fabulous on you.' The DJ decks were set up in the hall, and it was packed tight, men and women dancing, grinding hips, roaming hands looking for soft flesh to fondle. She tried to manoeuvre her way through the heaving mass of bodies, flinching as a cigarette burned against her bare forearm. She walked into the lounge, to find three women with French-manicured nails sitting around the glass-top table, chopping out lines of cocaine. 'He wants Imogen to go to Gordonstoun in September,' one was saying, 'but it's so far away and she's so little. It's a beastly idea.' She bent over the table using a silver straw to snort the coke. She sniffed, rubbing her nose with her fingers. 'Oh, hi, Keelin,' she said, passing the straw on to the woman next to her. 'Want some, darling?'

'I'm OK, thanks.'

'Your son is over there,' she said, pointing at the open door behind them. 'He's rather tight, I'm afraid.'

Keelin turned to see Alex standing in the hall, a bottle of champagne clasped in both hands. He was pale, sweat patches blooming under his armpits, and he looked disorientated, as if unsure of where he was. 'Will you excuse me?' she said to the women, closing the door behind her.

'Alex,' she said, placing her hand against his back. It was damp, the shirt sticking to his skin. 'Are you OK?' He took a swig from the bottle, wiping his mouth clean with his hand afterwards, and belched loudly. She'd never seen her son drunk before. She and Henry had encouraged him to have an occasional glass of wine with dinner – that's what the French did, Henry said, it was far more civilised – but Alex always refused. He didn't like the feeling of being out of control, he said, and Keelin had been secretly relieved. Her ex had always been at his worst when he drank. 'Alex,' she tried again, but her son continued to ignore her. *You're only seventeen*, she wanted to say, but it would be hypocritical of her, considering her own age when she and Seán and Jo had started sneaking sips from her father's bottle of Powers. But they'd never had access to champagne, and it made her uneasy somehow, that Alex would have access to such luxuries before he had earned the right to, like she had. Or be exposed to other things, she thought, hoping Alex hadn't seen the drugs drawn out like battle lines. 'I think it's for the best if you—' she began but her son backed away, telling Keelin to leave him alone.

'You've had too much to drink,' she said.

'Fuck off, Mam,' he roared, shoving her away from him. She fell against the edge of the door frame, bone against wood, and although it didn't hurt much, she was so stunned she almost burst into tears. She stood up straight before anyone could notice what had happened, but her son was gone, disappearing into the crowd. Keelin hesitated, then went to follow him, smiling at the guests as they said hello, wishing her a happy birthday. These strangers, with their pupils rushing black, hugging her and saying they loved her, radiating euphoria and sweat as they came up on the same batch of pills. Who were all of these people? And where was Henry?

She found him in the sunroom, with Miles Darcy, the man he considered his best friend from school, although

Miles often gave the distinct air that he was only tolerating her husband until someone more amusing came along for him to play with. Keelin had been bemused the first time she was introduced to Miles, recognising in him many of Henry's distinctive mannerisms, the expressions her husband used, the stories he told, but she had instantly understood that it seemed more natural when Miles did it, less practised, somehow. Watching the two men together, she had the unnerving impression that her husband had modelled himself on his friend but wasn't brave, or perhaps stupid, enough to perform the imitation in front of him.

He was showing Miles something on his phone now, and the other man was laughing, punching Henry on the upper arm, saying, Well done, old chap. 'Henry,' Keelin said, and he put the phone away as soon as he heard her voice.

'There's the birthday girl,' Miles said, kissing her on both cheeks. He was so handsome, with his tanned skin and slicked-back hair, his jaw the sharpest she had seen outside of a superhero comic. She breathed in that familiar scent of oranges and mint, the cologne he had handmade by a tiny perfumery in Tuscany; nothing as gauche as a shop-bought fragrance for him. 'You look ravishing, as ever,' he told her. She had a flutter in her stomach when he looked at her like that, his eyes gleaming, and she hated herself for being an easy target.

'Babe,' she said to Henry, 'I need your help. I've just seen Alex and he's very *drunk*.' She widened her eyes as she said the word 'drunk', so her husband would understand the severity of the situation. 'I think we should put him to bed before he gets any worse.'

'It's a party, Keels. Let the boy get blotto if he wants to,' he said, discreetly pressing his knuckles against the side of his nose. She gritted her teeth. Henry had promised he wouldn't do coke tonight, not with her son in the house, but Miles never turned up to a party without a few grams and Henry never could say no to Miles Darcy.

'Do you have a cold, darling?' she asked him. 'You seem to have a bit of sniffle there. Same one that you have, Miles – what a strange coincidence.' She looked around, searching for someone in a white shirt and black tie, preferably holding a tray of champagne flutes. 'Where are the waiters gone to?'

'I sent them home,' Henry said. 'The weather was getting worse, so I thought it might be for the best.'

'That was a good idea,' she had to admit.

'But not to worry, lovely,' Miles said, one hand on her elbow. 'Come, let's get you a proper drink. Can't have the birthday girl getting parched, now, can we?'

She began to thank him but he wasn't listening any more, he was staring at something behind her. A slight downturn of his lips, a dip of the head. 'Well, well,' he drawled, arching an eyebrow at Henry. Keelin glanced over her shoulder, just in time to see Nessa Crowley walk into the room. She was wearing a short black dress, a slip of a thing, her cat-like eyes accentuated with heavy silver shadow. She had a bottle of wine and a card in hand, and Alex was beside her, his face ecstatic, as if he had been waiting all night for her to arrive.

'If you'll excuse me,' Miles said, raising his glass to them both, 'I'm going to say hello to Alex. It's been yonks since I've seen the boy.' Keelin yanked Henry by the elbow before he could follow suit, pulling him over by the patio door where she glared at him. 'Darling,' he said, 'you're not going to let Miles go and chat up Nessa Crowley, are you? Poor Alex won't stand a chance once Darcy has her in his sights. Do we really want a heartbroken teenager pining around the place for the foreseeable future?'

'What is *she* doing here?'

'Keelin.' Her husband's face became weary. 'I thought we'd moved past all that nonsense.'

'Oh, I'm sorry that I haven't "moved past" this "nonsense" quickly enough for you. I'll try to hurry up in future, meet your exacting schedule of when and how I'm supposed to process my feelings.'

'I don't know what else I'm supposed to do. I wanted you to have a good time tonight. I did all of this for you.' He threw his hands out, gesturing at the room, the patchwork bunting, the helium balloons, the gold banners with *Happy Birthday, Keelin!* printed on them. 'I organised this party. I invited all of our friends, and—'

'You invited all of *your* friends, you mean.'

He left the champagne flute on the windowsill, then put

his hands on her shoulders. 'I love you, Keels,' he said. 'Only you. I've never loved anyone else but you. I've tried to be the best husband and father I can possibly be and I would never do anything to hurt you, especially not with a girl who doesn't know her arse from her elbow. Please –' he leaned in until she could taste his breath on her lips – 'don't do this. You're the love of my life.'

'I –' She moved towards him, almost kissing him, but then she remembered that photo and that tattoo and she pulled away. 'No. I don't want that girl in our house, Henry. Tell her to leave, please.'

'You know I can't do that,' he sighed. 'She's Alex's guest; it's not my place. Just try and have a good night, OK?'

He walked away from her, joining the other group and clapping a hand on Miles's back with more strength than was strictly necessary, causing the other man to jolt forward, spilling champagne onto his shoes. Henry patted his breast pocket as he leaned in to say something to his friend, and the two men disappeared, probably to find a toilet so they could shove more cocaine up their noses, leaving Nessa and Alex behind. Alex was whispering in the girl's ear, his forehead gleaming with sweat, while she looked at the ground, her face vacant.

I need a fucking drink. In the kitchen, Keelin opened a fresh bottle of Pouilly-Fuissé that was in the wine cooler and poured herself a generous glass. She exchanged terse hellos with the young women perched on the counter-top, their high heels in a heap on the floor. 'Sorry,' she said when one of them waved a mobile at her in desperation. 'The reception is shocking on the island, I'm afraid.'

She couldn't remember their names although they had been introduced earlier that evening. Two of Henry's London friends were recently divorced, and they'd each turned up for the weekend with a blonde barely out of her teens, delighted with themselves. Is this how things would be from now on? Henry's friends would get older but the women they dated would stay the same age, swapped out for a younger model once they hit their twenty-fifth birthday? It was such a cliché, Keelin thought, but more than that, it felt unfair. She knew if she turned up to a party with a younger man, she wouldn't be greeted with elbows to the ribs and a muttered 'well done'. She'd be stared at with pity and a hint of derision. Poor Keelin, they would say out of the side of their mouths. She looks like that chap's mother, doesn't she?

She drained her glass, then poured another one. She drank the second glass in three gulps, swaying a little as the alcohol rushed to her head. She would get drunk, she decided. That was the only way she would be able to endure this night.

'Keelin?' a soft voice said. The left strap of Nessa's dress was falling off her shoulder, a creamy shimmer highlighting the sharply outlined collarbones. Keelin had a strange urge to touch them, to see what it would feel like, those delicate bones beneath supple skin, and she suddenly felt ashamed. Ashamed that her own collarbone was not what anyone would describe as thin. Ashamed of her soft belly straining at the material of her dress, ashamed of the empty glass in her hand. The shame felt corrosive and horribly familiar, and in an instant she saw herself in that house in Carlow again. Take off your clothes, her ex-husband would say, his face twisting with revulsion as she did as she was told. You fat bitch, he said when Keelin was standing in front of him, naked. You fat, disgusting bitch.

'I wanted to give this to you,' Nessa said, holding out the wine and the card. 'In case it gets lost. I'm sure things can get pretty hectic at these parties.'

'Yes,' Keelin said, looking at the bottle. It was a cheap Chardonnay, a ten-euro special from the shop in Baltimore, she guessed, not anything Henry and his crowd would drink. 'How are you, Nessa?' she asked. 'And how on earth did you manage to make it across the island in this weather? And in those shoes?'

They both laughed and Keelin wondered at herself, making polite chit-chat with the young woman who had sent her son such a lewd photo. But she couldn't help it – she was Cáit Ó Mordha's daughter and she'd been taught to be polite to guests. She would smile at Nessa and she would make the girl feel welcome in her home, even if it killed her.

'I only came from Maria's place; I didn't have far to travel, really,' Nessa said. 'Don't worry, Evie was in flying form – she loves my cousin almost as much as me,' she said, as Keelin opened her mouth to enquire about her daughter.

'Maria's a great babysitter. They were all watching some Disney movie when I left.' She nodded at the card. 'There's another present in there.' She brushed off Keelin's protestations with a bashful, 'Ah, would you stop, it's only tiny.' Keelin opened the envelope and found a silver chain inside, an ice-cream charm strung on it.

'It's stupid,' Nessa said. She rubbed her hands against the thin material of her dress, causing it to pull at her breasts and making it very obvious she wasn't wearing a bra. 'I remember waiting at the pier with Seán to welcome you home from college, and you would always buy me a 99 cone in the siopa afterwards.' She looked down at Keelin – she was so tall, she must be easily over six foot in those heels – and her skin still had that perfect plumpness that seemed to vanish once you hit your mid-twenties. 'I thought . . . I hoped the two of you would end up together. My sisters did too. We wanted you to be our aunt.'

'It was never like that with Seán and me,' Keelin said abruptly, putting the silver charm back in the envelope and tucking it into a side drawer in the dresser.

'I know,' Nessa said. 'I just . . .' Her eyes flicked to the door then back to Keelin. 'I don't know why I'm here,' she said. 'Alex said it would be fine, but it's not right. I . . .'

She looked as if she might cry, and, despite herself, Keelin couldn't help but feel sorry for the girl. 'Are you OK?' she asked as Nessa nodded a half-hearted 'yes'. Her eyes on Keelin again, and she was about to say something, there was a weakening there, an unravelling of sorts on her face. 'Keelin, I need to—'

'Awww,' one of the blondes behind them said, hopping down off the counter. 'You two are so cute! Did you say she's your aunt?' she asked Nessa, who was dabbing her eyes with the tips of her fingers as delicately as she could, trying not to disturb her make-up.

'No—'

'That's not—'

They both hurried to deny it, speaking over one another, but the blonde was either too drunk or too high to pay much attention. 'Adorable,' she cooed, aiming her iPhone at them. 'Smile!' The woman was almost cross-eyed – definitely pills, and strong ones – as Nessa wrapped an arm around Keelin's shoulders, her hair swishing past Keelin's face in an inhale of apple shampoo. Keelin pulled her mouth into a rictus smile, wishing it was all over and she could go to bed. Why had she allowed Henry to talk her into this stupid party in the first place? 'Oh my God, you look amazing,' the blonde said, holding the photo out so Nessa could admire her own beauty. 'Wait.' The girl tried to grab Keelin's arm as she walked away, fingertips grazing flesh. But she didn't turn back.

Upstairs, she locked the bedroom door behind her, falling face first on the mattress with a groan. She lay there in the dim room, concentrating on her breathing. A crack of thunder outside and the sky was lashed with lightning,

346

burning bright for just a second. She hated this. She hated the small talk and the slurring voices, the same, boring tales being told over and over, smiling blankly because she couldn't hear what the other person was saying and she didn't want to ask them to repeat themselves for the fourth time. She hated feeling as if she was a 'bore' because she didn't do drugs and would rather Henry abstained in front of her teenage son. She hated all of it. When she was younger, Keelin would have made herself stay downstairs and pretend that she was having fun. She would have kept refilling her glass of wine, hoping no one noticed her discomfort and thought her strange. She would have smiled through it all, silently wondering why she couldn't just relax and enjoy a party, like a normal person, what was wrong with her? That was partly what had drawn her to Henry in the first place, how gregarious he was, how comfortable he seemed in any social situation. She had hoped some of his confidence might rub off on her, and even if it did not, she could hide behind him, bask in his reflected glamour. But she was thirty-seven now, and she didn't have to pretend any more. She was who she was; she had nothing to prove to anyone. She sat up on the bed, and tied her hair into a high ponytail. She would stay here for the night, and she would watch the storm tear the sky apart. It was her birthday. She could do whatever she wanted.

The guards would ask about that decision, when all of it was done. They'd wonder what Keelin was doing when a young woman lay in the grass outside their house, dying alone in the dark.

I was in my room, she would tell them. I don't know what happened to Nessa Crowley. I swear.

She said it so many times she nearly believed it herself.

CHAPTER FORTY-FOUR

No, we said, when we first heard the rumours about Alex Delaney and Sinéad Crowley.

No, it can't be.

We refused to believe it was true because memories have always been long on the island; the past was a country we kept close to our hearts. We could remember Alex and Nessa, the way he would look at her. We remembered the boy's grief when she died, his bloodless face as he stood at her grave. We knew he had suffered as much as we had done and we forgave him because of it. The son shall not suffer for the iniquity of the father, we said to each other. The boy is an innocent in all of this.

But the boy is now a man, and he has set his eyes upon the youngest sister. They have made plans, we hear, plans to leave Inisrún together. They will never come back.

And there will be no Crowley Girls left on this island then. Not a one.

CHAPTER FORTY-FIVE

The day after Keelin had gone to the Crowleys' house to beg Sinéad to have some sense, she had to watch her son leave her. Alex packed another bag, a larger one this time, shoving his favourite clothes and books into it roughly. He picked up a framed photo of him and Evie and wrapped it in a Superdry hoodie, placing it on top of his belongings, then zipped the case up. He took no other photos, not even the one from his first day at primary school, Alex resembling a miniature businessman in his shirt and tie, flanked by his mother and his grandmother, both women holding back their tears. He looked at the frame for a second, hesitating, then turned it face down on the bookshelf. Keelin tried not to be hurt by that.

'Please,' she said. She stood at the front door, her son halfway down the rose path, wheeling the suitcase behind him. 'Alex.' Her arms outstretched, reaching for him, for her baby, but he had gone too far from her. She couldn't bring him home now.

Henry's hand on her shoulder. 'We have to trust him,' he said, as she choked back a sob. 'You have to let him go, darling.'

But she had lost so much, was it wrong that she didn't want to lose Alex too? Evie rarely came home now, and it would only worsen when she went to university, when she started earning her own money and met a partner of her own. She would forge her own life, she would forget this island, and she would do so with frightening ease. All Keelin had ever wanted to do was to be a good mother, and it was clear she had failed with both her children.

Henry pulled her back inside the house and she tensed at the feel of his fingers on her skin. *You're dangerous*, she thought. *I don't know what you are capable of. I am afraid of you.*

But she said nothing. She let her son walk away. Alex would leave Inisrún that day and he would take the last Crowley Girl with him. Bríd and Brendan would be alone in that house, surrounded by photos of their dead daughter, nothing but their grief to sustain them. And it would be her fault, yet again.

As Henry led her into the kitchen, she thought about the Sunday morning after the party. The body had been found in their garden and Brendan Crowley was told to get there as fast as he could. Keelin never did find out who made that phone call. Perhaps it had been her, she thought afterwards; perhaps she had been the one to ring the Crowley house. *There's been an accident*, she imagined herself saying. *It's an emergency*. Brendan arrived within twenty minutes, running into the hall, his breathing laboured. Where is she? he shouted. He was wearing two different shoes, his hair sticking up at odd angles, his eyes wild. He looked around at the guests, the beautiful people shivering and crying, pale-faced. The debris of the night before around them, stale smoke, sticky floors, shards of broken glass glittering like diamonds. Where is my daughter? he said again, but quieter this time, as if he knew already what the answer would be. A woman raised a shaking hand and pointed outside. Henry tried to hold him back – he was a father himself, he would say to the guards later, he only did it to protect the man, he wouldn't have wanted to see Evie in that condition if the roles were reversed – but Brendan pushed him off, forcing the double doors to the patio open, looking left, right, Where is she, where is she? And then he saw her.

No, no, Brendan said. He sank to his knees beside the body. *Nessa*.

There were no words after that. A noise came from the man and it was primal, gut deep, like an animal with its leg caught in a trap. His head pressing against the girl's, her blood smearing across his forehead, like stripes of war paint. Daddy's here now, he whispered. He scooped her up, cradling her limp body to his chest, but his legs buckled, giving way beneath him, and he fell to the ground, still carrying his daughter in his arms. He had only wanted to take her home, he would explain to the guards, when they asked why he had contaminated a potential crime scene in such a foolish manner. And he hadn't known it was a crime scene then, Brendan told them. He had assumed it was an accident. All he'd wanted was to bring his daughter home, where she would be safe.

When it was over and Keelin could still hear that man screaming in her dreams, when she awoke, sweating, with the words '*Nessa, Nessa*' heavy on her tongue, she would ask herself: was it worth it, what she had done?

Yes, she would whisper to herself, for she had to believe that it was.

It was worth it.

CHAPTER FORTY-SIX

The Crowley Girl

Keelin stayed in her bedroom the night of her thirty-seventh birthday party, and it was peaceful there, watching the lightning lick the earth clean until her bedside lamp began to flicker. A stutter at first, on–off, a whisper of a *what was that?* Barely perceptible, unless you were looking for it. Then on–off, and staying off, the island tumbling into a darkness so deep it felt as if her eyes had been cut out of her head. The music stopped, a roar of voices – 'What?' 'Fuck.' 'Shit.' 'That's my foot, you ass.' Above it all, she could hear someone calling her name.

'Keelin? Keelin?'

Footsteps on the stairs, too slow to be Alex's, and not deliberate enough to be Henry's, she wasn't sure who this person was. A knock at the door – how did they even know she was in here? – then another one, more insistent, then a voice. 'Keelin.' It was Miles. He sounded sober, despite the coke; his capacity for drugs had always been much higher than Henry's. 'Are you awake? My apologies for disturbing you but we're in rather a bind. The power has gone out.'

'Miles?' she said, making her voice sound sleepy. 'Sorry, I had too much to drink and I . . . I must have dozed off.' She was wearing her pyjamas and dressing gown, her face slick with night cream. She didn't want him to see her like this, she would have bet good money he'd never seen his own wife without perfectly applied make-up. 'Can you get Henry to fix it?'

'We don't know where he is, I'm afraid,' Miles said.

'OK. I'm coming.' She swung her legs off the bed, cursing as she walloped her foot against the bedside locker. Using the light from her phone, she changed into leggings and flat boots, pulling her Musto rain jacket over a threadbare geansaí. 'Right,' she said to Miles when she opened the bedroom door, hoping he wouldn't notice her oily skin, 'let's get this sorted, shall we?'

'Don't worry,' she reassured guests as she passed them, downstairs and through the hall and into the kitchen, their worried faces illuminated by phone light. 'We have it under control.

'Have you seen Henry?' she asked but everyone just shrugged in response. No, no, not for a while now, they said. Wasn't he with you, Keelin?

'There's a small generator for Misty Hill,' she told Miles as she hoisted herself up onto the counter in the utility room, feeling around the top shelf of the cupboard for a torch. She handed him the three flashlights she found there, along with two boxes of matches and a plastic bag of tea lights left over since Christmas. 'But it needs to be switched on and I'm not sure where it is, Henry's always taken care of that kind of thing . . . I don't understand where he's got to – it's not like him to miss a party.' She took Miles's outstretched hand and jumped down, the bang of the cold tiles reverberating through her shoes and into the soles of her feet. 'Right,' she said. 'You distribute those – and tell people to be careful with the matches, will you? The last thing we need is for the house to go up in flames. I'll go look for that husband of mine.'

Henry wasn't in Evie's bedroom, and Alex's was locked, as it always was on nights like this, her son squeamish at the thought of strangers wandering into his room and touching his things without permission. She retraced her steps, feeling her way downstairs and through the hall, but it was so dark she could barely see, even with the candles twinkling on windowsills and tabletops. She called out his name again, but it was lost in the chatter of voices:

– we're stuck here, this is such a –

– this is what you get in the country, I suppose, but *really* I –

– bloody Ireland. I don't –

– Do you have *any* signal yet? This is absolutely –

And then she realised. She still hadn't seen Alex, and she

356

hadn't seen Nessa either. The girl had probably pulled her son into a corner, whispering that she wanted him, now, hoisting up her dress to show him how ready she was. She would care little that they were in Keelin's house and could be caught at any time. That would be half the thrill for a girl like that, she bet. Keelin imagined Nessa pressing her body against Alex's, reaching her hand down to – no, she said to herself, queasy. She wasn't going to think about that. She spotted Miles lighting a row of tea lights on top of the mantlepiece, his forehead creasing in concentration. 'Have you seen Alex?' she asked, but Miles shook his head. 'He wouldn't have gone out?' he asked, recoiling as a gust of wind punched against the windows. Was the glass strong enough to withstand the pressure; should she be warning people to stay away from them in case they shattered? 'Not in this weather, surely?'

'I don't know.' Keelin tried the handle to the patio, and the door flew open, almost taken off its hinges. 'Shit,' she muttered, struggling to close it behind her. She pushed against the wind, feeling as if she might be knocked off her feet with the weight of it. 'Alex,' she yelled. 'Alex!' The sky was on fire, like shooting bursts of fireworks. A cracking whip of light and then an ear-splitting grumble of thunder, too close together for comfort. The storm must be right above the house, she could hear her father warning her; she needed to get inside immediately. She stumbled, the wind slamming her into the garage, her spine straightening in pain as she felt the wallop of the wooden wall against her back. She could barely see now, blinded by the heavy rain, but she fumbled until her fingers grasped the iron handle, trying frantically to slot it sideways. She nearly had to crawl into the garage, using all of her strength to pull the door closed behind her. 'For fuck's sake,' she muttered as she pushed herself to standing, shaking the wet off her like a dog.

Then, with a prickle against the nape of her neck, she could feel that something was behind her. She turned around, trying to see in the shadows, but there was nothing. Still, she could sense a presence, a person. Someone holding their breath and waiting for Keelin to move first.

'Henry?' she said uncertainly. 'Is that you?'

'Darling.' She heard her husband come towards her, his steps heavy on the wooden floor. 'I came to get more food – the caterer's left the platters out here and we've enough to feed an army, but the weather was so frightful I thought I should stay here and wait it out. But I don't think it's going to get any better, is it? What rotten luck.' His hand on her waist, nudging her towards the door. 'Let's go back to the house, shall we?'

'But we have to get the generator sorted and I can't find Alex, where –' She stopped, inhaling deeply. *No,* she thought. It couldn't be. *No.* She took another breath in through her nose, until she was sure, *she needed to be sure.* But she had been correct. It was the scent of apple shampoo.

A flare of lightning, double quick, throwing the room into

relief. The shape of a person standing beside her husband, tall and thin. A woman. She disappeared into the night again but Keelin pressed the keys on her phone with trembling fingers and held it up, pointing it in their faces. Smeared lipstick and an unbuttoned shirt and a short black dress, bunched around the woman's waist, showing lace knickers and long, lean thighs.

'It's not what it looks like,' Henry said, and Keelin couldn't help but laugh, because of all the stupid, clichéd things her husband could have said when she caught him fucking a twenty-one-year-old, that had to be top of the list.

'Shut up,' she said. 'Just shut up, just, just –' And she reached out and hit him across the face as hard as she could. She did it again, scrawling at him, wanting to feel his skin under her fingernails. She would draw blood from this man. 'I'll kill you,' she shouted. 'I'll kill you, you piece of shit.'

'Keelin . . .' The young woman's voice. 'Stop it. You're hurting him.' Nessa stood in between them, wincing as Keelin's flailing hands struck her too. 'Henry.' She crouched down. 'H, are you OK?' As Keelin kept her mobile light trained on the two of them, she could see the girl stare at her husband like she had loved him for years. It was then she realised this wasn't a one-time thing, a drunken snog after too many glasses of wine. This had happened before, and more than once. The worst of it was how good they looked together – they made sense in a way Keelin suspected she and

Henry never had. Both tall and beautiful and infinitely desirable. How long had this been going on for? she wondered, suddenly nauseated. How could she have been so blind?

'Get out of my house right now,' Keelin told Nessa Crowley. 'Or I'll kill you too.'

CHAPTER FORTY-SEVEN

Maria Crowley, Nessa's first cousin

MARIA: I wasn't a Crowley Girl, not really.

NOAH: How do you mean?

MARIA: Ah, you know. I lived in Dublin with my mam in those days – I was only on Inisrún during the summer. And I didn't look like the girls either; I wasn't going to be darkening the door of a modelling agency any time soon, let's put it like that. And they were weirdly innocent in lots of ways. They didn't drink, they never had boyfriends. Nessa used to think everything from Dublin *had* to be better. She'd want to see what kind of clothes I was wearing, what music I was listening to. I told her she was the lucky one, growing up full-time on the island, but

361

she didn't listen. (laughs) Nessa never listened if you were telling her something she didn't want to hear.

NOAH: Were the three of you close?

MARIA: Róisín and I clashed a bit – we were probably too alike, to be honest – and Sinéad always seemed so much younger than me back then. But there was just the year between me and Nessa so we were inseparable.

NOAH: Would you tell us about the Nessa Crowley you knew?

MARIA: Everyone talks about how smart she was, but Nessa could be silly too; she loved stupid jokes, the sort of thing you'd only find funny when you were still in fourth class. She was a good singer too, better than half the chancers who came to record at Misty Hill over the years. When Saoirse sings now, she reminds me of Nessa.

NOAH: Saoirse is your daughter, correct?

MARIA: Yeah. I got pregnant when I was seventeen. He was staying at Misty Hill, a musician. He's pretty well known in Ireland but he never made it anywhere else, much to his eternal disappointment. (laughs) I would have been screwed if it wasn't for Keelin.

NOAH: In what way?

MARIA: When she heard I was pregnant, and it was a Misty Hill resident who was responsible, it was Keelin who insisted the Kinsellas step in. She knew what it was like to be a single mother, how scary it could be, you know? She persuaded Jonathan and Olivia that the retreat needed a hairdressing salon and I should be the one to run it. I try and remember that when . . . well, I try and remember it, anyway.

NOAH: We heard it was you who told the guards about Nessa having a relationship with Henry Kinsella. Is that true?

MARIA: (pause) It is. I was in shock when they came to talk to me and I just blurted it out, but the guards promised it was all 'confidential'. Confidential, me hole – sure, who else could have leaked everything to the press later on?

NOAH: When did Nessa tell you that she was in a relationship with Henry Kinsella?

MARIA: It was the autumn of 2008, maybe September or October? She was back at college anyway. I kept saying, you're only messing, this is a joke, right? Like, everyone thought Henry was a ride, but he was almost twenty years older than us and he was married! To *Keelin* – our uncle's best friend. It was mental.

NOAH: Did you tell anyone else?

MARIA: No. Maybe I should have. But Nessa swore me to secrecy and I didn't want to betray her trust.

NOAH: Did you ever tell Nessa to end things with Henry?

MARIA: Did I what? I begged her to break it off from the very first moment she told me, but there was no talking to her. She was *weak* for that man. She kept telling me how sweet he was, how amazing he was in bed, how he made her feel things she didn't know were possible. She couldn't see beyond him.

NOAH: Were you shocked by their relationship?

MARIA: Shocked? I don't know about that. Nessa could be . . . she could be determined. If she wanted something, she would go to any lengths to get it. Everyone on the island was in love with her, but sure, of course that wouldn't be good enough for Nessa, of course she'd have to set her sights on one of the Kinsellas, just to prove she could.

NOAH: Were you jealous of her?

MARIA: Jesus. You're really asking the difficult questions, aren't you? (silence) If I'm being honest, I suppose I was a bit. No, I was. I was . . . The three of them were so beautiful and I didn't want that to matter to me, because it didn't matter to them. But it's easy not to care about your appearance when you look like those girls. And I didn't.

NOAH: Do you miss her?

MARIA: Ah, come on. Of course I do. The pain never goes away. You'd have yourself driven demented thinking through all the different scenarios, the what-ifs and maybes. Wondering what our lives would be like now if Seán hadn't suggested Nessa as a tutor, or if I'd refused to babysit Evie Kinsella on my own that night, made Nessa stay in the cottage with me to mind the two girls. What would she be doing now?

NOAH: What do you think happened to Nessa that night?

MARIA: Do I believe Henry Kinsella did it, is that what you're asking? Well, he had more reason than most, didn't he?

NOAH: Because of the affair?

MARIA: Not just that. I'm talking about the reason Nessa went to the Kinsellas' house that night. What she was going there to tell Henry.

NOAH: What was she going to tell him?

MARIA: Nessa said she was pregnant. And it was Henry Kinsella's child.

CHAPTER FORTY-EIGHT

Keelin's life would forever be broken up into two halves: before that night and afterwards. That was the barometer by which she measured the passing of time now, by how many days, weeks, months had passed since Nessa Crowley's body was found face down in their garden. Six weeks later, the State Pathologist would declare what everyone on the island had secretly been thinking all along, that this wasn't an accident – Nessa Crowley had been killed. The garda inquiries officially became a murder investigation, Henry Kinsella the prime suspect. The guards were preparing the Book of Evidence, compiling their no doubt compelling reasons why Henry ought to be prosecuted, and that time should have been a period of relative calm for the Kinsellas, a lull in which they could lie low until the DPP made her final decision, but Henry had different ideas. You did what? Keelin demanded when she discovered her husband had given an impromptu interview to a journalist, a young woman chancing her arm by turning up on the doorstop of Hawthorn House, saying she'd heard a few rumours and wanted to give Henry the chance to tell his side of the story. He invited the woman in for tea and answered all her questions, saying yes, he was the main suspect in the Misty Hill murder, but he was an innocent man. This was a miscarriage of justice, but he believed in the integrity of the Irish legal system and he knew his name would be cleared in good time. Once Henry had outed himself like this, and on the record too, the media had carte blanche to use his name in connection with the case, printing his photo, and Keelin's too, robbing them of the anonymity they would have been afforded until Henry was formally charged. What were you thinking? she asked him, but she already knew. She had searched for the journalist's name online, a Fionnuala Cronin of the *Irish Daily*, shaking her head when she came across a photograph of an attractive brunette in her early twenties. Henry never could resist an opportunity to talk about himself to a pretty girl. After that, it was months of fielding endless phone calls, trapped in the house when other journalists began to arrive on the island, giving a curt 'no comment' when she had to push past them to take her daughter to school.

She remembered so clearly the day their solicitor delivered the news that the Director of Public Prosecutions had decided the case against Henry Kinsella wasn't substantial enough to convict him beyond reasonable doubt. They were in a bright, airy suite of a Kinsella Hotel on the banks of the River Lee in Cork, where they'd spent the last week awaiting this very phone call. They were alone. Keelin hadn't wanted her daughter to see any of this; Evie was anxious enough as it was, constantly on the verge of tears, jumping out of her skin whenever she heard a loud noise. A grind school in the city had agreed to allow Alex to repeat his Leaving Cert there for he hadn't been able to sit his exams the previous June, so ruined with grief was he after everything that had happened. My Nessa? And Henry? Alex had said when he heard about the affair, going mute once more, as he'd done when his grandmother died. But there was no suggestion of a psychologist this time. Therapy would require Alex to tell the truth, and none of them were allowed that luxury now. 'It's done, there's no case against me,' Henry said when he hung up the phone with the solicitor. 'It's time for us to go home, Keelin.' She asked him to arrange for the Misty Hill helicopter to pick them up in Cork but no, Henry wanted to drive to Baltimore and set sail to Rún. Like old times, he said. It was early February, almost a year after Nessa Crowley's death, and the cold air was merciless when she opened the car door at the pier. She tucked her hair under her hat, pulling her scarf over her face, as much to disguise herself as to protect her skin from the stinging wind, but Henry took no such precautions. 'Just me and the wife,' he said, handing cash to the teenage boy who was collecting fares. The boy paled, looking around him for assistance, unsure of what to do – should he allow the Kinsellas onto the boat? What was the right course of action? – 'Is there a problem here?' Henry asked, and the boy panicked, stepped aside and let them pass. When the boat docked, the boy jumping onto the pier to throw the thick, twisted rope around a rusting bollard, Henry walked ahead of his wife, carrying their suitcases. There was a hand on Keelin's elbow, yanking her back. It was Niamh Murphy, her pink scalp visible through her thinning hair. 'You should be ashamed of yourself coming back here,' she hissed. 'After what your husband did to that poor girl.'

That poor girl. That poor family. That's what everyone kept saying. Things like this didn't happen here, not on Inisrún, not to people like them. It was inconceivable and yet somehow, it was true. One of the Crowley Girls had been murdered, and the man responsible was back on the island, refusing to leave.

'Sorry,' said Tadgh, the man who drove the island taxi. 'There's no room.' Keelin peered through the windscreen into the half-empty minivan but she said nothing. 'Are you sure?' Henry asked, taking a leather wallet out of his pocket and tucking two fifty-euro notes into the man's palm. The taxi driver didn't even check to see the amount. 'I don't want your money,' he said, tossing it at Henry, his lip curling in disgust. 'It doesn't matter,' Keelin said, her hand on her husband's chest, reminding him to stay calm. 'Let's go.' They walked up the boreen together, dragging their suitcases behind them. It had begun to rain and by the time they reached Hawthorn House, their clothes were drenched

369

through, Keelin's socks squelching in her low-heeled boots. Johanna was waiting for them; she had the heating on, she said, Evie was upstairs taking a nap, and there was a smell of something delicious wafting from the kitchen, cinnamon and sugar, bringing back memories of lazy afternoons spent in the Stein cottage. 'You're frozen,' Jo said as she hugged Keelin, refusing to look at Henry. 'What were you doing, walking in a downpour like this? Was Tadgh the Taxi not running today?'

Keelin was too miserable to reply, so she just clasped her friend's hands. (They'll hate you for this, she had said when Johanna offered to take a week off work and mind Evie while they were in the city, awaiting the DPP's decision. I'll survive, her friend had replied. And I'm not doing this for *him*, I'm doing it for you. You're the one I care about.) She embraced Jo at the front door, urging her to take one of Henry's golfing umbrellas for the walk back to her parents' house. She waved Jo off, holding it together until her friend was out of sight, before she sank to the ground, weeping. 'Please, darling,' Henry urged her. 'Evie can't see you like this; she'll be frightened. Everything has to go back to normal now.'

But none of this is normal, she wanted to say, and it was only going to get worse. It must have been the guards who leaked that information to the papers, Henry would insist later. Who else could it have been? The decision not to prosecute him left the media free to say whatever they wanted, now there was no trial to jeopardise. There were breathless editorials about the 'evidence', the scratches on Henry's face, the bonfire that had been lit, the fact he and Keelin were nowhere to be found when the young woman had died. A friend of the victim had disclosed details of Nessa and Henry's 'inappropriate' relationship to the guards, with anonymous sources claiming Henry Kinsella had been afraid Nessa was going to tell his wife about the affair and he was determined to shut her up any way he could. The tabloids' headlines were screaming: 'Naive Nessa' and the 'Kinky Kinsellas', how the 'Perverted Pair' had lured the innocent young girl into their 'Millionaires' Sex Lair', detailing the hardcore pornography that had allegedly been found in their bedroom, the sex toys and BDSM equipment. In every article, Henry's net worth was referenced, the cost of Keelin's designer handbags highlighted, photos of their 'sumptuous home' used to further enrage the Irish public. Phone records were referenced, how the guards discovered her husband had spent hours talking to Nessa in the months before her death, thousands of text messages exchanged. And then, finally, they talked about the deleted photograph which was recovered from Henry Kinsella's computer by IT experts. A picture of a naked young woman with blonde hair and long legs and a swallow tattoo on her ribcage. It was deliciously salacious and yet, even with this wealth of material at their disposal, it was still Keelin herself who garnered the most column inches.

Could a woman really enjoy that kind of depraved sex life? One would have to wonder if Keelin Kinsella was simply desperate to keep her man – it hasn't escaped our notice that he was attractive, and only becoming more so with age. But if that was the case, why

371

did Mrs Kinsella allow a woman so much younger than she into her home? Why place temptation in her husband's path? Surely Mrs Kinsella could have guessed that something like this would happen. But the biggest mystery of all is this – why, after this public humiliation, has Keelin Kinsella stayed with her husband? Standing by your man à la Tammy Wynette is all very well, but when he's been accused of murder?

Henry wanted to sue the newspapers for defamation and invasion of privacy, and perhaps he should sue the guards too, for leaking the information in the first place, but Keelin persuaded him that was a terrible idea. Who knew what else they would find, given half a chance? They had enough on their plate trying to keep this mess hidden from Evie, and worrying about what seemed to be her son's inevitable nervous breakdown. She couldn't deal with much more.

That was when the phone began to ring.

'Hello?' she said as she answered the landline. 'Hello?' There was a muffled not-quite silence at the other end of the phone. 'Hello?' she said again, but there was still no reply, so she hung up.

The phone rang again and the phone rang again and the phone rang again and the phone rang again. Evie, staring up at her with troubled eyes, asking who it was. No one, Keelin told her daughter. It's just a wrong number. Nothing to worry about, pet.

'Hello?' she said, answering the phone. 'Hello?'

'Hello?'

'Who is this?'

And then, finally, a voice. Telling Keelin to leave this island and to take her murdering bastard of a husband with her. There was no place for the Kinsellas on Inisrún any more. Kids, Henry said, ignore them. But she thought she recognised the voice, the rhythm of the language had a familiar cadence, like a piece of music she had heard years ago and could not remember the name of now. She was haunted by that, the half knowing of this person who hated her so much. Maybe if she closed her eyes and listened more closely, she could solve the mystery of the phantom phone calls. But she didn't do that. She didn't want to know.

After putting her daughter to bed and sending Alex yet another unanswered text, Keelin lay awake in bed, Henry snuffling gently beside her, the sheets pulled up to his chin; she marvelled at how serene he looked. It was then she heard a knocking at the front door; a fist against wood. *One, two, three.* It heralds death, she explained to her husband when Evie left for school the next morning. My mam heard the knocks the night before Daddy died. We've had enough death in this house, he said. Just forget it, Keelin.

She tried to forget it, but each night she heard the knocking, and each day the phone calls came. She and Evie looking at one another, the colour draining from the little girl's face, her fingers curling tightly around her crayons. I'm scared, Mummy, she said, staring down at the table. Make it stop.

Henry took matters into his own hands and cancelled the

Eircom account. Who needs a house phone in this day and age? he said. The mast had been erected by then, the service was good, they even had Wi-Fi on the island now. They would just use their mobiles from now on, he said brightly.

Keelin tried to forget it, but the emails were pinging into her inbox every day, telling her she was fat, she was ugly, she was an unfit mother and her children should be taken away from her. Henry asked her to hand over her passwords so he could delete any unsolicited emails before she had a chance to read them. I hate seeing you so upset, he said. But what did it matter if he did that, when the postman arrived every lunchtime, unable to fit all the mail into their letter box? Hundreds and hundreds of envelopes, the postmarks from all over the country but the words were the same, declaring them murderers, perverts, monsters. The photo of Keelin and Nessa from the party cut out of newspapers, with captions written in red ink in the margins, pointing out in precise detail Keelin's physical shortcomings in comparison with the Crowley Girl, how much prettier, thinner, younger Nessa had been. It should have been you who died, one person wrote.

Henry came home one day to find his wife sitting in the hall, surrounded by piles of post. He went into the kitchen, she could hear him riffling through the drawers, and he returned with a black plastic bag. Evie mustn't see any of this, he said and he picked up fistfuls of letters and stuffed them into the refuse sack. When he was finished, he sat beside her, the two of them with their backs to the door, legs stretched out before them. We can't leave this island, not now, Henry said. You have to try. For me. For us.

She did her best. In front of her daughter, she tried to behave as if nothing had changed. She phoned her son every evening, asking about his studies, how he was settling into his new apartment near the grind school, checking that he was taking his meds. Alex, you know— she said at the end of the day's call, and each time he cut across her. Yes, Mam, he said. I know. I won't say anything.

She learned to ignore the stares, the sudden hush cutting through every room she walked into, as sharp as a scalpel, and the whispered conversations that would start as soon as she left. 'That's . . . you know, the . . . Yeah, she's the wife . . .' They said Keelin was afraid of Henry, and that was why she didn't leave. They said she knew too much and she was petrified the man would kill her too if she opened her mouth. They said she didn't want to give up the Kinsella money, she would never divorce Henry and risk losing access to his bank account. Some of them even said that maybe she had murdered Nessa Crowley herself, driven mad with jealousy, swinging for the beautiful young thing trying to steal her man.

Keelin wished she could tell them that they were wrong. They were wrong about all of it.

She lost her job in the women's shelter soon after, years' of study and training dismantled in one awkward, five-minute phone call. It wouldn't be appropriate for her to continue, her boss said gently. We have to think of the optics. You understand, don't you, Keelin? And she said yes, of course she understood. There didn't seem to be much point in arguing, reminding the other woman that Henry hadn't been convicted of anything, he hadn't even been charged in connection with the murder. Everyone had already made up their minds. She told her husband she didn't mind about her sudden unemployment – the commute to the city had become too demanding anyway, she reassured him, and it was better that she concentrate her efforts on Evie and Alex now, they needed her. But she was lying. Keelin had constructed so much of her identity around her work, it had become the one thing she could point to and say, yes, I am a good person – and now it was lost to her. She didn't know who she would be without it.

A Kinsella family meeting was called soon after as a matter of urgency. Jonathan and Olivia arriving to the island first, followed shortly by Charlie. Henry's parents hadn't been to Inisrún since news of the murder broke; they stayed in Scotland until the DPP's decision was made – it wouldn't look good for the Kinsella Group, they explained, and Keelin said, we have to think of the optics, I suppose, and Jonathan said yes, that's it exactly, Keelin. At least *one* of you comprehends how dire the situation is. Before the family arrived, she lit the stove in the kitchen, arranging freshly baked butter cookies onto a china plate and brewing Darjeeling tea in a ceramic pot, the way Olivia preferred. 'Do you want to watch the *Wizards of Waverly Place* or *Hannah Montana*?' she asked Evie as she turned on the television, anything to keep her daughter distracted until her grandparents had left again. The Kinsellas wouldn't ask about Alex, they never did, and for once Keelin was glad of their ambivalence towards her son. How could she explain that his heart was broken and she wasn't sure it would ever be possible to fix it, or him?

'They're here,' Henry said as the door-bell rang. He wrapped his arms around her, his mouth close to hers. 'It's just you and me now, remember,' he whispered. The doorbell rang again and she hurried to greet the visitors. Keelin took her in-laws' coats with a 'hello, good to see you, thank you for coming all this way'. She ushered them through to the warm kitchen, offering them tea and biscuits ('I made them myself this morning!' she said) but Jonathan waved her off in irritation. 'I hardly think it's the time for fucking baked goods,' he said, and Olivia didn't frown at him, the way she usually did when her husband cursed. Charlie refused to sit, standing by the door with his overcoat on, glowering at his brother. Keelin drew a stool towards the table and she stared at the plate of biscuits she had put so much effort into baking, her gaze following the swirls and folds of the creamy mixture, while Jonathan told Henry what a disgrace he was, how he had brought shame upon their good name, the damage he had done to the brand they'd spent decades creating. Her father-in-law slumped down onto one of the stools, and Keelin could see how tired he was. The man was in his seventies but he'd always seemed like he possessed infinite reserves of energy and would live forever. But now he looked old, depleted. It was a hard thing, she thought, being a parent. Loving another person that much weakened you, in a way. It made you vulnerable.

Olivia put a hand on her husband's knee. She waited until the room was quiet before she spoke. 'You will leave here,' she said, in a tone that brooked no argument. Not that she was used to anyone arguing with her, what Olivia Kinsella said was final in this family. 'We will sell Misty Hill and the old house and you will sell this place too.' She sniffed. 'It was always too big anyway.'

'Where will we go?' Keelin asked, surprising herself with the hope in her voice. A fresh start, somewhere where no one knew them. Evie could make new friends, and Alex could go to university abroad, Paris, maybe, he had always been good at languages. That way, she could take care of her son, make sure he was safe, that he didn't—

'No,' Henry said, moving behind Keelin, both hands on her shoulders. The smell of him straightened her spine, reminded her of the pact they had made. What she had promised him that night in the shadows. 'We're not going anywhere. Inisrún is our home.'

Jonathan spluttered but Olivia shushed him. 'And what do you think of this, Keelin?' the older woman asked. Henry increased the pressure on her shoulders, just enough so only she would notice it, and she smiled at her mother-in-law. 'I am staying here too, where I belong,' she said. 'With Henry.'

She repeated the same line to Johanna, who begged Keelin

to reconsider, and later to Seán, who waited until Henry had left for the mainland before arriving on the front porch of Hawthorn House. She opened the door just a crack, fearful of who might be there, what trouble they might have brought with them, but it was only Seán Crowley, in threadbare jeans that were far too big for him; he had lost an alarming amount of weight. 'Leave him,' he pleaded. 'I don't know what I'll do if he hurts you too,' and then he started to cry, tears running down his cheeks. Keelin looked him in the eye and she said, 'I'm never going to leave Henry.' She shoved the door closed, stuffing her fingertips into her ears to block out the sound of him calling her name, Keelin, Keelin . . . Johanna phoned a few hours later. 'I heard Seán was round to see you today,' she said, her voice stiff, 'and you threw him out. After everything he's been through, do you really think that was fair?'

'He was getting upset.'

'Of course he's upset – his niece has been murdered. He's fucking devastated. And your husband is a—'

'My husband is what, exactly?'

'I don't . . .' Jo's voice quivered. 'I don't how much longer I can do this.'

I love you, Keelin thought. *You are my favourite person in this world, Johanna Stein.* 'You don't need to do anything,' she said. 'But don't call me ever again, do you understand me? We are no longer friends.' And she hung up the phone.

She told her best friends in the world to leave her alone and they did. She understood their reasons – it had become

379

too difficult, being associated with Keelin Kinsella. You could only tell someone to leave so many times before you began to wonder why they're staying. Maybe it's what they want, these women in these marriages, you think. Maybe it's their choice, you shrug, but what you're really trying to say is, Maybe it's their fault.

The seasons kept turning over on the island, the trees sprouting buds, blossoming green then shrivelling to rust, drifting off to leave the branches naked, shivering in the cold. 'Many happy returns, darling,' Henry said when she woke up on the morning of her thirty-eighth birthday. 'Thank you,' she said, pretending that she wasn't thinking about Nessa today, the first anniversary of the murder. The weight of a stone in her hand, craving skin to break open. The scream of *What have you done?* A body on the grass, a life seeping away. Her birthday and Nessa's death, bound together forever.

As time passed, she became increasingly frightened of slipping into the unknown dark where Brendan Crowley was waiting for her, screaming his daughter's name. Sleep wasn't for women like her, not any more. Sleep was for people who had nothing to fear in the night. She began to dread leaving the house too, weary of pretending she didn't notice the other islanders, people she had known since she was a child, staring at her with undisguised contempt. We'll build a gym, Henry suggested when he found her at the front door in her walking shoes, unable to go any further. We'll get the hairdresser to come to you, he said when her roots were showing and she refused to get the ferry to the mainland for her appointment at the salon. You can Skype Alex every evening rather than travel to see him, he said. I'll order the groceries online and have them delivered. Anything to make this easier for you, darling, he said. Her husband took such good care of her, finding more and more inventive ways to turn Hawthorn House into a haven, a cocoon within which Keelin could bury herself and never emerge. You won't have to go outside these four walls ever again if you don't want to, he promised her. The thought of what leaving would entail – getting out of bed, showering, blow-drying her hair, choosing an outfit – became too much for Keelin to even contemplate. She would stand in front of the mirror and look at herself, the bones picked out beneath her flesh, the bruise-like shadows under her eyes, and she thought she looked like a hag, a Cailleach come to steal children from their beds while they slept. Henry called a doctor, and then another one, continuing up the coast of west Cork until he found a practitioner willing to ignore the Kinsella name and make a house call to the island for a hefty fee. The doctor, a grim-faced man with a thick thatch of grey hair, spent less than two minutes with Keelin before he prescribed the same antidepressants Alex was taking to help him cope after Nessa's death. And what about sleeping tablets? her husband asked. And maybe some Valium too, I think she could benefit from that. The doctor added both to the list, warning Henry to keep the medication out of harm's way.

His wife might be at risk of doing something 'stupid'; she seemed the type, he said.

Don't worry, darling, Henry said when the man left to catch the ferry. I'll take care of you. Her husband doled out the tablets, asking to see her tongue afterwards to make sure she had swallowed them. He did extensive research on what foods would help ease her symptoms, deciding they should cut alcohol and sugar from her diet. He chose the time she was to take her sleeping tablet, and he set the alarm clock to wake her at an hour he deemed appropriate – we don't want you staying in bed all day, he said. That wouldn't be good, now, would it? He chose clothes for her, advised her on how she should wear her hair and her make-up. I think it's important to make an effort, he said. You'll feel worse if you hang around all day in your tracksuit, won't you? And Keelin nodded and said yes, Yes, Henry, you're right, Henry, because she didn't want to have to think – thinking meant remembering; apple shampoo and swallow tattoos and blood smeared on hands and the weight of that stone in her hands and a voice screaming, *What have you done? What have you done?* – and she was grateful to Henry because he had taken away the need for her to think about anything any more. She just did what he told her to do.

'I'm going insane,' she said matter-of-factly. 'I'm losing my mind.'

'Don't worry, darling,' he said. 'I'll take care of you.'

That was the beginning of it all, she would realise later, but by then, it was too late.

CHAPTER FORTY-NINE

When the Tuatha Dé Danann came to Ireland, they stood on these shores and they looked at these lands and they thought, *Yes, yes, we will take this place for our own.* And they burned their ships and they set fire to their oars so there would be no turning back.

And so too did we bring flames to Misty Hill. We did so in the shadows, waiting until all eyes were closed and the last breath had settled for the night. The reporters had left our island by then, bored of the tragedy that had happened here. The artists had gone too, taking their money with them. All that was left on Inisrún was this cluster of empty cottages and the Crowley Girl's bones rotting in the graveyard beyond. We were despairing and we were angry. And so, on the second anniversary of her death, we gathered.

Afterwards, none of us could remember who lit the first match, or, for that matter, who lit the first house.

It was none of us.

It was all of us.

In the end, it didn't matter. We stood together in silence and we watched that cursed place burn to the ground. Ashes to ashes.

There would be no turning back.

CHAPTER FIFTY

Barbara Phelan. CEO of Lighthouse Éire, a charity helping victims of domestic violence in Ireland

BARBARA: I've been working with Lighthouse Éire for almost twenty-five years now. Our mission has always been the same, to make Ireland safer for women and children. Violence against women is a global epidemic, it affects one in three homes worldwide and—

NOAH: We should probably acknowledge there are male victims too.

BARBARA: Of course. I tend to use the pronouns 'he' for perpetrators and 'she' for victim because while women can, of course, be abusers, and violence also occurs in LGBTQI+ relationships, the statistics bear out that the majority of victims are female. In the twenty years since we started monitoring femicide in this country – that is the broadly accepted term for the killing of women and girls by men – one in every two victims is killed by a current or former male intimate partner. Failing to note the gendered aspect of these crimes does us a grave disservice. It prevents us from moving forward and finding solutions.

JAKE: Yes, I agree. (pause) According to our research, Keelin Kinsella worked for your organisation for a number of years.

BARBARA: She worked in the Cork branch, yes. She volunteered there when she was a student and she took a job as a support worker in 2001. After she was married, she remained with us but in a part-time capacity until 2009.

JAKE: Did you know her well?

BARBARA: Jane Maher was the coordinator of the Cork centre, but I did meet Keelin on a number of occasions. She came to Dublin for training sessions, conferences, et cetera. She disclosed to me her own experiences of domestic violence in her first marriage. She spoke very publicly about that, I should say, including giving a paper at a national summit on this issue. This isn't a violation of her confidence.

NOAH: Her ex-husband categorically denies any such abuse.

BARBARA: Have you spoken to him?

NOAH: Not on camera – he refused to talk with us. But he sent a strongly worded statement refuting Keelin's allegations.

BARBARA: I see.

NOAH: You don't believe him?

BARBARA: I believe women, Mr Wilson. This is what we're trying to fight here at Lighthouse Éire. We're trying to dismantle the myths around domestic violence. That victims lie about being abused, for one. Or we assume it only affects a certain 'type' of person, which is deeply classist and, as a case such as Misty Hill proves, also incorrect. Domestic violence excludes no age, no socio-economic background, no race or religion. It is found in every stratum of society, and our organisation is working to shine a light on that. We want to eradicate intimate partner abuse for good.

JAKE: How would you characterise Keelin's relationship with Henry Kinsella?

BARBARA: I'm not in a position to comment on that. It would be highly unethical of me to do so.

CHAPTER FIFTY-ONE

Kimberly Singer, leading expert on intimate partner violence with Soul Spirit Sisters, Sedona

KIMBERLY: After reviewing the tapes you sent me, I must admit I was quite concerned by the dynamic of Henry and Keelin Kinsella's relationship. I've never treated Keelin – that would be difficult, considering my practice is in Arizona! – but there were certain behaviours I found troubling. She's hesitant to talk during the interviews; she often looks at her husband before speaking, as if to make sure she has 'permission' to do so; she's palpably nervous around him.

NOAH: She's also on camera. That makes a lot of people nervous, especially if they're not used to it.

KIMBERLY: True. But if a client came into my practice

exhibiting those behaviours, I would see it as a red flag. In my expert opinion, these are typical signs of abuse.

NOAH: We told Henry Kinsella that you had reviewed their tapes and we outlined your concerns, giving him the right to reply. He told us he'd never been violent with Keelin. He swore he had never raised a hand to a woman in his life. The idea made him feel ill, he said. (pause) You're shaking your head at me, Kimberly. Have I said something you disagree with?

KIMBERLY: It's a common mistake, presuming violence has to be physical. That's why even the term we use, 'domestic violence', is so woefully inadequate.

NOAH: What term would you use?

KIMBERLY: Intimate-partner terrorism is my preferred choice, although of course that does exclude the abuse of children in the home.

NOAH: Terrorism? Isn't that a bit well, dramatic?

KIMBERLY: Not for the women trapped in these relationships. When I started my practice, I would ask clients to share the worst thing that had ever happened to them. I was expecting to hear horrendous stories of physical violence, but do you know what they told me?

NOAH: What did they tell you?

KIMBERLY: Each one of them swore that while the beatings were devastating, the mind games were worse. The manipulation, the isolation, the control – emotional, financial, sexual – the humiliation; these were the things that took women years to recover from, and yet these particular wounds left no visible scars; there was nothing to show to the world around them and say, 'See, look what he did to me.' Coercive control—

NOAH: Coercive control is psychological abuse?

KIMBERLY: Yes. I've seen a massive increase in such behaviours reported by my clients over the last number of years. People have a better understanding today that *physical* violence is wrong; they don't dismiss a neighbour beating his wife as a 'private family matter' the way they might have done in the past, so abusers have had to adapt their methods of torture. We call it terrorism because abusers turn their homes into a war zone, with the women and children as their hostages. They won't let them go without a fight.

NOAH: If they're not in any immediate physical danger, why don't these women just leave? If their partner isn't hitting them or—

KIMBERLY: Don't you think it's interesting that we always ask 'Why do these women stay?' We never think to ask, 'Why are these men violent?' or 'Why won't these men stop terrorising their partners?' (pause) OK, Mr Wilson. I'm going to ask you to do something for me.

NOAH: Sure.

KIMBERLY: I want you to put a few things on the table. Your house keys to start. You got that? Now, your car keys. Your wallet containing all the money you have in the world, and every one of your credit cards. I want your passport and your driving licence too. And last of all, I want the shoes off your feet. We good?

NOAH: Yes.

KIMBERLY: From here on out, these items belong to me. You can't touch them again without asking for my permission. Is that clear?

NOAH: Crystal.

KIMBERLY: Now tell me, Mr Wilson. Why don't you just leave?

CHAPTER FIFTY-TWO

'This is outrageous,' Henry said to Keelin as the show broke for ads. They had been waiting for tonight to come ever since Channel Three's publicity machine had swung into action; it'd been two weeks of long-form features in the Sunday papers, interviews with Jake and Noah on afternoon chat shows and feminist podcasts, debating the issues with shock jocks on national radio stations. Henry requested an early preview of the documentary, but all they'd received back was an oddly formal note from Noah, saying a preview wouldn't be possible at this time but he hoped Henry would agree it was a fair representation. What does that mean? Keelin asked, but her husband shrugged. I don't know, he said. We'll have to wait until June to find out.

'Don't you think it's outrageous?' he asked now, waving his hand at the television.

Kimberly, she thought. It was so . . . American, but it suited that therapist, with her suspiciously wrinkle-free forehead and the oversized necklace she wore to disguise a crêpey décolletage. 'I can't believe she's allowed to just *say* things like that,' her husband seethed. 'I've a good mind to phone my solicitor right now and tell her to start legal proceedings. It's defamation, surely. That woman is impugning my good character by implying I'm abusive.'

'You'll have a hard time suing her,' Keelin said, 'given she's in the States. Free speech is enshrined in their constitution.' She snuck a look at him. 'When did Noah give you the right to reply? You never told me about that.'

'Oh, he rang a couple of months ago, babbling about some American therapist, and I told him it was nonsense, obviously. Imagine, to be lumped in with men like your ex. I would never do *anything* like that.'

'Well, Channel Three is covered then, legally, if they—'

'What if Evie is watching?' he said, ignoring her. 'And hears that woman accuse her father of being an *abuser*?'

'She's not going to watch it. And she would never believe that of you anyway.'

Of course she wouldn't, their daughter thought Henry was perfect. She always had done. She remembered when Evie had begged for a smartphone for her twelfth birthday; she was the only girl in her form who didn't have one, she'd complained. Henry, disregarding Keelin's misgivings, ordered the latest iPhone and had it delivered to the school in Scotland.

Within hours their daughter had googled the Misty Hill case, even though she was strictly forbidden to do so, and discovered about the affair. But it had been her mother whom she had rung that day, screaming down the phone that she hated her, that this was all Keelin's fault, she was pathetic and old and no wonder Daddy had gotten sick of her, she'd probably *driven* him into Nessa's arms. She waited until her daughter's voice went hoarse and the girl began to cry instead. It's not true, is it, Mum? she said. Please tell me it's not true. And Keelin told Evie not to believe everything she read. Her father loved her very much. It's OK, pet, she had said. It's all going to be fine.

'All I've ever tried to do is protect you and the children, is that so wrong?' Henry reached for the bottle of red wine warming by the open fire, pouring some into his glass. 'You wouldn't have survived in those early days without me. I'm hardly one of *those* men, am I?'

'No, darling,' she said, fingering the ice-cream charm hung around her neck. 'Of course you're not.'

'Then why did that therapist insinuate that I am?' He yanked her hand away with force. 'Would you *stop* doing that, Keelin, for God's sake. I'm on my last nerve here,' he said. 'You know I find it annoying when you're playing with that bloody thing. Why would you insist on wearing it tonight, of all nights?'

Henry always said the charm looked cheap, like something she'd found as the prize in a Christmas cracker. You have

394

boxes of beautiful jewellery upstairs, he protested. Why on earth do you insist on wearing that gaudy little knick-knack? He didn't know Nessa had given the necklace to her, nor did he understand the meaning behind it; he just thought it was naff, and unbecoming of a Kinsella woman. But as she had gotten dressed today she had picked the chain up from her jewellery box, watching herself in the mirror as she fastened it around her neck. She wanted the Crowley Girl to be here with them, in a small way.

'Shh,' he said as the commercial break ended, pushing Keelin's feet off his lap. He leaned forward, his elbows resting on his knees, staring intently at the television. Why wasn't he more afraid? she wondered. Surely he must know the danger this documentary put them all in. 'I don't think that's the most flattering colour on you,' he said as the camera zoomed in on Keelin's face. 'I told you to wear your pink Hermès scarf with that suit. It needs something to lift it.'

'I must have forgotten,' she said. She did look pale on the screen, her face angular and tired, the make-up doing little to disguise the dark circles under her eyes. What would the people watching think of her? Would they wonder who that woman was, this perfectly groomed, middle-aged woman with her chic clothes and neat hair and legs crossed primly at the ankles? Her face and her voice in millions of homes all over Ireland and the UK tonight – *The Crowley Girl* was the most anticipated documentary of the year, *The Times* had said, guaranteed to get a huge audience share. The viewers would be mostly female, the columnist wrote, questioning why these gruesome true crime reports appealed so much to women, given they were the primary victims of such crimes. But Keelin could understand it. Women had always been taught to be afraid; it was embedded in their very DNA, passed down from mother to daughter, a poisonous heirloom. Women wanted to hear these stories of rapes and murders so they could search for the clues, the warning signs the victim had missed but which would ensure their own survival if such a threat befell them. They needed to hear of the mistakes, the dark road walked down at night, the door opened, the lift taken from a smiling stranger. I wouldn't do that, they would whisper, incredulous at the victim's stupidity. Hoping it would be enough to save them when their time came.

Would Jonathan and Olivia watch the documentary? She knew Evie wouldn't. There had been a FaceTime call that morning where her daughter had informed her scornfully that no one watched television any more except for 'like, old people', but if this show sold to Netflix, she would have to kill herself, and her mother would be to blame, naturally. Everyone in Ireland would be glued to the documentary, and Keelin knew too that if she walked the island tonight, every living room would be lit up, each body to a one planted on sofas and chairs as this documentary – their home, their history, their shame – played out for all to see. Suffering through the indignity of having their greatest tragedy picked apart by outsiders for sport. Were Bríd and Brendan sitting in their mausoleum on the far side of Rún, listening to Keelin swear that her husband was innocent? Would Alex and Sinéad be watching it, wherever they were? They'd been gone from the island a full week before her son deigned to phone her, reassuring Keelin they were safe and happy. 'Ta sé ar fad taobh thiar dúinn anois,' he said, speaking in Irish because he knew Henry would insist Keelin put her phone on loudspeaker so they could both listen in. 'Tá sé ar fad thart.' *It's all behind us now. It's all over.*

And maybe it was. The Australians had gone home months ago, and they obviously hadn't discovered any new information to justify reopening the case; the guards hadn't come knocking on the door of Hawthorn House, search warrants in hand. The gardaí had always been sore about their failure to prosecute Henry for the murder, embarrassed by the international criticism of the investigation, the skewering of the sloppy mistakes that had been made, both in the Irish media and abroad. If there had been a shred of evidence in the programme that incriminated Henry, the guards wouldn't have wasted time in arresting him. They must be safe, she thought. And she didn't need to worry about Alex either, as Henry kept reminding her. He would never tell Sinéad what he had seen that night, because if he did, he would lose her, and her son wouldn't survive losing another Crowley Girl.

Keelin's face disappeared from the screen, replaced by other, heartbreakingly familiar ones. Maria Crowley. Bríd.

397

Alice Buckley. Seán. Johanna . . . *Oh Jo* – how she missed her friend. Henry was talking now, handsome and forlorn. It had been difficult, he explained, these last ten years, paying the price for a crime he didn't commit. He had cared for Nessa Crowley, of course he did, and he regretted their unfortunate, er, dalliance. The truth was that he loved his wife more than anything in the world but it had been a difficult time in their marriage, she hadn't been well in those days, *psychologically*, and he'd been under immense pressure to keep everything together for the sake of the children. It was a stupid mistake, but it wasn't a crime to have an affair, surely? And while he was devastated at what had happened to the young woman – and in his own home too! – he was an innocent man and deserved to have his name cleared. He wanted an apology from the state. An acknowledgement from An Garda Síochána that they had attempted to frame him with the flimsiest of circumstantial evidence. I don't know what happened to Nessa Crowley the night of the party, Henry said, wiping tears from his eyes. I swear to you on my children's life, I don't know.

He was convincing, Keelin thought. It was almost unnerving how skilled at lying her husband had become, or maybe he had always been this good and she hadn't been paying enough attention.

They watched the rest of the documentary together, the talking heads and the opinions for hire, the outlandish theories and the wild speculation. Henry's phone started to light up, dozens of missed calls and texts and notifications on social media. 'Look at all these friend requests on Facebook,' he said, holding his iPhone out for Keelin to see. 'And my Twitter followers, crikey. I can't keep track. I'm at twenty thousand . . . Keelin, I'm at twenty-five thousand, oh my God, thirty thousand followers.' Henry jumped off the couch, knocking over his glass. Keelin sat there, staring at the red stain seeping into the cream carpet and she did nothing. She was good at that.

'"The guards had nothing on Henry Kinsella",' Henry read aloud. '"Yet another cover-up to save their incompetent arses".' He punched the air triumphantly. 'Go on Twitter there,' he told her, gesturing at his iPad resting on the arm of the sofa. 'Come on,' he said when she didn't move, clicking his fingers in front of her face. 'Search for the hashtag TheCrowleyGirl. This is amazing, Keels. The tide is turning, I can feel it. I always knew this documentary was going to save us. I'm a bloody genius.' His phone rang again, Henry grinning when he saw the name on the screen. *Emma,* he mouthed at Keelin. 'Well, hello there,' he said as he answered. 'How's my favourite solicitor doing tonight?' Keelin could hear the woman's voice on the other end of the phone, excited, speaking rapidly. 'I know,' Henry said. 'It looks good, doesn't it? Should we set up some interviews for next week?' He paused, nodding at whatever the solicitor was saying. 'Have you seen the response on Twitter? The Crowley Girl is trending at number one,' he said. 'It's incredible. I've over thirty thousand followers now.' He laughed. 'Maybe I could have a second career as one of those influencers that Evie is obsessed with – my kingdom for my teenage daughter's approval.'

Keelin tapped the screen of the iPad, clicking into the Twitter app. #thecrowleygirl, she typed in, deliberating over every letter. Giving herself enough time to go back, if she wanted, to save herself, but she knew she wouldn't. She was unable to resist the temptation.

@GrahamLFC19 I think the wife did it. Hell hath no fury, etc #thecrowleygirl

@MaireadNiR #TheCrowleyGirl theres something not quite right about Keelin Kinsella. She knows more than shes saying like

@SarahFitz63 I don't know why it's the Crowley *Girl*. We don't call men *boys*, do we? It's so sexist and reductive #Thecrowleygirl

@TrionaSunshine why do these women stay with men like that? I'd be out the door before you could catch me, its mad #thecrowleygirl #toughloveisland

@DubsFiveInARow96 wudnt of kicked nessa crowley outa bed for eating crisps, would ya? What a ride 👀👀👀 #thecrowleygirl #nessa #ride

@Styvesain I'm not being funny, but what is going on with Keelin Kinsella's face?! 😳 Easy on the botox, Joan Rivers #TheCrowleyGirl

*

'I think we bloody well did it,' Henry said to his lawyer, collapsing on the couch beside her. She exited out of Twitter quickly, placing the iPad on the coffee table. 'I'll email you tomorrow,' he said. 'We need to get our strategy in place, we should take advantage of this publicity . . . Yeah, I get you. I know . . . yeah, I agree. OK, bye. Bye.' He hung up.

'Emma said it couldn't be going better,' he said. He frowned as he looked at his wife. 'Are you all right? You look a bit peaky.'

'I went on Twitter, like you told me to,' she said, touching her fingers to the ice-cream charm again, holding it close, 'and people were saying *awful* things about me. Why would you want me to see that, Henry?'

'Oh, stop.' He nudged his shoulder against hers. 'Darling, you're being too sensitive. Look.' He picked up his phone and scrolled through the app. 'There are lots of kind comments about us – you must have just skimmed past them without even noticing. Don't be so negative, not tonight. I'm not in the mood.' He peered at the screen again. 'Bloody hell, I have forty-five thousand followers now! This is incredible.' He looked at her again and frowned. 'Keelin, come on. This is a good thing, for both of us. We should be opening a bottle of champagne to toast our victory, not pouting because of a few trolls on social media.'

'There's still –' she checked her Cartier watch – 'fifteen minutes left in the programme. Isn't it a tad premature to be celebrating already?'

'Don't be such a worrywart,' he said, scrolling through his feed again, turning the phone around to show Keelin more tweets. There were no comments about Henry's appearance, she noticed. He was allowed to have aged within the last ten years, but for her to have done so was a crime against humanity, apparently. Keelin had never been a great beauty and she had long made peace with that fact; she'd recognised as a teenager that she would have to rely on her personality rather than her looks to get by in life and she always felt that decision had served her well. Most people didn't care about that stuff; it was superficial nonsense. It wasn't until she was being blamed for her husband having an affair with a woman young enough to be his daughter that Keelin realised how wrong she had been.

'If the Australians had anything new, they would have revealed it by now. This –' Henry waved at the television, barely looking up from his phone. 'This is just summing up.'

The camera panned across the barren landscape, a bleak sky bleeding into a grey sea, a thick mist crawling down the briar-covered hills on its hands and knees, rocks slashing out of the water by the pebbled beach. Noah's voice-over, the camera zooming out and away, showing an aerial view from above the island. 'During my time on Inisrún,' he said, 'I have spoken to many people about the Misty Hill murder. Some were intimately connected with the case, others witnessed the aftermath from a distance, and yet all of the people on this beautiful island off the coast of west Cork have been deeply impacted by the death of Nessa Crowley. I came here looking for answers, and yet I leave with none. Instead, I have even more questions about what happened here on the night of 14th March 2009. And I'm not the only one.' Bríd Crowley's face appeared on TV then, a tiny sore in the corner of her mouth, her eyes red-rimmed and tired. 'No one could get onto the island that night,' she said, staring down the camera lens. 'And no one could get off it either. It was someone here who did this, someone on Inisrún.' Her voice broke, and she held back a sob, nodding at the person behind the camera that she was able to continue. 'If it wasn't Henry Kinsella who killed my daughter, then who did?' she asked, and the screen faded to black.

The credits rolled – a film by Noah Wilson, Keelin saw, 'assisted by Jake Nguyen'; Jake must have been demoted for his loyalty to her – mentioning the assistance of the Kinsella family and thanking the people of Inisrún island for their cooperation.

'It's done, darling,' her husband said, and she attempted to smile at him. It was over. They were safe. So why did she feel so . . . dissatisfied? She'd been living on her nerves for the last few months, the last ten years, really, waiting for a moment of reckoning, one that meant she would have to pay the price for her sins. And now the moment had passed, and this was all that was left, this gnawing feeling inside her, this widening gyre of emptiness. She felt utterly hollow. Maybe she had wanted something to happen, she thought. Maybe she had wanted to be punished.

Henry's iPhone lit up again, and he took call after call. 'Yes, of course I'll sit down with Piers. I'm a huge fan of his work,' he said, making a rapturous face at Keelin, reading out emails to her in between – *The Late Late Show* wanted him as a guest the following Friday, as did *This Morning* on ITV. The *Sunday Times Magazine* was looking for an in-depth interview – 'six pages with photos, Keels, I'm going to suggest they take the pics here; it will be great publicity for the Misty Hill relaunch.' Her husband smiled, baring his teeth, and she almost recoiled from the euphoria that was radiating from him like oil spitting off a hot frying pan. She started to speak but his phone rang again. 'Well, hello there,' he said, standing up and walking to the fireplace. He stared at his reflection in the mirror above the mantlepiece as he spoke. 'I haven't heard from you in a while.' He laughed. 'I'm joking, Seb. Relax.'

Keelin eyed her own phone, recharging in the corner of the room. She didn't unplug it, check to see who had been contacting her, how many friend requests she had on Facebook, what invitations for interviews were waiting in her own inbox. She didn't care about any of that. There were only two people she wanted to hear from and the longer she avoided her phone, the easier it was to pretend that perhaps there would be a message from Johanna waiting there, one from Seán too. *We watched the documentary*, she imagined the texts saying. *We love you, Keelin. We miss you.*

She wouldn't reply to either of them – it wasn't safe; it was best to keep the people she loved at arm's length, where they couldn't get hurt – but it would be enough to know they were out there, thinking of her. That someone in this world remembered Keelin Ní Mhordha, that the woman she once was didn't die alongside Nessa Crowley that night.

She started to shake, her teeth chattering so loudly that Henry looked at her in alarm. 'I have to go,' he said to his friend, hanging up and throwing his phone onto the sofa. He grabbed the cashmere blanket from the other chair and wrapped it around her body. 'Are you all right? he asked, muting the television. 'It's fine, darling,' he said, putting an arm around her. 'It's just the shock. But it's all over now. We're safe. All of us. I promise you.' She rested her head on his shoulder, catching that word – *safe* – and holding it to her heart.

'It's just you and me now,' her husband said, and as she closed her eyes she could picture the rest of their life together. How quiet it would be, just the two of them rattling around this enormous house, the years stretching out before her in an endless series of days and nights, and days and nights, over and over again, until she died. She would never leave this island again.

'Thank you,' she said to him. 'Thank you for everything.'

CHAPTER FIFTY-THREE

The Crowley Girl

After Keelin had threatened to kill Nessa Crowley, there was a stunned silence. The three of them standing in the garage, wondering who would be the first to run out into the storm. Keelin kept her phone aloft, still pressing on the keys to light the room as best she could. She needed to see this. Nessa, staring at Henry. Reaching out to touch him again, but he didn't look at her, pulling away so the young woman's fingers grazed off his shoulder. She was waiting for Henry to defend her, Keelin realised, to tell 'the wife', the frigid bitch, the nag – what had he told this woman about their marriage? What excuses had he made for his wandering eye? – in no uncertain terms that Keelin couldn't treat his girlfriend in such a fashion. Nessa was expecting a proclamation of love; she wanted a planting of a flag at her feet, calling her home.

'Henry,' the girl said in a small voice. 'Your face is all scratched up. Let's go to Maria's house, she won't mind. We can wait there until the electricity comes back on.'

'Excuse me? You think you're bringing my husband to the house where my six-year-old daughter is staying? Are you out of your fucking mind?'

'I didn't mean it like that,' the younger woman cried. 'I thought it would be better if we left until you calmed down. He's hurt. You hurt him, Keelin.'

Had she hurt her husband? she faltered for a moment. She shouldn't have hit him; there was never any excuse for that. She was as bad as her ex, resorting to physical violence to make her point. 'Henry,' she started, but then she saw Nessa take hold of her husband's hand, interlacing her fingers through his, and Keelin wanted to hit her across the face. She never knew she could have such a fierce desire to inflict pain on another human being.

'You should go,' Henry said, dropping Nessa's hand. 'My wife and I have to—'

'But, but, what about us?' Nessa said. She tugged on the ends of his shirt, like Evie did when she was desperate for his attention. 'What about . . .' She broke off, glancing at Keelin. 'What about what I just told you,' she hissed. 'About the . . . the *baby*.'

'The baby?' Keelin asked, looking between the two of them. 'What baby?'

Nessa whimpered, looking to Henry for help but he refused to meet her eye. 'I'm sorry,' she said. 'I didn't mean for you to find out like this. It wasn't supposed to happen. I—'

Keelin put her hand up to stop the younger woman from talking and she started to laugh, growing more hysterical as she saw the bewildered expression on Nessa's face. 'Oh, sweetheart,' she said. 'You're saying Henry got you pregnant? That's not possible, I'm afraid. He got a vasectomy two years ago, didn't you, *"H"*? Not that he consulted me about it – I'm just the stupid wife, amn't I? He told *me* he had to go to the mainland for some "business", arrived home a few days later with –' Keelin made a snipping gesture with her fingers – 'and acted like I should be grateful. Said he didn't want to risk me getting depressed again, like after Evie was born. It was a good thing, he said, he did it for me. I didn't know the real reason for my husband taking away my chance to have more children was because –' Keelin was screaming now, spittle running from the corners of her mouth, but she didn't care – 'he wanted to fuck twenty-something-year-olds without using a fucking condom.'

Nessa's face crumpled, her mouth quivering, and she ran past Keelin, throwing the door of the garage open. 'Shit,' Henry muttered as the wind tore in, whipping against the garden furniture and knocking the folded chairs to the ground with a bang. Without thinking, Keelin went to follow Nessa but she didn't get very far, bumping into Alex by the back door, his mouth gaping open in shock. 'What happened?' he cried, looking in the direction the girl had disappeared in. 'She was crying. What did you do to her, Mam? What's *wrong* with you?'

'I didn't . . .' she started to say, but her son wasn't listening. He was running after Nessa, calling her name. 'Alex, come back, it's too dangerous in this weather.' She tried to go after him but there was a hand around her waist, restraining her. 'Get off me,' she said through gritted teeth, elbowing Henry in the ribs, but he held her so tightly she couldn't move. 'Let go of me, you piece of shit.'

'No,' he said, spinning her around so she was facing him, clamping her arms to her sides. 'You have to let me explain.'

'Explain what? That you've been fucking one of the Crowley Girls? I don't think that needs much explanation.'

'That's not fair,' he said and she couldn't be sure if he was crying or if it was just the rain running down his cheeks. 'Things haven't been the same between us since Evie was born, you have to admit that.' She didn't have to admit anything, for she had thought they were happy, thought their marriage was a good one. 'And I was there for you during all that, wasn't I?' he said. 'Throughout the depression and the—'

'Are you actually using my post-natal depression against me?' she snarled. 'What is wrong with you?'

'Darling,' he said, leaning in to kiss her, but she turned her face away from him. 'Keelin. Please. I love you.'

409

'Oh, fuck you, talking about *love* while you shagged the both of us at the same time. What if you've picked up some sort of disease from her? You'd be happy giving that to me, would you?'

'That's not possible.'

'And how, prey tell me, do you know that?'

'Because she . . .' The rest of his words were muffled.

'She what?'

'She was a virgin,' he muttered.

'Oh, Jesus Christ, what is wrong with you?' she said, the bile rising in her throat at the very thought. 'And what about Alex? How could you do this to him?' She stopped. 'Oh, shit,' she said. 'What if this baby is *Alex's*? What are we going to do?'

He hesitated, and with a sudden heaviness in the pit of her stomach she knew the truth. 'No,' she said slowly. 'Of course not. She was never with Alex. That was just an excuse, wasn't it? You used my son as a way of deflecting attention away from the fact you've been cheating on me for months, didn't you? *Didn't you?*'

He didn't say anything, his mouth set in a grim line. He looked more annoyed than remorseful, as if irritated he had to explain himself in this way. Keelin dropped her head; she couldn't bear to look at him any more. How could she have been so stupid? Obviously that photo had been for Henry, not Alex. The excuse her husband had concocted was pathetic, it was such a blatant lie. And she had known it too, on

410

some level, of course she had known, but she didn't want to believe it. She hadn't wanted to believe that Henry could do this to her. She had loved him, and trusted him when he said he would never hurt her. And with Nessa Crowley, of all people! Keelin had been blind, hadn't seen the girl for what she was – a snake in the grass. A worm needling its way into the heart of their family.

She slumped, her body going slack, and she would have collapsed if it were not for Henry rushing to hold her upright. He rested his forehead against hers, breathing in when she breathed out, recycling air, until it felt like they were one, the way they had on their wedding day, when they promised they would belong to each other for the rest of their lives. They stood there for what felt like hours, Henry whispering, 'I'm sorry, I'm sorry,' into her ear, while she said nothing, shivering against him in her wet clothes. *I loved you,* she said silently, as her husband held her close. *I loved you so much.*

'What the –' he said, spinning around on his heel at the flaring of something sharp behind them. 'What was that?' he asked, but Keelin told him to be quiet, for that sound had been too familiar, echoing in her bones. She stood still, listening. And then it came again and there was no doubt in her mind this time.

'Alex,' she said, and fear snapped inside her, breaking her breath in two. She started to run without knowing where she was running to. She looked around her, rubbing the rain out of her eyes, but she couldn't see him anywhere. Henry ran past her, disappearing into the darkness, and she tried to chase after him but she kept slipping, hissing through her teeth as she pushed herself up from the mud, her scraped knees stinging. 'Alex,' she shouted, the thunder drowning out her voice. 'Alex!'

She almost wept when she saw him in a flash of lightning, standing in the rock garden, his hands loose by his sides. 'Alex,' she said, 'what are you doing? What happened? I heard you scream.' He was shaking, she realised, as if he was having a fit. 'Calm down, sweetheart,' she said, pushing his wet hair off his face. 'Tell me what's wrong.' He pointed towards the garden, and he turned his head away from her, gagging as he fell to his knees. Keelin crouched beside him, rubbing his back while he vomited onto the grass. 'You're OK, pet,' she said. 'You've had too much to drink, that's all. You'll be fine tomorrow.' The clouds shifted, breaking apart, and the moon became visible for the first time that night. Keelin blinked, her eyes readjusting in the dim light. It was only then that she saw her husband. Blood on his hands, standing over something – a collection of limbs, a scrap of black material – staring down at it with a blank expression on his face.

'Henry,' she said, fear unspooling in her stomach, loose and wet. It was a body, she realised. The body of a young woman.

'Henry, what have you done?'

CHAPTER FIFTY-FOUR

Joseph O'Shaughnessy, retired detective sergeant

JOSEPH: With a case like this, the first thing you'd do is set up jobs in order to track the movements of the deceased in the hours before death. Who they were with and where, what time, et cetera. After that, we spread the net wider in the victim's life, talking to their friends and family. You're trying to forensically take their life apart, in a way, to see if anything, or anyone, flags as suspicious. When there's so little DNA evidence, you're depending on witness statements, but witnesses are subjective, like. Their memories can be frail, and their recollections can be coloured by an agenda – you'd want to be mindful of that. Some might believe they're telling you the truth, but what they *think* they remember isn't actually what they *saw*. But all the same, usually there'll be a few witness statements that catch our attention. From there, you'll compile a list of persons of interest.

NOAH: Who were the persons of interest in the Misty Hill case?

JOSEPH: I can't be naming any names now, but in a case similar to that one, there could be people who might point the finger at another party guest. A man who was a friend of the host's and was flirting with the victim, 'had his hands all over her', one witness said. A man like that, he mightn't be the sort to take rejection lightly.

JAKE: Are you talking about Miles Darcy?

JOSEPH: Jesus, lad, I'm not talking about anyone in particular here now. I'm just talking in general, d'you get me? No one was charged for Nessa Crowley's murder, were they?

JAKE: OK. If this 'friend' was ruled out, where would you look next?

JOSEPH: Hypothetically now, the guards might decide that a young man who was friendly with the deceased could be an interesting prospect. A possible motive to be found there, if you were looking for one – if he was in love with the victim but found out the stepfather was sleeping with her, betraying the mother too. But you know, if there happened to be multiple witnesses who saw that young man unconscious in bed at the time of the murder, then the gardaí would have to look further afield, wouldn't they? Hypothetically speaking, like.

414

NOAH: That leaves Keelin and Henry. Was Keelin ever a proper suspect?

JOSEPH: Lookit, I wouldn't be the one to confirm or deny that. That wouldn't be in my gift at all. But I will say if I was investigating a case and it was similar to the one you're mentioning, then I *suppose* the wife could be a suspect. As a guard, you'd be looking for a motive – her husband was having an affair, she was jealous, she wanted the young wan out of the way. That kind of thing. You'd have to be checking if she had a decent alibi.

NOAH: Keelin didn't – sorry. What happens if 'the wife' doesn't have an alibi?

JOSEPH: I'd be looking at a few factors. Physical strength for one; was the wife capable of delivering a blow like that? And if she wasn't, then who was? Was anyone behaving in an odd manner? Doing things like, I don't know, lighting a bonfire in the middle of a storm. That might be seen as strange behaviour, couldn't it? Deleting text messages and emails. Scratches and bruises, that kind of thing.

NOAH: It's all circumstantial evidence though. The DPP said it wasn't enough to convict Henry Kinsella.

JOSEPH: You're right, lad. So a guard would then be looking at motive and alibi. With many of these cases, the alibi given is the wife, and that doesn't amount to much if she's a suspect too.

JAKE: And motive? Maria Crowley told us Nessa went to the

party that night to tell Henry she was pregnant, but the autopsy didn't find any signs of pregnancy, did it?

JOSEPH: No. And I can't talk about the specifics of this particular case, obviously, but if I was a guessing man, I would say there are two reasons a young girl might tell her boyfriend she was pregnant when she was not: a) she was mistaken due to her, eh, monthlies being late, or b) she was trying to force someone's hand. What do you think a man would do if he heard news like that? If he was desperate, like? But as you said, this is all conjecture! Henry Kinsella is an innocent man in the eyes of the law and that's that.

NOAH: What do you think, personally?

JOSEPH: It doesn't matter what I think personally – that's not what being a detective is about. It's about the facts. I will say one thing to you now though . . . I was a guard for a long time and I've learned to trust my instincts. When we bring a person in for questioning, we watch them carefully. You might have one person who's distraught. She can barely speak, she's in such a state of shock. I've seen enough throughout the years to know when that's genuine. But sometimes you'll get someone and the way they react is . . . *unusual*, d'you get me? They seem to be almost enjoying the whole thing. Such a person might fit the profile – narcissistic, lacking in empathy, unnaturally calm. I retired only two years ago –

NOAH: Congratulations.

JOSEPH: Thanks, lad. So, yeah, I'm retired, but there are

some cases that never leave you, and Nessa Crowley's murder is one of them. (coughs) It haunts me.

NOAH: Not just you, Mr O'Shaughnessy. Everyone I've spoken to during my time in Ireland is obsessed by this case. They all want to know what happened to the Crowley Girl.

JOSEPH: It's funny. Young women go missing in Ireland all the time. Some of them turn up dead, others are never found. You never know which cases are going to take a hold of the country's imagination. Which girls will be the ones we decide we're all going to care about, like.

JAKE: I suppose it helps if they're white, right?

JOSEPH: I don't know about that, lad. But it definitely helps if they're good looking.

NOAH: Which Nessa Crowley was.

JOSEPH: Yes. Which Nessa Crowley was indeed.

CHAPTER FIFTY-FIVE

The Crowley Girl

Keelin would replay this scene in her head thousands of times in the years to follow, and each time she would still remember the sensation of being stuck, her feet welded to the earth beneath her, leaving her unable to move. Henry, looking up from the body, and saying, 'What?' His face shocked. 'I didn't do this, Keelin.' Blood roaring in her ears as she understood the implications of what her husband was saying, of who was responsible instead. 'It must have been an accident,' she said, her breath catching in her throat. 'She's fine. Isn't she fine? We just need to get the nurse. This will be fine.' Alex's panicked breathing beside her, whimpering, 'Mam. Mam, please do something.' Henry crouching down beside the body again. 'Nessa,' he said. 'Nessa, can you hear me?' Shaking

418

the girl's shoulders, and feeling for a pulse on her wrist, and then sitting heavily on the ground, a whispered, 'Fuck. *Fuck.*'

Keelin felt as if she was being dragged out of her body, her fingernails scraping her insides as she left her skeleton, floating into the sky and looking down on the scene below. She was observing this taking place before her and it was like a play unfolding: the boy having a panic attack, gasping for breath; the man with a hand over his mouth, to stop himself from screaming, it seemed. A young woman lying in the grass, oh so very still.

'What happened?' the man said, standing up again. 'Tell me *exactly* what happened. Did she fall?'

'I didn't mean to. She wouldn't stop laughing at me.'

'Alex. Did you push Nessa?'

The boy was weeping openly now. 'She was laughing at me and I . . . Is she going to be all right, Henry? Please, I—'

'Shh,' the man said. 'We'll take care of this.' He looked at the woman standing there. 'Darling,' he said, and she looked around, wondering who he was talking to before she remembered that she was the woman, the 'darling' to whom he referred. This man was her husband and this boy was her son, and there was a dead body lying in her front garden.

'Keelin,' Henry said, taking her hands in his. She looked down, his flesh against hers, the pressure of his fingers too heavy for a dream. 'I need you to take Alex upstairs.' He fished a set of keys out of his pocket and handed them to her. 'Go around the back and use the fire escape.' That had been installed when a Hollywood actress insisted on staying in Hawthorn House while rehearsing for her West End debut, instead of the cottages; it was deemed necessary for insurance purposes. Henry had been furious, she remembered. Health and safety nonsense, he complained. It utterly ruins the facade. 'No one will see you that way,' he said now. 'Alex, you need to get out of those clothes immediately. We'll burn them in a bonfire.'

'We can't light a bonfire tonight – we're in the middle of a storm,' she said, and she felt furious with him for even suggesting it. 'Do you have any ideas that aren't completely ridiculous?'

'Keelin,' he snapped, 'we're going to have a bloody bonfire, all right? Just get Alex upstairs. I'll deal with this.' He grabbed the boy by the wrists and pulled him to standing. 'Alex,' he said, 'you stay quiet, do you hear me? You don't know anything. You drank too much beer and you passed out in your bedroom before the lights died. You don't know *anything* about this, OK? When the police come, you say nothing. Do you understand me?'

'Yes,' Alex tried to say, but he collapsed, his knees buckling. Keelin ran to her son, wrapping her arm around his waist and telling him to lean his weight on her. 'Come on, mo stoirín, you can do this,' she said. 'I'm here, I'm here now.' Alex's entire body was convulsing, and she had to limp with him as far as the fire escape, shouldering his weight. As she hauled him onto the first step of the metal structure, she turned to

420

meet her husband's gaze. He nodded at her and she nodded back. A decision made, in that moment, she would think later. One that could not be undone without ruining them all. Keelin had chosen her son, and Henry had chosen her.

'Get up, a stór,' she said, as Alex fell on the steps. 'Come on,' she urged him as they reached the top of the fire escape. She unlocked the large window, dragging him in with her, and locked it behind her. 'Stay here,' she told Alex, holding her hand out for his room key. She crept down the landing to his bedroom, using her phone as a torch. She gestured at her son to hurry after her, closing the door behind them. Alex collapsed onto the bed, trembling in his wet clothes. He rolled off the mattress and vomited beside the bed, spewing yellow bile onto the wooden floor. The bitter smell curled in her direction; she could taste it at the back of her throat.

'Tell me,' she said.

And he did. He thought this was going to be *the* night, he said, the night he finally told Nessa how he felt about her. They'd been having a great time, dancing and drinking, and someone passed them a joint; he'd never smoked one before, but he didn't want to look stupid in front of Nessa so he inhaled deeply, swallowing the haze inside him, losing himself. When he came to again, she was gone, and he couldn't find her. He met Miles coming out of the bathroom and he asked the older man if he'd seen Nessa. No, Miles had said, although he wasn't sure Alex was going to have much luck with that girl, she seemed rather a prig, and he pulled Alex back into the bathroom with him. Sprinkling cocaine on the cistern, chopping it finely with a credit card, holding out a rolled-up fifty-pound note for Alex to snort it with. It'll help you talk to her, Miles had promised. You'll feel more confident. The lights went out then, and Alex went to find Nessa, to make sure she was all right, and that was when he saw her running away from the garage, crying. He had followed her into the dark, stumbling on wet leaves, his heart beating in his mouth. She was sitting on a large stone in the rock garden, her arms wrapped around her legs. It was as if she was waiting for someone to rescue her, he told Keelin, and he wanted to be the one to do it. She looked surprised to see him, her face breaking in disappointment, and she cried even harder, make-up running down her face, but she was still beautiful, he thought. He wanted to comfort her, that's all. He hugged her then, and he couldn't believe how good it felt to finally hold one of the Crowley Girls in his arms. This was his chance, he thought, his opportunity to claim Nessa as his own. He had dreamed of this for so long. You're lovely, she said, sniffling, and that's what girls are supposed to want, isn't it? Why do girls always say they want nice guys if they don't? He'd tried to be patient with Nessa, he didn't want to pressure her, but he was tired of waiting now. He leaned in and he kissed her, but she pulled away. Alex, she said. Alex, I— And he kissed her again, because he knew that she could like him too if she just tried hard enough, she wasn't even *trying*. No, Alex, she said, and she pushed him off. He told her he loved her, he said it over and over again, but the girl wouldn't listen. No, Alex. So he said it again – I love you, Nessa, I love you. And she laughed at him then and she turned away, still smiling. She was going to tell her sisters, he realised. They would laugh at him together, call him pathetic; as if Nessa Crowley would ever be interested in someone like him, a loser with no friends, whose own father wouldn't have anything to do with him. And there was a rock in his hand and he didn't know how it got there and he didn't mean to hurt anyone. He just wanted to stop her – to stop the girl from walking away, to stop her laughing at him. To make it all go away. *Mam, you have to believe me, I didn't mean it. It was like I was out of my body and someone else was doing it.* But Nessa was falling, to her knees first, and then to the ground, and she hit her head. *That wasn't my fault, was it? That wasn't my fault.* He watched as she lay there, blood blooming like flowers in her temple, staining her eyes pink. He watched her die.

'I'm the same as my father,' Alex said, and he began to hit at his body, punching his legs and clawing at his chest. 'I'm a monster, I'm a monster—'

'Don't say that.' Keelin grabbed his hands so he couldn't inflict any more harm on himself. 'You're nothing like that man. I can't . . .'

She would still be with Mark in that house in Carlow, if it hadn't been for Alex. She had left her marriage to save him. She couldn't have allowed her son to be brought up in the carnage of that relationship, to stand by and watch as violence crackled down Alex's spine like electricity too, sparking in the palms of his hands, itching for girl flesh to satisfy him. She had left that night in order to break the cycle and she had. *She had.* Alex was nothing like his father. He was a good boy. She could not believe anything else.

'This was an accident, Alex,' she said. 'It wasn't your fault.'

He looked at her, and there was something ruined in his eyes. 'I'm going to jail, amn't I?' He bent over, his shoulders racked with sobs, and Keelin's heart twisted inside her chest with the savage fear of losing him. *He's a baby*, she thought. *He won't survive without my help.* 'No,' she said, lying down beside him on the bed. She curled around her son, as if he was still in the womb and she was the barrier between him and the outside world. 'Henry will take care of this. I promise you.'

Alex handed his mother the clothes that needed to be disposed of and she waited until she heard the tap turn on in his en-suite bathroom before she shoved her hand under the mattress, patting frantically until her fingers closed around the hard edges of the same notebook she had found all those months before. She threw it down the fire escape to Henry, along with the clothes, whispering at her husband to pull the buttons off the shirt and jeans. She had seen something about that on an episode of CSI. They wouldn't burn, re-appearing in the ashes, like breadcrumbs that would lead the guards back through the forest to their front door. She crept into Alex's room again and she sat with him until he fell asleep, humming a lullaby his grandmother used to sing when he was a child. She kissed the tips of her fingers and pressed them to his forehead.

'Is he all right?' Henry asked as she walked into their bedroom. He was sitting on top of the duvet in a dressing gown and slippers, his hair still damp from the rain. He'd lit a couple of scented candles, one on her bedside locker, another on his own, and the heady smell of bergamot and basil made her feel lightheaded. She crawled onto the bed beside him, lying on her stomach. She thought she would cry, would have welcomed the release, in fact, but she found she could not. Henry touched her neck and she shivered.

'I'll talk to Alex tomorrow,' he said. 'I'll explain what to say when the guards get here.' Keelin half moaned at the mention of the police and he shushed her. 'They won't be here for a day at least, we'll have time to clean up properly,' he said. 'The weather will work in our favour. I'll delete my messages, and I got rid of Nessa's mobile. I threw it over the cliffs into the sea. No one will find it now.'

'But they don't need the phone to figure out about your . . . your *involvement* with her. There's no way Nessa didn't tell her sisters about it, they're as thick as thieves. Those girls will blab to the guards and then they'll—'

'Blame me?' Henry asked. 'They can try. But there won't be any evidence. How could there be?' He half-laughed. 'I

425

wasn't the one who killed her.' He rested his hand on her head, began to stroke her hair. 'What was in that notebook? The one I threw on the bonfire?'

'Nothing,' she said. 'Just something that needed to be burned.'

She felt her husband get up, could hear his footsteps walking away from her, a drawer being opened. Then there was a delicious heaviness over her, a caress of cashmere. 'There,' he said, tucking the blanket around her body, 'I don't want you getting cold.'

'We had to do it, *we had to*, didn't we? It was an accident, Alex loved that girl, he wouldn't have . . . he would never . . . He wouldn't last two minutes in prison, he's not—'

'Shh, darling. You're getting yourself worked up.' He kissed the back of her neck. 'I think it's time I told you a story, Keelin.'

'Henry . . .'

'No,' he said. 'It's important you hear this.' And she could hear in his voice that it was, so she listened. 'Once upon a time,' he began, 'there was a man called Henry.' She propped herself up on her elbows at the mention of his name, but she still didn't look at her husband. 'The man was in his late twenties when this tale begins,' he continued. 'The world at his feet, some might say. There was too much of everything – too much money, too much sex, too much drink and drugs. One night, Henry and a young woman called Greta, they were at a family wedding in Surrey. Henry had been taking cocaine and Greta didn't like that. He became aggressive, she said, and even though Henry loved the young woman very much, he didn't like being told what to do. So he took more coke, just to prove he could. Greta came into the bathroom to find Henry and an old classmate snorting lines and she yelled at him, demanded they go back to the nearby manor where he'd booked a room for them. Henry didn't like that either; he didn't like being made a fool of in front of his friends. Fine, he said to Greta. If you want to go, then let's go. Outside, Greta tried to take the keys off him. You're blotto, she said. But he told her to get in the car, that he was perfectly fine to drive. Once they were inside, he yelled at her. How dare you! he said. You made me look like a fucking pussy. He drove faster, the windows open, Greta trembling in her thin summer dress. She begged him to slow down, her hands gripping at the sides of the seat. And then . . .' Henry paused. 'Well, I think you know what happened next, don't you?' he said. 'When I crawled out of that ditch, there was blood and glass everywhere, I could taste metal in my mouth and I was almost deaf, just this high-pitched ringing in my ears that wouldn't stop. Greta was trapped in the car, her head at a ghastly angle, and I knew . . . I knew she was dead.' His voice wobbled, and he took a breath to steady himself. 'And my first thought wasn't about her or her family, but about *me* – about the drink I had taken, all the coke. How my life would be over if the police found me there like that. My future would be ruined.'

'What did you do, Henry?'

'I got my father. I thought he would know what to do,' he said. 'And he . . .'

The car had crashed only five hundred metres from the hotel, so Henry ran back and slammed his fist against the door of his parents' room. His mother answered, her hair in curlers, and he told her to go back to bed, he needed to talk to his father. Jonathan took one look at his son, at his swollen eye and cut-up face, his stained clothes, and he nodded, as if he had been waiting for this day to come. They went back to the car, abandoned there in that quiet country lane, and Jonathan explained to Henry what they were going to do. You stay quiet, his father told him. You don't know anything. You drank too much beer and you passed out in the car when I was driving you home. You don't know *anything* about this, OK? Henry started to cry, and he pretended it was because of Greta but secretly, he was just relieved that his father was taking control and he didn't have to worry any more. Stop it, the older man said sharply. The girl is dead, nothing will change that. I don't see the point in making things worse by having you locked away for the next ten years. When the police came, Jonathan bowed his head and said it was he who was responsible. Henry had too much to drink at the wedding so Jonathan – a lifelong teetotaller – volunteered to drive his son and his girlfriend back to the manor where they were staying. A dog ran out in front of the car, Jonathan explained, and he had tried to swerve but lost control of the wheel. He'd told Greta to wear her seat belt, he said. She mustn't have listened, the poor girl. No one thought to ask why Jonathan had emerged from the crash unscathed, without a scratch on his body. No one asked the other wedding guests if they had any comment to make, although a number of them had seen the couple drive off alone, Henry behind the wheel of the car. It was much more convenient to simply believe Jonathan Kinsella was telling the truth – he was the founder and CEO of the Kinsella Hotel Group, after all, such a respectable gentleman – and to write it off as a tragic accident.

'That's what Kinsella men do for their children, my father said to me that night,' Henry told her now. 'We do what we have to do to protect our sons. And Alex is a Kinsella in all but name, he is to me at least. He'll be safe here, Keels. He'll be safe with us.'

She pushed herself up to sitting, trying to process what she had just heard. Only hours ago, she would have been appalled, disgusted at how her father-in-law had used his privilege and power to cover up Henry's crime, and how everyone else had simply looked the other way, all because of the Kinsella money. Is this what she had brought Alex into? she wondered. A family who believed they could buy their way out of any crisis, and never face the consequences? What would she be teaching her son if she allowed Henry to cover up for him too? But she was going to allow him to do just that, she realised. There had never been any real doubt in her mind, she would have died before allowing them to take her child away from her. She wasn't the person she had always thought she was, but then again, neither was Henry. How little she had known her husband, even after all these years. How many secrets he had kept from her.

He reached out to take her hand. 'And –' he hesitated – 'you're not going anywhere either, are you?'

'No,' she replied. She thought of Alex, asleep in his narrow bed. *Safe*. She knew she would do whatever was necessary to keep him that way. 'I'm not going anywhere.'

She could see the outline of her face reflected in Henry's eyes, the shape of her head drawn across his irises. She stood up, and he did the same, and she pushed her body against his. Skin against skin. They knew too much now; they had seen each other's broken bones, had learned each other's darkest secrets. The night had bound them to one another, stitching their hearts together with a black thread slicing so fine they couldn't be sure where one of them ended and the other began. Keelin had sworn her allegiance to Henry the moment she had walked away from Nessa Crowley's body without a second glance. *What God has joined together, let no man put asunder*. Henry and Keelin Kinsella had held hands in the shadows and they had set fire to the ship that had brought them to this land. There would be no turning back.

'What do we do now?' she asked her husband, her face against his chest.

'We wait.'

He lay down on the bed and she did the same, aligning

her body with his. She curled her little finger around her husband's. *Pinkie promise.* 'It's just you and me now,' he whispered as they waited together. The wind howling outside, voices chatting downstairs – she could hear her name, and then Henry's. People wondering where the hosts were, no doubt, *bloody rude* to leave their guests alone *with just a bunch of bloody candles.* Footsteps on the stairs. 'Oops,' she heard an American accent say, walking into Alex's room, 'the poor kid is out cold.' (Good, Keelin thought. There would be a witness afterwards, someone to swear that they had seen the boy in his bed, asleep. Innocent.) The woman giggling – 'Sweetie, we can't! – and then a low moaning, a thumping rhythm beat out against the door frame. The party winding down, voices petering out except for a few coked-up heads talking at one another, throwing stories at the walls like mud, seeing which ones would stick. They lay there, watching each other as the light turned grey, seeping steadily into the room, folding around them. In time she could hear the stirrings of morning, mattress springs creaking as someone turned over in the bed in the room beside theirs. A yawn, a tap running, a toilet flushing. A husky voice, barbed with cigarette smoke. 'Oh, do brush your hair, you look like a terrible slut,' she said. 'I need some air,' another woman said. Footsteps on the stairs again. The sound of the patio door swishing back and Keelin could almost feel the sting of the wind on that woman's cheeks, the deep inhale of breath as the morning air slapped her awake. Shifting from one foot to the other,

431

shaking the cold off her shoulders. Lighting a fag, coughing as the nicotine hit her lungs. The woman was looking out over the angry sea, and she would think how marvellous it all was, how beautiful the island was even on a day as desolate as this. How lucky the Kinsellas are, she thought, her eyes skimming past the rose-lined path and the rock garden to the water below. And then she saw something – she wasn't sure what, exactly, at first. Was it a doll of some sorts? A plastic bag? – her brain calibrating and recalibrating, unable to make sense of what was before her. She crept closer to it, disbelief turning to horror when she realised what this thing was, thrown at the edge of the Kinsellas' property. And she opened her mouth and screamed.

'Henry!' someone shouted from downstairs. 'Henry, get down here now!'

Keelin had been waiting for this moment all night, had known it was coming, yet she couldn't help but flinch at that scream. It was real then, she thought. Nessa Crowley was dead.

She looked at her husband, and she waited for him to tell her what to do.

'It's showtime, darling,' Henry said, and his eyes were bright with something she couldn't quite name. Not then, at least, but she would in time. 'Are you ready?'

When we woke the morning after the storm, we could smell death on the air.

Our young complained of a restless night, bogeymen waiting under beds, teeth sharp. They had been thrown from their dreams by a cry, the children said, and we laughed at their vivid imaginations but we could feel it too, like a quickening in our bellies, a wishbone caught in our throats. Something was stirring on Inisrún.

There's a girl missing.

We counted heads, hoping it wasn't one of our own who had been taken. That was before the news spread across the island.

It's one of the Crowley Girls.

Which one? we asked, as if it mattered. As if anything mattered, now that she was gone.

We saw Nessa everywhere for years after that, no matter how far we travelled from these lands. In New York, in Brisbane, in London, or Tokyo; every girl with tight jeans and a sweep of blonde hair was her, and we would say, Nessa, Nessa Crowley, is it you? Is it you? But then the girl would turn to us, and we would see the face more clearly, and it was never her. Her name trapped in our tongues forever, sewn there, swollen-full.

Other children were born on the island after she died, children who had never known Nessa or Misty Hill or what had taken place on Inisrún that night. We told them our stories. It was to keep her alive, we said, but maybe it was to keep ourselves alive too, the people we had once been before death had come to our shores.

Gather close, we said to them. And listen to our tale. For there were three of them, in the beginning.

We called them the Crowley Girls.

434

ACKNOWLEDGEMENTS

Juliet Mushens's initial notes on an early draft of this book were exceptionally sharp, and I have been blown away by her energy, drive, and work ethic. She is a powerhouse and I'm lucky to have her as my agent.

It's been a privilege to work with everyone at Quercus/ riverrun, particularly my brilliant editor, Jon Riley, who took such care with this book. Thanks also to Jasmine Palmer, Bethan Ferguson, Hannah Robinson, Dave Murphy, Talya Baker, and everyone else who worked so diligently on my behalf. Thank you to the team at Hachette Ireland, and to those who have worked on the foreign editions of my novels.

I've been fortunate enough to visit the West Cork Women Against Violence Project on numerous occasions and it's impossible to overstate the centre's importance. If you want to see what a vocation looks like, then look no further than

Marie Mulholland, who has dedicated her life to helping some of the most vulnerable women in our society. Thanks also to Susan Hurley and Colette O' Riordan – the work they are doing is extraordinary and necessary. If you are in a position to do so, please donate what you can to your preferred domestic abuse charity. These organisations are often underfunded and overworked, even though they are saving people's lives.

Thank you to Bertie Gillan of Inis Mór, Síle Foley of Inis Oírr, Áine Baker of Arranmore, and Neil O' Regan of Cape Clear for telling me their stories about growing up on the islands. Thanks also to Eibhlín Leonard of Ard na Gaoithe, Cape Clear, for her hospitality.

Thank you to Professor Marie Cassidy, the former State Pathologist of Ireland, for being so patient with me and my many questions. She was kind enough to read the relevant chapter in this book and offered incredibly useful suggestions. Thanks to Garda Brendan and to Mick Clifford, an investigative journalist with the *Irish Examiner*, for taking multiple phone calls and helping me shape the narrative in a way that was (hopefully!) true to life. Any inaccuracies are my own.

I am so grateful to Richard Chambers for his support and advice; writing this book would have been a very different – and much more difficult – experience without him. Thanks, Traolach Ó Buachalla, for translating the Irish phrases, proof-reading the manuscript, as well as giving me feedback as a documentary maker. Thanks to Niamh Ní Dhomhnaill for helping me figure out Keelin's psychology career, Simone George for pointing me in the direction of books and articles I might find helpful, and Michael O' Neill Jr from Fernhill House Hotel for taking a random phone call about generators and storms. Thanks to Rory Macken, for his guidance on Australian slang, and to Liberty of the *Liberty on the Lighter Side* blog who told me about life as a woman in her forties. Again, any mistakes are mine.

None of this would be possible without my friends and family. Special thanks to Anne Murphy, one of the strongest women I've ever known, and to Jim and Lorna Brooks, who were there for me when I needed it most.

Thank you to my greatest cheerleader, Marian Keyes, and to Catherine Doyle for being an excellent beta reader (and for coming up with the title!).

Thank you to everyone at the Tyrone Guthrie Centre in Annaghmakerrig, where much of this book was written. I am glad such a place exists.

The greatest thanks must be given to the survivors I met to discuss their experiences of domestic abuse and coercive control. I left every meeting humbled by their courage and strength. I was honoured to be trusted with their stories and I carried them with me in every word that I wrote.

Finally, *After the Silence* is dedicated to my beloved grand-mother, Margaret Murphy, who died on the 26th of January 2019. The garden in this book, with its roses and monkey puzzle trees, is hers. I hope she would have been proud.

AUTHOR'S NOTE

In chapter 33, Keelin refers to the idea of 'learned hopefulness' rather than 'learned helplessness'. I came across this theory in a *New Yorker* article called 'The Radical Transformations of a Battered Women's Shelter', by Larissa MacFarquhar.

In chapter 51, the analogy Kimberley Singer uses to illustrate coercive control is taken from Evan Stark's superb book, *Coercive Control: The Entrapment of Women in Personal Life*. It's the technique a prosecutor, Sarah Buell, used to explain this kind of abuse to judges.

BIBLIOGRAPHY

No Visible Bruises: What We Don't Know About Domestic Violence Can Kill Us by Rachel Louise Snyder

Why Does he Do That?: Inside the Minds of Angry and Controlling Men by Lundy Bancroft

How He Gets into Her Head: The Mind of the Male Intimate Abuser by Don Hennessy

Not to People Like Us: Hidden Abuse in Upscale Marriages by Susan Weitzman

Coercive Control: The Entrapment of Women in Personal Life by Evan Stark

Operation Lighthouse: Reflections on our Family's Devastating Story of Coercive Control and Domestic Homicide by Luke and Ryan Hart

Crazy Love: A Memoir by Leslie Morgan Steiner

On the Edge: Ireland's off-shore islands by Diarmuid Ferriter

Oileáin: The Irish Islands Guide by David Walsh